THE
WAVE MAN

© **1993 Times Editions Pte Ltd**
Published by Times Books International
an imprint of Times Editions Pte Ltd
Times Centre
1 New Industrial Road
Singapore 1953

Times Subang
Lot 46, Subang Hi-Tech Industrial Park
Batu Tiga
40000 Shah Alam
Selangor Darul Ehsan
Malaysia

Printed in Singapore

ISBN 981 204 461 2

THE
WAVE MAN

CHRISTOPHER BATES

TIMES BOOKS INTERNATIONAL
Singapore • Kuala Lumpur

The author gratefully acknowledges the help in reading the novel provided by family and friends, and particularly Meik and Diane Skoss, Dave Lowry, and Ellis Amdur who caught many gremlins, large and small. Thank you.

Dedicated to Ling-li,
Clever Jasmine that she is.

PROLOGUE

"Impressively efficient," the tall, well-tanned European said to the nut-brown, Thai-Chinese "officer" dressed in jungle khakis. "I hope all your laboratories are this well-managed, Colonel."

"They are, of course," he said, observing the Occidental's discomfort in the oppressive jungle heat, sweat rolling down his creased forehead into his large, tawny eyebrows, wet oval patches of shirt sticking to his back. "I hope you are as certain of your procedures as we are of ours," the Thai said, referring to a plan to export their refined opiate, knowing that success would double their cash flow.

"With the complete cooperation of the Thai government, how can we fail?" the tall Northern Italian replied casually, hoping to encourage the expectation of large orders, and, so, the willingness to talk the price down.

The busy insect sounds of the jungle were pierced by gunfire from the southeast corner of the encampment. One, ten, fifty guns opened fire in return as the colonel's men responded to the unseen enemy.

"*Cristo!*" the European cursed. "I thought you said this base was secure." He glared at the surprised soldier.

"Probably just some Burmese bandits," the Thai replied, trying to be casual, cursing all unreliable government officials, knowing that someone, somewhere, would have to be eliminated for letting this ambush occur, while someone else would have to be paid more to prevent a repetition. "You're lucky. They have come in from the side opposite your chopper." He grabbed the Westerner's arm and moved him through the refinery toward the small obscure landing pad that had been cut only days before into the dense foliage.

The pilot had heard the shooting begin and had started the engine of his aircraft. He was holding its rpm just below takeoff speed and looked about nervously for his employer. Danger was accepted with the high pay of the job, but he did not want to die; not here, not now. Within a minute the European was in the cockpit, and they lifted off the level matting of fronds laid on the ground and headed away from the dangerous reports.

In forty-five minutes they would be safely descending into another temporary landing pad in the Thai interior. After replacing the helicopter's magnetized serial numbers and removing the outboard mounted machine gun, they would return south to Bangkok, another week of prospecting completed.

Jo: Beginnings

In Japanese aesthetics, anything from a sword stroke to a brush stroke, a single musical note to a symphony is divided into *Jo*, *Ha*, and *Kyu*; beginnings, progression, and conclusion.

ONE

Theodore Bergman settled into the narrow airline seat and accepted a cold towel from the stewardess. Cool and comfortable, he was glad to be on his way out of Myanmar. He liked the Burmese, if not their obstinate government with its predilection for changing currencies and the name of the country with precipitous overnight announcements. He liked Rangoon, with its casual air of delayed development, but the week spent there had been taxing, even for a young American businessman.

Each trip is better than the last, though, he reflected. The sales will come in eventually. His profession was to travel throughout Southeast Asia as the regional sales manager for an American company. That did not leave much time to work on sales support and development in marginal markets like Burma, but he persisted nonetheless. As his friend at the U.S. Embassy had noted, the Japanese and the Brits were constantly staking the country out. The United States had to prepare for its share.

Now in an economy seat of a Boeing 727, with Rangoon 200 miles behind him and a lunch of boiled lobster tail *en salade* in front of him, Ted evaluated the business done. Two tenders were to be written up using the specifications of his equipment with potential sales of about $50,000 for each tender. A worthwhile market to keep an eye on, he concluded to himself.

When lunch had been cleared away he asked the stewardess for a copy of the *Far Eastern Economic Review*. Fifteen minutes passed, and as the descent into Bangkok's Don Maung International Airport began, she returned with the prior week's issue and apologized for letting it slip her mind.

Honey, with an ass like that, memory's not important, he thought, watching as she returned to the forward part of the cabin, her firm buttocks pulling the tight silk uniform to and fro.

He opened the magazine and a random headline caught his eye: "Thai assault foiled by modern drug arms."

Apparently, rebel forces were investing their drug revenue in modernizing their armaments. A Thai lieutenant-colonel, who had successfully routed several Communist cells in the south near Malaysia, and his troops had been secretly moved to the "Golden Triangle" area at the border of Thailand, Burma, and Laos. However, their surprise attack on a drug laboratory had come up empty. The Thai government troops had been beaten back by heavy rifle and mortar fire. When the shooting ceased, they moved in again, only to find that all the equipment for processing the poppy sap, weapons, and ammunition had been quickly removed into the jungle. No rebel soldiers were taken alive. Some of his advance guard reported having seen an armed helicopter take off when the fighting began. The reporter concluded that Thai bureaucracy and a recent change in government would probably slow down any appropriation of extra funds to meet the escalation.

Soon they'll have 747s to deliver the shit in, Ted groused, disapproving of the situation and feeling pity for the thousands of husks of human beings he felt had been wasted by heroin. He visualized photographs he had seen of junkies strung out in ghetto halls, needle tracks up their arms. So many victims of the drug trade, he thought darkly, glad that he had avoided its complications in high school and college. Going to high school in Japan had helped. Though drugs were available to the expatriate community in Tokyo, they had been less prevalent and considered more taboo than at home in the United States.

The jolt of the aircraft landing gear hitting, bouncing, and hitting the runway again jerked Ted from his reverie. He put his shoes on and gathered his case and documents as the taxiing was completed. When the plane stopped, he was up immediately and slid around the other passengers to get to the curtain separating first and economy classes. As soon as the stewardess whose posterior he had so admired pulled the curtain open, he was through it and out the main door.

He prided himself on making it to the immigration lines before the first-class passengers did. Years of international travel had led him to conclude that this was essential to getting through an airport quickly. He did not fail on this day and got into a line with three people ahead of him. Rule No. 2, he had learned, was to avoid lines with unwashed, unshorn, scantily clad young people in them. He had nothing against "hippies," as they were still called in Asia — he had looked like one himself in college — but he did not want to wait in an immigration or customs queue while their financial resources and onward air ticket or fully stuffed rucksack was carefully inspected. He had better things to do.

A Hong Kong businessman and his wife were promptly cleared through and an Australian had his passport chopped in less than a minute. Ted stepped up to the wood and glass booth, set his attaché case down on a shelf attached to it and slid his documents through a hole in the window, a passport smile on his face. The bored officer thumbed through the many spent pages. What do they look for in there, Ted always wondered, confession to a felony? The man looked at the photo, up at Ted's face, and back to the passport. Satisfied that the two matched, he abruptly stamped the travel document, the immigration card, and the government's copy — chop, chop, chop — and handed the passport back, waving Ted onward with a limp motion of his hand.

Entering the baggage claim area, he stopped at another immigration checkpoint installed to remove the government's copy. Ted went to the luggage carousel and began a ten-minute wait for the bags to begin to spill off the conveyor onto the moving stainless plates. He was in luck. The seventh bag to emerge was his, a charcoal grey Samsonite. Rule No. 3 was to carry combination-lock luggage, keys being a nuisance to keep track of when going in and out of countries and hotels. He checked the tag on the suitcase. It read "Burt Theopoulos." Rule No. 4 was to mark all checked baggage this way because a friend had once told him that theft rings operated out of airports, reading the names and addresses of people going out of town and striking at their houses. It was a minor precaution on his part.

After proceeding to an appropriately peopled customs line and being waved through without having to open his bags, he carried his things to the airport limousine counter and purchased a ticket with the Thai baht he had left over from his last trip. Not having been certain when he would return from Burma, he had not notified his distributor of his arrival time.

In the arrival hall, he first felt the Bangkok weather, heavy and oppressive. There were about 200 people pushed up against the stainless steel barrier trying to catch a glimpse of friends coming out. Some shyly held out pieces of cardboard with names scribbled on them, wondering if Ted was the guest they were supposed to meet. He joined a group of perspiring foreigners waiting for their limousines. He felt a gentle touch on his shoulder and turned around to see an effeminate porter wearing an airport uniform.

The young man smiled at him. "I take your ticket and call you for the car, OK?"

Ted gave the ticket to the man behind the appropriate counter instead. When his car arrived, his bag was carried by the same fellow who had tried to help him before.

"What hotel you stay at?"

"Tell the driver to take me to the Dusit Thani, please."

"Can I visit you?" the cheeky man asked, raising his eyebrows slightly.

Ted scowled and a playful pout was returned. He got in the sedan and settled into the sagging black upholstery, giving a last look at his admirer as the automobile pulled into a stream of taxis leaving the airport.

At long last the highway from the city to the airport, which had been under construction for as long as Ted could remember, had been completed. However, Thai driving had not improved. He chuckled when he remembered a friend's story of a Thai chauffeur who had burned a set of four tires down to the rims during an emergency stop from 180 kilometers per hour. On the road ahead it was the usual melee of cars and motorcycles competing with lorries and buses for a minuscule advantage.

After thirty minutes of high-speed near-collisions, he finally arrived at the hotel. As he entered the lobby the sales manager happened to walk by and greeted him. "Mr. Bergman! *Sawadee krap.* You have come to visit us again. Let me check to see if your registration card is completed." The short, plump, and balding Thai waddled to the lobby counter and snapped his fingers. A girl appeared shortly and bowed slightly, an attentive expression on her face on being summoned by the manager.

Ted merely signed the card and followed the bellboy to his room, which was appointed with all the five-star details expected by frequent international travelers, as well as a view of Lumpini Park. A large basket of fresh fruits was delivered as he opened his bag and pulled out his trip file. He took off his shoes, loosened his tie, and sank into the dark blue lounge chair next to the window. He selected a rambutan from the basket and peeled off its red, hairy skin, then popped the translucent, mutton-fat jade pulp into his mouth and savoured the sweet, sticky flavor. That done, he tried to turn his attention to his scheduling for the week.

His job, as Regional Manager — Southeast Asia, with Petrotools International required he maintain a flexible outlook. Being part of the worldwide scramble for natural resources, his schedule had to be sufficiently flexible to respond to urgent calls from the oil companies to have some tool or other sent out or supplied. He had to be flexible to deal with the temperaments and cultural quirks of distributors and customers in eight distinctly different Southeast Asian nations. Being a lone corporate representative in the area, he had to perform many diverse functions. Some were rather mundane — typist, copier, and repairman — while others required tremendous perspicacity; when he performed credit analysis or negotiations, for example. He also had to be flexible enough to balance corporate, customer, and personal interest.

He felt the last demand was his weakest point. For the past three years, he reflected, he had steadily surrendered more of his personal life into the hands of the corporation and his customers.

There was little time for self-development, for friends if he had made any, or for love even if he had found it. Could he have found it? Did he really want to find it, he wondered. Ever since he had lost his true love ten years before, no one else had sparked the same desire. Of course, he had rutted his way through Asia, but that merely satisfied a physical yearning whose fulfillment was only temporary. So many demands, so little time, and he felt the pressure more and more each day

What was it Butcher Obara had told him? To be like the mountains and the water. To be flexible but elemental like water and imposing but natural like the mountain. How did it apply? There was so much he had forgotten, so far he had gone astray.

Realizing that he had daydreamed long enough and feeling the worse for it, Ted tried to turn his attention back to his schedule for the week. Didn't the Butcher tell me to apply his words to my daily life, that only in that way would they become a part of me rather than a separate meditation? But Christ! It's so hard. So concentrate already.

He got down to serious planning. First, he had to check on the results of several tenders on which Petrotools had submitted quotes. Khun Sarasin would be waiting to hear from him and they had to visit a customer or two. He pulled a note from his file. It was a request for a technical call. It read:

> Ital-Siam Exploration
> Prospect for aerial surveying, Petrol. Prospectors
> Italian/Jap/Thai JV

He thought for a moment, trying to remember where he had come by this information. He recalled that two weeks before, while he was still preparing for the Myanmar–Thailand trip, he had met Terry Jones at the American Club in Singapore. Terry was a single fellow like himself, working for a local aircraft firm handling sales, leasing, and repair of corporate jets and helicopters to service the petroleum industry. This connection had led them to compare customer notes on several occasions. Over cocktails, Terry had told him about a customer in Bangkok, a new exploration consortium of Italian, Thai, and Japanese investors who were breaking into the oil and natural gas exploration field. They had budgeted to procure up-to-date equipment and had leased a used corporate helicopter from his company under a hire/purchase plan.

Ted put the note down on the coffee table and thought as he peeled another rambutan. First he would run a background check on the company at the American Embassy to see if anybody else was getting business from them, what were the company's resources, who owned it, did he know any of them, etc. While he checked on the tenders with the government, he would also talk to the people in charge of exploration concessions. In that way he would know where they were looking for what in Thailand and could prepare a sales presentation around equipment they should obtain for the application. Only after he had qualified the prospect and readied himself to confront the requirements head on would he call for the appointment. If under-the-table payments or guarantees of local servicing had to be made, he would invite his distributor in for the second call. Otherwise, he competed with Khun Sarasin, a fact that kept their relationship healthy.

This type of meticulous preparation was Ted's forte. Customers were rarely unimpressed with the background knowledge he had about them and his rate of success in closing sales with new qualified prospects approached 85 percent, of which he was justifiably proud.

He pulled a name card out of the file. It was one of his, but he had written the name of a Bangkok club on it. He vaguely remembered a conversation with a British expatriate from Thailand he had met once while flying from there to Singapore. The man had sung high praises about this club. The girls were clean and attractive, the setting unusual, and, he said, any type of pleasure could be obtained there.

Ted tucked the card into a shirt he had set aside for the evening, walked to the bed, and sat down. He picked up the receiver of the telephone and dialed the number of Khun Sarasin.

"*Weii* ... Ten Hong Wu Jin," the voice at the other end blared. It was Sarasin's wife, a native Chinese from Yunnan whom he had married after World War II. She always answered the phone in Chinese despite having lived an Bangkok for over twenty years.

"Khun Sarasin, please. This is Mr. Bergman."

"*Deng yi sya.*" The phone went silent.

"Hello, Ted? You're here early. You are in Bangkok, isn't it?"

"Yes, got in this afternoon."

"Do you have dinner plans? Of course you have dinner plans with me, yes?"

"No and yes. That would be nice."

"What's that?"

"I mean, I would enjoy dinner with you tonight."

"Good. What time will I pick you up?"

"How is 7 o'clock?"

"Seven? Fine."

"Is Mrs. Sarasin coming along?"

"Aiya! Don't mention the old tigress! I get no rest except when I go out with customers. ... You are just coming from Burma, isn't it?"

"Umhmm."

"No fun there, eh? May I assume your one-eyed monk wants to break his vows tonight?" Sarasin asked with a laugh.

"It's no wonder a man of your perception is such a success."

"Eh?"

"Yes, I would like to go out with you."

"Good. Seven. See you then."

The phone went dead. Ted replaced the receiver with a smile on his face. Sarasin was quite a character, he thought, and he admired him tremendously. The son of a Chinese immigrant to Thailand, Sarasin had struggled hard from very early on. His father paid no attention to him, Sarasin being the fourth son of eight children, and he had fought for every advantage. Immediately after the world war, he had set up a hardware shop selling chain, tools, nuts, and bolts. Now, at fifty-eight years of age, he was a millionaire several times over. Though he had not completed middle school, he had taught himself English and written Chinese. He used the knowledge to try to learn what was new that might be profitably sold in Thailand. In the 1950s, he had acquired the exclusive distribution rights in the country for several American and Japanese product lines. His business expanded, and when U.S. participation in the Vietnam War escalated he was in an excellent position to supply many urgently required tools, all at premium prices. With the pull-out of America from the region, he had been forced to diversify his business to stay solvent. The creation of OPEC and news in the press of increased energy exploration in Asia led him to quickly grab up product lines related to petroleum exploration. During an offshore exploration symposium in Houston, Sarasin had visited the Petrotools International booth. Representing many American manufacturers of search, survey, and drilling equipment and seeking increased overseas sales, Petrotools offered him everything he wanted from one source.

With the expansion of their Asian sales in the mid-Eighties, Petrotools had sought extra personnel to develop the market. Ted had been selected and so he had come to know the amiable Chinese-Thai. Though Sarasin was old enough to be Ted's father, they nevertheless got along well as trading partners. Ted was justifiably full of respect for Sarasin and his rags-to-riches climb. Sarasin, likewise admired Ted's appreciation of the Far East, his product knowledge, and his ability to help him pull through sales.

Ted lay down on the bed and closed his eyes. Placing his hands palm down together over his navel, he tried to relax. He felt caught in a cruel trap. The discipline of martial training he had undergone in his youth had succeeded in increasing his willpower. It had not made him free, though, or even flexible. He could not overcome the contradictions. Discipline was required for concentration. In order to concentrate he had to relax; in order to relax he had to clear his mind; in order to clear his mind he had to concentrate.

Since finishing college and going out into the 'real world' of business, he had devoted less and less of his time to his internal work. It was not that he felt it unimportant, but rather that he was unsure of its importance. He had a good career path. He was welcomed by distributors and accepted by customers who helped him make his sales numbers. They did not care about his internal work. But viscerally he knew it must serve a purpose for him, so why not keep up the training.

He began to review the reasons he could no longer train. Most had to do with his workload. Up early, out all day, being entertained at night, and living out of a suitcase all were contributing factors. Hotels were not conducive to martial or spiritual training.

Bullshit Singapore regulations, which required police registration of all students of fighting arts, made Ted uneasy.

That's bullshit too, he cursed to himself. He felt that if he were really strong internally and cut out for the road ahead, these would all be small problems. He denounced himself as an undisciplined rake, not the "warrior" he wished to be. He recognized his excuses and backsliding as the conventional impediments they were, but the recognition left him more depressed than he had been when he started out. He wondered if he would ever have the time, the will, to reach his goal. Is it possible to be of this world and also devoted to self-cultivation? Is this some Quixotic venture that wastes my time only and leads to ultimate dissatisfaction?

Troubled to find neither answers nor repose forthcoming, he dragged himself from the bed, stripped quickly, showered, and put on a fresh Indonesian batik shirt, cool slacks, and light shoes. He went downstairs to wait for his associate. The activity in the hotel lobby did not seem to change from one country to another: strained executives checking in after long flights, groups of tourists assembling for their free "tropical cocktails" and instant culture shows, and customers meeting suppliers. He was in the latter group. Moving now in the business world, he shed his gloomy ruminations and adopted his commercial mindset.

As Sarasin pulled up in his luxurious Citroën Pallas, Ted stepped out the hotel door to the curb and got in, the powerful air conditioning a sharp contrast to the heavy, wet heat he had just traversed.

Sarasin shook his hand, his grip light but friendly. "You get fat," he said jocularly. "We work that off tonight, eh? But first we eat. How about seafood?"

"You're the expert," Ted replied as Sarasin pressed on the

accelerator and quickly pulled out into the heavy traffic on Rama IV Road, cutting off two motorcyclists who consequently had a minor collision.

"How about after dinner?" the older man asked with a grin.

"There's a place I was told about," he said. "Perhaps we can try it. The Chaophraya Palace."

"Where did you hear of that? I thought it was Bangkok's best-kept secret. I've never seen a *farang* there."

"You can keep no secrets from me," Ted replied mysteriously.

"I see," Sarasin said, looking at the American eyes askance, wondering if his favorite house of sexual adventure had gone so far downhill as to cater to the half-hour pleasure seekers. "Well, let's change dinner plans then. They will serve us there first."

Driving west on Rama IV Road up to the massive portico of the capital's train station, Sarasin turned directly west and soon to the south, heading for the river. The streets became smaller and darker. He pulled the car over.

"We'll have to walk from here. Please, lock the doors."

They got out of the car and walked together down the narrow street. At the end was a single, flickering streetlight struggling to stay on, its light reflecting off the damp pavement. Rounding a corner, the river came into view. Ted smelled it before he saw it. He followed his companion to a series of stone steps which led down to a dock several yards below. Lean Thai rivermen looked on — eyeing his Rolex, Ted felt, and he regretted wearing it. No reason to tempt a tiger with raw meat attached to one's arm.

Sarasin spoke loudly over the sounds of splashing waves and roaring engines into the ear of one of the men whose long-tailed Thai riverboats were docked there. They boarded one together, being careful not to slip on the slick dock. The boatman pressed a button and his oversized, swivel-mounted, six-cylinder engine thundered to life. He engaged the transmission without warning and the boat swiftly accelerated away from the platform, almost spilling Ted overboard. He grabbed the edge of the wooden seat and cursed himself for being caught off guard.

They headed south, with the flow of the river but diagonally, and had soon crossed it from bank to bank. The view, although not to be compared with the Hong Kong harbor at night, was still attractive. At a distance behind him Ted could see the grand old dame of Thai hotels, The Oriental, whose old face and glittering new body sent reflections dancing in the wake of their craft.

The pilot soon turned into a *klong*, one of the canals in the old Thonburi section which still served as well-used water roads. Sarasin looked out pensively over the waters.

"I didn't realize this place was so far away," Ted apologized to the Thai.

"You mean you haven't been before?"

"No. I've only heard about it."

"Aiya! Then you are in for a treat!" he exclaimed, his mood suddenly more alive as he thought about which girl would be most suitable for his American friend.

The boatman had pulled into another, much smaller side *klong* — an alley, Ted mused — and came to rest at a dock. The engine became silent and Ted could hear the soft sound of Thai string instruments being played by experienced fingers.

Sarasin spoke to the riverman who tied up his boat as they got off. Ted was led up a short flight of wooden steps through large wet leaves hanging into the path which led to several renovated traditional Thai river houses. Large trees and dense greenery grew around all the dark wooden buildings which were connected through the

24

undergrowth by well-trodden paths.

They were greeted outside by a middle-aged Thai woman who struck Ted as possessing a rare sensuality. This woman was dressed in a tight-fitting Thai silk gown which, although covering her, revealed her still-firm curves to the observant male. What pleasure she could impart, Ted thought, following her and Sarasin to the door. There they removed their shoes and were led through a candlelit hall to a small room. She sat them on the floor cushions at the low table in the center of the room and spoke gently with Sarasin in Thai. Occasionally she looked at Ted and a brief smile would brighten her face. She then gracefully rose from her kneeling position and left the room.

Ted observed that the "palace" was quite quiet and subdued. None of the garish lights, makeup, or music that one found at the pay-for-play centers which covered Bangkok were in evidence here. There were no electric lights on, only candles, and besides the occasional rumble of a boat passing on the *klong* or a distant taxi's horn, the only sounds were of the string music, some muffled laughter coming from another bungalow, and the night sounds of the insects calling each other.

"You are not alone tonight," Sarasin said in a low tone.

"I know. You're here."

"What I meant was, there is another *farang* here. A Japanese businessman. Quite unusual. I hope not too many of you find this place. It will be spoiled, if I may say so without making you feel offended," Sarasin said sincerely.

"No offense taken. I know as well as you that the run-of-the-mill *farang* would kill the atmosphere here. I hope you will treat me as an exception."

"I already have. I brought you here. ... Ah! Dinner is coming."

25

A young girl in her mid-teens quietly padded into the room, a tray of food on each arm. She knelt by the table and placed the platters on it. Ted did not recognize some of the dishes. He could discern the rice, chili sauce, minced pigeon soup, and a platter of sliced raw vegetables. Sarasin introduced the rest.

"This you must try," he said, pointing to a bowl of shrimp. "These are a freshwater variety, raw, soaked in chili, garlic, and vinegar. Not unlike your *sashimi*, yes ... and this is quite hot, be careful. It is call, umm ... beef in hot jungle curry with spices."

Ted tried the shrimp first. It was delicious and not a bit heavy in fish taste, the spices chemically cooking the flesh, he presumed, like Philippine *kinilaw*. He tried the beef. To call it "quite hot" was a dangerous understatement. More like devastating, he grieved, as the fiery stew burned down the length of his throat. He took some tea.

He caught Sarasin grinning at him. "Something cold to drink?" Sarasin asked, barely able to contain his mirth.

"An ice-cold Singha, please," he replied, ordering a beer. "The rice will help," Ted said evenly, maintaining his composure while shoveling a forkful of the dry, long-grained Thai rice into his mouth. The flavor of the beef was actually good, once flavor could be distinguished from pain, he thought. To his companion's surprise, he took another spoonful of the beef, this time avoiding the small, green, pea-sized chilies that hid like mines in the sauce, ready to explode in unsuspecting mouths.

They continued eating, both enjoying the mix of bland and spicy, raw and cooked, hot and cold. When they had finished, the same young girl cleared the dishes away and brought a platter of fresh fruit, with sections of pineapple, watermelon, and whole rambutan on it.

"Shall we have some durian brought out?"

"I don't think they have any. I can't smell it," Ted quipped, referring to the heavy — some said disgusting — aroma of the fruit.

"I guess that means no, isn't it? Tell me, have you ever tried durian?"

"I am aware it is the king of fruit, and an Indian will gladly trade his last pair of *dhoti* for a quality specimen, but when I had it I was not impressed. Shall I describe to you what I tasted?"

"Please," the Thai urged, eager to hear his friend's appraisal.

"It had the approximate color, taste, and consistency of a large, honey-dipped oyster left on a city sidewalk for two hot days."

"It couldn't have been Thai durian," Sarasin said with mock indignation.

"Even so." They both laughed.

At that moment the sensuous woman who had greeted them at the entrance came into the room followed by four attendants. Ted determined them to be between nineteen and twenty-three years of age. All were attractive and emitted a maidenly aura not found on the streets of the Patpong entertainment area. They seated themselves around Ted and Sarasin. As the one on Ted's left took a toothpick and selected a piece of pineapple for him, another poured a thimble-sized shot of Mekong whiskey.

He ate the pineapple. It was just ripe, sweet and full of juice. The other girl brought the whiskey to his mouth and he drank the potent liquid. It, too, burned a path down his throat.

This process of fruit and whiskey was repeated for both Ted and his partner. Soon he could feel the presence of the girls more strongly; their smell fragrant but not perfumed, their touch light and unhurried, their heat adding to the heat of the night and the spices he had consumed. He began to daydream as he bit into a

27

peeled rambutan the girl had just proffered. It was soft, sweet, juicy … his reverie must have shown in his eyes for, the drinking suddenly stopped and the girls rose, taking him gently by the arms and helping him up. Sarasin was likewise brought to his feet and both were led out of the room and down the hall. Going through a back door they walked on a veranda to another section of the building.

"Take your time, my young friend," Sarasin said as he was lightly pulled through a hanging partition into his room.

Ted obediently followed the two maidens into another room reserved for him. It was sparsely furnished, with a large wooden bathing tub, big towels, a bed set low to the floor, and a view of the moonlight on the *klong* through a straw blind. The meal was finished; the feast was about to begin.

The Japanese man in a nearby candlelit room groaned quietly and gutturally as four oiled hands skillfully kneaded his muscular body. Yes, one of these girls would have to be recruited for a trip to Japan, he thought, listening to the distant sound of a boat chugging along the *klong*. A two-week stint would cover all her expenses. Ninety percent of the income from the remaining seven weeks would be pure profit for his organization.

So far it had been a very enjoyable and encouraging trip. The European was ready to start supplying the white powder, many women had been personally "interviewed" by him for nine-week working vacations in Japan, and they had finally taken over a travel agency to mask some of their activities. His uncle would be pleased.

He owed so much to his uncle, who had given him a job when he failed to enter college, who had overseen his growth in the organization, and given him a chance. More than once. He had made quite a mess several years back. Kidnapping, rape. Yamashita had extricated him. Now, ten years later, he was being given another opportunity to earn the respect of his peers and bosses. He would not screw it up, he concluded determinedly. Girls like the one massaging his male root with two soft, oiled forearms would be part of his success.

The two attendants had been talking in Thai about the "Eastern Sea Devil" on whom they worked. One thought him cute and well-built for his age, which they guessed to be about thirty-eight. The other thought him to be too fierce in his eyes for comfort. Both of them were amused by the large, intricate, and colorful tattoo which set the curves of his back alive. Neither knew what type of fish it was that swam up the waterfall in the fleshy tapestry, nor that this was the mark of a *yakuza*.

Ted woke abruptly to the harsh report of an alarm clock, his head aching as he reached to switch it off. He felt terrible. His stomach was sore, his tongue was raw and sour, and the act of opening the curtains brought agony to eyes which blinked stupidly in the raw light. He could not remember ever feeling so spent before. As he lay back down on the bed and covered his eyes with the crook of his elbow a worse day came to mind, the day after his first lesson with Butcher Obara, master of the knife. But that was different, he thought. I learned from that pain. I came out of it better. What have I learned from a drunken night with pretty girls who probably hate me for what I enjoy them to do? That two is not necessarily better than one? That a lay is a lay is a lay? Love it ain't.

These were lessons he had been tutored in repeatedly, he reflected. Still he persuaded himself to continue the search for

29

something special in the experiences. He did not really hope to find an end to the search, because then he would have to establish the reason for a beginning. He did not want to face it, least of all on a hungover morning in Bangkok with a busy day ahead. But he continued to lay in bed, now staring at the ceiling, now minutely examining the texture of the blue fabric on the chair next to his bed, now facing the window and looking at the glare of sun reflected on morning clouds.

He was lonely. That was the reason for the beginning of the search. He needed companionship, a warm body to hug and kiss and talk to. He stopped in his thoughts. He knew he was lying. He could not have talked at all to the girls the night before. They didn't speak English.

He started over. I don't have time for love. With my schedule, I have no spare moments to invest in love, and so I spend. A value-for-value relationship. She gets rice and a roof, and I get my rocks off. This did not satisfy him either, since he was obviously dissatisfied with the experience.

A thought, a memory, slowly emerged, forcing its way up through his consciousness despite his efforts to bury it. I cannot love. I have only loved Mieko. Nothing can match the purity and joy of that love which is no more. I seek brief physical release as a minor compensation for the void of emotion in my heart. He was surprised by the weight of the language his mind used to consider these feelings and decided he had probably found the real reason for his "search for the ultimate lay." He also knew that it was not the first time that he had gone through this mental exercise, nor would it be the last.

The phone rang, startling Ted out of his semiconscious meandering.

" 'Lo," he muttered, not being prepared for a gracious greeting.

"Ted? Sarasin here. You sound bad, boy."

"Is it 9:30?"

"Nine-thirty? We agreed last night when I dropped you off to get started at 8:30."

Ted could recall nothing of the conversation at first, then scraps of the late evening before came back and he vaguely remembered jokes about trying to rouse themselves the next morning.

"Are you OK? Last night you lost your dinner on the way back."

That explained the unusual flavor in his mouth. "Yeah, thanks, Khun Sarasin. Can you give me twelve minutes?"

"I'll be in the coffeeshop."

"See you there."

Ted got hold of himself and went to the bathroom, looking at his watch on the way. He calculated how long each action should take and challenged himself to meet his friend within the promised time. Jumping into the shower, he let the hot water dash against his face as he soaped up his body. He rinsed quickly, dried himself, checked his beard, which he was glad he had shaved the night before, and brushed his teeth. After applying deodorant and body powder, he returned to the bedroom with six minutes remaining.

Feeling refreshed, he pulled on his underwear and a short-sleeved fitting shirt, socks, and a pair of lightweight business slacks. The most time-consuming action was arranging his tie. He slipped out the door, attaché case in hand, and headed for the elevator, reaching the lobby as twelve minutes elapsed.

Sarasin was sitting at a table for two, a cup of coffee raised to his lips. Ted noticed that the night before was still evident on his face, which was tired and ashen.

31

"You don't look so good either, old man," Ted commented as he sat down.

"Aiya, don't complain about me. I didn't puke in the boat," he said, choking weakly on a laugh. "But seriously, I don't know if I can keep on entertaining young ones like you this way. It's too much for me."

"Can you think of a better way to die?"

"Umm … let's go again tonight!" he replied lustily.

"No, no. You're too important a distributor; I can't lose you now."

"Your concern is appreciated. Now, are you ready for the day?"

"Brief me again."

"The training at the refinery."

"Ah, yes. The flow equipment. OK. And we are going to introduce some new accessories, yes?"

"If there is time. We have an hour and a half drive ahead, so we should get going."

Ted signed for his friend's coffee and they went out into the morning heat. This time Sarasin's driver was at the wheel and Ted sat with the jovial businessman in back.

"How did you enjoy the Chaophraya Palace?" the Thai-Chinese asked.

"On my back," Ted replied with a grin.

"Huh? Oh," Sarasin chuckled. "Lovely girls. Played me like an instrument."

"A flute, I'll bet," Ted returned.

"Ho ho, you're full of jokes this morning! Better than the serious side you usually show us."

Serious? Ted was not aware that he struck others that way. He wanted to seem easygoing. And yet Sarasin's comment was unguarded and probably true to his observations. Why did he appear dour?

"You know, Ted ... perhaps I should not say this, but the girls last night said that after your bath you drank some more and after they screwed you up and down you started to speak Japanese and then cry. They didn't know what to do with you."

"Tears of joy, no doubt," Ted said, trying to cover for himself, wondering what he had said and why.

"You need to settle down. Get a wife. Oh, I complain about the tigress, but through her I have five good children, and that is lasting happiness."

"Besides, without a wife, there is no one to cheat on, right?"

"Ah, that too."

The Japanese man wearing white golfing trousers, white leather shoes, and a garish batik shirt emerged from the lawyer's office closely accompanied by two Thais. One was his driver, a former Thai boxer with a powerful, lean build and a slight limp caused by having had his ankle shattered in a bout several years earlier. He was grateful to have a decent-paying job and the perquisites one could earn doing the odd dirty job for his boss. The other man was the bodyguard and interpreter of Thai into English for the Japanese. The bodyguard's English had become as fluent as his assassination and defense skills while training in jungle warfare with American military advisers a decade before.

The final meeting with the lawyers had gone as expected, Nishida thought to himself as he ducked into the car, his eyes darting behind to make sure there were no threatening-looking Thais about. He had signed on behalf of Great Star Tours Japan Ltd. to become part-owner of a local travel agency. His first objective in Thailand had been achieved and was ready to begin earning revenue for his boss. A steady flow of Thai women he had personally recruited to service Japanese men in the love hotels that had spread through his country would apply for their visas, buy air tickets, and pay a small commission to this particular travel agency. His group would profit coming and going. And proper relations at the embassy would ensure that there would be no problems getting visas for these "tourist" women.

Glancing down at the briefcase on the seat next to him and seeing the symbol of the Great Star Group, a stylized five-pointed sparkle within a circle, Nishida thought once again about this life he had found. He knew he could admire in only a limited way the scope of the business to which he devoted his life. Others, like his Uncle Yamashita, knew so much more. Their plans were far-ranging and all-inclusive. He was a part of the plans, he knew, though he did not know what part, nor of what whole.

Great Star Construction built, among other things, the hotels in which the girls he hired worked. Great Star Tours Japan arranged for all-male sexual excursions to Southeast Asia where those who remembered the unbridled lust of World War II campaigns could relive past triumphs over local peoples. Those who were too young to have tasted the spoils of war also came on tours and at least came to understand the glory and extent of the old empire. Those who liked the taste came back for more, without ever leaving Japan, by visiting the love hotels. A profitable circle was complete.

He was a spoke on that wheel. A soldier of new Japan. A *yakuza*. His allegiance to his group was as strong as the Divine Wind that had destroyed Japan's enemies centuries ago, and it would take nothing less to divert his energy from serving his *oyabun*. His devotion to the *oyabun* was channeled through and received direc-

34

tion from his Uncle Yamashita, who reported directly to the chief of their organization and had served under him since the campaign in Manchuria.

Until his uncle had taken him in, his life had been a miserable concession to weak, Westernized Japanese. During junior high school, he realized he was different from all the other students. They were preoccupied with grades and the tests that would lead to high school and college, not with serving their country, school, and family. They criticized their teachers and spoke of freedom. They wore their uniforms sloppily and got flabby while concentrating on their studies. They were no longer Japanese. They were mutants. Only he believed in his purity.

He was a model student in every aspect but his grades. He dressed with military precision, his buttons and shoes shining. He sat upright in class and never bothered the teacher with questions. He executed their instructions exactly. But he did not learn and he did not do well on the examinations. He blamed this on the Western bent to the texts and curriculum.

He excelled at sports and particularly at judo and kendo, at which he trained religiously. It was his basic skill in these methods that provided him with his proof that he was truly Japanese and his classmates something less. During training for an interscholastic judo tournament, he was paired up to practice with another student, named Itoh, a year older than he. The student, the best in his weight division for the school, looked to their teacher and rolled his eyes up in frustrated disgust. He did not want to risk injury so close to the tournament and had hoped their *sensei* would choose another partner for him. The austere discipline required in the *dojo* would never allow him to voice his concern.

Itoh's feelings reflected the unspoken view of most of the

35

other class participants. Bouts with Nishida usually ended up with one or the other player getting injured. Nishida, they whispered among themselves, enjoyed the pain and always came back for more. They wondered whether it was worth it to come back at all.

Sensitive to his partner's expression, Nishida fumed inwardly at Itoh's slight. Is he saying my technique is inferior? Then let him come to the mats with me. If I am to win, he should not go to the tournament anyway. If my skill is wanting, I will accept defeat with the strength of a man, not as a whimpering coward like him, afraid to even approach the woven wrestling mats.

As his driver swerved to avoid a motorcyclist who had dodged to avoid a pedestrian, Nishida looked about, suddenly aware of the Bangkok surroundings again. His fists were clenched and his face taut as he remembered the judo practice. The teacher had urged the hesitant Itoh to complete the *randori*.

Nishida and Itoh approached the center of the *tatami* and the *sensei* signaled for them to close and begin. They took firm hold of each other's heavy cotton *gi* tops and began to pace. Itoh was an orthodox *judoka* who believed in overcoming force only by yielding to it or redirecting its momentum. Nishida relied on his sense of touch and balance to tell him how to move and when to respond.

Nishida knew Itoh dreaded the power and unorthodox variations he used. Nishida stepped and sensed and stared deeply and fiercely into his opponent's eyes and knew that this time he, too, should use conventional techniques. He tugged sharply downward on his opponent's right arm. The reaction was predictable. The enemy jerked his arm up, resisting the pull, and in so doing shifted his weight to his right foot. Facing him, Nishida swept that foot out from under him with his right instep. This failed to fell Itoh, so Nishida pivoted quickly, reversing the direction of his right foot to reap the opponent's left leg out from under him. He appreciated the look of pain that gathered in Itoh's face even as he was in mid-air.

He considered what to do with him. He has made me lose face and should not go to the tournament, he judged.

As Itoh plummeted toward the mat, Nishida decided what to do and followed him down. When both bodies made impact with the woven *tatami*, Itoh slapped brusquely to cushion his fall, but it was not enough to avoid injury. Nishida came down atop him and led his fall with the point of his right elbow which drove hard into Itoh's sternum. A satisfying cracking noise filled Nishida's ears.

Itoh was hospitalized and his parents requested that Nishida be expelled from school. Rather than take such drastic action, the authorities stopped him from participating on the judo team. Smiling to himself now, nineteen years later, he knew he had made the right decision to quit school instead. How could he demean himself by continuing to study in a place where true victory was neglected and losers were indulged?

Yamashita had recognized the traditional drive of the dropout and had taken him in. I will never betray him, Nishida vowed as his driver pulled up to a stop. He looked out to see that they had arrived at his next destination: a meeting with the European.

A long, slow car ride, a spicy lunch on an empty, indignant stomach and patient discussions with the refinery engineer Boribboon resulted in him asking for a price quotation from Sarasin. Ted knew that meant the order was practically in his pocket. Boribboon was probably also thinking of what he could buy with his commission. Ted did not want to know, indeed was constrained by U.S. law from knowing about such activities. He did not feel bad or strange regarding assumed pay-offs. He was not involved. The equipment he was selling was not a rip-off, nor was it an essential. It was a useful luxury, and he had seen much more useless, not to mention dangerous, products being sold to men who were on the "take." He had a clean conscience; his products were good, many promoting worker safety and efficiency, and were well worth their cost.

When Sarasin dropped Ted off at the hotel after their sales call, they confirmed a schedule for the next day. Ted checked his watch and considered the time. It would take at least thirty minutes to get to the Ministry of Industry. He would then have only half an hour to get some questions answered before most of the people he needed to see would want to leave and would resent anyone who prevented them from doing so.

He walked down the driveway from the hotel entrance to the busy street below and tried to hail a taxicab rather than one of the expensive hotel cabs servicing the front door of the establishment. Several motorized trishaws sputtered past, their loud, high revolution, two-cycle engines emitting the characteristic blue smoke. He covered his nose with a handkerchief to avoid the fumes, but some dust was nonetheless blown into his eyes. Shortly, a battered blue taxicab pulled over to the curb. A sweaty, dark Thai leaned over to the left curbside window and smiled, his two front teeth missing.

"Where you go?" he asked, his arm reaching back to open the rear passenger door.

"Ministry of Industry, Rama IV Road. *Towrai?* How much?"

"One hundred baht."

"No. Last time only forty," Ted lied.

"Eighty baht."

"No. Only forty."

"Can't."

Ted began to straighten up from leaning into the window and started to beckon to an approaching driver.

"OK, OK. Fifty baht."

Ted climbed in and quickly wiped the seat with his handkerchief. More than once he had soiled clean clothes in dusty taxis with plastic seat covers.

The driver pulled out into traffic and then looked back at the American in the mirror. "You need come back? I wait."

"No, thank you. I have a ride," he lied again.

"You first time Bangkok?"

"No. Many times."

"Like Bangkok?"

"Yes, very much." Again a lie. Bangkok was a nice place to visit and do business, but he could never see himself having a permanent affair with the city.

"You like Thai girl?"

"They're very pretty."

"I know good girl. She do anything you want. Very pretty. After business I take you there, OK?"

"No, thank you."

"Good girl. You want she lick ice cream cone. Make love also can."

"I'm tired today. Maybe some other time."

The driver remained silent even when they arrived and Ted paid him. They parted without a word.

He approached the dirty cement building and a guard held the door open for him as he entered, considering what to do first. He asked a receptionist, who spoke English, where the Explorations Concessions Section of the Department of Mineral Resources was located. Following her directions, he took the elevator to the third floor and went to the left, passing several small offices inhabited by bored-looking bureaucrats who gazed up hopefully as he passed by. Reaching the end of the hall, he entered a large office space filled with a dozen or more desks and two noisy air-conditioners. Half the desks were empty, their tops cleared away save for tall stacks of forms piled neatly at the corners.

"I'm looking for Khun Phansaeng," he said to a secretary who looked up slowly from her fashion magazine when he spoke to her. Without looking, she pointed over her left shoulder to a desk in the rear and resumed reading.

"Khun Phansaeng? *Sawadee krap,*" Ted greeted as he walked to the man's table bowing, his palms raised together as if in prayer.

The bureaucrat smiled, returned the obeisance, and beckoned him to sit down.

"What can I do for you, Mr. ..."

"Bergman. Here's my card. My company sells specialized equipment for exploration and survey. We've even sold some to your ministry. Umm ... I understand all applications for oil and gas exploration concessions must be channeled through this office."

Phansaeng nodded generously.

"I was told you might be able to give me some details about a consortium recently formed for some up-country surveying and exploration."

"Possibly. However, some companies are sub-contractors to larger groups who won big concessions. I would not know about them. I am also afraid I cannot give you too much information which might be considered confidential to the surveying company."

"I understand."

"Is there a particular firm in mind?" he asked with a helpful smile.

"Yes. I am investigating Ital-Siam Exploration."

For a very brief moment the smile turned downward imperceptibly, then Phansaeng smiled again. "I am afraid that is one of those firms I have not heard of. What kind of work did you say they were doing?"

"From what I have learned so far, they've leased a helicopter and will be doing some inland surveying."

"And your interest in them?"

"Oh, I hope to sell equipment to them. For surveying," he added.

"I'm sorry ..." he said trailing off into a smile, shrugging his shoulders.

"Yes. *Mai ben rai. Khap khun krap.* Is there a card catalog or index in the ministry where I could get information?"

"Well, yes, but they would be closed by now and I am not sure they offer information to the public."

They rose together and Ted bowed again. "*Sawadee krap,*" he bid farewell in the best accent he could muster.

Phansaeng walked Ted to the hall and watched him as he headed toward the elevator, then continued himself down the passage until he found an empty office. Closing the door behind him, he picked up the telephone receiver. He consoled himself that it was probably nothing to worry about as he nervously dialed a number. He listened anxiously for the sound of his call connecting through Bangkok's half-aged, half-renovated switching system, then for the reassuring ring at the other end.

"'Allo."

"Hello. May I speak with Mr. Nero, please?"

"Who is speaking, please?" the accented voice queried.

"Phansaeng, Concessions," he answered .

41

"Yes. This is Mr. Nero. What can I do for you Khun Phansaeng?"

"We have to meet ... tonight ... please."

"What is the subject to discuss?" was the cool reply.

"I ... I can't talk about it now. Meet me at 7:30 at the Café Vientiane." He hung up, not really wanting the dialogue to continue, hoping the time until 7:30 would pass quickly.

Nero listened as the line went dead, then looked across his desk to Nishida and shrugged. "I am afraid I will have to cancel our dinner arrangements tonight."

"Problems?" Nishida asked, aware of the tone of the call and its abrupt end.

"No, I wouldn't say so. Just some unexpected 'entertaining' I have to do. The government, you know." Actually, he was concerned. Phansaeng had been paid off long ago and told to forget everything. What could he be calling for now?

"I would hate for anything to interfere with our arrangement," Nishida interrupted the European's considerations. "My side has invested heavily in this joint venture. I enjoy thinking about what my principals would do to you if there was any irregularity."

Why is it always violence with these *yakuza*, Nero thought. It's no good threatening me. I'm just a chemist. The *don* pulls my strings and pays my bills. At any rate, the delays had been beyond his control. Despite the flush of enmity he felt toward Nishida and his assistant Suzuki who smiled on by his side, he restrained an impulse to return a threat and instead smiled back. "Mr. Nishida, your *oyabun* has complete confidence in me, and besides, if any 'irregularities' occur it will be better for us all to work them out

42

together, yes?"

"Hmmph."

"Now. Where were we? Oh, yes. The government raid. Our contact at the refinery located the leak."

"Has it been plugged?"

"Terminally, yes," Nero said wryly. "Commander Khun Sarithep assured me that we would receive a steady supply of first-class opiate, uncut and ready for our own export processing as soon as we confirm."

Nishida looked coldly at the suntanned European, almost wishing the helicopter had been shot down during the unexpected attack of government troops on the refinery Nero had gone to inspect. He was repelled by the sight of his large, tawny eyebrows and aquiline nose. "We have been ready for eight weeks to take shipment. Our customers are quite anxious. If only our side had run the operation it would be profitable by now." *It is not only in technology that we Japanese are ahead,* he reflected.

"Don't you think if we started sending out drilling samples without having done any exploratory drilling that someone might get suspicious?"

Nishida scowled, the logic faultless, but he did not want to lose. "Let me deal with people who suspect us."

Nero rolled his eyes back in disgust. Dealing with his Japanese counterpart and his obsequious assistant, who bobbed his head and wagged his tail like a subservient dog, had become the most trying part of his job. Burmese bandits, corrupt bureaucrats, even Thai taxi drivers were more amiable and less psychopathic than Nishida. *He is a racist, a sadist, and a low-class thug. His kind would never get a choice assignment like this from the* don. *Yes, but I have no choice. He is the worthless nephew of a valuable officer in their* organization. So I shouldn't bitch. "Sorry about dinner. Perhaps tomorrow night," he said, standing up from his desk, concluding the discussion with the Japanese.

"I can interview some more recruits tonight. It's all right," Nishida replied with a cruel smile, his thoughts momentarily shifting to the image of a brown, naked body and his pleasure at first penetration. He felt an erection start to build as he walked to the door and mentally willed it down. Better to save it for tonight, he thought.

Too many dead ends today, Ted decided, sitting in the taxi on his way to the hotel. No one had cooperated with him at the ministry and he had come up empty-handed. But that Phansaeng was a queer bird, he considered. He swore to himself the man was lying when he said he had not heard of Ital-Siam. Why would he do that? He was surprised by the strength of the intuition that told him something was wrong. He had felt that way before and the Butcher had told him it was a good sign. Fighters rely on it to keep them alive or out of fights. But his vision was incomplete. He sensed something amiss; however, he was at a loss to determine what.

He was free for the evening and began to think about what he would do. The taxi driver had suggestions of his own. When they stopped at a red light he turned around to face Ted and handed him a color picture card.

"How you like massage? I take you. OK?"

Ted looked at the photo. A beautiful Asian woman was sitting nude in a glass tub shaped like a bowl. Her skin was well-soaped and slick. The name of the parlour was written below. Ted was unaware that his pulse had changed slightly as he started to consider the chances that this establishment might offer something really sexually special. He handed the card back to the driver and declined politely, but kept the name in mind.

He decided to spend a comparatively tame evening in the teeming city. After showering and changing into more comfortable clothes, he took a long walk down Silom Road, past the lively flesh and food area at Patpong and on to a smaller side street. He saw the light in a familiar shop window still on and went up to knock on the door. A corpulent Chinese opened the gate, a broad smile on his face.

"*Konbanwa*," he greeted in Japanese.

"*Hayashi-sama, konbanwa*," Ted replied.

Mr. Lin was an old acquaintance and had Thailand's largest private collection of Japanese antique arms. He was fluent in Japanese but spoke little English. They had become friends on Ted's first trip to Thailand when Ted had stumbled upon Mr. Lin's shop.

"Why didn't you call to tell me you were coming? I would have invited Mr. Tan to come over," he said, heartily grasping Ted's arm with his ham-sized hands and pulling him in.

"Just decided. My evening time opened up and I thought I would stop by to see you. How's business?"

"Not very busy. Have you taken rice yet?"

"I was hoping to ask you out."

"No, you must be my guest."

"Please, you treated last time. Let me invite you out."

"No. You are a guest in Bangkok, and at any rate we can have simple fare."

They went out to the curb and Lin hailed a trishaw. The motorized cab for two passengers sputtered to a stop and they boarded as the heavy-set Chinese barked directions in Thai to the

45

thin driver. They slowly accelerated and headed toward Chinatown, the traffic closing in around them immediately.

"You remember this place?" Lin asked as they pulled up to a movie-theater front.

"The best curry in Bangkok."

"Yes. You remember," he said with a grin.

Ted could not have forgotten. In the street entranceway to an old movie house currently under renovation, several hawkers had set up stalls. Ted and Lin sat down at a folding table on unstable plastic stools under the constantly changing glow of auto and street lamps. A boy dressed only in shorts and sandals brought a dirty wet rag and wiped the chicken bones off the table onto a plate used by the last diner. Lin gave him the order. Shortly, two plates of rice, generous portions of chicken curry stewed with bamboo shoots ladled onto them, were brought steaming to the table. A side dish of Chinese sausage and hard-boiled eggs was laid down next.

Ted took the serving spoon and put some pieces of sausage and egg on Lin's plate, at which the jocular man ceremoniously bowed his head and said, "*Domo arigato, Takabashi-san.*" After serving himself, Ted waited for his friend to take spoon to dish and begin the meal, whereupon he took his first taste. The curry was just right, as it had been the time before: not so hot it burned yet spicy enough to proudly assert its presence. By taking some rice any sting could be minimized.

Ted began to sweat and he smiled at Lin as he wiped his brow with a handkerchief. He had eaten at the best restaurants in Bangkok and a hundred times more had been spent on him for an evening's meal, but when all was consumed and the table cleared, he was just as satisfied having eaten here with a friend in the heat, among the roar of traffic and the cries of hungry cats that dodged between his legs searching for discarded bones. Lin belched his satisfaction and the dinner was over.

Back at his shop, Lin took Ted gently by the arm and led him to the rear where they sat around a small marble-topped table. Huddled between the stands and shelves displaying a lifetime's collection of ancient and old coins, weapons, ceramics, and bric-a-brac, they sipped Chinese tea and talked. Springing up with a lightness of movement uncharacteristic in a man his size, Lin went to an old safe, which he wrenched open. He returned to the table with several boxes covered in dark blue silk, custom-made to contain the treasures within. He handed one to Ted and smiled expectantly.

Ted opened the box slowly, with the decorum deserving of the art object he knew must lay inside. He found an exquisite iron *tsuba* inlaid with copper and gold figures — a crane and samurai eyeing one another. This was as fine a Japanese sword handguard as he had seen in any museum, he appraised, and he was handling it himself. He carefully examined it from all sides. A similar work had been auctioned for $5,000, but that was several years ago, he remarked to Lin. Lin proceeded to tell him the origins of the piece.

The two other boxes also contained *tsuba*, one plain iron but of unusual shape, one also inlaid. Lin gave him a longer box which housed a fine *tanto*. This knife, originally carried by a samurai, no longer resided in its customary lacquered scabbard with a wrapped handle. Rather, it was mounted *shira-saya* with a plain white wooden grip and cover. Ted removed the bamboo pin holding the tang to the handle and examined the whole blade. It was in pristine condition and of unusual craftsmanship. Distinct temper marks undulated up the cutting edge all the way to the tip. It was expertly polished and sharpened, so that when held to the light he could not distinguish an edge per se, only one side ending precipitously into the other at a steep angle.

"You know my weakness, neh?" he said to Lin.

"I knew you would look twice, yes."

"May I ask if this *tanto* is for sale?"

"To the right person."

Ted looked at him and waited.

"Yes, yes. You are the right person."

"And for how much?"

Lin raised his head up in thought, then looked down his fat, flat nose at Ted and said, "One thousand one hundred dollars."

Ted whistled and feigned surprise. "Do you have any documentation for it?"

"No."

It was a risk for him to buy an unsigned blade at that price. "Could you part with it for $400?"

Lin acted disappointed, clucking his tongue and replying, "You think it is so valueless!?"

"Without papers, you understand," the American shrugged apologetically.

"OK, for you a guarantee. If you take it to Japan and get it appraised and it is worth one yen less than what you pay for it, return it to me and I will give you your money back."

Ted evaluated the counterproposal. Taking it to Japan would involve its registration there and red tape, plus the cost of appraisal. He also was not sure he was ready to go back to Japan, even after so many years. "Five hundred dollars?"

"Eight hundred."

"I really cannot afford more than $550."

They carried on this parry and riposte for several minutes until

48

Lin gave in. "OK, my friend. Six hundred, but you pay my hospital bills when my wife discovers I have given away this treasure," he said with a smile of welcome defeat.

"I will return tomorrow at lunchtime with the cash. All right?"

"Of course. Now, we should go out. I have found a new house of the water world and …"

"Please, not tonight. I am still recovering from last night."

"You? A young cock!? Perhaps I can recommend some traditional potions, neh? Cobra blood soup will help you!"

"Perhaps. So tomorrow around noon, neh?"

"Fine. But I may still call the police. Only a thief could wrest this from me for less than $700!"

Even as he was led to the door and bid his acquaintance goodbye, Ted still wondered whether he was investing wisely. Had he known then that he would never know the monetary value of the blade, but that it would be invaluable to him, he would have set his mind at ease.

TWO

"Hey, dad! Why are those old men wearing bathrobes?" Ted Bergman exclaimed, knowing that the two aged Japanese gentlemen waiting in the lounge at Haneda Airport were accustomed to dressing in their kimono.

"Now, Ted, I told you not to look and point. You know what that is. We read about kaimonas in the airplane magazine," Sarah Bergman reprimanded with motherly consternation. "Your father's tired, so don't horse around."

Actually, even Ted's reserve of teenage exuberance was fast waning. Thirty-six hours before, amid final hugs and farewells from relatives and friends, they had boarded the westbound plane in Des Moines, Iowa, and flown to San Francisco. During a six-hour layover, they took a car into town and raced through the Pacific capital's attractions. Little Tokyo was not on the list. They would see the real thing soon enough.

The flight from San Francisco on Pan Am had been as bad as most Pan Am flights, Thomas Bergman had commented. His Bloody Mary had been served to him unstirred. Consequently the Tabasco sauce floated on the surface disguised as tomato juice when he drank it off the top. Despite wanting to yelp in pain, he scowled and called for the stewardess.

•

She was about his wife's age, but the years of travel had been unkind. She passed her deteriorating state out to the passengers, much as she did the salted nuts. "Yeah, what's wrong?" she asked accusingly.

"Miss," he felt foolish addressing her as "miss." "You gave this to me unstirred."

"You want another or what?" she responded curtly.

Thomas' patience, already worn thin, was broken by her insolence. "Yeah, get this shit out of here, and bring me a decent drink."

"Honey, please!" Sarah exclaimed, not wanting Ted to be exposed to such talk. The stewardess retreated to the galley.

Ted just turned his head to look down the aisle in embarrassed silence. He had learned such words a long time ago. He was bewildered because his mother did not expect him to know them. How could I, a grown boy of sixteen, not know them, he wondered.

It was like the movie the family had gone to see with a scene of a woman stripping to music. His mother had rebuked Thomas for taking all of them to see such filth. Ted was most uncomfortable because he felt he should act embarrassed to conform to her expectations. Actually, he stared at the screen, bouncing breasts in the background, and wondered when life would start for him.

That had been three years ago. Now he was older, sixteen. Dating age. He thought about his dates. He was leaving a lot behind in Ames, Iowa. He was not unpopular. He was tall and well-built for his age. His ancestry of Scandinavian giants and two seasons on junior-high-school soccer teams had guaranteed that. He had dated Judy Sodestrum for the last semester and had taken her to the sophomore dance in May. There they had kissed long and hard until a chaperone, Mr. Pinter, Ted's math teacher, tapped them on the shoulder and said, "Sorry." That had broken the spell.

51

A week after the dance he told her that his family would definitely be moving to Japan during the summer. His father had confirmed it during a serious talk with Ted. She was more surprised and hurt than he had been prepared for. Crying on his shoulder, she asked if she meant anything to him. Of course she did, he had consoled. They kissed. It was a Sunday and her parents had gone to a hospital in the next town to see an ill friend. They reclined on the couch in the living room and continued their play, the television on. After five minutes of nervous manipulation, he was finally able to unhook her bra. The flesh that had won Judy the nickname "Viking Queen" by the seniors, came loose into his cupped hand, hot and soft. They rubbed and kissed each other in clumsy bliss until the doorbell rang.

"Oh my God!" Judy cried as she sat up, hooked her bra and pulled down her shirt, scrambling for the door. Ted checked himself over, tucking his jersey into his jeans. He looked into a hallway mirror, as she had, and straightened his hair.

It was Judy's aunt at the door.

"Why, didn't your mother expect me this afternoon?" she queried.

"No, ma'am. They're at the hospital now. They didn't mention you'd stop by."

"Well, tell her I'll be back after dinner. Sorry to interrupt you," she said without malice, an understanding smile on her face as she left.

That had been the last time he and Judy had been intimate together. She had not wanted to go farther for fear of becoming too attached to him. He cursed his bad luck again as he saw the Pan Am stewardess return with his father's cocktail. Didn't the popular song run, "Don't it always seem to go that you don't know what you've got 'til its gone"? Ted reflected that rock and roll was deeper than adults gave it credit for.

The meals on the flight had been uninspiring and the cabin temperatures quite cold. He used one blanket while his parents shared theirs. After reading *Sports Illustrated* and watching the movie, he had dozed off briefly, awakening in time to wash up prior to landing.

Then came the descent, contact with the tarmac, and disembarkation. It was his first use of his new passport. He felt a certain thrill in passing through Immigration Control, as if he was a "Mission Impossible" agent on some special assignment. Though Haneda Airport did not look distinctly different from others he had been in, it did have its own un-American and, therefore, strangely exciting appeal. The men in kimono played their part. So did the Japanese food shops with plastic displays of rice and tempura. Of course, the unintelligible writing all around the airport added to the mystique.

Despite regrets about leaving Iowa and his girlfriend, he had a number of things on his mind to do in Japan. First, he wanted to learn the language. He had talked to his high-school guidance counselor who felt that learning a rare tongue would be a definite career advantage. Ted had done well in French, history, and chemistry, and the counselor felt this pointed to an aptitude for the type of memory coupled with flexible vocal talent which would be required. The career options the counselor suggested were also exciting: foreign service, international business, intelligence, military.

Another hope he held was to learn karate or kung fu or whatever it was they did in Japan. His imagination had been captured that year by the American television martial arts hero from the Shaolin Temple. Academies had sprung up even in his own town claiming to reveal the secrets of Asian masters to anyone who signed a one-year contract. He had kept away from these schools and now looked forward to studying with a real Asian master. The troubles of finding a good teacher and gaining his acceptance without being able to speak the language were lost on his teenage mind. The excitement of actually being in Japan, a place so different from Ames, was building, rapidly burying thoughts of home.

Thomas thought he had provided well for his wife and son and was happy when they approved of the small house he had put a rental deposit on a month before. It was his first international assignment and he was glad the commission was footing the bill for his housing and Ted's education. They would cost a pretty penny, he reflected. But, after all, he was there on an important job, potentially very lucrative to the State of Iowa. The Japanese diet increasingly included a higher percentage of beef. And why couldn't a larger percentage of that percentage be delicious, corn-fed Iowa steer, he asked himself as if asking a prospective customer. With luck, contacts, and entertaining, he could make Iowa a major source of meat and ensure himself a spot on the board of the Iowa State Beef Commission.

It had not been easy to persuade his family to give up their settled, secure life to come to Japan. The night he told Ted had been difficult for him. His own father had uprooted their family several times for different jobs with different railroads, and he remembered the hollow feeling of watching a home and friends disappear in the dust behind the moving van. But no move had been as exotic as this. Japan!

Ted had reacted with mixed feelings, one moment sulking about his lost chances to play varsity soccer, the next moment bubbling about some Japanese sport, then pouting again when he told his father more about his budding relationship with the Sodestrum girl. He had no doubts Ted would accept his decision, but that had made it no easier.

Despite having discussed the possibility of the move with Sarah on several occasions, she had been another problem altogether. Approaching the middle years of her life, having only known Iowa for the most part and some of the United States for the rest, she was culturally, spiritually, and emotionally unprepared to make the vast mental leap required of her. It was not only an ocean of water which separated her from her destination, but one of history, temperament, language, and mores; and being totally ignorant of what those customs might be made her more apprehensive, the differences compounded. He knew she lacked Ted's adolescent flexibility to break away easily from her current station in life.

It had taken much more discussion, much more persuasion, to obtain her agreement. Her final consent was not based on any increased confidence in her ability to cope with a new place and friends, but rather in the hope that after only a few years they would triumphantly return to Ames with a new title for Thomas. She made it clear that it was her sacrifice to him and his career.

But for now, they are at least happy with this house, Thomas thought, following them from room to room, listening to their comments. It was a medium-sized expatriate dwelling with comfortable, if functional, lines. The construction was sufficiently Western to make them feel as at home as they would be in Boston or Atlanta. None of the *shoji*, *tatami*, or squat toilets they had laughed nervously about when reading the guide book to Japan were in evidence. Ted had his own room and bath in the side of the house opposite the master bedroom, a feature felt necessary for a boy reaching adulthood. There was a library, kitchen, dinette, and family room. Some of their furniture was on the docks in Yokohama ready to be cleared through customs and moved in. They had sold some appliances and would get new ones with dual voltage in Tokyo.

The house was situated in the suburban Tokyo town of Miitaka. It was an area near the international school and the rail line that went straight into the city. Many foreigners lived in the area and Thomas felt that Sarah would have a chance to make some friends. Ted, too, could find peers there. It was mid-June and they had all summer to settle in, he concluded. Thomas prayed they would manage. He had to get to work.

The first two weeks in Miitaka were devoted to the countless insignificant chores which, in sum, transform a rented dwelling into the semblance of a home. When their articles had been unpacked from the crates, they had an enjoyable time rediscovering their familiarity with them. A favorite desk lamp here, jeans that fit just right waiting in the dresser, an indispensable iron skillet now on the stove again. Things seemed to fall into place. Shopping areas were found and neighbors introduced.

During the third week Ted and his mother enrolled in Japanese classes four times a week, two hours a day. Ted picked up the lessons quickly, and after several weeks could help his beleaguered mother do her shopping. As compensation for her troubles in the class, she was able to meet several other wives in the same bewildering situation as hers. It was a relief just knowing she was not alone: lessening the misery by sharing it.

Thomas immediately set about his business planning. He had selected an office space during a prior trip and a secretary after arrival. Though she was a college graduate with a degree in English, she had been selected for her overall talents, cross-cultural communications not actually being her strong point.

"Bugman-san, there is a phone for you. Rine two," she called to him through the open doorway separating his space from hers.

He picked up the receiver and punched the lit button "Moshy, moshy," he said, unsuccessfully trying to imitate the standard Japanese telephone greeting.

"Mr. Bugman?"

"Speaking."

"This is Yoshida Tsuji from Tokaido Meats. We met several months ago at the Jetro-sponsored conference on farm imports."

"Ah, yes, Mr. Tsuji, I remember. How are you?" Could he possibly forget the name of Japan's second-largest meat handler?

"OK. You are now settled in Japan?"

"Yes. Nicely, thank you."

"Wife and children?"

"Yes, also here."

"Good. Perhaps we can get together this week. You may have some questions about our market I can help you with."

"Yes, I would certainly like to have the chance to see you again. Perhaps you would come to dinner with me?"

"You must be my guest," Yoshida replied hastily.

"No, Mr. Tsuji, you are the customer," he stated presumptuously, acting the gracious host.

"I insist. You are a guest and a stranger here. Please allow me," Yoshida said firmly.

"Well, I'd be delighted. When?"

"Are you free this evening?"

Thomas thought for a moment. Technically, no. He was expected home for dinner. But he did not want to blow a big break on a technicality. "Yes, tonight would be fine."

"Good. I will pick you up at 6:30 in front of your office."

"You have the address?"

"Yes. Six-thirty then. Goodbye."

"Bye." Thomas returned the phone to its cradle without thought, the hand reaching unconsciously to the set. He was elated.

I thought Japanese were evasive. This guy came right to the point. And so soon. Maybe he just wants to pump me for competitive information. Hell! What can I tell him that he doesn't know anyway. So he is interested in us. But so soon? I just got here. An ally like him could cut through a lot of red tape. But Tsuji seems to be a bit different from the average Joe Japanese. Can't put my finger on it, but maybe that's why he came straight out ... . Jeez, I hope I can get an account with him."

The secretary interrupted his reverie to tell him he had another call. This time it was Sarah. He gingerly explained who had called and why and that he could not be home for dinner. She took it evenly, denying the inconvenience. On hanging up he put it out of his mind, having more pressing things to consider.

The remaining hour and half of his afternoon was spent reviewing the file he had put together on Tokaido Meats. There was not much. The company was formed in 1936 by Yoshida's father, Yoshida Risuke, who started with only a butcher shop. It emerged after the war as a growing force in meat slaughtering and distribution. Presently, two farms were owned by Tokaido, one in Kobe, one in Yuuki, and they had diversified into trucking. Yoshida Tsuji had risen through the ranks to become president in 1969. His father still held a guiding position as chairman of the board. The rest was numbers: dollars and yen.

Thomas called Jetro to ask for more information about Tokaido.

He was quickly informed that Jetro, Japan's External Trade Relations Organization, was not a telephone data bank. If he wanted more information he would have to go their library and do the research himself. Disappointed, he spent his last minutes trying to review some Japanese phrases. All too soon, 6:30 arrived.

With clockwork punctuality, the black Nissan President Deluxe pulled up to the curb and the rear door opened automatically. Thomas seated himself by Yoshida and extended his hand.

"Tsuji-san, cone ban wa."

"Good evening, Mr. Bugman," replied Yoshida, wondering who had taught Bergman his poor Japanese. "Are you learning to speak Japanese now?" he asked, feigned surprise in his voice.

"Thank you, no. My wife and son are though. I guess it just rubs off," Thomas said, satisfied with his coup.

That explains it, thought Yoshida. "It is a difficult language, don't you think?"

"Well, I hope that just living here, I will pick it up naturally. I've heard that happened to some executive acquaintances of mine who went to Europe; a two-year tour and they were fluent," he said optimistically.

He will learn painfully, Yoshida thought, that learning is not that easy. He must think my conversation with him perfectly unrestrained. I am still struggling, despite speaking with many soldiers for years after the war and my weekly English tutorial for the past five years. He will learn, painfully.

"What kind of food would you like?"

"I hardly know my way around. I think you had better choose the restaurant."

Yoshida gave the driver an address and settled back into the plush upholstery of his company's best sedan.

59

"This is some car," Thomas exclaimed. "Why don't you export some of these to the U.S.? I haven't seen any like it there."

"We are only in the meat business," the Japanese man said, a confused tone in his voice.

"Oh … I meant 'you' as in 'you Japanese,' the country," Thomas said, realizing the snag in the conversation.

"Oh, I think Japanese industry is preparing for an export …"

"Push?"

"Yes. Export push. But … 'we' save the best for home use," Yoshida replied with a smile. "We are going to a place called the Eight Fragrance Garden. Have you eaten there?"

"No, I don't think so."

"It is a contemporary restaurant built within the perimeter of a famous old garden."

"Japanese garden?"

"Yes, of course."

"I've seen a couple. They're nice. I like them a lot." Thomas said, not really sure of what to say. He had found Japanese gardens not particularly to his liking; unimaginative, from his point of view. He preferred the photos he had seen of the colorful, geometrically designed floral patterns built into European estates.

"Actually, Bugman-san, a Japanese garden does not usually evoke …" Yoshida paused to see if the word he had learned was well-chosen or not, "a strong feeling of like, or dislike. It is a place to relax and be. Perhaps there is another word … eflation?"

"Elation?"

"Yes, the garden makes one feel elated. Are you aware of the form behind Japanese gardens?"

Thomas had not been aware they had a specific structure. A pond, a waterfall, a hill, trees, and walls. He had discerned no

60

pattern.

Yoshida listened to the silence and said, "They are models of nature. The world condensed into a small, comfortable space. After dinner we can take a walk around the garden."

The automobile turned off the main road into a long, winding driveway that curved around an ancient tree, its branches lightly illuminated for the evening. They came to stop at the entrance where dozens of other diners were alighting. Thomas felt the entrance looked more like a hotel, such was the activity in the red-carpeted lobby.

He and Yoshida crossed the foyer and descended a flight of steps leading to the edge of the garden. They traversed a wooden bridge, shy branches of bamboo leaves touching the rail, and followed a path to another building. Entering, they were shown to a Western-sized table with a grill in its center.

"I believe you have had teppanyaki before."

"Yes, at Kanto's in the U.S. and once here during the Jetro meeting. I like it."

"You may find this a little different. Not so ... extravagant."

"Flashy?"

"Perhaps, yes. The food is excellent, the performance quiet."

An attendant brought them *o-shibori*, which were snow white and steaming. Both men delicately picked up the hot towels. Thomas tossed it from hand to hand, as he had seen Japanese do, to cool it down before wiping his face and hands with it.

First tea and then beer was served, and as the kimono-clad waitress began the preparation of appetizers, some pickled vegetables were brought. The execution was subdued compared to the circus-like atmosphere of some teppanyaki shops, but definitely got the stomach juices moving, the American concluded. Scallops, four

61

to an order, were placed on the grill where the shell served as a natural pan. They simmered in their own juice and were served with lemon. Other vegetables and seafoods were likewise prepared and cooked before them. Finally a fine piece of beef was brought out which the woman cut into thin strips and sizzled on the grill, seasoning them delicately. The meat was well-marbled and became quite juicy when set to heat.

Thomas tasted a slice and exclaimed, "This is some piece of beef!" He instantly regretted it as he detected a smile on the Japanese face. Oh, shit, he stormed, I bet this guy brought me here on purpose — knew I'd say something like that. He is a competitor anyway, not yet an ally.

"This is Kobe beef," Yoshida spoke up. "I am sure you are very familiar with it. This piece is from our ranch." The proud smile was soft, not threatening.

"Well, it is tasty. Like some of the Grade A Choice we produce," Thomas said, lamely covering for himself.

"Bugman-san, I did not bring you here to discourage you," Yoshida said, sensing the man's perceived loss of face. "If we are to work together, as I hope we can, you must understand the Japanese meat market. Customers will pay highly for a cut such as this. You must understand their taste, not try to change it. Someone else can do that. To sell your product we must create the perception that it has an acceptable balance of flavor, fat, and texture. Iowa beef will never be Kobe beef. Accept that. We shall search for the appropriate part of the market."

"Mr. Tsuji, I appreciate your frankness," he said, recovering, "which I understand from reading is not a typical Japanese trait. Although we are interested in joint marketing possibilities with Tokaido, I would like to know more about your reasons for wanting to work with us."

"I will be frank again ... please, have more," Yoshida said directing the woman to put more beef on Thomas' plate. "Yes, the reasons are clear. We do have two farms producing superior grades of meat for Japanese consumption. But our market surveys indicate the emergence of significant trends which we must respond to in order to maintain our position. Fast foods, your McDonald's buggers and others, will be pushing into our market. Several locally developed franchise operations similar to your roadside chains are also being contemplated, steak houses for the *sarary-man* on a fixed expense budget. Such restaurants cannot afford our beef.

"I will not deceive you. The Australian Beef Export Commission has been persuading me for a year to buy from them. According to our test marketing, the balance I mentioned before was lacking. Despite their entertainment and sincerity, I have turned them down.

"I now ask you to dinner and you are aware of the potential of our relationship. We have the warehousing capacity, the trucking network, and the contacts. And we are willing to help you overcome Japan's cumbersome agricultural imports process if that is possible. I believe your government is right, you know, complaining about our nontariff barriers."

Thomas had listened in silence for several minutes, stunned by Yoshida's directness and the market information he had gathered. It was a golden opportunity. But, he hesitated, where are the problems?

"May I see the results of your market survey and projections?"

"They are in Japanese."

"May I have them translated?"

"Yes."

Good, Thomas thought. Even if we don't get in bed with Tokaido, the information is powerful promotion for our beef. He was excited and tense. The possibility that he could sign them up as a major wholesaler of Iowa steer was a potent stimulant to the salesman in his blood.

"I think I would like to see the garden now," he said, meaning it.

The garden air, despite being in the city, was clear and refreshing. Chatting about business, they took a long stroll down to a traditional teahouse by a lower pond, then up through a small forest lit with stone lanterns and around to a waterfall cascading down from a miniature mountain. They stopped by the larger, upper pond and looked at the *koi*. The large goldfish swam together in bright orange, white, and black swirls. Unconsciously, a warm, quiet feeling prevailed in Thomas even as he was driven to his train station, silently contemplating the future.

Yoshida reflected on the meeting with Bergman as he sat in the back seat of the car, his driver picking his way through the evening Tokyo traffic. Yes, frankness was not a typical Japanese trait. But I am not a typical Japanese. I am not even Japanese, by their standards. I am an *eta* to them, and I despise them as they despise us still. Oh, they may call us *shinheimin*, "new citizens," but their feelings are the same as always. To them the difference between us is like that between Kobe beef and the grade Bergman sells. One is superior, refined, well-balanced, and unique. The result of exclusive breeding. The other, although also beef, is common and not of the same standard. We are the same though. They just cannot, will not, recognize it.

By August, life had settled down for the Bergman family. Thomas had concluded a marketing agreement with Tokaido Meats which won high praise from the commissioners on the beef commission. Some even began to wonder if it was necessary for him to be stationed there anymore.

Sarah had made two friends with whom she regularly commiserated. They spent much of their time talking about home and their children or how bad or funny life was in Japan.

Ted, on the other hand, was busy trying to fulfill his goals. He had surprised even himself. He could now buy items of interest, get train directions or greet neighbors in Japanese. He had dropped out of the group class in favor of a private tutorial the school had suggested. It cost more, but the commission was paying for it, so Ted did not worry.

Furthermore, he now had a chance to practice speaking several times a week at the Shorinji kempo training hall he had found. According to a book he bought, Shorinji was the Japanese reading of Shaolin Temple. What the students were practicing did not look like the Asian fighting art he had seen on television and in the movies, but he was too excited with the methods to care. There were no other foreigners in his class, not that they were unwelcome, and he used his limited Japanese as much as possible.

It was hot, tiresome training, and his five weekly sessions soon trimmed off what little fat he had and built up his chest and arms. The basics he was learning consisted of endless repetitions of stance, blocks, punches, and kicks, followed by more repetitions of combinations of these movements. He was a quick study and, though the teacher never gave any verbal encouragement, Ted's natural ability was recognized.

Ted looked at his body in the full-length mirror on his closet door as he dressed for a special Sunday outing. His stomach showed signs of the ladder of muscles he-men always displayed. He flexed his chest as he breathed out slowly and deeply. His pectorals, although not bulging, were visibly larger. He relaxed and stepped closer to the mirror as he inspected the progress of his chest hair. Satisfied that there was more than before, if only two or three bristles, he put on his shirt.

His father had told him to dress nicely; a tie was not necessary, but no dungarees. There was a picnic scheduled for many important meat buyers and their families. It was to be American-style all the way. Charcoal-grilled steaks, corn on the cob, both from Iowa of course, salad, rolls, chips, dips, and booze. Lots of booze. Ted regretted having to go because he had to miss his kempo class, but his father had stressed the importance of it.

The picnic could not be held in the countryside, so a hotel with a rooftop garden in the Shinagawa section of Tokyo was chosen. The Bergmans arrived early, and Ted helped his father with the final preparations. An awning had been erected and waiters were busy helping chefs set up their outdoor charcoal grills.

At 5:30, guests began emerging from ever-busier elevators. Despite the formal request for casual dress on the invitations, many guests arrived in their corporate uniforms — dark blue suits and ties. Men were given cowboy hats and the ladies bandanas with silver Iowa pins. There were two long photo displays of life in Iowa, stills of ranches, cross-country skiing, blue skies, and open grasslands. The second photo display depicted the life of an Iowa steer. Cleanliness, corn feeding, and the industry's scientific approach to cattle raising were stressed. Simple explanations in Japanese accompanied the photos. Seventy-five families, comprising the heads of restaurant, grocery, and fast-food chains, were invited. Iowa supplied the beef, corn, and spirits while Tokaido Meats funded the rest.

Before long the roof was alive with Asian cowboys sipping whiskeys and cognacs. Ted and Sarah were introduced to some of the guests. Though the invitations had suggested it would be a family evening, most of the men had come alone. Some had reluctantly brought their wives, few had brought their children. Ted felt quite out of place until Yoshida came up to Thomas.

"Please pardon my tardiness," he said with a bow to Thomas. Actually he was only three minutes late. "I am glad you brought your family. I have brought mine, as you can see." His wife stood meekly to his left rear and bobbed her head with a smile.

"I would like you to meet my wife Sarah and my son Teddy. This is Yoshida Tsuji, Mr. Tsuji, the head of Tokaido Meats."

"I've heard so much about you, Mr. Tsuji," Sarah responded with a smile, offering her hand to him to shake which he did momentarily.

It was Ted's turn. He bowed deeply and said "*Yoshida Tsuji-sama, hajimemashite.*"

Yoshida was taken aback by being addressed not only in Japanese but with the proper use of respectful forms. He looked hard at the handsome youth, wondering if this was the only Japanese he knew.

He asked in his native tongue, "Do you have a Japanese name yet?"

"My name is Takabashi. 'Taka' sounds like 'Ted' and 'Bashi' like 'Bergman.' 'Eagle Bridge,' Yoshida-sama."

"Let me introduce the rest of my family," Yoshida said in English as his wife stepped aside and his two daughters came forward.

It was Ted's turn to be awestruck. Both girls were cute and one

67

was his age. She was the picture he had formed in his mind of young oriental beauty. Long, straight, shining hair, skin unravaged by the teen acne, and a body that appeared firm and appealing to the eye.

"This is my oldest daughter Mieko and her sister Yuko." Both girls bowed.

"Yoshida Mieko, I am Takabashi," Ted said in Japanese with short bow.

She smiled shyly and covered her mouth with her right hand as she bowed again to him.

The picnic went all too quickly for Ted after meeting Mieko. A country band played some music and the U.S. Armed Forces square dancing club gave a demonstration, inviting guests to join in. It was the first time Ted was glad for the rainy days at elementary school spent learning reels rather than having recess. He offered to teach Mieko and they joined in the group.

As the sky darkened and the smell of grilled steaks sent everyone's stomachs rumbling, vast bowls of salad with side dishes of shrimp, bacon, beets, onions, croutons, dressings, and other condiments were set out on long buffet tables. Fresh, hot bread and stacks of corn with butter dripped on them were delivered steaming to the display. The Yoshidas and Bergmans sat together, Ted and Mieko side by side. Mieko's steak was quite the largest she had ever seen and there was no question in her mind that she would not be able to finish it. Ted's was the biggest he had in months and there was no question in his mind that he would relish every bite.

After eating, Thomas stood up to give a short speech with a simultaneous translation followed by another short talk and toast from Yoshida. They both then moved from guest to guest thanking them for their participation and giving each family a five-kilogram box of frozen Iowa steaks.

As the prospective customers departed, some a trifle drunk and being helped by wives or waiters, Yoshida faced Thomas. "They have enjoyed the evening. I believe we can call it a success."

"When the first container-sized orders start rolling in, I'll call it success," Thomas said wryly.

"Yes, yes. We would like to invite you and your family to our house for a taste of Japanese home life. Do you think you can make it?" Yoshida added congenially.

"Sounds great. When would that be?"

"How about two weeks from today?"

"That'd be the last Sunday of August. I'll make it a date then."

The photo displays would be disassembled by others and sent to Thomas' office later. There was nothing further to be done and Ted knew time was running short for him to ask Mieko out for a date. He was unsure of himself and of local customs. Mieko's mother came toward the young couple who were by the rail looking at the night lights of Tokyo Tower. Ted could feel the pressure mounting.

"Mieko, it's time for us to leave," she said, taking her daughter's arm.

Mieko said, "Goodbye, Takabashi-san," in her gentle voice and turned with her mother to leave.

"Yoshida-san, I hope we have a chance to see you again," he said slowly but desperately to the mother, the words trying to find his tongue.

He could not understand most of her rapid reply but he sensed it was friendly — something about going to their house. They bowed to each other and he joined his mother and father, his heart beating rapidly, thoughts of Iowa far, far away.

The cicadas hummed in the small garden at the center of the house as Yoshida kneeled on the *tatami* gazing out over the stones and moss, his eyes unfocused, his mind deep in thought. Why did that "attached horse" have to choose tonight to pay a call, his intent less than friendly? And why would he bring his boss, Yamashita? They could not want more than principal and interest. What more could he offer? At any rate, tonight was a bad night for such lowly visitors. He was expecting the Bergmans to arrive in an hour and did not want *yakuza* henchmen despoiling the atmosphere in his house while guests were there.

He heard the *shoji* slide open quietly behind him and turned to see his wife.

"Yamashita-san has arrived," she said gravely.

"Show him in."

The stout but solid Yamashita entered the room accompanied by a much younger man, the "attached horse," who appeared to be about twenty-six years old. Both were dressed in black suits with thin lapels and matching ties. Company pins adorning their lapels indicated they were employees of Great Star Construction, a holding company. Anyone even peripherally associated with Tokyo low-life recognized the company's extensive gangland ties and tremendous financial strength gathered through ever-increasing ownership of legitimate enterprises.

Neither man bowed or exchanged courtesies, but the "attached horse" started in abruptly, saying, "You are a month overdue in your installment."

"Forgive me. I can give you a check for it tonight."

"The last check you sent us was postdated. We don't like that," the young man said brusquely.

Yoshida recognized he was trying to please his boss with a

show of brazenness. "I am sorry, Nishida-sama. It will not happen again," he said meekly, appealing to the ego of the underling.

"We have heard that too many times to believe you, new citizen. Would you have us employ your daughters until their holes bleed?" Yamashita said forcefully.

Yoshida's stomach knotted at the thought. How such fatherless monkeys could look down on him as an *eta* when they themselves were so crude, he could not fathom. "Of course, that will not be necessary," he replied in a low, subservient tone.

"Now then, you will pay us on time?"

"Yes."

"No more readjustments in your schedule?"

"Yes."

"And no postdated checks?"

"Yes."

"You see, even godless *eta* can behave like real people if trained to," Yamashita said to his assistant with a cruel chuckle.

Yoshida went to a low writing table set near the wall and opened a drawer pulling out his checkbook. He checked it for the correct amount, dated it, and wrote the beneficiary's name, Great Star Finance, on the blank. He then pulled his chop out of its pouch from around his neck and pressed it into a pad of vermillion ink. When it was well primed, he pressed the chop evenly on the appropriate space and looked at the impression it had left. His seal was his signature. He handed the check to Yamashita.

"Please," he said with grave formality, gesturing toward the *shoji*, beckoning them to leave.

The two men departed without a word, shown out by Yoshida's wife who had returned silently to direct them to the gate.

Yoshida turned to face the garden again. The sun had burned

71

long golden rays into the sky above the house during the visit of the two men. He regretted having missed the glow of sunset on the pond. It was now almost night, and more insects had joined in with their busy nocturnal calls. However, the visit had unsettled him and he could not lose his mind in the sight and sound.

Would that I had never met Miss Matsubara, he lamented. How is it that the male root, a small muscle used for pissing, can lead one to such troubles? Yes, Matsubara was beautiful ... and young. But that beautiful? This prolonged agony? Yes, I took her best years, I enjoyed her best years. I so enjoyed pillowing with her ... but it has cost too much!

Eight years before he had entertained a client at the Colorful Flower Hall, a medium-class geisha establishment, to further a business arrangement. He knew his customer was just as interested in exercising his fifth limb in bed as he was in listening to ancient tunes being plucked on the *samisen*. Therefore, he had chosen this particular place where the girls were less proficient in the finer arts and more willing to entertain without their kimonos on.

While the purchaser became engrossed in an entertainer selected for him by the proprietress, Yoshida was cared for by a relative newcomer, Matsubara Aichiko. He was struck by her youthful gaiety and innocent but willing air; so struck that on paying for his customer's expenses for the remainder of the evening's private entertainment, he inquired about making an appointment to see Miss Matsubara again.

He had never sought a permanent sexual liaison outside of marriage, but he felt he had reached the time and financial position in his life when he could both enjoy it and afford it. He was entertained by her at the club for seven consecutive nights. On the seventh evening he reserved a room at a quiet Japanese-style inn and took her there after settling it with her manager. She acted just as he had dreamed over the past week that she would, only better. She refused to undress before him and instead helped him off with his clothes, meticulously folding and hanging them piece by piece. She held up the *yukata* for him as he slipped into the robe and padded with him to the bathroom, where she checked to make sure all bath materials were present, then left. He washed himself alone, rinsed, and settled into the deep hot tub to soak. Just as he began to get anxious, she came in wearing a *yukata*. Slowly, shyly, she untied the *obi* and hung it on the wall hook. She peeled off the cotton robe and revealed her form to him.

Despite the relaxing properties of the hot tub, he became suddenly aware of his pulse quickening and he began to feel his jade stem swelling. She stood just out of his arm's reach and began to wash herself, naturally, methodically, completely. As she soaped her breasts, he could see, could feel by her touch, that they were firm, the nipples small, but hard and definite. As she rinsed with a wooden dipper of hot water, he could feel the liquid coursing its way over her every curve, finding its way into her every crevice, rinsing through her pubic triangle, pulling the dripping mat of hair downward.

By the time she stepped into the tub with him he felt he had already experienced the ultimate intimacy that could be shared with her, but he was wrong. After their bath, she had dried him gently, avoiding contact with his maleness, which ached for her touch. She led him to the *tatamied* room and pulled him down to the *futon* lying on the floor. He took her, suddenly, and completed his desire. She cried out softly, the breath burning in his ear, and pulled him in. His burst of energy coincided with the rush of her high tide and was quite final, a warm glow succeeding it. He rolled

73

off her and slept deeply.

For the following year he had visited Aichiko at the Colorful Flower Hall on a regular basis, always seeing her at least once a month. On every occasion she had found some way to stir his passion as strongly as on the first night. She taught him things he had never known could be shared between a man and a woman. After a year, he approached the proprietress of the hall about buying out Aichiko's contract. Discreet negotiations took place, and within a month he had found and furnished an apartment for her. As her contract and taste in accommodations were not cheap, he had to dig deeply into his personal account to finance it. Nevertheless, he was satisfied with the transaction. Aichiko gave him more in a night than his wife had given him in a life, he justified.

"Why must the world change so fast?" Yoshida pined as he sat thinking of his current predicament. After two years of keeping Aichiko to himself and exclusively enjoying her favors, it became clear that the relationship would not work out. Although his wife had kept silent to him about her, he felt certain that she knew. His father inquired about his expenses and performance and implied he did not approve of the extravagance.

He resisted thoughts of deserting Aichiko for several more months but his father, a staunch critic of *shinheimin* who integrated with Japanese, no less Japanese whores, gave him an ultimatum, to give up his family and company or the "*daruma* doll" he kept. He bowed to his father's decree, and on one cold January night when he would have much rather been pillowing with her, he gave her a farewell present of a platinum ring with two natural pearls set side by side embraced by two diamonds of modest size.

"There is a pearl for each year of pleasure you have given me and a diamond's facet for each night spent burning in your arms.

There will be no more jeweled evenings after tonight, though."

Aichiko blinked her eyes innocently and smiled, "It is beautiful, like your words, but I do not understand."

"We must not see each other again."

"Again ... ever?" She was not ready for this eventuality, having only recently succeeded in extracting enough gifts from him to live according to her expectations.

Yoshida was silent, feeling her stare and his years, now paying interest on the renewed youth he had experienced with her.

"What am I now that you can let me go?" she railed. "Where can I go? We were lovers and bound together. What can repay the tenderness I showed you, myself an unpicked flower when you first smelled my fragrance. Do you think my petals can be pasted back on, that another man will take a second look now." As an entertainer she was an actress. As an actress she was now playing a desperate role. She could not let him get away cheaply.

Yoshida maintained his composure and direction through more than two hours of her pleading. He heard her wailing and felt her clawing at his pants' cuff as he closed her apartment door behind him. He assured himself that with two months on the lease yet to go, she would find herself another benefactor and be comfortably settled by the time the landlord politely insisted she move.

Aichiko was not to be swayed. She placed herself at the roadside entrance of the Yoshida residence through seven cold and blustery January days. On the seventh day she barged into the lobby of Tokaido Meats where Yoshida was informally discussing a management problem with their labor leader and personnel director.

He was shocked to see her appearance, having avoided looking at her when he left his house in the mornings. She was chapped and without a trace of makeup, her hair dry and disheveled.

75

"How can you treat me this way," she cried dramatically, collapsing at his feet, sobbing.

He drew away and looked at both of his subordinates, as incredulous as they.

She lifted her head and looked up at them and her face took on the expression of raw fear one sees in an animal about to be slaughtered. She drew a knife and, kneeling, poised it inches from her solar plexus.

"You were born to kill animals here. I should have known I would end up in this place too." She plunged the knife toward her heart.

The labor leader acted swiftly, kicking her elbow to the left and deflecting the blade so that it only tore the side of her coat and grazed her rib. The sharp knife clattered to the floor and Yoshida raced to grab her up and pull her away from the scene she had created.

Determined to prevent another such occurrence, Yoshida decided he had to negotiate with Aichiko. Her initial demands were far beyond what he had expected. From an outright purchase of the apartment for her and the establishment of a Ginza boutique which would surely have cost him 200 million yen, he bargained her down to an extension of the lease on her accommodation and the title to a small saké and snack bar in a popular area of Shinjuku. Still he had to find 100 million yen.

His father turned a deaf ear to his request for a personal loan from the corporate treasury. "I have never paid for a whore's cave, I won't begin now," he said severely. "Go get your floating-world gold from your Japanese friends."

Yoshida assumed he could not get a loan from a bank without a number of embarrassing and potentially damaging questions about the continuity of Tokaido Meats' leadership being asked in the financial community. Finally, he had turned to a private loan company. He dared not ask about the ownership, knowing that such small institutions frequently had ominous shareholders. He got his loan, but only at the usurious rate of 22 percent yearly interest with ten years to pay.

For the first two years, his father had sought to punish him. Raises and a dividend on their privately held shares were denied. Expansion capital requirements were given as the reason. Yoshida could only try to keep up with the interest on his debt. Satisfied that the loose nail had been driven solidly back into the corporate foundation, his father finally relented and promoted Yoshida to the position of president. However, headway was slow and he was getting more worried about clearing his debt as time passed.

He heard the sound of the metal hinges on the old wooden gate being opened to admit the Bergmans' car. He mentally submerged his long-standing predicament and superimposed the present business objectives he hoped to attain through Thomas. This was as it should be, he reflected. The past mistakes keep trying to float up, buoying my present outlook. I cannot forget those lessons if they are the foundation of my present. He stood up from the floor and went to greet his guests.

The dinner had been a quiet affair. Sarah had been politely silent through most of the meal, uncomfortable as she was sitting on the floor and eating disagreeable food. Thomas had made a number of clearly surface compliments about the house, while Mrs. Yoshida tried to make everyone comfortable through smiles, friendly nods, and attentive food service. Yoshida directed his wife and daughters and made small talk in Japanese with Ted.

Ted was oblivious to everything special and ordinary during the evening. His embarrassed attention was focused on Mieko. Embarrassed because he could not look at her enough and was afraid he was violating some ancient Japanese code. Focused because he had thought of Mieko constantly for two weeks since the barbecue and had only found out tonight that his reverie understated her attraction.

Mieko and her sister had been told to dress for the occasion and their mother had helped them don bright red-flowered kimonos. Mrs. Yoshida herself wore a subdued blue silk kimono with a bamboo pattern. All three were shod in silk *zori* matching their costumes.

Ted was first captivated by the short quiet footsteps of the three silken bodies as they walked from the entrance to the reception. He could not see them as they walked discreetly behind the men, but his hearing concentrated on the sound. The house was of traditional Japanese design and a rough hewn rock path led around from the gravel drive through several small evergreen trees and across a short stone bridge over a miniature pond. Six *nishi koi* swam in a school, their golden rainbow bodies reminding Ted of a Tiffany carnival glass vase he had seen once.

When the men had established themselves in the Japanese equivalent of a living room, a six-*tatami* space adjoining Yoshida's study, and the wives and daughters had busied themselves elsewhere, Ted sat quietly and examined the walls. They were a soft cream color and were divided into rectangular sections by straight smooth timbers brown with age. Evenly placed between the supports were hanging scrolls. There was a picture of a Japanese man or god, Ted was not sure which, who huddled closely with a deer in the snow, sharing warmth. Another was of calligraphy and Ted could not read it. Nevertheless, the flow of the lines appealed to him.

His eyes came to rest on an alcove set apart by a rustic heavy section of bamboo that rose from the floor to the ceiling as if it had grown through the house and sent its leaves above the roof. In the alcove was a light olive green china basin with a cracked-ice glaze pattern half-filled with water. In it was placed a single lily pad and flower. Ted carefully examined the flowers from across the room. He had never looked twice before at any arrangement — that was for fags, he had convinced himself — but this was different. They were not out of place or gaudy. They obstructed the view of nothing and added to the life of the room.

Yoshida had been talking with Bergman but gazing at Ted as the boy's eyes circled the room slowly. This lad does have a certain appeal. Much more at home here than either of his parents, he reflected.

"Do you know what that is?" he asked Ted, nodding toward the alcove.

"*Iie, wa karimasen,*" Ted replied.

"It is a *tokonoma*. An altar used by the family. Items treasured by my father's generation and handed down to us are placed here."

"I have not seen a flower arrangement like that before."

"Something I do in my spare time," Yoshida said. "Do you like it?"

"It's ... you did it? Its the first one I have seen that's ... I donno ... bold," Ted commented, searching for the right word.

Bold. Yoshida considered the word. Yes. The arrangement was bold through its understatement.

"You are right, Takabashi-an," he said smiling at the teenager. When Mieko re-entered, Ted's mind was lost on her again. He

79

tried to divert his attention, to tell himself that he was just a horny boy. But his eyes would find their way back to her as she looked down, coyly embarrassed, avoiding his gaze.

Mieko enjoyed his attention. Never had a boy looked at her more that once she felt. Perhaps it was because she was a *shinheimin*, she thought sadly, as if she had a mark that any nice boy could see clearly. Perhaps it was because, although she thought herself plain, the American boy had never seen a girl in a kimono and so he alone was momentarily fascinated. She dared not believe that he was attracted to her the way she was to him. But she enjoyed the eye games they played while they were to last.

Yoshida was acutely aware of Ted and his daughter's presence together in the room. The two served as catalysts; a space devoid of one lacking any reaction, but together energizing the whole area. He felt that Bergman was oblivious to what was going on and that Ted's mother, though aware, did not approve. But he approved. Ted, although American, had shown a creditable awareness of true beauty. Yoshida approved.

After dinner Ted felt himself in the same quandary he had been in at the end of the barbecue. He fretted over how to ask Mieko for a date. She hasn't looked at me once all night, he stewed. She probably has no interest in a *gaijin* foreigner like me. I bet she thinks I'm a jerk.

As everyone approached the main gate to say their farewells, Ted blurted out in imperfect Japanese, "Yoshida-sama. I would like to invite Mieko to see the movies next week."

"Excuse me," Yoshida said, testing the boy's mettle.

"Umm … may I take your daughter to the movies next week?"

"She does have her schoolwork," he said as Mieko's eyes darted to her father's, a beacon of urgency in them. "But I think it would be all right."

Both Ted and Mieko glanced directly at each other for the first time that evening and brief grins flashed across their faces. They parted highly elated with thoughts of the next weekend.

In the automobile returning home, Sarah asked Ted what he had said to Yoshida when they were leaving.

"I, uh, asked if I could take Mieko to the movies."

"Teddy," she scolded disapprovingly, "of all the girls you could ask out, did you have to invite her, the daughter of your father's most important business connection?"

"I think it'll be OK, honey," Thomas interceded with more assurance than he felt. "You won't get into any mischief, right son?"

"I only invited her to the movies!"

"Just be a gentleman, son," Thomas said, closing the matter.

Later that evening as they prepared for sleep, Sarah rolled to her husband's side of the bed and whispered her concerns about the date and for his business.

"Honey," her husband replied softly," he's a growing boy. He's always shown good judgement and I don't want to worry about it, OK?"

"But your work here is hard enough without Teddy making trouble for you. You promised me we would try to go back to the U.S. as soon as possible. I don't want him to be a risk to your success. Besides, I just don't think it's right here for Teddy, exposed to all these foreign ideas; he's so impressionable. You remember that TV show with all the fighting in the U.S.? Well, now he's turning himself into some kind of killing machine. Have you looked at some of the books he's been buying? They're all about maiming and murdering. It just concerns me," she said resignedly, sensing that Thomas had either put up a mental wall to her protestations or had gone to sleep.

She settled back into her pillow and troubled thoughts of Ted marrying an Asian pulled her across a rocky path to a disturbed sleep.

Ted and Mieko dated steadily through the fall, suffering only two minor setbacks. After their first trip out together to the movies, Ted's mother had taken him aside and asked him, in tones implying a parental command, not to see the Yoshida girl again. Quite disappointed, Ted called Mieko and told her that his parents wanted him to concentrate on his studies more and he could not ask her out again.

Two weeks passed, when one evening after dinner Thomas called his son into the study.

"How are your studies going, son?"

"OK. Fine."

"Have you seen Mieko lately?"

"No. I am not supposed to."

Thomas was baffled by the remark, but replied, "Don't you think it's time you asked her out for another date? Practice your Japanese."

It was Ted's turn to be confused. "OK. I guess so. Does ... does Mom think it's OK?" he asked cautiously.

"I wouldn't worry about her. Now, go along and call your friend," he said with a smile. His wife's concern about Ted was unfounded, he felt. A week after his son's first date with Mieko, Yoshida had asked about Ted during a business lunch. How was the boy doing in his studies, was his Japanese improving, had he enjoyed his date with Mieko? Finally, Yoshida had said, "Your son seems to be a very nice young man. I want you to know I have no objections to him inviting Mieko out again and he is welcome to visit our house any time."

After a hard look from his mother when he was preparing for his second date, he was not bothered by his parents again about seeing her. He never knew what had changed their minds. However, he was ecstatic that they had.

He had created a minor rift for himself when watching a movie with her on their fourth date. Having no intimate friends nor an older brother to coach him, he was at a loss when trying to determine the proper protocol for kissing a Japanese girl. She would be only the second girl he had kissed, and she was so different from Judy. Judy had experience. He knew that. Everybody said she had. But Mieko. He knew only her, none of her friends, and he worried that she was the daughter of his father's important client. She always seemed so shy, yet interested. During a romantic scene on the screen, Ted had turned and looked at her. She turned her head towards him and looked into his eyes. Feeling that the moment was right and the opportunity about to disappear, he leaned toward her and pressed his lips over hers, experimentally probing with his tongue.

She recoiled, obviously shocked and looked about to see if anyone was watching. After the show he apologized to her, but she said nothing. When he called her again to ask her out, it was as if nothing had happened. She was eager to see him. Since then they had enjoyed each other's company, going out and helping themselves in their language studies. But there were no more kisses and Ted was the shy one now.

Ted's life became as satisfying as he could ever remember it being. Every day was an adventure. He was doing well in school.

Many of his classmates at the international school he attended, he observed, were burned out as students. Having been dragged through half a dozen countries during their matriculation, they were tired of the pace, tired of expecting to leave friends, of the dreaded anticipation of a new country, a new language, and a different set of restrictions be they religious, governmental, or parental. They were the children of the lifetime expatriates, those executives who stayed out of the corporate mainstream too long to make it to the top, forever exiled, sometimes gratefully, to the overseas post. But to Ted, it was all new and his mind collected data and images like stamps in an album. His studies improved as he reveled in new teaching methods, new teachers, exotic subjects, and a seeming lack of real competition. Of course, there were serious students. They formed a clique as distinct as a thermocline in a lake: above, warm fertile water where ideas, like algae, grew, and cold clear water below; between the two a strict demarcation.

He joined neither group and found he really had little time for socializing with his peers. Three nights a week he had a Japanese tutorial. His teacher was a patient, matronly Japanese woman who had been educated in college during a spate of feminist sentiment in occupied Japan. She was from a wealthy family and sometimes told her student of her gratitude to the Americans for their moderate reconstruction of her country. Being unmarried, she tutored foreigners to earn extra money, but mostly to have people with whom to talk and who depended on her.

During three other nights of the week he attended his training at the Shorinji school. His teacher had found Ted's drive to learn and improve his skills unflagging, which had surprised him, and eventually invited Ted to attend a special Sunday session for senior students. Initially, Ted was used as a live dummy for the demonstration of the techniques by the teacher. But Ted put up with the pain and he learned through observation. He realized now he had to demonstrate his perseverance at every step in order to be initiated into more advanced techniques.

He had learned several basic drills and had conditioned his body so that it was ready for further learning. He sometimes let his pride get the best of him and thought that because he had tried a technique, he had mastered it. He would usually end up on the floor looking up at his training partner, wondering what had gone wrong. Undaunted, he would practice the method repeatedly at home until he felt it was internalized. In this way, his progress was rapid, pleasing both himself and his silent, praiseless instructor.

On Christmas Day, the Yoshidas were invited by Thomas to attend a traditional holiday feast. Sarah had initially protested that Christmas was not a time to invite business guests. However, Thomas gave her a short lecture on the Yuletide spirit and his hopes to draw closer to Yoshida through such contact.

When the Japanese family arrived, they started to take off their shoes, but Sarah smiled and said, "Don't worry about a thing. In America, we wear our shoes in the house."

Yoshida's wife looked to her husband for a cue and then returned a nervous smile and stepped through the door onto the carpet. As the men went to the living room and sat down on the long sofa next to a brightly lit tree that reminded Yoshida of a night on the Ginza, Sarah was followed into the kitchen by Mrs. Yoshida and her daughters.

Sarah felt clumsy and uncomfortable working on her turkey with six eyes staring at her and unintelligible gasps, chuckles, and comments being traded behind her back. Actually, Mrs. Yoshida was impressed. She had previously understood that all American

85

home cooking was instant, canned, or frozen. The manipulations she saw taking place were all strange and new to her, and though the sight of the huge, ungainly, golden bird did not appeal to her, she appreciated the work that had gone into it. She asked Mieko to compliment Sarah on her cooking.

"My mother wishes to says that this chicken is beautiful and smells good."

"It's a turkey, not a chicken. Thank you. *Domo arigato.*"

The Japanese women laughed when Mieko told them their mistake.

During dinner Mrs. Yoshida reported to her husband what she had seen. They concluded that the meal tasted better than it looked and the raw tartness of the cranberry relish especially appealed to them. They found the sweet potatoes with marshmallows too rich, but were completely enthralled with the mincemeat pie. After their repast, they retired again to the living room.

All afternoon, Ted and Mieko had felt uncomfortable under their parents' supervision. They could speak neither Japanese nor English to each other without someone understanding. Finally, in the living room, Ted pulled out a gift brightly wrapped in red paper. He gave it to Mieko, who covered her mouth as she giggled in embarrassment.

"Oh, that reminds me," Thomas exclaimed, snapping his fingers as he rushed back into the bedroom. He came out with three other small packages.

Mieko who was sitting on the carpeted floor next to the coffee table, raised the gift to her eyebrows and then bowed her head to the floor. "Thank you, Takabashi-san," she said.

"Well, go ahead. Open the gifts," Thomas said enthusiastically.

The Yoshidas hesitated. Usually they would wait until they had returned home to open them lest they accidentally express any disappointment, making the giver lose face.

"Go on!" Thomas encouraged, an expectant smile on his face.

Mieko waited for her father and mother to open their gifts first. Yoshida unwrapped his to find a small, golden steer on a marble pedestal to be used as a desk accessory to hold paper clips. A gold plaque was inscribed with the words, "Iowa Beef, The Best Beef!"

"Yes. Thank you, Bugman-san," he said, holding the trinket to his forehead with a slight bow.

Mrs. Yoshida had a French silk scarf, which she tried on with shy but obvious pleasure. Yuko had a traditional Raggedy Ann doll. She laughed as she pointed out the bright red hair to her mother.

Finally, Mieko opened her gift, slowly peeling the tape from the red paper, careful not to tear it. The wrapping gave way to reveal two books. One was a simulated-leather-bound diary with a small, ineffectual lock. The second book was a practical dictionary that Ted had found very useful.

She opened the diary. "It is empty," she said, puzzled.

"It is your book," Ted replied in Japanese.

Yoshida looked on, thinking warmly that the red wrapping paper was auspicious, signifying a wedding. He hoped that her book had a happy ending. He laughed to himself and then shook the thought from his head. They are just children, he mused.

"By the way, Bugman-san," he said addressing Thomas. "My wife and I will be taking the girls on a trip to a snow resort. I will do some business and they will ski. Do you think Ted would like to go?"

"Well, that's awfully nice but ..." Thomas began.

"Dad! Could I go? When is it? It's not during school, right?" Ted exclaimed, eager not to let the moment pass.

"No, part of New Year's actually."

"That's too kind, Yoshida-san. Are you sure Ted wouldn't be an imposition?"

"None at all. A relaxing weekend is all, and I am sure we will more than profit by practicing our English, yes, Mieko?"

She looked down with a smile and nodded.

It was Ted's first time on the slopes that year and he quickly regained his ski legs. Mieko, though not unfamiliar with skiing, was not as sure as Ted, and they stayed on the intermediate slopes during the morning. Yuko awkwardly tagged along, and Ted patiently gave her some pointers. She only playfully followed his instructions, ending up more tipsy as she tried to draw his attention away from her sister.

They had their lunch at a noodle shop adjacent to the lift and ran into Mieko's mother on the way out.

"Mama-san, can you ski with Yuko? Takabashi-san and I want to ski on the advanced slopes and she is not ready."

"I am! I am!" Yuko interjected.

"Mieko-chan, I think you should take care of your little sister. If she is ready she can go with you," her mother decided. "I will be visiting a temple this afternoon and cannot ski with her. Remember, we have dinner with your father at 7:30."

"Yes."

Ted and Mieko caught the lift bar to the top of the advanced slope and prepared for their way down. They spoke English to avoid Yuko, and she continually cried out, "No fair, it's no fair, big sister."

They ignored her, teasing her further.

Halfway down the run, Mieko pulled away quickly from Ted and Yuko and headed into a less-traveled section of the course. Occasional trees dotted the incline and Ted dug his poles in hard to catch up with her. Her sister, already barely able to keep up, was left trailing behind.

After a minute, Ted caught up with Mieko whom he had seen take a tumble in a drift of deep powder. When he slid to a stop next to her she held out her hand to be helped up. She got halfway to her feet again and slipped, pulling Ted down too, embracing him as he fell.

Shocked, Ted pulled away but felt the insistent tightening of her arms around his waist. He looked deep into her eyes and followed their message to her lips. They kissed and the anxiety of the months since he had last kissed her were forgotten. He was forgiven.

Yuko came to an abrupt stop and, spraying snow in their faces, fell on top of them giggling. They glowered and stood up, brushing the whiteness from their suits. She followed them down the mountain in silence.

Dinner was at the rustic, old *ryokan* where they stayed. It was famous in the resort of Zao for its attention to tradition. Nothing noticeable had been changed in eighty years, though steam heat had been installed beneath the *tatami*.

Ted was quite hungry and devoured what was brought to the table. He was seated on the floor, adjacent to Yoshida at the head of the low, rough-hewn table. Mieko was next to him, with her mother facing them.

They ate thick, hand-pulled whole wheat noodles in a broth that both warmed and nourished. Wild vegetables prepared several

89

ways, seaweed, and short, marinated braised ribs completed the repast. Mr. Yoshida called for more saké as he finished his third small bottle.

"Takabashi-san, you are not with your parents or in the United States and I will not hold it against you if you share some saké with me," he proffered for the second time that evening. "A man who drinks alone is too lonely. Pour for him, child."

Mieko gracefully took the bottle and poured a trickle of the hot wine into his thimble-sized cup.

"Now. Drink with me." They raised their cups and Yoshida drank his down. Ted put the liquid in his mouth and moved it around with his tongue. It was sweet, but made his tongue feel dry. It was not a taste he expected.

"What do you plan to do about college, Takabashi-san?,"

"I think I would like to keep studying Japan."

"In Japan?"

"I donno. Maybe."

"What can a young person do with a background like that?"

"Business, I guess. Something like my father."

Not much like your father, I hope, he thought as he considered that Thomas' success was in spite of himself. "What is it you like about Japan?"

"Well, I'm training some Japanese *budo*, a fighting art called Shorinji kempo. I like that a lot."

"Shorinji. That is a Chinese name. Isn't that a Chinese art?"

"I guess you're right. The headmaster brought it here a while back, after the war."

"Then what do you like about Japan?"

"The people. Sometimes all the formality is a little stuffy, but I feel more comfortable here than I did in Iowa with my friends."

"Isn't it lonely here sometimes?"

"Not so long as I learn new things. It's exciting and … and your daughter and I are friends."

"And we are friends," Yoshida said with a fatherly smile as he directed Mieko to pour Ted another cup of saké. "I would like to hear more of your views on the Japanese people."

"I only know what I see. Everybody works hard. I don't see any problems like in the States with some lazy people living off the government. And, of course, there's no problem with racial discrimination like we have in the U.S."

Yoshida chuckled, but his face had tensed. "What you see and what is are not always the same. A very Buddhist concept, I think. Would you believe me if I told you that there is a class in Japan that are looked down upon, who are discriminated against in admission to the finest schools and best corporations and who for centuries have been restricted to performing only those jobs that the pious rulers found most disgusting?"

Ted was bewildered by Yoshida's sudden change of mood and tone. "If there are groups like that they don't stand out."

"Yes, you are right. But as you're learning, Japan can be a very subtle country. And the methods of discrimination can be as indiscernible as the physical differences between one group and another."

Ted was more confused. "Is this group all the poorest people or what?"

Yoshida laughed inwardly at the thought. "No, rich or poor, they are despised by many."

"Is this what the riots were about a couple of years ago?"

"No. No one has ever rioted for our rights."

Ted heard the "our," but was afraid to ask. He remained silent.

"The group are called the *shinheimin*, 'new citizens,' the *burakumin*, 'the hamlet people,' or worse, *eta*, 'the dirty ones.' We were legislated into existence centuries ago by a Buddhist ruler who did not want good people to have to slaughter animals for food and leather. A section of society was set aside to do this dirty work. Centuries later, we are still doing it."

"Sounds like the castes in India with their untouchables."

"The comparison has been made before. And as the U.S. has found, you cannot completely legislate equality back into the people's minds. We are '*eta*,'" he spat the word. "For over ten generations my family has been locked in this ... classte?"

"Caste."

"Yes, caste. Butchers. Spillers of blood."

"But the samurai killed, too," Ted said, noting the irony.

"They certainly did not group themselves with us. Only in the past hundred years has the government made us the 'new citizens' and restored our rights ... technically. But if my nephew were to try to join one of Japan's big trading corporations for a junior management position, his background would come to light, and reason would be found to reject his application."

"Boy! I never imagined ... . But you're so successful."

"I am still just a butcher. A rich, powerful butcher. Some are not so well off."

The lacquered wooden plates and bowls had been unobtrusively cleared away as they spoke and tea was served. The proprietress poured for them and then left the room.

"After such a delightful meal and depressing discussion I feel like a bath, and I must insist that you join me, Ted. Wife, if you please," he said as he offered his arm for her to help him up.

They all walked silently down the wood-floored hallway, and

when the Yoshidas reached their room Yoshida said, "Come into the bath as soon as you can."

Ted went across the hall into his small cubicle and noted that the *futon* and quilt were already lying on the *tatami* ready for him to snuggle into for sleep. A clean, crisp blue and white *yukata* was laid out on the pillow. He stripped and put on the *yukata*, then stepped into his slippers and went to join the Yoshidas.

Yoshida had taken the largest accommodations at the *ryokan*. He and his wife shared a room while his daughters stayed in an adjoining room. Between the two was a hot tub for each separated by a sliding wooden *shoji*. Ted was glad for that. He was sure he could not face Mieko naked in front of her parents, or even alone perhaps.

"You know to wash before you get in the tub?" Yoshida asked.

"Yes, sir." Ted was thankful for the reminder.

He sheepishly took off his robe under Yoshida's gaze and poured three dippers of hot water over his body. After soaping up and rinsing, he tested the water in the tub. It felt scalding hot to him.

Yoshida removed his robe. "Too hot?"

"No," Ted said bravely as he put his leg in up to his knee and contained a wince.

While Yoshida washed, Ted slowly moved his body deeper into the tub. The move from his groin to his armpits was the hardest, he reflected as he sat neck deep in the steaming bath.

Yoshida joined him. "Isn't this relaxing?"

"Yes. My muscles were sore from the skiing. This feels good."

"I thought your martial training would keep you in shape."

"Different muscles, Yoshida-sama."

"You did not say why you train kempo."

"It's fun."

"Is that all?" Yoshida queried, disappointed with the answer.

"No. It's a kind of training I haven't had before. It makes me feel powerful, but at the same time I always keep in mind that I'm not supposed to pick fights," he added solemnly. Ted could hear Mieko, her mother, and sister washing themselves on the other side of the screen and his attention was temporarily distracted. He imagined Mieko there in full view. He swallowed and continued, "Control, too. A lot of my generation seems to be out of control, but in this I have to have perfect control."

Yoshida stretched out and said, "There is a man I would like you to meet when we go back to Tokyo. He is a fighter. A very good one, but you won't find his method in any book. I don't believe he has ever taken any students, but if he would accept you I think you should study with him."

"I like what I am studying now, but I appreciate your offer. I would like to meet the man. What does he do?"

Yoshida was not sure how to answer and replied, "A method of knife fighting. He works for me at Tokaido Meats. Why don't we plan to see him next weekend?"

"*Domo arigato, Yoshida-sama,*" Ted said bowing his head into the water.

Suddenly, Yoshida called out to his wife, "Woman, rub my back, won't you."

Momentarily, the wooden screen separating the two baths slid open and Mrs. Yoshida leaned through, her breasts still dripping with trickles of hot water. She nodded to Ted and began to press her thumbs into Yoshida's back.

Ted was taken by surprise and tried desperately not to express it. He looked through the open screen to see Mieko, who in her

94

surprise had raised her head up, briefly pulling her breasts out of the water. For an instant, Ted saw her taut nipples before they disappeared beneath the surface as she slid neck deep into the tub, embarrassed. They turned from each other and tried not to show their feelings.

After dreaming of Mieko that night, Ted was disappointed not to find her at breakfast. He had a bowl of rice gruel with dried fish and Japanese pickled radish. Yuko sat down next to him and chattered on about her plans to spend the day with him and Mieko while she ate her bowl of gruel and stole pickles from Ted's platter. Ted half listened to her small talk while waiting for the sound of Mieko's footsteps.

As he finished eating she came in and silently took her meal. Afterwards she went back to her room and put on her skiing suit, then came out and called impatiently to her sister to get ready to leave for the day. As Ted emerged from his room ready to go, she pouted, turned, and walked toward the reception and main door.

On the ski lift to the top of the run he sat uncomfortably next to her. Finally he spoke up. "Are you angry or embarrassed because of the bath last night? I'm sorry, but I didn't intend to see you. Please don't be angry with me."

She looked at him and he could see she was trying not to cry. "Takabashi-san, I am not angry with you," she said as she sobbed and a tear rolled down her cheek.

"Then why?"

"What do you think of me today, Takabashi-san?" she asked looking at him again, the sun shining in her face.

He saw a beautiful girl, raven hair windblown, pink frosted

cheeks, and brown eyes moist with tears. He saw the girl he had dated four months and come to enjoy the lively presence of. He envisioned the most perfect pair of breasts he had ever seen floating momentarily on the surface of a steaming bath.

"I like you more than ever."

"Really?!" she said incredulously. "You don't mind I am a *shinheimin*?"

Immediately Ted understood her, why she had avoided him and her tears. "Oh, hell no!" he said jocularly. Then seriously, "To me you are Mieko first, the girl who kissed me in the snow yesterday."

She laughed in relief. "I did not kiss you. You kissed me," she said, drying a tear track.

He recognized this as a face-saving gesture on her part and did not comment, only nodding in silent bemused agreement.

True to his word, Yoshida arranged for Ted to meet his employee whom he promised was a great fighter. Ted was not impressed. He had given up a Saturday workout to go to Tokaido Meats after their working hours to meet Yoshida. It had been a long train ride and he had thought of things he would rather have been doing. He daydreamed about his kiss with Mieko when a teenage girl sat across from him on the train and wished he was going to the Yoshidas' house instead. Still, he considered, if he could stay on good terms with Yoshida-san it might help him, maybe even his father. The man who came into Yoshida's office when called did not appear to Ted to possess much fighting ability. He had none of the rippling muscles of Ted's senior instructors nor the stout builds of the older teachers.

He walked in clutching a crumpled white linen hat he wore in the processing plant. He still had on a white apron stained a blood-rust color and a pair of similarly soiled white pants. He was short, only coming up to Ted's shoulder, and of slight build. His eyes darted keenly from Yoshida's face to Ted's and back again. Ted noticed he had a stubbly grey and black shadow of a beard on his chin.

"*Yoshida-sama, o-jama sasete itadakimasu,*" he said obeisantly.

"Don't be formal, friend," Yoshida replied. "I would like you to meet someone special, the son of the Iowa beef representative, Takabashi-san."

Then in English he said, "Ted, this is the chief of the meat-cutting section, Obara-san. He and I are like brothers."

Ted bowed and greeted the man with more formality than he felt was called for.

Obara looked at Yoshida, his obeisant expression gone, and asked derisively, "Is this the one you want me to teach?"

"*Hai.*"

Obara sucked air in between his teeth as he shook his head doubtfully from side to side. "I cannot teach a boy. It is not games I do, you know. Not flailing the air with powerless arms."

"Yes, he's a boy, but test him. I think you'll find him adequate."

"Adequate? For what? I do not want any students."

The exchange was fast and Ted only understood that he was considered a boy and the feeling was definitely negative toward him. Ted was glad. He could gracefully escape having to train with this fellow without Yoshida feeling slighted. The only one who would lose face would be himself, and he could afford it. He did not have time to waste training with an amateur.

"Obara-san, how long have we known each other? Thirty-five years?"

"Thirty-seven," he replied, meek again.

"Have I ever made such a request?"

"No."

"Then please, consider him as your disciple."

Ted was afraid the man was caving in to Yoshida's pressure. Obara turned and focused on Ted. He could feel every part of himself being evaluated and pronounced unfit by the eyes that drilled into him.

"Come here, boy," Obara ordered with contempt and authority. "Have you fought before?" he asked as Ted moved to face him.

Ted could see his cigarette-stained teeth clearly and could smell saké on his breath. "I have studied Shorinji kempo."

"Shorin temple boxing? What do priests know about fighting?" he sneered. "All right. Do something for me."

Despite himself, Ted wanted to impress upon Obara that he had studied hard. He executed a combination of three techniques; block, front kick, punch. His delivery was fast, fluid, and concentrated.

"Not bad … for a dancer. Can you protect yourself."

Ted nodded that he could, but became aware of a doubt in the back of his mind. He ignored it and said, "What would you like me to do?"

"Any attack you like. Do not stop until you have hit me, but protect yourself."

"Here?" Ted asked, his hands waving to indicate the furnishings, which obstructed free movement.

"I did not say to attack the furniture, but me."

"Don't worry about hurting Obara-san," Yoshida added in

English. "Do as he says."

Ted sighed and set his mind to the attack. He assumed a posture he felt was suitably aggressive, his feet shoulder width apart, one in front of the other, and positioned his hands.

Obara stayed as he was, feet together, hands at his side, relaxed. Even as Ted moved in with a step and a kick, the thin man moved swiftly but unhurriedly to the side. Ted turned to face him again and attacked, this time with hand maneuvers.

Obara deftly avoided the first two, but as Ted snapped out a third punch, he felt sure it would find its target. To Ted's painful surprise, Obara rapped his knuckles into his biceps and immediately the arm was filled with a burning paralysis. It shook uncontrollably at Ted's side and he found it did not respond to his mind's commands.

"You haven't hit me yet. Keep going," Obara chided.

Angry now, Ted renewed the assault. He led with a kick. The old man was never where he had been, never in range. Ted could feel control coming back to his arm and he thought he could surprise Obara by attacking with it again. He feinted with his left hand and swung painfully with his injured right arm. It never reached the target. Obara stepped in this time, driving his elbow into Ted's already weakened biceps while digging his right thumbnail deep between Ted's ribs.

The boy staggered back with the flush of agony that radiated from his lower chest and filled his body. He buckled over clutching his middle and winced, trying to hold in the tears which had begun to course down his cheeks.

"That was your first lesson, boy. Don't underestimate your opponent, no matter what he looks like. And destroy his weapons. It's easier to defend than to attack. Learn them well."

Ted remained kneeling on the carpet long after Yoshida had shown Obara out. He would hit that man some day. He swore he would.

THREE

The Café Vientiane was up a small *soi* off Chilom Road. Nestled between a bookstore and a French bakery, it was frequented by local connoisseurs and visiting businessmen in the know. Its owner had fled Saigon in November 1972, taking his life savings of 160 taels of gold, his family, and his knowledge of French cooking with him. After working for several years as a sous-chef to a European whom he regarded incompetent, he had saved enough to start his own restaurant again. The rise in gold prices had helped in no small amount and he was able to choose his location, decor, and kitchen with the proper attention to detail. There were only eight booths constructed of dark wood with comfortable, but not overly soft cushions, and four tables with hardwood, cane-back chairs. Fresh flowers were delivered daily and a homelike atmosphere was maintained by placing the cashier out of the sight of patrons.

Paolo Nero waited in the first booth on the right, facing the door. He sipped a Campari and soda and drummed his fingers on the table, unable to appreciate the relaxed mood of the establishment. It was 7:35. Phansaeng was late. If he wants more, he can't have it, he thought, but then considered that he might have no choice. Phansaeng was too smart for his own good. It would have been one thing to bribe him to arrange for the exploration rights on a choice territory. But to bribe him for a geologically complex, marginal plot had been absurd, and the first mistake of Nero's predecessor, Marconi. Phansaeng assumed there was something illegal about the operation, without having any idea of what, and had sought further compensation. Marconi had been sent back to Italy, perhaps exiled to some lonely graveyard in an automobile scrap heap, Nero thought melodramatically, and the *don* called me in.

Trained as a petrochemical engineer in the United States with a scholarship from the *don*, Nero had spent the first decade of his career in legitimate work for their organization. Only later had family and financial pressure been brought to bear upon him to accept this assignment.

Nero heard the sound of a delicate wind chime being moved by the door and looked up to see Phansaeng enter, survey the room anxiously, and head toward him.

"I am sorry to be late. Traffic."

"Yes, yes. Care for a drink?" he asked politely as a waiter came to the table.

"Iced lemon tea."

"Now. What can I do for you, Khun Phansaeng."

"I don't want anything further from you. I wish I did not ever have to see you again. My life has been hell recently. Despite what you may think, not all Thais are carefree. I worry."

"I'm glad you want no more. My partner has said that burial expenses are much cheaper than the deluxe accommodation you require, if you understand my meaning."

Phansaeng grit his teeth and swallowed. "I have some information for you."

"Well … I am listening."

"A man came to see me today. He knows about your com-

102

pany."

"So what?" Why did I come to meet this buffoon, Nero lamented.

"He is 'investigating' your company. He knows you have a helicopter."

"And?"

"And I think he knows ... about your ... what you are doing."

"Do you know what we are doing?"

"No. I don't want to know."

"Then what do think he knows."

"Our conversation was brief. I told him I had not heard of Ital-Siam. He said he wanted to sell you something, but ..."

"Probably just a salesman," Nero interjected, shrugging it off.

"I don't think so."

"Why?" Nero asked tersely.

"Because he did not ask about any other firms, only yours. And he did not try to sell anything."

"What is his name?"

"Bergman."

"Swedish?"

"American. Here is his card," Phansaeng said handing it across the table. "We spoke in English, but he greeted me in Thai. He may speak Thai, I don't know."

This was a problem Nero had not expected to come up so soon. They had gone to great lengths to maintain a low profile. If Bergman was a mere salesman, how had he heard of Ital-Siam? And if he was undercover DEA, well, Nero would have to convince him that their operation was legitimate. That was, after all, one of his main roles: to bring some legitimacy to the operation through his credentials in the petroleum industry. The refining of poppy sap was primitive compared to the hydrocrackers, pressure vessels, and stacks which broke crude oil into usable constituents. He could talk exploration equally well, if that was required.

Nero looked at the bureaucrat across the table from him, paused and said sarcastically, "If any more salesmen visit you, don't bother to call. I am not interested."

"But … "

"Yes, thank you for not sending him to us. We have bought all the equipment we need. I am sorry you can't join me for dinner. Perhaps some other time," Nero said, standing up and pointing the way to the door, his tone cold and nasty.

"Mr. Nero. I hope …" Phansaeng started, anger in his voice.

"Yes?"

"Goodnight," he finished, heading for the door, his back to Nero. He hoped it would be that way from now on, with his back turned to this affair. He had enough.

Nero sat down again and stared sullenly at the empty seat in front of him. He regretted being so brusque with the Thai, but he really did not need the additional trouble at this moment. The waiter came, set the tea down at the vacant spot, and left. He watched the waiter return silently to his station, then concentrated again on the problem at hand.

First, I should contact our shipping office in Singapore, see if this American checks out. *Cristo!* What about Nishida? If I tell him he will undoubtedly overreact, the bastardo. But if I don't tell him and something goes wrong then I have written my own suicide note. *Porca Madonna*, this business. Tell Nishida; you have to. Maybe this Bergman fellow won't even show up. But if he doesn't show that does not prove he is not DEA. DEA? What am I saying? I must be as faint-hearted as that clown Phansaeng. There is no reason to believe this American is anything more than what his card says he is. So, put a tail on him just to be sure.

The waiter had brought a dinner menu over and waited patiently by the table for European to look up. The businessman continued staring down at the table into his glass of Campari and the waiter was about to return to his station again when the man started out of his reverie. "*Eh. Ah si, prego.*"

The following morning Sarasin greeted Ted with some welcome news. A tender they had worked on together had finally been awarded to them after a three-month wait. Ted was relieved. He had counted on the sale when planning his forecast for the year. Although he could by no means coast for the rest of the year, nor was he so inclined; he felt physically lighter on hearing the outcome. He stopped to think about the feeling. Certainly he was not really lighter, yet there was a youthful spring in his step he had not experienced in a long while and his shoulders relaxed downward, the tension gone from his neck.

"I hope that's all right with you," Sarasin said seeking consensus for something Ted had missed.

"Excuse me?"

"Well, if you have plans, I understand, but I hope you can go with me to see this customer this afternoon. He's an American like you, and you know the story: he respects your words more than mine."

"OK," Ted said mentally rearranging his day as he spoke, "But you'll have to drive me by the bank. I need to get a cash advance. And ... oh damn, I forgot. Look, I'll have to call this antique store." He handed Sarasin Lin's name card. "Can you have your secretary call him and tell him I'll come by tomorrow to pick up my antique, not today."

"No problem," Sarasin promised. "How about going to the bank after lunch before we go to see this fellow."

"Fine, but I want you to drop me off at the U.S. Embassy afterward."

"I can wait for you there."

"No need, thanks. Personal business," Ted smiled.

They spent the morning with some of Sarasin's sales personnel, training them and answering their questions. The Thai-Chinese entrepreneur had found that to compete with aggressive supply houses in Singapore he had to be able to provide better service. His sales engineers were all college graduates and were paid well. However, Ted and others like him, provided his men with the specialized instruction born of field experience they required.

At noon Sarasin came into the meeting room and signalled for Ted to conclude his discussions. Ted thanked the field force for their attention and Sarasin led his group in a brief, but hearty, round of applause.

"How about lunch?" he asked Ted.

"Actually, I need to drop by the hotel to pick up my passport for the bank. Perhaps you would allow me to invite you to lunch there."

"I can take you somewhere nearby."

"Please, Khun Sarasin, you treated me to a marvelous feast night before last and you have won the tender. I must insist."

"Well, fine. Fine. Shall we?"

Lunch was heavier than Ted normally cared for, but he did not wish to inhibit Sarasin from selecting what he desired by ordering lightly himself. He had cold cucumber soup and a small steak *au poivre*. Sarasin ordered onion soup and chicken diablo. They shared a Caesar salad prepared at their table. They watched silently as the waiter meticulously prepared the dressing, adding each ingredient while continuously stirring.

"What did you call this?" Sarasin asked tasting the finished work.

"Caesar salad."

"Seize her salad?" he asked incredulously.

"Very funny," Ted replied in a congratulatory tone. "No. Caesar, like Julius Caesar, the Roman emperor."

"Is this a royal dish?"

"I don't know. Probably came from Caesar's Palace," Ted replied, leaving the Thai thinking he was eating the pride of an emperor's ancient kitchen, not of a casino restaurant.

When they had finished their meal, enjoyed their tea, and Ted had settled the chit, they went to the lobby.

"I need to get my passport."

"I'll get my driver and wait for you out front."

Ted went to the front desk and gave the woman there his key. After he had signed his release card, she led him into a private room, brushed stainless steel boxes lining the walls. Inserting the master key and then his, she turned the two simultaneously and opened the short, thick door. She let him remove the box himself.

He always felt a slight pang of anxiety whenever he opened his box, foolishly fearing, he thought, that the contents would be missing. As usual his passport case was in good order. He removed the blue travel document and closed the lid, handing the container back to the attendant. He took the key from her and slipped out the door.

On his way past the front desk he saw that the message light over his key cubby hole was illuminated. He stopped and asked the counter girl to hand him the message.

"Yes, Mr. Bergman, you had a caller several hours ago," the young woman said gently in her Thai way.

He opened the note. It read: "Mr. Viranathep called, will call back 2:30 p.m."

"Are you sure this is for me?"

"He asked for Theodore Bergman, yes," she said.

He knew no one by that name. Perhaps it was a prospective distributor who caught wind he was in town. Possibly there was a leak in Sarasin's organization. Ted decided to mention it to the Thai as he walked out to the car.

Across the lobby, a man seated on a lounge chair abruptly placed his glass of beer and a hundred baht note on the low table and stood up. He rushed to get outside and onto his motorcycle as quickly and unobtrusively as he could. He had just spotted his mark and there would be hell to pay to his boss if he lost him.

Ted's first stop was the bank where he used his VISA credit card to draw a cash advance from his account in the United States. The wonders of computerized global banking, he thought as he counted his U.S. $1,500. Only in his lifetime had such credit facilities been made available to the average man. He despaired at the thought of trying to be a trader in Marco Polo's time, or even in the age of the Yankee clippers.

Before giving Ted the money, the teller had cabled the United States, received a reply and an approval had been issued by her supervisor, all in twenty minutes. Even at that, Ted chided himself for becoming slightly impatient with the wait.

Ted rushed out to the curb and looked about anxiously for Sarasin's car. On both sides of the avenue, as far as he could see, the

108

traffic was moving at a painfully slow but steady pace. Gray clouds of fumes bellowed from motorcycle exhausts as delivery boy riders threaded their way through the automobiles. Impatient drivers revved engines and honked horns to no avail. Several minutes later Sarasin's Citroën pulled around the corner down the block and made its way back toward Ted. He walked down the pavement to meet it halfway and got in the car, the comparative solitude and coolness when he shut the door a welcome change.

"Sorry, Ted. We had to go around the block. Took us a half hour."

"How long do you think it will take to get to the customer's?"

"It's not far. Maybe another twenty minutes."

"Say, Khun Sarasin. Do you know a man by the name of Viranathep?"

"No. Who is it?"

"I donno. I had a message in my box saying he called and will call back." Ted handed him the message.

"Probably a tout."

"Selling what?"

"Antiques, tours, souvenirs, women perhaps."

"Just wondered if you knew him."

"Probably won't call back either," Sarasin commented, returning the note to Ted.

Their progress through the city traffic was slow and Ted anxiously looked at his watch several times, wondering if he would be able to visit the commercial attaché at the embassy. Forty-five minutes after leaving the bank, they arrived at the next destination. He and Sarasin were admitted to see the foreign manager of the company without the wait a Thai salesman alone would have experienced.

Being a courtesy call to cement relations with a company already purchasing his products, Ted made his demeanor as American, easygoing, boy-the-two-of us-sure-are-far-from-home-how-do-you-like-it as possible. On hearing the manager's voice he assumed a slight Southern accent from the start.

The manager, Gerald "Shakey" Robinson, was a short but muscular man with bushy, reddish-brown sideburns. His collar was open and the shirt tails were tucked tightly into his jeans, a thick, tooled leather belt with an ostentatious silver and turquoise buckle wrapped around his waist. Ted noticed his Tony Lama boots and complimented him on them.

"Shit man, you know how much these cost here? It's like wearin' gold on your feet. But I bought these in Houston 'fore I came out."

"You from Loosiana?" Ted asked slightly increasing the accent in his voice, but not enough that the man would feel he was being imitated.

"Sure as hell am. Slidell, the bedroom of New Orleans. How about you?"

"I did some pipe layin' and rig-monkey work in Texas and Loosiana for a coupla' summers. But I'm from Iowa. How long ya' out for," Ted asked, noting the casual similarity to the first question inmates ask each other.

"Well, I been here 'bout ten months. Figure we'll finish this project in another eighteen or so."

"Family?"

"In Singapore. I get down every three weeks or so to see 'em."

"I live in Singapore, too. Near Goldhill Plaza."

"We're out toward Jurong. Company flat."

Ted got down to business and reminded the man of the products he had already bought from Sarasin, thanked him for his patronage, introduced a new product they had recently taken on, and expressed his hope that Petrotools International and Sarasin's company could be of continued service.

As Ted wound down his presentation, the man spoke up.

"I 'preciate y'all droppin' by. Say, you two free tonight?"

Ted was ready to say no, but Sarasin broke in. "Ted and I were planning to go out together and we hope you can join us."

"That'd be fine. Where're you put up at?"

"I'm at the Dusit Thani."

"Shall we meet there?" Sarasin enjoined.

"Sounds good. I figure I'll get off 'bout 6:30 tonight. That'd put me at your place 'round 7:15."

"We'll be there. Thank you, Mr. Robinson. See you later," Ted said.

"Call me Shakey! See you later!"

When they were out of his office Ted rushed to the elevator and toyed with his watch anxiously while repeatedly pushing the call button. It was 3:30 and he wanted to get to the embassy as soon as possible.

"No rush, young man," Sarasin said when he caught up. "I can ask my driver to defy all road regulations for you. No matter. You will make it! Calm down."

Ted examined his internal condition and took the old man's advice. Why should he kill himself, lead a frenetic, high-tension life for a company; not for a human relationship, but for one between a man and an organization? Because he wanted to do a good job. But doing a good job did not necessarily have to mean running himself into the ground. Perhaps because he considered himself to be a corporate warrior. Business, and especially international business, was one of the few predatory battlegrounds left open to fighters. The greater part of all other human relations was dominance oriented, posturing to frighten rather than relying on tested methods to eliminate the opponent. But a predator should be relaxed, like the tiger or the eagle. Relaxed, but alert.

As Sarasin looked on he saw Ted respond to his advice in a way he had not expected. First, Ted's shoulder's relaxed downward until his hands hung an inch lower than they had been before. Tense furrows on his brow disappeared and Ted rolled his head limply around, first chin to chest, then clockwise. Sarasin thought of a toy clown's bobbing head mounted on a spring. Most striking, he observed, was the change in the eyes. They opened up wider and, like an unclogged drain, took in everything they faced.

The elevator door opened. "Please," Ted invited Sarasin to enter first, feeling readier now to calmly face the business at hand, the Butcher's methods still at work in him.

His previous worries had been unfounded; they reached the embassy at 3:45, the traffic having temporarily abated in preparation for the 5:30 coagulation. Ted bid Sarasin adieu until dinner and turned down the Thai's second offer to wait around until his business was finished.

Entering the building foyer, he had his passport inspected by a Marine and his bag searched by a Thai. Another Marine called up to the commercial section and a secretary came to lead Ted further into the building. He gave his card to her and she went to arrange a meeting. He waited several minutes while looking at some American industry trade magazines that were on the waiting-room table next to the massive lounge chair in which he sat. The room was cool and quiet and had the pleasant nondescriptness of a dentist's waiting room. Only the sterile smell of alcohol was lacking, he thought.

An exceptionally tall man leaned through a doorway, a phone receiver to his ear. He must be six feet eight inches tall, Ted estimated. "Be with you in a moment," he said to Ted, covering the mouthpiece with his hairy right hand, his demeanor open and friendly.

A minute later he walked out to the waiting area, his arm extended like a spear. He shook hands with a firm, vigorous grip, as if he had taken training at a "positive mental attitude" course. "Gee, sorry to keep you waiting, Mr. Bergman," he conceded unnecessarily to Ted as he sat down. "What can the Office of the Commercial Attaché do for you?" he offered, his hands extended, palms up, toward Ted.

"Actually, I need some information about the Thai market in general and any projects coming up that would be related to our petroleum exploration tools, and any recently opened tenders."

"It's a tall order. Let me get my secretary to start pulling some files. Would you care for some coffee, tea perhaps?"

"Tea, thank you."

After Hatch had called their orders out to his secretary, they chatted for several minutes and Ted commented favorably on the uncharacteristically helpful attitude of the attaché.

"Don't praise too soon, you haven't seen what's in our files yet. But seriously, I used to work abroad, then I went to the State Department. I've a good idea of what businessmen want. At least better than some of the eggheads and blue-sky types who work for State. You look pretty young. How'd you get a creampuff post in Singapore?"

"Lucky, I guess."

"Speak any Asian languages?"

"Japanese."

"Fluently?"

"I think that term is overused, as you probably do if you speak a foreign language. I'd say I'm very proficient."

"Do you get to use it much down here?"

"Not use it really. I visit a lot of Japanese contractors. In the middle of a sales presentation, I can tell right where I stand by keeping my mouth shut. Then I answer, still in English, specifically to the resistance I hear the engineers voice among themselves. Occasionally, I'll finish by thanking them profusely in Japanese. They get a kick out of it — most of them anyway."

"Sounds like when I was selling 'dozers in 'Nam. I could hear exactly what the customer wanted and give them just that. Yeah, I know what you mean."

His secretary came back in with several file folders which she placed on the attaché's desk. She smiled at Ted and left the room.

Ted raised his brows as his eyes followed the sway of her skirt leaving the room.

"I think she works for the Soviets," the attaché joked, interrupting Ted's thoughts.

"How's that?"

"She's too good lookin' to've been hired by our people. Gotta be a plant. Now, what have we got here?" He reviewed the contents of the file folders, selected unclassified memos and passed them across the desk to Ted. Some of it was quite stale information, he found, being two or three years old already. Out of a whole stack of data, only three pages contained information he could use.

"You seen this?" Hatch asked, tossing a thick, stapled document toward Ted.

It was a complete list of all contractors and subcontractors in

Thailand who did petroleum, liquefied natual gas, or natural resource related work. It was a year old. Ted thumbed his way through it slowly, made some notes, and commented to Hatch on some changes that had taken place.

"I need some information about a new company, Ital-Siam Exploration. Do you have a more recent edition of this?"

"We're working on it. Miss Chai, can you get that stack of info I've been pulling together," he called out the door.

She brought in a large manila envelope and handed it to Hatch, leaving with another smile at Ted. His heart jumped, but, he admonished himself, this is Thailand: everybody smiles.

"Here we are," Hatch said in a self-satisfied tone. "Ital-Siam. But it's a short file; must be a new company."

Ted looked at the single page given to him. The company had been formed only six months before but exploration had not yet started as of the date on the report. The Italian company, BuonoPetro owned 45 percent; Great Star LNG (Japan), a division of Great Star Construction, owned another 40 percent. The remaining 20 percent was owned by Thais. They were not listed, and Ted surmised that they might be government or military officials brought in at cost to offer protection and assistance.

"Anything there for you?"

"Not much. It says neither where they are exploring nor for what."

The general manager's name was Paolo Nero. The address of their office and a phone number was at the bottom of the page. Ted wrote these down.

"Say, Ted," Hatch said, looking at his watch, "One of the guys here at the embassy and I have got an appointment and I gotta get a move on. Where are you staying?"

"Dusit Thani."

"If you're ready to go we can drop you off there."

"I'd appreciate that, thanks a lot," Ted replied, putting his notebook into his attaché case.

"Let me just buzz this guy," Hatch said picking up his phone. "Bill? Chuck here. Ready to go? … OK, see you out front." He hung up, then said to Ted, "Shall we?"

As they left the office Ted gave and received a smile from the secretary. A warm feeling prevailed until he reached the lobby and was introduced to Hatch's associate. Though he smiled and shook hands like a normal American, Ted sensed a cold, emotionless void in him. Or perhaps not emotionless, but so hateful as to numb all other emotions into regimented submission.

His handshake, like his haircut, was clipped and military in its precision and brevity. He introduced himself as William Brody. Ted stared at him as he took a name card from his pocket and gave it to the man. Ted's impression about Brody was so strong and so distinct it was startling to him.

Brody took the card and searched his pockets until he found one of his. It identified him as liaison between the U.S. Drug Enforcement Agency and the Bureau for International Narcotics Prevention.

"From what I've heard, you must have a tough job, Mr. Brody," Ted said conversationally.

"What have you heard?" Brody asked seriously.

"I only meant things I had read in magazines and so forth."

"Oh? Do you come to Thailand frequently?"

"Five or six times a year."

"Have you ever been approached by any dealers," he questioned.

116

"Mr. Brody. I am a young American, yes, but I am also an international businessman and I am very opposed to dope, if you please."

"Sorry. Always looking for details. Didn't mean to imply anything, but the job is like you said. If you do hear something, give me a call," he said by way of apology.

"I don't look for trouble, Mr. Brody, but sure, I'll give you a ring if anything comes up."

"Call me, Bill," he said lifelessly.

"OK, Bill."

The three of them walked to Hatch's automobile, an imported Ford LTD, and he called his driver, who ran over from a shaded area where all the drivers congregated. Ted and Bill sat in back together and chatted about Ted's background as they left the embassy parking lot.

Suddenly, Brody's eyes caught a glimpse of something and followed it as the car drove past. He turned and craned his neck to look out the back window.

Ted turned to see what had caught his attention, but could distinguish nothing extraordinary from the street scene behind them.

"What is it?" he asked, alarmed.

"Nothing," Brody replied unconvincingly. As they had left the embassy he had seen a Thai taking a picture of their car with camera and telephoto lens. He was not certain but it seemed the same man was now on a motorcycle a safe distance behind their car. Being a gargantuan American vehicle, there's no way we can blend into traffic and get lost, he lamented silently.

No one spoke for the remainder of the ride. As they approached the entrance to his hotel, Ted thanked Hatch for the information and the lift. As he was closing the door, he turned to Brody and said, "Goodbye, Mr. Brody. Hope you feel better tomorrow," and closed the door.

"What the hell is that supposed to mean?" Brody exclaimed, obviously irritated.

Hatch just chuckled and told his driver to proceed to the squash club.

As the night wore on, Ted found it increasingly difficult to remain pleasant company. Shakey Robinson had rather crude taste in entertainment and Sarasin indulged him fully. They had eaten at a seafood supermarket restaurant popular with tourists and afterwards had gone to Soi Cowboy, a nightclub area rivaling Patpong but with cheaper, sleazier fare. While smiling and trying hard to reflect his customer's state of mind, Ted maintained a constant, angry, internal dialogue about what he would rather be doing and where he would rather be. He also thought of the *tanto* he had not had a chance to pick up that day and longed for the simple pleasure of talking with Lin and seeing his antiques.

Sarasin had boisterously pulled the two Americans into the Mon Cherie Amour Go-Go Bar, telling them about a new live show they had on stage. They drank two cocktails each while watching five different girls of varying age and appeal try to sensuously remove the little they wore on stage. Three girls had been brought to the table and sat close to the men, cooing nonsensically in their limited English. The girl with Ted was probably between eighteen and twenty years old. She wore a tight polyester blouse and a miniskirt without panties. Her nipples were as long and apparent as the shadows they cast on her shirt front from the colored lights above.

She crossed her legs slowly and looked down to attract Ted's attention to her crotch, which was momentarily offered to his sight. She looked at him with half-closed eyes and drew her tongue across her lips slowly. He thought sardonically about what would happen if he vomited on her.

Sarasin had directed the most buxom of the three to sit with Robinson. She put his arm around her, leading his hand to her breast. "These girls are right friendly, eh, Ted?" he said with a wink as she dragged her full lips across his hairy chest at the opening of his shirt.

The lights went down and room became silent. The live show was about to begin. A slick foam mat, not unlike one a gymnast might use, was brought out onto the go-go deck wetted and soaped. Two girls of better than average appearance were brought to the center by a man dressed like a referee. Ted recognized the girls' costumes as those Thai boxers would wear. They had flower garland headbands and wore blue and red satin trunks. They also had on T-shirts and boxing gloves with stretch cuffs, but were braless and barefoot.

As Thai music strained the audience's ears, the two combatants went to each corner and kneeled, bowing low to the mat, coincidentally briefly allowing the spectators see their busts hanging large and firm. They returned to the center and the referee started the match. The martial theme music from a Bruce Lee movie started playing and the two fighters closed on one another. They punched and jabbed without great skill. Occasionally a kick was attempted, but on the wet slippery surface it more often than not ended up with the kicker falling down. Soon both girls shirts were damp and clung fast to their skin, revealing more of their form to the men who watched and cheered. The opponents clinched and jumped, thrusting their knees into the ribs and kidneys of the other. Every hit, every slap of glove on skin and gasp of breath was amplified to heighten the excitement of crowd.

When the bell rang, two stools appeared in the corners and male seconds seated the girls, fanning them with towels. They wiped their faces and began to massage the girls' legs and arms. Hands slipped under the T-shirts and rubbed the girls' chests. As the seconds began to put their hands down the satin trunks, the bell rang for the start of round two.

Midway through the round, the girls clinched again and tripped each other, falling heavily to the mat which had been soaped up again between rounds. They wrestled about, sliding and rolling, pulling and grabbing. One shirt was ripped off, then the other. The gloves were cast aside. One girl tried to regain her feet and her shorts were pulled down. Each piece of clothing was thrown to the audience. Soon they both wrestled completely nude, each trying to control the other on the slick surface.

They finally embraced, lying on the mat, their chests heaving, each trickle of water, each throaty breath heard by all. The lights came down by half and the music changed to a quiet piano and saxophone piece. The combatants began to kiss and caress each other. As their performed passion grew, they slid on top of one another, chest to chest, legs to legs. The girl on top executed a graceful turnabout. Using the lower girl's stomach as a slide, she spun around until she faced the girl's navel. They continued to touch and lick. Shortly, they found each other's sex and their impassioned groans and clicking tongues filled the club with the sound of oral love.

Robinson looked on at the performance with undivided attention. He had not noticed Sarasin whisper into his escort's ear and hand her a baht note. He had barely been aware she was no longer seated next to him. As the girls on stage began to kiss each other he felt hot breath forcing its way through his blue jeans to his own crotch. He did not dare lift the table cloth to look as his pants were unzipped and swollen member given freedom. The rhythmic heaving of the breath from the stage almost matched the pulse he could feel throbbing as he himself was consumed below.

Ted looked toward Robinson to see if he was enjoying the show. His eyes were half-closed and seemed glazed over though he still stared at the girls on stage who were now both close to their mutual play orgasms. He saw Sarasin smile and put a finger to his lips, then point back to the stage, and he knew not to distract the guest, though he did not know why. Robinson shuddered, closed his eyes briefly and let out a breath as the performance climaxed.

Afterward, Robinson's girl emerged from nowhere, it seemed to Ted, and Shakey said he had a great evening and was ready to head home. When Sarasin and Ted had dropped him off, Ted was still unsure what had happened, why Robinson had not taken the girl back to his hotel, and why the evening had ended so abruptly.

"Do you think Shakey had a good time?"

"I know he had a great time," Sarasin replied, beaming.

"How come?" Ted asked, not knowing the humor in his question.

"Well, where do you think his companion was during the love bout?"

"Taking a leak? I donno."

"Licking his ice cream cone."

"No shit!" Ted exclaimed, laughing. "Christ! I hope she's clean. If he gets the clap he'll never buy from us again."

"Don't worry. That's taken care of."

121

Ted had been told that before, but was still concerned. Then a thought came and he laughed again. "I've heard of under-the-table pay-offs before, but this is too much!"

Nishida knew something was wrong when he had received a call from Nero for an urgent meeting. That was at 5:30 and in the past two hours he had discussed with his assistant, Suzuki, what might be amiss. Nero had not given any indication, only that they should meet at the office at 7:30. They talked about the inept backwardness of their Mafia counterpart and the torpid intellectual prowess of Europeans in general and Italians in particular compared to the unrivalled celerity of the Japanese mind. Their anger had grown as their speculations began to reflect more dire circumstances. By the time Nero arrived, their anger had turned into black humor as they wondered into what dangerously stupid situation the "Count," as they had nicknamed Nero, had put them.

Nero entered the office and was surprised to find Nishida and his obsequious assistant smiling. He expected to find them in their usual sour moods, criticizing his every proposal and threatening his life and limb. He knew they would not be smiling for long. The news he brought them was ill-timed and very disturbing. He asked them to bring their tea and come to sit at the small conference table at the side of his office.

"So, Nero, what's the problem?"

"Yes, well, let me start at the beginning. It seems someone knows about us, or is at least investigating our operation."

"*Sooo desu nehhh!*" Nishida jumped. The news was worse than they had joked about. "Who? How did you find out?"

"You remember Phansaeng?"

122

How could I forget the hungry worm, Nishida thought. "Him again?"

"He called me up yesterday, you remember, very nervous, and said we had to meet. I saw him last night at the Café Vientiane. He said a man had come to see him about Ital-Siam." He handed Ted's name card to Nishida. "This is the fellow."

"Where is he from?"

"U.S."

"It says he is just a salesman. So what?" Nishida scoffed.

"That's what I said. But he told Phansaeng he was 'investigating' us. And he didn't ask about any other companies. Also, Phansaeng didn't think he was a salesman."

"Phansaeng wouldn't think a whore had lost her virginity," the Japanese sneered.

"Well, I'm glad, then, that I showed better judgement and more caution than you, friend. I had this Theodore Bergman tailed today."

Nishida was sorry he had opened his mouth only to bite his own balls. I should have known this Italian snake would hold back and bait me. "And what did you find out?"

"My tail caught him at about 1:30. The first place he went was our bank. He stayed there twenty-five minutes."

"What did the bank say?" the Asian interrupted.

"The officer in charge of our account said he was not contacted by this Bergman. But that does not mean Bergman did not invoke some legal pressure to silence him, yes? Then he proceeded to the Sukhumvit Towers office building."

"How?"

"By car."

"Obviously! Whose car, a taxi, what?"

123

"A Thai man's car, a Citroën. I am having difficulty tracing the plates. After spending half an hour there …"

"Doing what?"

"How the hell should I know? It's a big building and my tail couldn't just follow them up into the elevator. As I was saying, after a half an hour they left and he was dropped off at the U.S. Embassy."

"Really!"

Nero took out a manila envelope and removed some photos. He passed them out to Nishida and Suzuki. They looked at one shot of three men in a parking lot. "Bergman's the one in the blue shirt and red tie."

"Young."

"I thought so, too."

"Do you recognize the one with the close haircut."

Nishida was cautious. If he said no he might reveal his ignorance. If he said yes the same might apply. He settled for a long, inconclusive scratch of the ear and sucking in of breath.

"That is 'Wild Bill' Brody."

"*Sooo des!*" Both Japanese exclaimed their dismayed surprise simultaneously.

"Yes."

"What were they doing?"

"These pictures were taken as the three came out of the embassy together, and left together." He pointed out a photo of the rear window of a departing automobile, Brody's face to the camera, Ted next to him.

"Who is the tall one?"

"I haven't found out yet. But we do know who Brody is. He's bad news."

124

The two Japanese talked quietly, occasionally giving hard looks at Nero.

"So. What is your plan, Count?"

Nero hated being called that and wondered who had thought up the name. Their English was not so good that they could have made it up themselves, he felt. "Keep an eye on him. If he comes here we try to convince him we're legitimate, a petroleum exploration firm."

How could a naive bird like Nero have been sent out for this job, Nishida wondered. He's much too green. "Firmer action is necessary."

"Look, I called our office in Singapore. They checked his number out. No one answered. Of course, that's suspicious, but he and his company are in the 'U.S. Firms in Singapore' listing."

"A cover?"

"It couldn't be a cover just for us. The list was published before we registered our corporation."

"I think you're being too loose. We should have known about him long ago and crushed him before we became a factor in his investigation."

These Japanese swine can't wait to screw me, Nero regretted, and they are just as much at fault as myself. They have a bigger army here than I, more ears on the street. Why do they pick on me? Sometimes I regret not being a seasoned criminal. I could cope better with the likes of them.

"Mr. Nishida. If we eliminate him, don't you think the people he reports to will know even more clearly where the dirt is swept under the rug? And if he is just a salesman, should he die?"

"I thought we had concluded that he is definitely undercover DEA? What is this *bakana* about a salesman?"

125

"We can't be sure!"

"We can't be too careful."

Nishida's assistant spoke up. "We have orders to step on ones who get in front of us. We *yakuza* are not afraid to do it."

Nero, exasperated to his limits by their obstinate hostility, reached across the table and surprised himself by seizing the younger one by the collar, pulling him violently from his chair and slamming him up to the table's edge.

"Listen, you snotty little leg breaker, I am the boss here. Your *oyabun* has said so. Unless you want to spill your chicken guts in front of him, then you take my orders, do things my way!"

Suzuki glowered back at him and reached for his pocket. Nero acted quickly, shoving him with both hands toward Nishida, who was still seated. Suzuki reared back toward his superior, toppling them both. They jumped to their feet from the floor and stared down the barrel of a Baretta drawn hastily by the European.

Nishida spoke first. "We are partners. The *oyabun* has told us to follow your directions, and we will do that."

However, in his heart Nishida knew the European was as good as dead. The *oyabun* would never condone lax security for an important operation. He would have to take matters into his own hands. He would enjoy planning the end of this Bergman, and Nero as well.

HA: PROGRESSION

FOUR

The first day of the last year; that's how Ted reflected excitedly about his return to his senior year at the international school in Tokyo after a two-month summer absence in the United States. The contrasting feelings he experienced when he left Tokyo and on his return only four days before were intensely vivid to him. His departure had filled him with the hopeless anticipation of one who is leaving a beloved to return to a once familiar, but now strangely unchanged, place. His thoughts had focused behind him during the whole vacation, toward Mieko, the Butcher, and Japan, and toward what he found of his past waiting for him.

His hometown friends were all unchanged. He had seen nothing in them that was not a necessary extension of what they had been a year before. They had not grown, merely kept pace with their development. They had no new passions, only sharper or duller versions of the same feelings shared before among themselves. Some had begun to drink or smoke, cigarettes and marijuana, but no one carried it to excess or showed any strong tendencies one way or another. They were muddling through, waiting for graduation, and the hopes of escape to college.

They had not accepted him into their confidence as they had before. Ted had felt they were constantly holding back on him.

129

They did not remark that he had changed, but he knew — felt — by comparison with them that he was no longer what he had been.

His life had taken a radically altered course, and just in time, he judged, comparing their lethargic lingering to his dynamic rush toward a vision he could as yet only touch but not grasp, taste but not consume, see but not comprehend. The vision was of his molding into a sublime warrior in the hands of Butcher Obara, and into a man through his love for Mieko. He was conscious of the course he had chosen and knew what he should do. He had been surprised to see no similar direction in the lives of his old friends, and disappointed to discover his life had been so shallow only a year before.

His mother had brought him back first to Iowa while Thomas followed a month later. She had insisted that Japan was no place to spend a summer and that she was afraid Ted would get bored with nothing to do in that strange land. Before he realized that he was to return, it was all planned and he could raise no objection. Thomas took him aside and asked him to accompany his mother and take care of her. The boy resented what he felt was her attempt to separate him and Mieko and stop him from training.

He had carried a framed portrait of Mieko which he kept on his bedroom dresser. Occasionally, he would return from a shower and after removing his towel would remember her picture was there. His heart would race as he recalled the night in the bath when he had accidentally seen her exposed flesh, and he imagined she could now espy him. It was not a feeling he found unpleasant.

He had thought about her daily, and written her weekly in Japanese. She returned letters in English. They wrote of everyday events, and any trace of love was so subtle that it cried out from the page. No one else would have read anything into the letters, but to him, her feelings were apparent and true.

Ted trained hard every day on what the Butcher had taught him. One afternoon he showed his friends some of what he had learned and told them about the Butcher. He never heard the end to jokes about karate (pork) chops and hamburger kung fu. He never demonstrated for them again. His training became solitary and stark. Obara had promised that if he demonstrated improvement after he came back, the old man would begin the real teachings. Ted earnestly repeated the methods for long, hot summer hours at a time.

Ted had taken a five-foot log from his uncle's back yard and swung it around his head in large circles until his back, chest, and arms ached. He worked to develop speed in his hands and the ability to see a small moving target and strike it. He strengthened his thumb for the unusual gouging techniques the Butcher had mastered. He also continued a rudimentary study of the anatomy on which Obara had insisted.

Returning to Tokyo, he had felt as elated as he had been depressed on leaving. He knew better than to talk incessantly to his parents about Mieko and Obara. His mother had already been cross with him several times, her hostility no longer skillfully suppressed. However, he could not help but tell them how excited he was to be going "back home." Sarah looked to her husband and rolled her eyes in disgust.

His first four days back had been kept occupied by parental demands that he help settle in again. He cleaned and bought groceries. He only had time to call Mieko. When he dialed the number the first time, he likened each digit to a step toward a curtain behind which she stood quietly waiting. The phone ringing was the curtain being raised tortuously slowly. When she answered, it was as if he could see her clearly before him. His hands trembled as he held the receiver and said simply, "*Konbanwa, Mieko-chan.*"

Her reply was equally anxious in its total restraint, "Good evening, Takabashi-san." Had they exchanged vows of eternal love they would not have been happier than to have only heard each other's voices simply acknowledge the existence of the other and the mutual value of that existence. Neither stopped to consider the source or quality of the emotions they felt. They were too young and too much in love to examine foundations.

They talked about the summer and the present and the future until Sarah came and told Ted to get off the phone. When he reluctantly said goodbye to Mieko, his mother could not leave his room without reinforcing her parental authority.

"We haven't been back one day and you're already calling that Yoshida girl. Tonight you tied up the line since dinner."

He examined his watch. Dinner had been two hours ago. He had called Mieko at 8:30. It was now 9 o'clock. He ignored his mother's lack of consistency and looked at her with the slow painful eyes of a day laborer anticipating the crack of a whip.

"Don't you look at me that way, young man. We can't have you monopolizing the phone just so you can talk pretty with your girlfriend," she commanded, a shrill edge building to her tone.

He remained silent. He did not mean it as a silent protest, like a verbal sit-in, but rather he was silent because there was nothing rational he could say to her that she would appreciate, understand, and agree with. He could not comprehend the virulence she had increasingly displayed toward his relationship with Mieko. The girl he had chosen to date was intelligent, well-educated, courteous, pretty, and — if there was nothing else she could appreciate — from a rich family. Not finding anything deficient in Mieko, he assumed he had done something to deserve his mother's ill will.

He studied hard in school, helped her on occasional errands requiring spoken Japanese, did not begin to smoke or degenerate, and even endeavored to keep his room neater than in the past. Perhaps, as he had seen in a movie once, she was jealous seeing her son grow up and begin to have an interest in girls outside the home. Having no better reason, he decided that was what she was experiencing. He could not sympathize, but he decided to avoid arousing the feeling in her, as one avoids letting blood when swimming around sharks, by hiding his growing attraction to and for Mieko.

"From now on I want you to limit your calls to five minutes," she proscribed.

"Yes."

Had she known he was not defeated, but had already decided to do so anyway, she would not have felt the brief, tense victory that flared in her heart.

Now back in school, he was doubly elated. It was the first day of the last year. It was also the day he was to see Mieko. His concentration shifted frequently from the description of the semester's course work the biology teacher was presenting to his notebook in which he had repeatedly written the Japanese kanji for Mieko's name, "Bright Child." When the bell rang he left class faster than the others and rushed to his locker, where he deposited some books and then ran to the train station. He had wanted to meet her at the entrance to her school, but she had turned down the suggestion quickly. Instead, she wanted to meet him in Shinjuku.

He waited at the east entrance to the Shinjuku station. Although not yet the rush hour, people streamed past him, moving with solitary, purposeful expressions. Those who looked at him quickly averted their glance back to the steps ahead. In the distance he heard the telegraphic-like clicking of the ticket takers' hole-punch shears as they repeatedly snapped them shut between tickets. A bum walked past Ted about five feet away. The smell of fermented sweat and old saké first attracted Ted's attention, forcing him to turn to the spectacle. Bums, their still figures leaning against pillars and walls, were neither uncommon nor numerous in Japan's large rail and subway stations. They did not look different from the panhandlers and hobos he had seen in the States. He wondered idly if this one was a *burakumin*.

He felt a shy tap on his shoulder and turned to see Mieko's smiling face. She retreated one step away from him as he turned and he looked at her entirety. She was still dressed in her school uniform, a crisply ironed, blue, pleated knee-length skirt and white blouse buttoned up to her neck. The conservative cut of the clothes was designed to conceal blossoming teen figures, but it merely made the mystery of what was not defined more alluring in Ted's eyes. He shook his head from side to side in wonder and smiled more broadly than he had in months as the tenseness in his stomach gave way to a light, energized feeling.

"Mieko-chan."

"Takabashi-san."

They realized that they did not want to create a scene in the train station and both grinned nervously as they looked to see if anyone was paying attention. Ted took her schoolbag and they walked out onto the sidewalk, talking freely now and just following the surge and flow of the crowds of pedestrians They broke out of the tide and entered a Western-style coffeeshop. They went up the steep, winding steps to the second floor and sat next to each other in a booth in a corner; alone, but overlooking the street below.

After a waitress had taken their order, they sat quietly for a moment and looked into each other's eyes. "I so missed you this summer," Ted said breaking the silence. "I have never missed anyone so much. And seeing you in the station just now was ... you were even prettier than the first night I saw you at the dinner."

She had read his letters all summer without embarrassment, but she was shy to hear him speak so fondly of her. She looked down at her hands folded in her lap and thought. She felt the same as he, yet something told her that their love was too private to mention aloud, even to him. "I am not pretty, now or then."

"Please, Mieko. Don't stop me from speaking my heart," he said in Japanese.

"Takabashi-san. What do your parents think of me?"

"Oh, I donno," he lied, switching to English. Realizing his lack of frankness he continued, "Well, I think my father likes you. But my mother, she just can't get used to the fact that I'm growing up."

"That is all?"

"I think so. Why? What do your parents think?"

"My father encourages me to see you. My mother is silent but does not seem to object."

"I'm glad to know that. Are you worried so much about them — my parents?"

She looked up at him again. "I know I am too young to love, but I don't want my hopes destroyed by something I must not oppose. I have revealed more of myself to you than to anyone. It makes me feel insecure."

"That I'll tell others?"

"No, that what I have put in you of me will be taken away. I will lose myself."

Ted closed his eyes and felt inside himself. He thought he

135

could sense the part of her that had grown inside him in the past year. It was a warmth, an energy that bordered on laughter. He had never loved anyone before. Not this way. The cold, regimented love he felt for his relatives was almost an obligation. It was not self-renewing. This was a new sensation, and he knew that nothing could destroy their bond save their own incapacities.

"Mieko, don't worry about my parents. You mean more to me than they do."

"You mustn't say that," she commanded.

"But it's true!"

"If your parents object, then I will not be able to see you."

"It's up to us."

"Not here."

Ted's line of thought ricocheted off her words and bounced into considerations of Japanese culture. Of course she would worry about his parents' objections. From her point of view he would have to follow their wishes. But he did not believe he would make that choice. He realized too, in a flash that made him blink his eyes, that what he was considering was marriage. He had never let the thought of marriage enter his mind with any girl he had known before. But sitting in the quiet booth, looking into her sincere eyes, he knew he could spend his whole life with her. The finality of his future, knowing he had found someone, the right one, so soon, was both frightening and exhilarating.

Yoshida heard his daughter enter the house, returning home from her date. He heard the chatter of the three women in his life, his wife, Mieko, and Yuko. Mieko was chided for not being home for dinner and Yuko added rival sibling remarks. He wished he could

136

feel light-hearted and gay about life, but his affairs were not going well. At least his business was not as well as anticipated, and he was being continually pressured by the collectors to maintain regular payments on his debt.

Only the night before he had been visited by Nishida. The stress had begun to affect his work. Usually very astute at sounding out his manager's opinion's and coming to a proper, balanced choice, he had of late made several decisions at odds with recommendations. None had turned out well, and, though the errors probably went unnoticed by most, he amplified the severity of his lack of conscientiousness and preoccupied himself with past failings.

Most upsetting, he thought again, was his lost zeal for sexual contact. He was not sure if the problem was age, stress, or fear, but he could no longer summon the previously stalwart member between his loins to seek its entertainment. Momentarily, he vindictively accused his wife of losing her appeal, but just as quickly realized the problem lay outside the home. Perhaps he was punishing himself for his previous dalliance which had cost him so much.

If there was guilt, it was not towards his wife; that thought was not even a consideration. By having been indiscreet, perhaps taking the wrong lover, and definitely having caved in too easily to her demands, he had weakened his fiscal health and undermined his leadership capacity. Hadn't his father punished him by denying him a promotion and profit-sharing for several critical years?

The appointment the night before with Nishida had been brief but ominous. He was short of cash, and his debt was increasing rapidly. Nishida told Yoshida to expect a call from him and Yamashita the following week to set the terms of a final settlement. Nishida stated no terms other than to threaten that "the bankrupt *eta* insect would eat bitterness." Somehow Yoshida had to manage to obtain special financing. As chief corporate officer now, he could arrange a loan from the corporate treasury. However, all available capital was being used in their expansion and promotional projects and Tokaido Meats was already considering increasing its long-term debt to an unmanageable percentage. Somewhere he had to find a cheap source of money for his company, and for himself. Sitting sullenly in his dimly lit study, a possibility with half a chance came to mind. He smiled softly and went out to see his daughters.

"Tell me the truth, Takabashi-san," Obara said to Ted. "Whom did you go to see first, me or Yoshida Mieko-san?"

Ted grinned nervously and avoided his teacher's intense stare.

"You see, what kind of student are you? And yet you insist you trained 'religiously' all summer. I think you exercised your palm all vacation long playing with yourself," he chided. "I hope you are not too exhausted to show me how much you have forgotten."

"Please let me show you how much I have forgotten," Ted said with the mock solemnity of a costume-drama samurai, bowing his forehead to the floor.

From his kneeling position facing Ted, Obara slapped the back of his right hand out to the right side of his student's still-bowed head. Despite the speed of the surprise attack, Ted's head bobbed up even faster, the hand a blur passing beneath his chin. Having missed in his first attempt, Obara reversed the direction of his hand and returned with a palm slap to the left side of Ted's neck. Ted gave him a numbing block into the fleshy part of his wrist and pulled a thumb attack just short of a nerve in Obara's biceps.

"How many times have I told you, Taka-ko," he said regaining his posture, "that your nerve strike must be accurate to within the

138

size of a hundred yen coin?"

"Many times."

"Just so. Even that you seem to have misplaced in your memory," he said with a smile. He had expected his strikes to make contact at least once. He was pleasantly surprised to discover his student had indeed progressed. "Show me all the basic drills."

Ted had found Obara's teaching to be extremely unusual but eminently practical. They had always met at Tokaido Meats to train and for the first month Obara had directed Ted to labor with the other employees moving sides and quarters of steer. Thomas was encouraged to see Yoshida take a personal interest in his son, allowing him to be a part-time apprentice in the meat room. He did not understand why Ted did it, though, but never asked. Obara watched Ted closely that first month. The boy was hostile but determined. Seeing that he neither quit nor complained to Yoshida after a month, he then put the boy under the direction of his assistant. Though powered meat saws were used in the modern packing plant, Obara and his assistant had begun work as butchers in the age of knives. Ted was put to work cutting scraps with a butcher's blade. At first he was given sections of fat and cartilage to work on. He was told to cut smoothly and cleanly. Later he graduated to ankle joints. These were difficult for him. Butcher Obara moved his knife effortlessly through the cartilage and between the small openings between bones. Ted forced his way between the joints, sometimes cleaving his way through. Obara would look on sadly and point out repeatedly that he wanted to see no marrow. After a month of cutting, Ted began to sense the way to move the blade, while realizing his skill was still vastly inferior to the Butcher's. The Butcher then gave Ted more active tasks. After moving meat and cutting ankle bones for an hour, he would drill evasive stepping into his pupil for another hour each session. Though he had yet to learn how to attack, he could not forget the intense pain with which Obara had incapacitated him and knew the teaching would come if he was patient.

By the end of March, Obara had begun to show him blocking methods. These differed from what he had learned at the Shorinji school, which was slow by comparison. Obara's intent was less to stop the momentum of an incoming blow than to strike out at a sensitive part of the attacking weapon. In order to employ these techniques successfully, Ted had to do drills in evasive stepping to avoid the power of the attack, conditioning several parts of his hands and elbow to serve as striking points with speed and accuracy in order to hit the small, swiftly moving targets.

As Obara watched Ted review the old drills they had practiced in the spring, he was silently impressed with the progress his student had made and his token criticisms softened into thoughtful comments on a stance or the safety of a method. After an hour of review he called Ted over to sit with him.

"I never thought you would be ready for more advanced learning. Well, you're not really, but we will start tonight. Go then and take that push broom." It was the kind with a wide face and short bristles. "Now hold it out."

Ted grasped the handle in two hands and held it out parallel to the ground.

"No, no. One hand."

Ted released his left hand and the end of the broom dropped to the floor. He strained to lift it.

Obara stood up and took the handle from him. "Like this," he ordered, holding the pole firmly in his right hand, the end sticking out motionless. "When you can hold it motionless then move your hand, but keep the tip in one place," he said, as his hand described a U-shape while the brush remained fixed in space as if suspended from above, "when you can do this, come back. Not until."

Thomas felt he had learned a lot about Japan in the fifteen months he had been there. Although significant progress in meat imports had eluded his organization, he was able to report more intelligently on what was preventing their inroads and could reflexively cite over ten specific nontariff barriers in his defense. During the year, he had frequent contact with Yoshida and had grown to like him with the aloof camaraderie traders maintain for each other. At least every two weeks he attended one function or another with the president of Tokaido Meats, but he had rarely spent time alone with him. This made Yoshida's offer for private discussion over dinner seem all the more special, perhaps out of place.

Yoshida had picked him up in a company car and they had driven to a very small and delicately appointed restaurant in Akasaka district which specialized in nouvelle cuisine.

When the maitre d' had shown them to their private room with flowered silk wallpaper and fine rosewood dining table, Yoshida broke the tempo of their conversation, which thus far had centered on polite banter. "I thought the time had come for us to have dinner again as we did last year. At that time you were new here and valuable discussions led to our current relationship. Our dinner then was Japanese. Tonight Western. This restaurant specializes in appetizers. We have worked together twelve months since the rooftop party. We will have one appetizer for each month."

"Certainly sounds like an unusual dinner."

"I hope you enjoy it. This is a proper mix of East and West:

141

Japanese modular approach to food with Western ingredients and decor."

Over a dry white wine, they enjoyed the first three selections the chef had chosen for them. Still Thomas wondered what the real purpose of the dinner was.

"Yoshida-san. That was the best paté I have ever had. I must compliment you on your choice of restaurants."

"It's nothing."

"I'm really quite flattered that you invited me to dinner with you tonight, but surely I don't deserve special attention yet, and you did indicate you had something important to discuss."

Correct on both counts, Yoshida thought. "Yes, but I think we eat first and talk later. OK?"

"Of course," Thomas returned jovially, still wishing to find out what the real purpose of the dinner was.

"How is your son's training going?"

It was not until the coffee service was removed and after dinner drinks were brought to them at two leather high backed smoking chairs that sat overlooking the soft lights in a small temple garden below that Thomas' curiosity was satisfied.

"Now. Where are … were we?" Yoshida said with a stammer.

"An important matter you wished to talk to me about."

"Oh, well, important? Yes, I suppose so."

He removed an envelope from his coat pocket and handed it across the antique burl walnut table to Thomas.

"There are some accounting numbers. What we have spent the past year as part of our expansion and promotion. The second page is our projected expenses for next year." He paused and gave the American several minutes to look at the figures.

"I certainly hope that your efforts are rewarded," Thomas said, hoping Yoshida did not want anything other than encouragement.

Yoshida smiled, but wished Bergman was the type of man who was perceptive enough to make this easier on him. "Yes. The risk is not small to my company. These expenses represent a not-small portion — do you say 'not small'?"

Thomas nodded that he understood as he sipped his cognac.

"A not-small portion of our potential revenues in sales of your state's beef for the same period."

"Well, we all hope that our market entry will be eased somewhat and your sales will exceed these projections, which, by the way seem conservative to me."

"Bugman-san, I'm sure you are aware that the beef we had tonight in the eighth course was not Iowa steer. It was not even from our ranch as was the piece last year. It is from a rival company. This restaurant, a prestigious one, you can imagine, does not buy our beef now."

Thomas could feel bad news on the way but he was not sure what it would be. Did Yoshida want to give up on their marketing agreement? "Your sales projections do not indicate a drop in volume for your domestic product," Thomas said, probing.

"Yes, but the market kilogram consumption is expected to expand 4 percent next year while our costs will increase 6 percent. We believe our sales by kilos will be down as much as 10 percent."

"Yoshida-san, I am sorry that your business in domestically produced beef is hurting, and you might say I wish the reason for the decline was because of the impact of my product, but I'm not sure what more I can do to help. Do you have any specific proposals on how we can improve our chances of breaking in while not draining too much out of your organization."

"Bugman-san, you have had a chance to see what we are doing

to sell your product here. This year you worked with my people. You know we are on your side. Our promotional program is set."

Thomas felt Yoshida had left the statement without a conclusion. He tried to think of what Yoshida was driving at. "But ..." he finally added to draw the Japanese man out.

"But Tokaido Meats requires greater cooperation from the Iowa Beef Commission."

"What kind of cooperation are you proposing? Investment?" Thomas asked fearing the worst.

"Investment? Not necessary at this time. It was our original intention that continued increasing revenue from our beef business would fuel our growth with you. As you can see we cannot shift resources without damaging our sales there. It would be appropriate for the beef commission to arrange a low-interest loan to Tokaido Meats to subsidize the cost of promotion."

Thomas sat and silently considered the proposal as he took another taste of the cognac. The idea was not without merit or justification; however, the commission had never done anything like it before. It would certainly give him a chance to wring more concessions and greater effort from Tokaido.

"The commission might be willing to arrange a loan subject to some conditions. How much are we talking about?"

"I shall think at least a million dollars."

Thomas whistled and raised his eyebrows. "That's a lot of meat not yet sold. I don't think I can swing it."

"The alternative would be a personal setback for both of us. Tokaido Meats would have to give up on the imported meat program or go to a better-financed organization ... like the Australian government." Yoshida felt he had to finesse Bergman, but not too much. If he pushed too hard he might end up with nothing.

"Yoshida-san, if it is your intention to jack us around on a yearly basis with this threat of Aussie beef, then I don't think there is a lot of room for cooperation," Thomas said coldly.

"No, Bugman-san. I have been frank with you. You have seen the figures. You know the market. Tokaido Meats does not want to sell Australian product and I do not want to give up the imported meat program. But we need your assistance. Think of the potential for sales if we are successful compared to the modest cost of a loan."

"All right Yoshida-san. I'll report to the commission on your proposal. I can't guarantee anything, and I'm sure the commission will set conditions."

"Such as?"

"Such as accountability for the funds. They won't want it used in any way to promote Japanese meat. It will all have to go toward our promotion."

"Yes."

"The commission may demand that I play a greater role in your organization."

"Yes."

"Of course, if the loan was tied to specific purchases from Iowa it would be easier to get their acceptance."

"Please put the proposal to your commission. To further our relations and improve the chance of your beef being marketed here successfully, I am willing to consider any reasonable request."

They toasted each other their last taste of cognac and prepared to leave, each feeling a victory of sorts had been won.

Yamashita waited. He did not think Nishida would keep him long. Besides, it was a comfortable, cool night and he was content to sit on the bench in Korakuen Park and watch the hundreds of people going everywhere on the sidewalk-at the park entrance. Their lifestyle had certainly changed, he thought. He could only pick out one woman in a hundred who wore a kimono and fewer men. More women were smoking, too. Tramps.

Life had certainly been different when he and the *oyabun* had returned from the war on the mainland. As a private to his *oyabun's* rank of sergeant, they had marched together through Manchuria and Korea. Life was tough then. The winters were bitterly cold and the Asian brothers on the mainland were not always hospitable. He remembered more than once having to kill for food.

Then the foreigners had taken over Japan. They proved their naivete almost at once by being so gentle. Japanese are patient and durable. Anything less than our destruction only serves as a fertilizer for our renewed growth. Not only did they not destroy us, they helped us.

Upon his repatriation with the *oyabun* from the mainland, they had set up a small construction company to rebuild whole neighborhoods that had been leveled by the war. The *oyabun* organized his men as he had in the army and soon had a disciplined team of hard workers with simple tools. Many people who could not afford the reconstruction of their homes became indebted to the *oyabun* and repaid him over the years with priceless information, deeds, land, and occasionally with their lives. Until 1951, they had remained busy with legitimate work, but the *oyabun's* growing influence had caught the attention of a local gangster who tried to extort protection money from him. The *oyabun*, employing his network of indebted contacts, learned the extent of the gangster's operations. One dark autumn night at 3 in the morning, the *oyabun* and his men struck. The sleepy, half-sober men they found had been no match for the burly construction crew whose jobs had been threatened. None of the gangster's men there survived the night. Within a month the *oyabun* had taken over the operation of three houses of prostitution and continued to extort protection money, but at lower rates, making the merchants of the area actually grateful to him. Soldiers of the dead gangster came to join the *oyabun*'s new organization.

Together they had seen the transformation of Japan. The *oyabun* oversaw a construction empire with land and hotels in every major city in the country. They had expanded into the travel industry, sports promotions, and agriculture. Of course, there was a dark side of the business, too. Anything in the world must have its dark side. That is the principle of *inyo* — shadow and light. The *oyabun* merely excelled at meshing the interest of both into a workable, synergistic enterprise.

He wondered what was keeping his nephew Nishida. He was fifteen minutes late. He should know it is not polite to keep one's elders waiting, he considered, especially when the elder is also your boss. He looked anxiously toward where his two bodyguards were supposed to be standing a discreet distance away. They were still there. No foul play. I really shouldn't suspect Nishida of doing me in. You're just too suspicious, old man, he chided himself.

Thus far Nishida had shown himself to be a good recruit, if only a little too overzealous. Collections from street people who owed them had gone up 10 percent after word got out that Nishida had blinded one debtor and shattered the knee caps of another. Actually, the stories were overblown. He had half-blinded and crippled one man, two were not involved, but such was gossip and it was good for business.

He saw Nishida enter the park and look for him. As the

147

nephew approached Yamashita, the two bodyguards, on recognizing him, closed their orbit around Yamashita to provide him with privacy.

"Yamashita-san, excuse me for being late. The *oyabun* himself had an errand for me to run."

"Really? You were successful, I hope."

"The task was completed. I had to deliver a package to the boxing coach." The *oyabun* maintained a stable of kick-boxers who competed regularly at the Korakuen area.

"You gave the package to the coach?"

"Yes."

"Good. You are performing adequately in your collection duties."

"I will try to work harder."

"Yes. Remember that this is a business though. Force is only occasionally necessary to obtain what is due and only from the low class. Other methods may work better and maintain the upright image of our organization. Do I need to explain?" he asked with the formal and insistent demeanor of an old teacher.

"I understand."

"Who is the most in debt of your accounts?"

"The *eta*," he said contemptuously.

"Yes. He is long overdue and does not even keep up with interest."

"I told him last week that you would see him next time and that he should be prepared to repay us in short order."

"Good. We must handle the *eta* carefully. He is a rich man and can repay us. He is just playing with us. Do you understand?"

The thought of the *eta* looking down on him enraged Nishida, though his attitude remained unchanged. "Yes," he barked.

"However, we may not want money from the dog. He has other things we want."

"Will you discuss this with him tonight?"

"Perhaps. Shall we go?" he said standing up from the park bench.

They walked to the large avenue outside the park, followed by Yamashita's aides. The driver was called and shortly a curtained, standard-sized black American limousine — only the *oyabun* had a stretch model — pulled up to the curb.

Nishida sat in back between one of the guards and Yamashita.

"Are you still training?" the older asked.

"Yes. Kendo and judo."

"Nothing new?"

"No."

Suddenly Yamashita's voice grew deep and stormy. "Do not lie to me, child. I have heard of your attempt to join the Yagyu Shinkage Ryu. Tell me what happened."

Surprised, Nishida blurted out the story. "I entered the *dojo* as any student and sought tuition. After training six months the headmaster expelled me."

"Expelled you? You are such a bad disciple?"

"I trained hard. But a member of the school knew I worked for Great Star and had heard of my job. The teacher said that the Ryu would not admit anyone lacking in moral character."

"This is truly insulting. Have you any desire to continue seeking a master?"

Nishida had long hoped to begin training in a traditional school of swordsmanship. Kendo, the Japanese sport of fencing, had taken his ability to a level far short of that required for the skillful use of live blades. "Yes. I will persevere and continue my search."

"Do not allow yourself to be expelled from another school."

The vehicle had ascended a long ramp to reach the overhead expressway that crossed Tokyo city. The flashing neon signs of countless shops intermittently colored the view. Although it was 7:30, many office buildings they passed were still brightly lit and occupied with busy workers seated at their long rows of desks. They both looked out over the city, each with his own thoughts. After picking through the evening traffic, which congested even the highway, they descended again to street level and entered the residential area where Yoshida's house was situated.

As the limousine pulled up to the sidewalk across the street from the walled-in traditional house, Yamashita spoke to Nishida in a grave tone. "It is not fair for this *kabu* to live so graciously when he owes us so much, neh?"

"Yes."

"This is a serious situation with a big customer. I am counting or your proper assistance to clear the matter up."

"I understand."

"Good."

They walked to the gate and rang the doorbell.

Inside the house Mieko responded to the call and ran out the front door, not hearing her father's call to let him see who was there.

She opened the gate and asked the visitors if she could help them.

"We are here to see your father on business, little girl."

Her father again called from behind her, "It's all right, Mieko, I'll get it."

"Father, these men are here to see you."

"Thank you, child," Yoshida said, approaching the gate. "You

150

may go inside."

"Yes, father."

Yoshida said, turning to the men when his daughter had returned up the stone steps to the house, "You did not tell me you were coming tonight."

"We don't owe you the courtesy of an appointment," Nishida commented brusquely.

"What if I had been away?"

"Then perhaps we would have talked with your wife and children. ... Have you forgotten your manners toward your betters or are we to stand here all night?"

Having doffed their street shoes at the main door, they padded into the *tatamied* room and knelt down around a small table. Yoshida closed the *shoji* and turned on his knees to face the two unwelcome visitors.

"How can I apologize enough for the tardiness of my payments?" Yoshida began conciliatorily.

"You cannot. Apologies don't buy saké and rice."

"Here. I will write you a check for what is overdue and next month's payment as well," Yoshida said hastily, not knowing where the funds would come from to cover the withdrawal.

"No. We are calling in your loan in its total amount. You are behind in payments and your interest due has grown to an unacceptable percentage of the total debt," Yamashita said coldly, his tone leaving no room for discussion.

Yoshida swallowed hard and laughed uneasily, his right hand reaching up to scratch his head vigorously behind his left ear. He sucked the breath in audibly between his teeth and replied, "You know I cannot pay you back in a lump sum so soon."

"You have no choice. The loan contract you signed was very

151

explicit. Continued tardiness of payments would be grounds to call in the loan. We are only businessmen. You have been tardy. We are recalling the debt."

"Perhaps I could pay you a quarter at the end of the month and another quarter every two months."

"Unacceptable. There is only one alternative if you cannot make it. We would be willing to accept part-ownership of Tokaido Trucking."

Yoshida's heart sank, though his composure remained fixed. Tokaido Trucking was an associated firm of Tokaido Meats, but was wholly owned by himself. He had built up the company to expand the meat business delivery range and market size. Both firms had become very successful through the arrangement. Because of accelerated depreciation allowed on the vehicles, the use of 1958 land values in accounting for the real estate on which his depots were built, and the intrinsic, unaccounted value of the permanent contracts with Tokaido Meats, the actual value of the firm was grossly underreported. This meant that the scum facing him could legitimately seize a third of his firm, by book value, he calculated. His mind raced to think of a source of money and he remembered the dinner he had invested in Thomas Bergman and his proposal for a loan. He had indeed planned to use funds to take the financial pressure off himself, so he could pay the *yakuza* back. But he had been totally unprepared for the devastating proposal they had brought so abruptly. "I understand. And if I can pay you back?"

"It would not be wise to pay us back," Yamashita said, a menacing hue coloring his voice.

"I'm … I'm not sure I understand."

"We would prefer a percentage of your trucking operation."

"But surely you would prefer cash."

"You cannot come up with the money, no one will loan you more with your record, and we do want our share of Tokaido Trucking. … Thirty five percent, I believe."

"Can you give me until the end of the year, three months only. I guarantee you I can pay you back by then, or I will give you your share of Tokaido Trucking."

Yamashita considered the counter offer. "Until December 1. Our lawyers will be in touch in late November to arrange the share transfers."

"Yamashita-san …" he began to implore, then stopped. "I will wait to hear from your side. Please," he said formally as he opened the *shoji* and beckoned them to leave.

Ted pulled the collar of his coat up around his neck as the cold dry wind blew swiftly down the train platform. In early November, the weather had turned sharply and unexpectedly colder, and he still found himself underdressing for it. A fully loaded train came to a stop precisely at the designated marks and its doors slid open to each side depositing a mass of pushing Japanese commuters onto the platform. He shoved his way through the wave of businessmen, secretaries, students, and wives to find a place to stand on board. The warm, dank cabin contrasted sharply with the dryness out-doors, and he pulled his collar back and partially unzipped his lightweight down jacket.

It was early on a Friday evening and he was leaving the Butcher on his way to see Mieko. They were the focus of his two current loves, and the thought that he could indulge in both in one evening made him feel that he was truly in the best of all possible worlds. Everything else he did was to support these passions or

153

appease those who would keep him from them. He had become the best in his Japanese class, through the extra effort he made with his tutor, because he wanted to be able to communicate with and about his loves on a level undisturbed by the hesitation of translation in his mind. He had achieved that. He knew his mother would stop him from pursuing his "extracurricular" activities if his grades slumped, so he maintained the high average he had started with at the American school. He strove to meet all demands the Butcher placed on him and he felt he had been successful.

He tried always to keep Butcher Obara surprised. Obara had been astonished when Ted had returned only a week later in September able to hold the broom out horizontally and move it as he had directed. This had been a prelude to training in seizing techniques. He had learned to couple the sidesteps he had drilled in before with a tight block and grip of the opponent's arm.

Later the Butcher showed him how to grab and press specific points that hid below the skin's surface. More than once Ted lost the effective use of his arm for several minutes at a time when Obara showed him the application of a method. He had pleased his teacher, though, by training at home and returning the next week with the skill learned, if not mastered. Obara then went on to grabbing other areas of the body. Ted systematically studied how to seize the throat, ear lobes, nostrils, eye sockets, testicles, and the loose skin over the kidneys, and to break the neck.

That evening the Butcher had closed the session with a reflection on what Ted had studied and what was left. "I have taught you basically all I know about empty-hand combat against a weapon. You must avoid the opponent's weapon at all costs, so you have learned evasion. You must destroy his weapons — the hand that holds the knife is a weapon — so you have learned to strike and seize. You must destroy your opponent, never let him have another chance to meet you on the field of combat, so you have learned ways to destroy him. But, I am a butcher, and butchers use knives. They are easily hidden, easily drawn, and easy to do damage with. Of course, they lack the range of gun, but I am a butcher, neh? Not a soldier. So from here on you will train with the knife. We will review your empty-hand skills, which are the basis for use of the knife, every session, but your new learning will concentrate on the blade. For now, remember this: Anything you learned to poke at with the thumb, you can thrust at with the point."

"I understand," Ted had said bowing his head to the floor, ending the session.

He always reviewed Obara's closing remarks as he rode on the train. Looking into the window pane, he did not see the reflection of the people packed up close to him but the face and actions of his teacher. Occasionally he looked at a person standing by him and picked out, point by point, the areas he had been taught to attack: a weak vertebra that could be dislodged with a properly targeted punch, a vein throbbing beneath the surface of the skin, a pressure point in someone's wrist.

It was doubly important for him to review Obara's words on this evening since he would not have a chance to immediately write down what he had learned. The train was pulling up to his stop, and his thoughts were turning to Mieko, whom he knew would be waiting for him just outside the station.

He zipped up his coat as he stepped out of the car and walked down the grey cement platform, being propelled by the crowd toward the staircase which led up over the tracks to his exit. It was 7:30, and as he descended back to street level and toward the ticket table, he picked out Mieko's face among the pedestrians. She was standing by a kiosk looking at magazine covers. He approached her quietly from behind without her noticing.

"Could you give me some directions, miss?" he asked in English, assuming a heavy Southern accent.

She turned around expecting to see a young, lost tourist but was happy to see only Ted. She preferred to save her English for his ears only.

"Good evening."

"*Konbanwa*," he returned. "Have you eaten."

"No."

"Good. I'm starved. How about some *yakitori?*"

"Yes," she said, taking hold of the arm he offered her.

They walked out of the station and crossed the street, turning left into the first small alleyway they saw. One pub and one *yakitori* stall had wooden signs hanging out into the alley advertising their business. They walked into the small restaurant, ducking through the cotton curtain that hung down to chest level.

They sat in the last two seats at the bar and looked at the assortment of raw meats and vegetables on skewers that the chef had prepared.

"You order," Ted suggested.

Mieko told the grill man what they wanted.

"What would you like to drink, Takabashi-san."

"How about saké?"

She ordered one small porcelain carafe of hot rice wine and two of the thimble-sized cups, then turned to Ted and asked, "How was your training tonight?"

"I enjoyed it. The Butcher is going to start teaching me to use a knife next session."

"Is Obara-san good?"

"I think so."

"You know, I have heard stories when I was a child about a man just called 'The Butcher,' too. He was something like a ... a Robin Hood for *burakumin*. I heard once that a sidewalk shoe repairman was set upon by street hoods. 'The Butcher' came along at the same time and killed two of them and maimed three others. Does that sound possible?"

Ted tried to imagine Obara in such a situation then replied simply, "Yes, I think so."

"This man was like a god to us, like a temple guardian spirit. I heard some *shinheimin* even burned incense and prayed for his intervention in their troubles with the Japanese."

"Do you consider yourself to be Japanese?" Ted asked, switching to English for privacy.

"I think myself a Japanese, but they, if they know, probably think of me as a lower person."

"I just don't understand how they can feel that way about people who look, talk, and act the same way."

"Remember, Takabashi-san, I think I am a Japanese, but my father thinks we are *burakumin*. Also remember, the Japanese are a very pure race. We are on an island and have been safe from invasion until you Americans came," she said adding a smile. "Japanese feel their success is because of their ..."

"Japaneseness?"

"Yes. They feel no one in the world is like a Japanese; even a Chinese person growing up here or a Japanese growing up outside will never grow to be a true *Nihon-jin*."

"But what about you? You were born and raised here, you speak the same language, go the same schools, have the same manners. Why don't they see you as the same?" Ted asked, not willing to accept this inequity, which he perceived as being more insidious than discrimination against blacks and Mexicans in the United States.

"Japan's history is long. In history, we are a lower class. Tradition changes slowly in a country with a long history," she concluded thoughtfully.

"Then, there is nothing to do but suffer?"

"Suffer?"

"Endure pain."

"Well, once there was 'The Butcher.' Now there are social organizations I hear of who are trying to make us truly equal. Do you think 'The Butcher' I heard about and Obara are the same?"

"I don't know. Perhaps I'll ask some day."

The grillman brought fresh Japanese mushrooms, chicken skin, and okra cooked on the spot to the young couple. Mieko ordered some more and then prepared the sauce for Ted.

"What would you like to do tonight," she asked.

"Be alone with you," Ted said quietly, but without hesitation. He had known Mieko for well over a year, but he had never known her in the biblical sense, he mused. He did not regret it and did not want to make her feel self-conscious about her commitment to herself. He liked to feel he understood Mieko and tried to love her as he supposed she wanted to be loved, not the way he would have corralled an American girl in high school. The fact that his eighteenth birthday was approaching and he had not yet lost his virginity did not concern him as much as he imagined it would have were he in the United States.

"Can we be alone tonight in such a city?" she asked.

"Yes. All alone."

"Will you take me there?" she asked quietly looking up into

his eyes.

"Yes." He could not believe she understood what he had asked. He poured her a glass of saké and toasted her. "To my forever partner."

"To my forever partner."

Yoshida stared sullenly out the window of the high speed train as the landscape of suburban Japan rushed past. Blue tiled roofs blurred into drab cement buildings set close to the line. The train was moving at 150 kilometers an hour and had not reached top speed, yet the noise, movement, and sway were less than conventional trains at much slower speeds. The Shinkansen, the "New Quick Line," was a symbol of national pride and it daily sped across the face of a Japan changing with equal haste.

Looking out over the densely packed apartments, factories, and office buildings which only infrequently gave way to the farm-land they had crowded out, Yoshida was not certain in his heart that it was all progress. Modern life, he felt when he was depressed, did not agree with him.

Why can't I be a simple pilgrim traveling from temple to shrine to temple. Donate a little here, eat a specialty there, rest, enjoy the scenery, and have no trouble. No one goes on pilgrimage anymore it seems, at least not on foot. I could do good deeds for people. Philanthropy. What a luxury! No one has time today.

But I guess I can't complain. If it were 200 years ago, any samurai could cut me down for a sideways glance. The roads weren't too safe to walk on. And ... and I am a *burakumin*. I would be less than nothing. A bored warrior would probably use me to test the sharpness of his sword. Mieko would have no chance in life. Why should I want to be a pilgrim anyway? It is because of Buddhism that I am an *eta*.

Have things really changed? I am one of a fortunate few who could succeed, and that only through the work of my father. The rest of us are still less than Japanese. Mieko may test into a good school, but as an *eta* woman what chance does she really have? No good Japanese boy would marry her; his family would never allow it.

But Takabashi-san, he is good. The Butcher was impressed that he did not pass out that first day he struck him. And since then he has trained hard. He has not violated my daughter and shows the proper respect. Yes, some things modern are good. His mind lingered on the glow of young love's memory.

He tried to return to the line of thought he was pursuing before he became distracted by the view from his train seat.

The meeting he was returning from in Nagoya had just brought more unwelcome news at a time when things were not going well at all. Sales in the area were being attacked by another group headquartered in Osaka. Tokaido Meats, it was explained, had fallen behind the other firm which had aggressive salesmen offering prompt delivery through a more localized network of cold-storage facilities using more modern refrigeration and insulation than Yoshida's company. Extra sales and logistics expenses were offset by a more efficient plant. To regain the lost market share, Tokaido would have to cut prices, possibly leading to a meat price war, or invest in new plant and more salesmen. Either way, Tokaido was in no position to invest in their current cash situation.

A snow-draped Mount Fuji filled the window, but the view failed to raise his spirits. The snow only reminded him of winter, December. It was already December. It was already time to pay off the *yakuza* dogs. With what, he shrieked silently within. He did not

160

have to worry about losing Tokaido Trucking. He had talked to his father who had agreed to "buy" it. His father would not let him forget his past mistakes. "You are still my child, my empty-headed boy, and as a father I will protect you," he had said, relieving Yoshida despite the invective. "I will buy Tokaido Trucking from you. Sign it over to me and they cannot get it." He had waited for his father to mention what form of payment he would receive, not wanting to insult the man by raising the question. Finally, he had said, "Thank you, I will use the proceeds to pay off my debt to the *yakuza* cess and bury that dark part of my past." Suddenly his father added anger to insult. "You think I will pay so you can go live a dissolute life again with some other rented cunt? By the spirits of the mountain and the sea I swear I'll not finance your whoring," the old man had raged. "Then … then what do you mean?" the son had asked, lost. "Let's say I'll give you an non-negotiable IOU, payable in Tokaido Meats stock in five years or at my death, whichever comes first."

"How will I pay off the loan?"

"I will help you protect your interests, our company. How you protect yourself is up to you."

His father was a shrewd bastard, Yoshida considered in retrospect. In five years I will have paid off the *yakuza* or be dead myself. If my father dies, the debt is payable in stock which I will receive without inheritance tax. Tokaido Trucking was safe. But Yoshida was filled with dread.

He had an appointment tomorrow with Nishida. He could not imagine what would happen when he told the thug with canine intelligence that he no longer owned the assets they wanted to collect. He expected the worst.

His only hope waited for him twenty minutes beyond this

train ride, he thought, as the space-age locomotive approached the Shinagawa section of Tokyo and began to slow down for its final stop at Tokyo Central Station. Thomas Bergman. He hated to have to rely so heavily on such a man. He also abhorred the thought of owing anything to him. But if Bergman came through with the loan from the beef commission, it would indeed save Yoshida and he would feel a heavy burden of social debt, but not gratitude. Bergman was not the type of man one could feel grateful toward.

The past months since he had broached the subject of the loan with the American, they had discussed the progress of the approval on several occasions. For the first three weeks Bergman claimed the stateside commission would not have even received his report. Then, when he had gotten a reply, it was to gather more information from Yoshida. The questions had been many and concerned private aspects of his company's financial history. Yoshida had grudgingly replied to all but two of the questions, the answers to which he felt were too confidential and superfluous to any loan agreement. After that, he had waited. Weeks had passed, and all the while Yoshida had been tortured by the tyranny of the deadline on his loan.

Yesterday Bergman had called him and asked that he come to his office. He had not indicated what the topic of discussion would be, but Yoshida was certain he had received word from the United States about the loan. Yoshida uttered one more silent prayer to the spirit of the fox who guides merchants. He felt the chances were very good. Had not Bergman said, weeks before, "By the looks of this questionnaire, I'd say there's some interest from the commission to go ahead with the loan"?

The Shinkansen glided to a stop and Yoshida retied his shoes, grabbed his attaché case and disembarked. A cool, dry wind blow-

162

ing down the platform hurried him to the stairs, which led down into the warm recesses of the station proper. He joined hundreds of other passengers walking briskly to the exit. Is there any waking hour when this station is not crowded, Yoshida wondered as the blue-capped ticket taker politely snatched the stub from him when he passed through the narrow gate. He walked to the taxi stand and entered a waiting vehicle. After telling the driver his destination, he settled into the seat and reconsidered his situation.

If Bergman did come through with the loan, he supposed he would have to be at least a little grateful to him. Yes, when he comes through it will really change my opinion of him. I'll know he is on my side. Tomorrow I will be able to look Nishida in the eye and tell him I will be able to pay off principal and interest within the week. Just to see the look in his eyes then will be worth the agony of the past and danger of not handing Tokaido Trucking over to them. Even the problem in Nagoya would be lessened by the cooperation of the beef commission.

Yoshida left the taxi in a more optimistic frame of mind, and as he took the elevator up to the floor where Bergman awaited him, he felt lighter than he had in months. He could sense a new beginning was in store for him. When he entered the reception area Bergman's secretary took his coat and told him Bergman would be with him momentarily. He sat down and relaxed a moment while scanning an American farm-industry magazine.

"Yoshida-san! Glad you could make it. Come right in," Thomas said as he came out of his office with his hand extended in greeting to Yoshida. "Sorry you had to wait in the reception, I had a call. Have a seat," he said, pointing to the chair facing his desk.

Thomas continued to exchange pleasantries for several minutes. Yoshida appreciated the warm tone in Thomas' voice and felt he must have good news for him. However, he was anxious to learn what the news was. During a break in the conversation Yoshida decided to ask, knowing that Americans appreciate directness. "I thought when you called me about an appointment it might have something to do with the loan we had discussed. Any news yet?"

"Well, I have some good news and some bad news. Which do you want to hear first?" Thomas said easily.

I wish these Americans would refrain from playing stupid games in business, Yoshida grumbled internally. Then he considered a moment and said dryly, "I would like to know the good news first."

"The good news is that the commission has decided to give you the extra discount on multiple-container orders of beef," Thomas said with a smile.

The news was not unexpected. Yoshida understood there was a beef surplus. A discount on prices negotiated under different circumstances was only apropos. "The bad news?"

"I'm sorry to say the commission turned down your request for them to arrange financing."

"No loan?" Yoshida asked incredulously, his eyes growing wider.

"I did the best I could," Thomas said, lying easily.

"Do they understand the consequences, was it explained completely clearly to them?" You cannot possibly understand the consequences, his insides screamed.

"Yoshida-san, I told you I tried the best I could but they feel it is the vendor's responsibility to finance promotion. And frankly, they were concerned that you did not answer all the questions on the form they sent out."

"You said you thought it was all right that I leave those answers blank."

"Leave the questions blank," Thomas corrected. "Well, I thought they could make a decision based on the material you provided, but I was wrong. The commission would probably want to wait until the government here opens up meat imports a little more before they commit a large sum of money to your marketing effort. Their reply also indicated that they felt that the State of Iowa had invested enough already through the introductory promotions we have had."

Yoshida's head was swimming. He realized too late he had put too much hope in the loan coming through. Now, not only was his life at stake, but the *yakuza* might also find some other way to lay claim to part of Tokaido Meats or Tokaido Trucking. He had not imagined that the guileless American facing him could be so treacherous. Selectively his memory picked out scraps of conversations with Bergman. The words he remembered told him that he had had cause for confidence before. That means Bergman must have been lying, he concluded. "But you had said that you felt the chances were good."

"I believe I said that I hoped the chances were good since I knew the kind of competition you face," Thomas said, having long been aware that the commission would reject the appeal.

"This is really quite disappointing and I hope you understand the consequences such as we discussed originally."

"Yoshida," Thomas said, consciously dropping the formal "san." "We hope that this will not strain our relations with your company, but we feel we have been generous with you in the past, and actually I am getting some heat from the U.S. because sales have not picked up."

"I may have to contact better-financed meat export groups," Yoshida said, trying to conceal his desperation.

"I should let you know as well that we have been contacted by other strong food-marketing groups about breaking your exclusive. One company in Osaka seems to have particularly good potential," Thomas added for impact.

"I see," Yoshida replied briefly, stunned by the double blow Thomas had dealt him. He sat silently waiting for Thomas to continue, which he did not. "We at Tokaido Meats had hoped that the loan would come through so we could put our best efforts behind the sale of your product. Now, I am afraid we will have to re-examine our targets and budgets. If you have further information for me, or perhaps the reconsidered opinion of your organization regarding the funding, please get in contact."

"Will do," Thomas said casually.

Yoshida was more frightened than he could ever remember being. His palms were damp and he felt a trickle of nervous sweat roll down his forehead into his eyebrows. His breathing was shallow and he wished he could somehow postpone the disclosure he had to make to Yamashita. Perhaps if I am frightened enough I will die of a heart attack, he thought hopefully.

The two men facing him were grim and their countenances revealed no mercy. They had expected to see Yoshida carrying something when he came to the quiet Ginza hostess bar they owned. Though it was the afternoon, it was dark in the lounge and they stared at him as he appeared the table. He had come completely empty-handed, not even carrying a briefcase or envelope, and they were slightly baffled. Surely he does not plan to renege on his payment, they both wondered to themselves.

"I do not know how to tell you this," he began. "I have some

166

bad news."

"It will only be bad news for you, *eta*," Nishida commented in a low toned snarl.

"Yes. As you can see, I am not carrying anything. I do not have the money."

"We will accept Tokaido Trucking shares as you agreed."

"I am afraid your records are in error," Yoshida replied, choking on the accusation. "I no longer own Tokaido Trucking."

Yamashita glared first at Yoshida, then at his surprised subordinate. "You do not own ... who owns Tokaido Trucking!?"

"My father, as he owns Tokaido Meats."

"You are dead," Nishida growled.

As he lost control of his composure and collapsed his face into his hands, his back heaving with choked sobs, Yoshida cried, "That would probably make my father happy, but please don't kill me. I am nothing, it is true. But my family, they need me."

"You should have considered that long ago, butcher. Your kind does not deserve life or Buddha's compassion. Death might be too good for you, though."

"I beg you," Yoshida sobbed, "Please, just give me more time. I am sure I can raise the money."

"We don't want the money. We want Tokaido Trucking."

"I ... I don't think I can get it. But the money. There may be some way."

"You'll hear from us very shortly, and you had better jump when you do."

"Of course," Yoshida said, confused but sobering up.

"Now get out."

Yoshida stood up warily and looked about. There were no immediately threatening people around, though Yamashita's bodyguards sat across the room sipping beer and keeping their eyes on their boss. He was free to go. Free. Why? He could not imagine the reason for their leniency. He was grateful for it though and slipped onto the elevator to the ground floor as quietly as he could.

When the elevator doors closed behind the debtor, Yamashita turned to Nishida, his eyes narrowing like an eagle focusing on its prey. "I don't know whose sight I detest more at this moment, yours or his. Why was I not informed about Tokaido Trucking?"

"I cannot even find an answer to that."

"Yes, you are bumbling. What you should know, you do not know. What you should tell me, you do not tell me."

"Yes, I am deficient."

"You are more than deficient, you are less than useless. You are a liability to our organization."

"I do not deserve a second chance."

"Yes, you do not." Yamashita paused and looked at his nephew's bowed head. He looked penitent. "Did you even remember to prepare for this contingency as I asked you?"

"I did not forget."

"Everything is ready?"

"Yes,"

"Then go ahead, make your phone call. And, Nishida, succeed in getting what we want from Yoshida and I can forget today. Fail, and I never will."

For several weeks two pairs of eyes had been watching. Tracing movements. Noting habits. Detailing routine. Today they waited outside the girl's high school as closing time approached. They had received word from their boss Nishida that today they would act.

After the bell rang and the front doors to the building sprang open, a tide of blue skirts, blue coats, and red caps swelled out onto the sidewalk and divided, some going left, some right. They knew their mark would go left, and waited, their car parked by the curb.

They saw their mark trot down the steps, chatting with friends, her schoolbag embraced to her chest and waited as she turned predictably and walked toward them.

"Yoshida Mieko-san?" a man asked deferentially as she passed.

She turned from her friends and looked at the businessman standing next to the black sedan. "Yes."

"We are from Tokaido Meats. Someone in your family has taken ill and your mother sent us to take you to the hospital. I am sorry."

She paused and looked to her friends for some sign of comfort or advice.

"It is really quite urgent, Yoshida-san."

She pursed her lips, waved goodbye to her classmates and stepped into the sedan. The two men entered from left and right and sat on each side of her. The doors closed, the car pulled from the curb, and the locks clicked shut automatically with the acceleration of the vehicle.

"What has happened?," she asked.

"We're not sure Yoshida-san. Perhaps an accident."

"Who is in the hospital?"

"We're not sure. If you can wait until we arrive."

Mieko was worried and confused. No one had been ill that morning. Her mother was all right. Maybe her grandfather had unexpectedly gotten sick. Or her father. Her stomach churned as she imagined her father dying. She had never given any thought to his age before, never considered the possibility he might be taken

169

from her, never to be seen again. She wished someone besides strangers had been sent to tell her and that they had more specific information. She sat in silence as her thoughts grew more morose.

The car first took city streets, then pulled onto the highway and drove away from Tokyo, finally exiting from the expressway a half hour later. Suddenly the car pulled into a garage. A gate was closed behind the vehicle and the floor began to descend with the car and passengers into the parking area.

The two men escorted Mieko to the elevator, followed her on, and pushed the button for the top floor, the tenth. The elevator had bright pink carpeting and smelled of cigarettes and saké. She wondered if this was a hospital or just a clinic.

The doors opened to reveal a dimly lit, smoke-filled world she had not imagined existed. No one who cared heard her scream.

Yoshida returned home that evening happy to be alive and whole, but fretting uncontrollably about his debt. It had consumed his entire afternoon as he tried to call in all personal loans and favors. He had only been successful in raising a quarter of the amount needed. Almost as soon as he got home the phone rang. His wife answered it and called him.

"Yoshida Tsuji?" the unidentified voice asked.

"Yes."

"Yoshida Tsuji, the *eta* debtor?"

He paused. "Yes."

"Your daughter Mieko has taken a part-time job with us to help pay off your debts. Not a pleasant job for a pretty, young, virgin child. You have a week to pay before she goes on full-time duty. Do you understand? A week."

170

"But …" Yoshida tried to interject but the phone went dead.

Yoshida sank into a chair and gripped his head in his hands. He could not believe, would not believe they would do this. But his head knew better. They would use Mieko. His beloved Mieko.

He called his wife, who came out of the kitchen, surprised to see him sitting so sullenly.

"Bad day?" she asked.

"Woman, a very bad day. Has Mieko come home yet."

"No."

"Do you know where she is?"

"No."

"She's not with Takabashi-san?"

"She told me she would be home by 5 this afternoon."

"And you are not concerned about her whereabouts?!" Yoshida lashed out vindictively, wishing he could transfer some of the blame onto his wife.

"I am sorry. I will call her friends."

"No need. I think I know where she is. She won't be coming back tonight."

"Where is she?" his wife queried, puzzled.

"You must remain silent about this. Tell no one."

"What?" she asked, shocked.

"Mieko has been taken by the *yakuza*."

She sat quietly for several moments as the weight of his words sank through several years of memories. Memories of losing his touch, and finding it had been given to another woman. Memories of his father's intervention and the gifts her husband had given the whore, the likes of which she had never received. Who was owed more, the fallen flower or the bearer of his children, she had raged within. Memories of the many nights the *yakuza* thugs had visited their household and the fear and contempt she had for them ... and now this. Her precious Mieko. Heaven only knew what price her husband's creditors would exact on their daughter. When she could contain her rage no more she vocalized her sentiments. "Yoshida Tsuji, you are a disgusting and lecherous old man. I want you to get whatever the *yakuza* want as fast as you can and be done with them. But no matter what the outcome, I swear you'll live the rest of your life without my love." She then turned away and left him to his thoughts and regrets.

The Love Hospital was a theme love hotel that had been built in 1969 on the outskirts of Tokyo. Located near the highway, it attracted businessmen at all hours and crowds at night. There was a bar and restaurant, an indoor hot tub and private steam-bath cubicles, an area where couples could discreetly check into honeymoon suites, and another where lone men could find satisfaction.

They would be attended to by young women dressed in miniskirted, low-cut nurse's uniforms with crisp, white, paper nurses' caps pinned in their hair. Newcomers were always delighted to discover that when the waitresses leaned over to serve their neighbor, their lush bottoms flashed uncovered into view. The neighbor was also afforded a peek at the girl's chest as his drink was offered. This kept the volume in spirits and snacks at a high level and raised the desire of the guests to go upstairs for more intimate and costly sport.

On one floor were "operating rooms." Here, for a fixed hourly sum, the amorous man could look at a fully exposed woman who lay on an examination table underneath a clear, curved plastic lid. By putting his hands into any of six thin surgical gloves which entered the lid and sealed it off from the outside, he could touch, squeeze, and probe as he wished. A "nurse" stood by to make sure it did not go too far. She was also available (for more yen) to touch and lick the guest as he did his operation. Most opted for this extra service.

On a still higher floor were the "therapy rooms." A guest chose from a wide selection of "therapists" who were also clad in easily doffed nurses' attire. The rates per hour for therapy were higher still, and the guest had to negotiate with the doctor for special service. The rooms were of standard hotel quality and had large bathtubs.

On the top floor were the most expensive services. The visitor would choose a "psychiatrist" who would first lie him down on a couch with a drink. There, with the lights down she would coax his deepest sexual fantasies out of him. Based on what he had related, they would move to another theme room appropriate to his fantasy. Many guests dreamed of being a samurai using a sword to threaten a kimono-clad virgin maiden into satisfying his lust after battle. Some wanted to be approached by a blond Western woman and asked to bed, where they would fulfil her wildest fantasies with their oversized organs. This could be arranged. Others lusted after their secretaries and so they had an "office" complete with desks and typewriters. Then there were the standard bondage requests for which there were several rooms.

For four nights Mieko had been encased in an operating-room cubicle. Hour after hour, drunk and sober, old and young men had come to touch her; some gently, some not so gently. One time the nurse had to intervene when a frustrated customer had tried to cut through the surgical glove with a pocket knife. The nurse had sat the man down and gave him some free extra service to calm him until his hour was up.

Mieko had resisted violently the first night until a man whose name she learned was Nishida told her two things: one that she

173

could not believe, one that she could. He told her that her father owed them a lot of money and that he had agreed to sell Mieko to them, that she was to obey Nishida and earn her keep, and that in three months she would have paid back her father's debt. Not believing her father would do this to her, she continued her struggle. Then Nishida asked her. "You have a foreign boyfriend, yes?"

She thought for a moment. "No."

"He goes to the American school. He is tall and blond. You ate a snack with him three nights ago after seeing a movie." He watched her expression change from defiance to horror. "You see, your father told us. We know all about you. And if you don't treat our customers nice, we will kill the *gaijin*. You do believe we can kill him, don't you?"

She nodded her head.

"And you will not struggle or he will die and your father will be disappointed."

She nodded again, now sobbing deeply.

Nishida signaled two nurses to undress her. He watched as her school blouse and cravat, skirt, and undergarments were removed and stored. As each piece was stripped from her, he felt a growing rush of blood sensitizing his sex. She was beautiful and everything he wanted but had never had. She was a virgin, or at least virginal, he concluded. He had only lain with whores. She was too young to lay with him, yet too mature for him to pass up. He knew she was rich, educated, and *eta*. The combination was too irresistible for him to deny himself the pleasure of deflowering her in such a way that she would know her education and money meant nothing, and that the sexual mystique of being born *eta* had value only in the bed of a man who could harness it for his own satiation.

For four days, when she was resting from her ordeal in the

operating room, she was kept locked in a suite. It was Nishida's private domain, and he had made it clear to his guards that none of them were to enter, none of them were to touch her. Only "nurses" came in to talk to her and bring her food, most of which she refused. The nurses sometimes bathed her and dressed her only in a *yukata* robe. Then she knew Nishida would come soon and her nightmare would start again.

On the fourth night, as she was lying in the operating cubicle staring at the subdued pink bulb that bathed the room in pastel coral light, trying to imagine herself with Ted, or away, or dead, the "nurse" spoke to her.

"Mieko-chan?"

"Yes."

"We probably have a few minutes before the next man comes. You want to come out for a while?"

"No."

"Trade places with me if you like."

"No," she replied, repelled by the thought of having to touch so many strangers. Actually touch.

"Mieko-chan, we have worked together these few nights and I have heard about you. I feel sorry for you."

"Thank you, Ohtsu-san," Mieko said, beginning to cry. No one had really said anything to her that one would expect humans to say the whole time she had been there.

"I heard about how your father sold you into this. And at such a young age. Disgusting," the twenty-eight-year-old attendant said, staring through the plastic at the trembling girl in the case. "Me, I believe it was my choice to be here. The pay is not bad and I ... I can't do much else. But you. No pay and I hear you're educated ... Look, the boss plays tough and we should not even be talking but I

175

believe Buddha remembers good deeds, and if you'll promise not to tell anyone, I may be able to help you."

Mieko's eyes opened wide and stared through the cover up to the face looking down at her. She had thought she would never see a sympathetic face again. "Ohtsu-san, I beg you, I beg you. Please. Help me escape from this torture," she entreated, her palms now pressed against the plastic, trying to reach out and touch the woman.

The next morning Ohtsu was admitted to Mieko's room dressed in her nurse's uniform. She silently approached Mieko's sleeping form and gently shook her shoulder. Mieko rolled over, bringing her hands to her face, crying out in her nightmare, "No more, please."

Ohtsu shook her again. "Mieko-chan, wake up."

Mieko's eyes opened slowly and peered through her fingers at the woman's face. "Ohtsu-san? Is it morning?"

"Late morning, yes. We must go."

She helped Mieko wash and don her robe, took a table knife from a tray of breakfast foods Mieko had requested the night before, then knocked on the door for the guards to let them out. They got on the elevator and went down to the third floor and entered the operating room they had occupied. Ohtsu unzipped her uniform and pulled it off her shoulders, suddenly standing naked before Mieko who looked shyly at her body.

"OK. Put this on," Ohtsu said, handing the dress to her. She put it on and zipped it up looking at herself in the wall mirrors. Her young form filled the material too fully and she began to despise what she saw, hating her body for becoming attractive to such terrible people and putting her through vile ordeals.

"Mieko-chan," the older woman said, breaking into her reverie. "Here is 10,000 yen. It is all I can spare but it will get you away from here. Don't go to your father and don't go to the police. And don't tell anyone I helped you. You understand?"

"Yes. I know where to go and there I will tell no one," she choked now beginning to sob again.

"Don't cry. You must look like one of us when you walk out the front door. Get the first taxi you see and go someplace to buy a bra and panties."

"Yes, Ohtsu-san. Thank you."

"Now lock me in the operating chamber."

"Ohtsu-san!" Mieko cried, embracing the woman, remembering the embrace of her mother and wishing she could see her again.

"Call the elevator when it is downstairs. Less chance someone will be on it if you summon it up," Ohtsu said as she pulled away from the girl and lay down on the table. "Lock me in and leave the breakfast knife on the floor. Go."

Mieko peered through the doorway. No one was in the hall and the elevator was downstairs. "Goodbye. Buddha will remember you," she said as she went swiftly to the sliding doors.

She entered the elevator, pressed the button for first floor and took a deep breath as the doors closed and she began her descent. When they opened she walked as steadily as she could, her eyes fixed on the tinted glass doors that led to the outside. To reach the door was everything and she was oblivious to anybody who may have stared at her as she made her exit.

Once outside she blinked her eyes painfully in the first sunlight she had seen in four days. A taxi was waiting and the passenger door opened as she approached the curb. She got in and told the driver to take her toward Tokyo, then settled back in the seat as he pulled into the traffic. After riding for twenty minutes she got off at a stationery shop from where she wrote and posted a letter.

She took to the streets again and searched for a subway entrance, unaware of the stares her attire produced. Ahead she saw the stone archway and white plastic sign that led downward. Each step down brought with it the memory of some time she had ridden the underground train before. She recalled her fright as a young girl when she had become separated from her mother in a crowd getting off a full subway car. She saw in her mind's eye the image of her father and sister dressed in kimono as they took the rail to Asakusa Kannon temple on New Year's Day many years before. As she bought a ticket, the faces of her schoolfriends surrounded her as they frequently did on the way home after class.

When she reached the platform stretching in a long, grey granite curve ahead of her, she saw Ted standing there, his clothes informal and his face serious, but smiling. He was handsome, she thought. And love showed in his eyes. She wished her coffee-colored eyes could express love as his did. She so wanted to show her love to him. Even on their last night together, he had not demanded anything of her though she had wanted to give everything to him. He stood there on the platform, his hand outstretched. She walked slowly toward him, not wishing to attract attention, and extended her hand to him. Their fingers touched and her body was filled with warmth. She looked up into his eyes and smiled as he was smiling gently down at her. She turned her head to see the subway car approaching swiftly, and then she and her beloved stepped out into air, into nothing.

FIVE

Bill Brody woke up with a start. His face was damp with sweat. An automobile in the alley outside his compound had honked its horn and sped away.

His eyes darted about the dark room as his hand groped for the Colt .45 Commander on the night table. Taking it in hand, the cool, familiar precision of its lines calmed him down and brought reality back into focus. He realized that there was no one, no danger, beside him. It had only been the same old nightmare.

Brody shuffled to the bathroom and closed his eyes as he turned on the lights. He opened them slowly and peered in the mirror at his perspiring face. It was drawn and unrested. In brief flashes he could see his wife standing there beside him, brushing her teeth or combing her hair. He blinked his eyes.

Flashes of the nightmare also came back. A chauffeur-driven car was inching its way over a muddy road lashed with rain. The vehicle rocked violently as the wheels fell into unavoidable pot-holes. Brody stood in the rain watching the car, feeling that something terrible was about to happen to the people inside. His stomach churned with tension. As the car passed him, he could see his wife in the back seat waving goodbye. He could not move, and the frustration of the nightmare built up as he tried to cry out, but could not. The automobile continued onward. The front wheel dropped into another pothole and the car was suddenly thrown into the air by a blast of fire. The vehicle vaulted upward, disappearing into the clouds above. At this point he always awakened.

He had been tortured by this dream for too many nights. He found it ironic that his mind should punish him so brutally by letting him see repeatedly what reality had spared him the sight of. Four months earlier in Chiang Mai, his wife had died in a car bomb incident. It was probably intended for him, but the drug lords who had arranged it had sent him messages afterward, saying he should leave or follow her. They capitalized on their botched attempt to eliminate him by flagrantly taunting him. His superiors in the United States had brought him back for one month of debriefing, rest, and relaxation.

While in the United States, he had seen to the burial of his wife's remains, then disappeared for three weeks. He drove west and he drove north. He drove without direction. He drove through wilderness and through ghettos. When he had seen enough to remind him of the beauty of his country and its need for him to do his job, he had returned to Washington, not happy, but sane. He had been sent back to Thailand, but to Bangkok, not Chiang Mai. For that he was grateful. Not because he feared for his person. He would give anything to face the animals who had destroyed his life and engage them in mortal combat. He was not afraid of them or of death. However, he did not feel he could rationally continue his job surrounded by the scene of his love's execution and in the midst of an all-pervasive evil. At arm's length from the tragedy, he could maintain his sanity and function effectively.

Still, the nightmares came.

He wandered back to bed and put the pistol on the nightstand.

He lay back and looked at his watch. The luminous face read 5:35. It was almost time for him to go jogging before the sun rose too high, making the heat more unbearable. He remained still instead.

Brody looked at the empty pillow beside him. No one had ever occupied her place there; not during marriage, not after her death. Despite the numerous opportunities he had to bed any number of women, he had never succumbed to the temptation. His chosen professions had always put a strain on his wife. The hours, the environment, and the danger conspired to disintegrate a marriage. He had vowed to her to be faithful. He was, even now.

Tears welled in his eyes and dripped to the sheets, spotting them. He grit his teeth and tried to contain further anguish, but memories flooded his mind's eye.

In 1966, his younger brother Mike had been drafted into the Army for service in Vietnam. Brody had always been very close to his brother and had helped raise him, their parents having divorced early. Hoping to help his country fight Communist expansion and keep a watchful eye on his sibling at the same time, he had dropped out of college and enlisted in the Army as well. Brody had been sent to junior officers' training school, and by the time he caught up with Mike, the boy had been on two extended excursions.

Vietnam was like nothing they could have imagined. Experiences swung on a pendulum between the nightmare of an alien culture begging and trying to kill simultaneously and the garish dream of unlimited sexual debasement. The two unreal worlds had only been punctuated by sleep, often unsteady, and the occasional letter from home that pulled one back temporarily to a recognizable perspective.

Brody's concern over his brother had been well-founded. He had only been able to arrange a pass to see Mike every month or so, and at each visit he noticed signs of change. The initial visits had been quite special. Mike had made an effort to show his brother off to his platoon buddies and warm moments were shared. However, after five or six months and several engagements with the enemy, Mike showed the strain. He had become distracted and sometimes hostile. When Bill looked into his activities, he had become very cold and refused to see him again. Two months later Brody had determined that his brother was a heavy drug user. Brody knew many of the soldiers under his command used drugs to varying degrees. He had been advised to ignore the off-duty use of "pot and other mild hallucinogens." But it was evident his brother had graduated to much heavier use. He had spoken to Mike's commander, who had shrugged it off. His request to have his brother shifted to his command had been rejected immediately. He had tried to have him transferred to another unit.

For several months his petition had gathered dust. He had then learned that Mike had died. During an R & R trip to Saigon he had overdosed on heroin. Brody had found the doctor who had made a cursory examination of the body before tagging and bagging it. The doctor said that Mike had probably been mainlining heroin for two months.

That had been Brody's first loss to heroin. After unenthusiastically completing his tour of duty, he returned to the United States where he finished his college degree. He joined a police department and soon had maneuvered himself onto the drug squad. Seeing his attempts to foil trafficking in his area were to no avail, he applied to join the Drug Enforcement Agency in 1982. They sent him and his wife to Chiang Mai several years later.

Now he wondered why he should stay on. Drugs flowed out of Thailand as they had before. Warlords financed their feuds with the white powder. Nothing had changed despite his vigilance and best efforts except that the two people most dear to him were gone. Did the people in the United States really care?

Nevertheless, he tried to justify staying on as he lay in bed clutching a pillow damp with his tears. Anything that could cause me so much tragedy and loss must be evil, he reasoned, and being evil, it must be worthwhile trying to destroy. Such thoughts helped keep his despair at bay. He had to believe there was a purpose for the suffering he had endured for his country. Once more he prayed for the strength to defeat his godless foes.

Ted was grateful that Shakey Robinson had not wanted to stay out too late the night before. He woke up refreshed after an eight-hour slumber and took a luxuriously long shower. He felt so much better than the morning before. Everything felt right. The cool tiles in the bathroom tickled his feet and the dense oversized towels hugged his body dry. He took his nicest pink, French-cut shirt and tie from the closet and donned a pair of underwear. Standing before the mirror, he felt none of the remorse of the day before. His body looked OK, at least not flabby, and his hair was at the length he liked it, between cuts. He slipped into a pair of slacks and carefully tucked his shirt tails in to accentuate his slim, muscular lines. He looked again at his reflection, smiled, finished dressing and went to breakfast. He felt great.

When he returned, he phoned Lin to see if he could pick up his antique. The man's shop was his home. He was there and agreed to open the steel shutters when Ted arrived.

Ted dialed again and waited for an answer.

"Ital-Siam Exploration," the receptionist chimed.

183

"Yes. This is Mr. Bergman from Petrotools International. May I speak with Mr. Paolo Nero, please?"

"One moment, please."

After being passed through Nero's secretary, he made contact with the general manager.

"Nero speaking."

"Hello. Mr. Nero? This is Ted Bergman from Petrotools International. Terry Jones in Singapore told me I might be able to help you select some exploration accessories for your helicopter."

"Jones, you say? Yes. What can I do for you?"

"Would it be possible for me to visit you this morning? I realize it's short notice."

"Let's see. I have an opening around 10:30."

"That would be very good. I'll be in to see you at 10:30, then. Thank you very much."

"Not at all. See you soon." Nero hung up the phone and sat thoughtfully for a moment. Bergman sounded innocent. His repose was interrupted by Nishida.

"Bergman, yes?" he asked.

"Yes. He will be here at 10:30."

"You still want to sit and wait for him to arrest us?"

"We will follow my plan. Listen and see what kind of person he is. I am still waiting for more information from Singapore. Until then, you and ..." he was prepared to berate Nishida's assistant, "your helper will do as I say."

The two Japanese were silent. Nero did not like that. "Do I make myself clear?" he pressed them.

"Yes, Count."

Ted was happy his call to Ital-Siam had gone so smoothly. He got out his attaché case and began to select brochures for products in which he felt they would be interested. He checked his watch and prepared to leave. It was 9:10.

Walking quickly to the antique store, Ted noted that the street scene was completely opposite from the previous night when he had followed the same sidewalk. No touts approached him and no neon signs flashed messages to tourists that live shows, massages, and sex were available on tap. It was just a busy city sidewalk with bright sun glaring off its uneven concrete.

Arriving at Mr. Lin's, he banged his palm on the steel shutter. Shortly, Lin's wife came, peeked through the mail slot, unlocked the shutter, and pulled it up with a loud clank that reminded Ted of the sound of a rising drawbridge in the movies. She smiled and led him in.

Lin came down the stairs wearing a T-shirt and boxer shorts, slippers on his feet. "*Ohiyogodzaimasu, Takabashi-san,*" he greeted in Japanese.

Ted returned his welcome. "I have brought the cash for the *tanto.*"

"Yes, yes. Would you like tea?" the proprietor replied, not wishing to rush the transaction.

"No, thank you. I have had my breakfast and I must leave soon for a morning appointment."

"Always racing about."

"Perhaps someday when I am a rich, happy man like you I can slow down and enjoy life."

"Rich? Where?" the older man chuckled as he turned the dials on his safe. He brought out the silk-covered box and handed it to Ted.

Ted opened the box and withdrew the knife once more. He felt a rush of excitement as he slowly pulled the blade from the wooden scabbard. The flawless sheen of the body flowed into the distinct undulations of the forge marks that had been so carefully fired into the steel edge centuries before. Instinct told him he should make the purchase without reservation. The blade spoke to him of its authenticity.

He opened his briefcase and got out half the American dollars he had obtained the day before. He counted them carefully and handed it to Lin, who also counted them.

"I have prepared a receipt for you for Customs," Lin said, turning over to Ted the invoice with his shop's seal. "Are you sure you would not like some tea?"

Ted looked at his watch. "No, thank you. I am afraid that with the traffic I might be late for my appointment. Can't keep the customer waiting."

"Sometimes they'll buy more if you do."

"Perhaps in the antique business. Take care, Hayashi-san. I'll see you in two months or so."

"Goodbye. Take care of that *tanto*. I am beginning to regret selling it."

Ted shook his hand warmly and stepped out to the sidewalk and hailed a taxicab. After the customary bargaining, he climbed into the back seat and settled in for the long, hot ride.

He mentally reviewed what he knew about the prospective customer with whom he was scheduled to meet. The meager bit of information he had gleaned so far disappointed him. He preferred to go on initial calls well-armed with background data. The more specific he could be from the start on his equipment recommendations, the more professional he would appear, and the more time he would save. Nevertheless, there was a break-even point on the amount of time he could spend researching, and he had reached it with Ital-Siam. If he spent any more time collecting data, as opposed to facing the client and trying to sell, Petrotools' return would be decreased.

He had not any business dealings with Italians in the past. He wondered what their primary buying motivation was. Impress the boss? Save money? Reduce the risk of downtime? Increase exploration efficiency? Bells and whistles? Usually he could determine within the first five minutes what a person's purchasing motive was and could play on it. Those whose key eluded him were frequently seeking kickbacks or entertainment and his selling job stopped there. The distributor handled it. He merely convinced the customer that he would not go wrong selecting a Petrotools product.

The taxi had made slow progress up Silom Road to Lumpini Park and the traffic lightened when the driver passed through the intersection to Rajdamri. The eagerness and optimism Ted had felt earlier was still with him and he began to fidget impatiently with his Rolex. To him, the watch symbolized several virtues he believed in. Besides punctuality, it represented elegant ruggedness and functional simplicity. Both were rather traditional Japanese virtues. Perhaps Swiss as well, he thought; nevertheless, they appealed to him. He had bought the timepiece three years before when he had received his first substantial bonus. He had never lost his fondness for it. He wondered, though, in a moment of self-doubt, whether he still stood by those strengths himself. He banished the thought. The cab had pulled to the curb and he had to be as confident as possible. Cold calls were the hardest.

"Mr. Nero," his secretary called over the phone, "Mr. Bergman is here for his 10:30 appointment."

"Send him in."

Nero stood up as the American businessman came through the doorway. Despite having seen the photographs the day before, he was struck by Bergman's youth. He extended his hand across the desk. "Mr. Bergman, yes?" he greeted as Ted grasped his hand and squeezed it firmly, tugging it lightly three times and releasing it.

"Yes, sir, Mr. Nero. Thank you for meeting with me on such short notice," he said, handing the prospective customer his name card.

"It's all right. What can I do for you?"

"Well, my company promotes a wide range of tools and instruments used in the search for natural resources. Frankly, I'd like to know more about your business so I'll have an idea of what to recommend. What are you searching for and where, that sort of thing."

Nero was alarmed at the pointedness of the first question. He sipped on a glass of water as he thought and said finally, "We have a concession up north to search for land-based oil and LNG reserves."

"You know, I tried to get information from the Thai government about where you're exploring, but they hadn't heard of you," Ted laughed.

"Par for the Thai bureaucracy, wouldn't you say?" Nero's smile was strained. "Yes, we started several months ago."

"May I ask what techniques you are employing?"

"Mr. Bergman, as you may be aware, exploration techniques are often proprietary and your company does not exactly have the reputation of a Schlumberger."

"I understand your concern, sir … "

"Call me Paolo. May I call you Theodore?"

"Ted, Paolo — however, I understand the helicopter you leased was unequipped for survey work and wanted to know just a little bit more about your operation so I can fine tune my suggestions. Save us both time."

In the adjacent room, Ted could hear two men carrying on a conversation and was distracted by it. If they had been speaking Thai he would have ignored it as just more white noise, but subconsciously bits of the sentences lodged in his brain. They were not speaking English, but he could not hear them clearly. He turned his attention back to Nero who was halfway finished with his answer.

"… that system coupled with the radio seismology and infrared units rounds out our package. It's adequate for our purposes." Nero was still uncertain of what to think about Bergman. He had noticed the young American's eyes dart about the room taking in everything. He had seen his distraction a moment before as his attention turned to the quiet talk in the other room between Nishida and Suzuki.

This worried him. Bergman was neat and dressed in the kind of clothes that pointed out his nationality. He could not be mistaken for a Frenchman or Italian. Clean but unfashionable. He wondered what it was about North Americans that made their salesmen so flairless. Purchasers sometimes had more verve; rarely the peddlers, he noted. The bulky Swiss watch was typical, too; possibly a pirated model, he judged.

He looked Bergman in the eyes. "What can you do for us?"

Ted placed a catalog on the desk facing Nero and, as he opened it in one move to the correct page, he returned a deeper stare into the Italian's eyes, saying, "You need this to be a success

189

here in the jungle."

Nero blinked away from the intense gaze returned to him. Bergman's eyes had widened and, like a Gypsy's, seemed to have a captivating magnetism. He would normally have been put off by a statement like Bergman's, but he found his eyes on the page in front of him.

"You are no doubt familiar with this technology, but not with the special microprocessors we have built in to speed up your data delivery rate. The bottom line: reduced survey time."

Ted launched into a discussion of the product features he thought would appeal to Nero most as the general manager of operations.

Nero found himself absent-mindedly considering the purchase of the equipment when he remembered that this interview had another purpose. "I am afraid, Ted, you are too late. I wish I had seen this before we bought the system we have. It looks good."

"What kind did you get?"

"Umm ..." Nero had not bought any remote topographical analysis systems and found himself with the tables turned. He had wanted to test Bergman's knowledge. "I believe it was a Fairchild TA-60. Does that ring a bell?"

"No, I'm afraid it doesn't." Ted had never heard of the system. "Is it British?"

"American, I think," Nero said, hoping to unbalance Ted.

"I'll have to look it up," he said, writing down the name on his notepad. "The reason I'm curious is because we also sell accessories to upgrade most any brand of RTA gear. In Thailand's dense jungles up north you might want to look at our portable drilling rigs, truck-mounted or helicopter-lifted to the site," Ted continued as he placed another catalog on the Italian's desktop. He started to introduce it when Nero interrupted him.

"I signed a P.O. for this kind of gear last month. It might have even been this manufacturer's."

Although Petrotools had exclusive sales privileges for the product in Southeast Asia, it was possible the distributor in Hong Kong or Houston had set someone up in Bangkok. "From whom did you buy it?"

"We'll check with my secretary later, all right?"

"Thank you."

Nero leaned back in his chair and called casually through to the conference room, "Nishida, you might want to meet this fellow."

Nishida and Suzuki came through the door and avoided looking at Nero, staring immediately at Ted.

Ted knew as soon as he heard the man's name that the conversation he had caught bits of was in Japanese. These two men had to be representatives of the Japanese investors, he reasoned. The man introduced to him as Nishida reminded him momentarily of the Butcher, or what the Butcher must have been like as a young man. But his perception quickly reversed and he realized that the man facing him was exactly unlike his mentor. This man had a strong grip which he tested on Ted's hand. Ted gave him the same stare he had shocked Nero with and equaled the pressure. Their shake was not a greeting but a contest. While staring in the man's eyes he had seen the ruthlessness of the Butcher, but not the intelligence. He had met this type of businessman before. They were always hard to sell to, he remembered. As they released their grips, Ted noticed that the Japanese was missing part of one finger. Industrial safety did not used to be emphasized so much in Japan before, he recalled.

191

The second man introduced to him had less personal power than Nishida. He was obviously the underling, with small, ferret-like movements, nervous and excitable. Also a hard sell, Ted knew, unless he could be made to see how a product would benefit his personal future. He decided to conceal his knowledge of Japanese to see if he could key in on any buying motivations.

"Why don't we all have coffee," Nero said as the two Japanese pulled up chairs and sat down to Ted's right.

The secretary brought in a tray with four cups of coffee and bowls of powdered creamer and sugar. Nero told the newcomers about the products Ted had introduced.

"Your card says you are stationed in Singapore, is it?" Nishida asked him.

"Yes. I've been there for almost six years now."

"You like it there?"

"Yes. It's clean, well-organized, but rather boring."

"You prefer the nightlife in Bangkok, eh?" Nishida continued querying.

"Hmm," Ted replied with a short noncommittal smile. "Tell me. Do all of you go to your work site up north?"

"Yes," Nero said, looking to Nishida.

"It's dangerous, isn't it?"

"We haven't had any incidents," the Italian replied with a shrug.

"I mean, what with the drug people and all up there."

"We did not say northwest Thailand, Mr. Bergman," Nishida snapped coolly.

"What he means is our concession is not in any particularly dangerous areas. I don't think the government allows survey work where there is a lot of trouble. Well, I do remember one time we

192

had a close call. In camp one night several rough-looking fellows with *dhas*, those Thai swords, slung over their backs ..."

Ted started to listen to a quiet dialogue between the two Japanese next to him and lost track of Nero's story. This was part of the thrill of having mastered a foreign tongue, he mused: eavesdropping.

"Does the American look like a salesman to you?" Nishida asked.

"Looks can be fabricated. Of course, he looks and acts like a salesman. But I don't think he is a salesman."

These Japanese are always ready to steal industrial secrets from others, Ted considered, and they probably suspect I'm here from another oil company to get information from them. What a bunch of bozos.

"His questions before and after we came in were pretty pointed. Indirect enough so the Count wouldn't detect anything, but their direction was clear enough to me," Nishida said.

"I agree," replied the ferret. "Don't forget the embassy yesterday."

"If he is from the drug investigation bureau, then he must be eliminated. I don't think we can take the chance that he is not an undercover agent."

"Shall we proceed to have him killed?"

"Yes," Nishida decided. "No tie to us, neh?"

"What about Nero?"

"If the police think Bergman died in a traffic accident or street robbery, why should Nero suspect? If he ever finds out, I will handle it."

Ted listened with increasing horror as the words he should not have understood became clear to him. He rushed to seek alternate meanings for what he knew could not be the intent of what they had said. But he knew their vocabulary and their conversation had only one meaning. He wanted to cry out that it was all a mistake, but caught himself; then they would know he knew what they had decided. He tried desperately to maintain his gaze at Nero who continued with animated gesticulations relating the story of some danger he had encountered. His only hope, he realized as momentary calm hit him, was to exploit his knowledge as much as possible. First, he had to get out of the office, out of Thailand.

He looked at his watch. "My! I'm sorry Mr. Nero. I have a luncheon appointment I just remembered." Even as he spoke he knew the words sounded stiff and theatrical. He could not control it.

"Eh," Nero blurted, caught in mid-sentence. "Oh, yes. Well, if you have no further products to discuss then perhaps you can send us brochures of new items when they become available."

"I'll do that," Ted assured as he stood up, testing his knees. "Mr. Nishida and Mr. Suzuki. Umm. Have a nice stay in Bangkok."

The two men bowed slightly and remained silent.

As Ted turned to leave the office Nero spoke up, "Didn't you want the name of the company we bought the portable drilling gear from?"

"Huh? Oh, yes. Thank you."

He followed Nero to his secretary's filing room and the Italian told her what to retrieve.

Ted waited, his foot twitching and his hands restless. He wondered if they would try to kill him right there. His mouth turned downward tautly as he imagined his blood sprayed across the walls he faced, a bullet in his chest, his heart ejected behind with his blood. The seconds it took her to find the paper passed at an excruciatingly slow pace. He licked and bit his upper lip and looked first to Nero. Did he know these Japanese were criminals?

Yakuza! He suddenly remembered the name for them. Images from Tokyo television of gangster rituals and activities flashed through his mind's eye. He saw them cutting off one joint of the little finger in payment of mistakes made. He saw Nishida's hand pulling away from his and its partial digit. He wanted to gasp, but maintained his composure.

"Mr. Bergman," he heard the secretary say. She was standing right in front of him with a sheet of paper to hand to him.

He shifted his focus to her. She was a pretty woman in her mid-twenties, unmarried, he felt, and she smiled up at him pursing her lips slightly as he took the paper from her. He looked down at her blouse, at the soft curve of her breasts, and down to where the tight skirt she wore defined her pubic mound. She might be the last person he would ever see, he realized desperately. He banished his morbidly sexual thoughts and thanked her as best he could for writing down the company's name.

"I'm sorry we could not do any business, Ted," Nero said holding the door for him to leave. "Perhaps another time. Stay in touch, OK? *Ciao.*"

"Goodbye," Ted said stiffly as he walked to the elevator. He cringed, imagining the barrel of a pistol leveled at his spine — or head. The elevator doors opened and he quickly slipped in, first pushing the button to close the door and then the button for the ground floor. Perhaps they would be waiting at the ground floor like a movie he had seen. The doors would open and he would die in the elevator. Die. He had dealt with the concept and mechanics of death so clinically with the Butcher. This was very different from what he had imagined a self-defense encounter would be like.

As the lift descended past the fourth floor, he quickly pushed the button for the first level. Stupid to be totally predictable. He had to think. He knew he was supposed to die. They did not know he knew. They knew nothing about him, he reasoned. If they wanted to shoot him he hadn't a chance. He had to stay around people. Crowds. That would reduce the likelihood of firearms. He was better equipped to deal with silent weapons: knives, garrotes, clubs.

He stepped off the elevator at the first level and found the staircase. He walked down quickly, expecting that if his opponent was waiting at the elevator door, he might get alarmed should the lift open empty. The stairwell door opened into the lobby facing the bank of elevators. He could see no one suspicious. There were two secretaries chatting as they waited and a guard by the door.

Ted walked briskly to the front door, looked to each side and stepped out onto the sidewalk and the bright noonday street scene. He weighed the risks of getting in a taxicab versus walking. If he was in a cab he could not get out quickly should an assassin pull up beside the car. He might be on a motorcycle for a fast getaway. If he walked he had freedom of movement, the protection and danger of the crowd, and the possibility he might spot the opponent. However, it was lunchtime, and there were so many people pouring out onto the streets that he would have difficulty singling out anybody or getting a cab.

He decided to stay on the street. He turned right and looked back at the front door of the office building. He noticed no one in particular but tried to note the special features of the potential opponents he could see. He decided to look about two blocks later to see who was still there.

A middle-aged man in a Thai-style shirt and baggy pants

shuffled toward him. Two young businessmen chatted as they waited on the sidewalk. There was a young Thai man about twenty three years old carrying a mailing envelope, probably a messenger. Behind him was a schoolboy with a book bag. A handsome Asian tourist walking arm in arm with a Thai hostess dressed in brief attire also caught Ted's attention. He continued walking up the street.

Unnoticed by the American, a tall, dark, well-dressed Thai man had stepped out from behind a food stall. He had watched Bergman come out of the building, look for a taxi, and decide to walk. Suvannathep would continue to observe to make sure the job was done correctly. His boss, Nishida, was a severe taskmaster regardless of whether he was interpreting or taking care of wetwork. Of course, Nishida was no more a taskmaster than the Green Berets who had trained him in jungle warfare. Observation, stalking, assassination, small-group tactics, survival: he had mastered their lessons well. So had the two he had hired to dispose of Bergman. They did not know who they were working for, nor who Bergman was. They only knew they had a year's pay each for a day's work and that it had to be done quietly, with no guns, like a common street robbery. If possible they were to deposit the body of the "salesman" in a *klong* or otherwise delay the discovery of his drained corpse.

He watched the two men follow Bergman up the street. Bergman walked stiffly, he noticed, and did not look left or right. Suvannathep almost felt his presence was not required, so easy would be the hit. Two armed men ambushing a sheep of an American. It was short work. Nevertheless, he wanted to practice stalking himself and should they do a messy job he would pay them less. If they were as good as he had been told, he would keep them in mind for future work.

Ted had walked three blocks when he decided to step suddenly into a photo-processing store. He counted to five and stepped out onto the sidewalk again and walked in the direction from which he had come scanning all the faces and clothes as quickly as he could. He tried to look confused as if he did not know where he was going. He did not want his unknown future assailant to suspect what he knew. He saw four of the same six he had noted before: the old Thai, the messenger, the tourist and his girl, and the schoolboy. He glanced again at the schoolboy. He had a young, boyish face, but a mature body. That was the man who was to take his life, he sensed.

Ted continued walking back over the steps he had taken and considered the unamusing joke his life had come to. I'll die at the hands of a Thai schoolboy for not being what I am, and I can't tell them I am not what they believe because then they'll know I know too much anyway. He realized his mind had given up on survival. His intellect was laughing at his body's demise. That was something the Butcher had commented on. The mind getting in the way of survival, when that is the most just and basic consideration; all the mind games, religion, externally imposed morality — everything that impeded valid action.

He decided he had no time to consider the philosophical aspects of his dilemma as he saw the schoolboy step into a stationery shop. Ted passed the shop and walked up the steps of a pedestrian bridge that crossed the busy avenue. When he had reached the other side and turned to go down the steps, he had a clear view of everyone crossing after him. The schoolboy had emerged from the shop and was approaching the bridge. Ted felt relieved to know he was right. Then he saw that the messenger boy was already crossing the bridge and that the old Thai man had stopped to hail a taxi, it seemed. His moment of elation crumbled into desperate confusion.

He trotted down the steps and made his way up the sidewalk faster than the crowd, now a businessman late for his appointment, checking his watch constantly. He pushed his way around others and dodged oncomers who were not looking where they were going. He kept up a quick pace for two long blocks. He turned around suddenly, ostensibly to look at a passing truck, but his eyes fixed on the path behind. He saw no one he recognized.

Ted wondered if he had let his imagination have too much free rein, if the people he had thought were shadowing him were innocent. He thought hard again about the Japanese conversation he had overheard. Could he have heard unclearly? Or mistranslated a single word that then set up a series of mistranslations; a bilingual Freudian slip of the ear, not the tongue? No. He thought in Japanese when he heard that language. He shifted into that mode. No translation occurred in his mind, he understood without thought, no room for error.

He looked down the sidewalk again. He did not see them. He did spot a public telephone nearby and that image registered quickly: he should call someone. Who? Who was the sour fellow he had met yesterday? Brody. He opened his attaché case and his eyes came to rest on the carefully wrapped box containing the razor-sharp *tanto* he had bought that morning. He had no time to unwrap it then nor anywhere to conceal it as he walked. He dug nervously into his name-card box for the card he had been given the day before.

Walking to the phone, he searched his pockets, found the correct coin, deposited it, and dialed. He stood with his bag on the ground between his legs and scanned the sidewalk up and down. Still no one in sight.

The phone on the other end rang. He waited for it to ring

again, two, three times.

"Hello, Embassy of the United States of America."

"Please connect me with Mr. Brody."

"Which Mr. Brody, sir? The one in … "

"DEA."

"Thank you." The line went blank as Ted fixed his stare on the faces emerging up the walkway.

"Mr. Brody's office. May I help you?" a woman's voice answered.

"May I speak with Mr. Brody? This is an emergency."

"I think he has gone to lunch. Let me check." Again the phone went blank as he was put on hold.

"I got him just as he was going out. He'll be with you in a moment. Who shall I say is calling?"

"Ted Bergman." Ted's stomach knotted as he remembered he had only three minutes to use the phone on one coin and no more change left. He waited anxiously.

"Brody here."

"Mr. Brody, this is Ted Bergman. We met yesterday."

"What's the emergency, son?"

"Someone's trying to kill me."

"Who?"

"They think I work for you or something. I was looking into their company for sales and they think I know something."

"About what?"

"Their drug operations! Oh shit. They're coming up the street. I'll call you later — or from Singapore." Ted hung up the receiver, picked up his bag and continued his fast walk.

Suvannathep watched on from a safe distance as the two men he had contracted continued to follow the American. They were not doing a good job. Of course, the American had not been easy to track unobtrusively. He obviously was late for an appointment but not sure where he was going in the strange city. The phone call had probably been to get directions. Suvannathep had wanted to double over with laughter when Bergman turned several blocks before and headed straight for the younger of the two killers. The man had very clumsily ducked into a school supplies store and waited for the salesman to pass. He should never have let himself be seen, even if the mark did not suspect he was to die as in Bergman's case. It was poor form, he judged.

Ted was wondering what his next move should be. He knew now that two young Thais were the ones who wanted to kill him. The older man he had last seen hailing a taxi was no longer in sight. The assassin dressed like a schoolboy had heavily muscular thighs, perhaps from soccer, Thai boxing, or long marches. Ted could not see that he was armed when he took quick glimpses back, but that did not rule out a knife or gun in the book bag which the schoolboy carried in his left hand.

The second man seemed to be several years older and Ted had reckoned him to be dressed as a messenger. The parcel he clutched underneath his left arm like a football probably had his weapon concealed in it. A quick look at the man's face was all Ted could stand. It had the methodical, purposeful expression of one who does not make mistakes. It also lacked any humanity: the job and its successful completion were all that mattered.

Knowing now the position, appearance, and projected skill of his opponents, Ted's thoughts leaped ahead, searching for an appropriate solution. He thought of the Butcher and tried to imagine what he would do. The enemy expected nothing of him, no resistance or guile. He could capitalize on that. He ruled out escape. That would leave him constantly worrying about his rear guard. A poorly executed escape might also tip them off that he knew of their intentions. He had to try to defeat his opponents decisively. He had once possessed the capacity. He was not sure he had it now. For one thing he was unarmed. He could not dare to stop and remove the *tanto* from its silk-lined box. They might be upon him before he could draw.

Ideally, he should give them an opportunity to move in on him in such a way that he could control them. He began to think of ways he might divide them.

Ahead the street took a sudden turn upward as it formed a bridge to cross a canal. The sidewalk split, one side going up the bridge, the other side continuing to the embankment above the *klong* beneath the bridge. Several alleys, narrow and shaded from the bright sunlight, emptied into the lower sidewalk.

Approaching the division ahead, Ted frantically tried to decide if this was the right place to make his move. His pulse had quickened and his legs began to feel weak. It was a decision he wished he did not have to make. He could continue along the street and wait for their move, or perhaps a better opportunity. If he went down the alley he could force their hand. He might not be the one to emerge though, he considered soberly.

Grimly, he was reminded of the poem about the path not taken. There was no snow here — indeed it was sweltering — and he was young, not old. He was not being drawn toward destiny like the man in the sleigh but rather was walking under his own power and soon knew he must make a decision wholly of his own discrimination. The result of his choice could determine the rest of his life, or the length of it.

These considerations occupied a split second. He was one

stride away from the divider between the bridge and the sidewalk to the water's edge. As his left foot moved forward he changed the direction of its momentum and stepped down. The first step was made. He stopped and looked slowly around in all directions, then continued in.

Three onlookers took particular interest in the sudden, awkward change of direction the American made. The two stalkers were relieved. They had only to close on the mark, stick him, and perhaps deposit him in the *klong* to float slowly away with the city's cess and garbage, another hapless foreigner who had foolishly flashed too much money.

Suvannathep was both amused and disappointed. The show was about to begin. This gave him a thrill he rarely had a chance to experience anymore; the thrill of watching or doing a job that is forbidden and getting away with it. Nishida's interpreter was bemused, too, by his assumption that the American was so afraid someone would see him enter the cheap massage and brothel area that he had walked until he reached the bridge, turned, stepped down, and surveyed the path behind before going on toward one of the alleys. These Westerners always had sex on the brain, he mused; fucking during lunch break! He was disappointed with the two hirelings, though. They were practically walking together now and had made no attempt to hide themselves when the American looked back.

He watched from a safe distance, standing behind a noodle vendor's stand as the American disappeared into the mouth of the second alley. The two assassins had started to walk briskly toward the alley and the chauffeur saw their right hands disappear, one into his manila envelope, one into his schoolbag. The two reached the alley. They stopped and suddenly seemed agitated. The one dressed as a messenger waved his hands in the face of the other commanding him to search the next alley. Something had gone wrong and Suvannathep decided it was time to close the gap.

Ted had seen the two who intended to kill him about half a block behind. Moving together, they stood out clearly among the other pedestrians. He walked past the first alley. There were too many people in it.

The second alley was quite narrow, being more a drainage and ventilation space between the backs of two buildings erected alongside each other. There was no place to hide, nor were there any people he could see. He ducked into the alley and immediately broke into as fast a sprint as his business-clothed, leather-shod, case-toting body would allow. About 100 feet into the alley it intersected with a small lane which led to the first crowded passage he had passed. He turned right and continued his sprint back to the first alley. This was wider and the entrances to two low-class massage establishments lay between him and the main road. There were some food carts and a fruit vendor also crowding the walkway.

He stood behind the fruit vendor and inspected a durian while keeping an eye on the entrance to the alley. The two killers walked past quickly, their eyes fixed on the alley into which they had seen him enter. He walked cautiously up the passage and carefully peered right around the corner of the building. He saw the schoolboy walking, his back toward Ted, in the direction of the *klong*. The messenger was not with him. He stepped out into the open and, walking over his original steps, went toward the second alley again.

As he ran, stopped, and began to feel in control of his opponents, his legs had regained their steadiness and his heart had begun to beat with only the demand for blood pushing it, not his fearful reveries. Had he had time to consider it, he would have decided he felt neither confident nor incompetent, neither courageous nor quivering with fear. He did not feel at that moment; his actions were guided by experience and trained instinct.

Reaching the first alley he stepped full view into it and stared down its shaded length. The messenger was walking up the passage toward him, returning from his search down to its end. Startled, the messenger had stopped for an instant and reversed the grip of the knife in his hand, holding the blade along his forearm.

Ted looked at the right hand of his attacker as a stray ray of light caught the polished edge of what was carried concealed there. It was a standard U.S. Army survival-type knife which had been polished and buffed to remove its camouflage blueing. Ted wondered why a killer would be so thoughtless as to buff his blade making it easier to see, but breathed a sigh of relief that the chosen weapon was edge rather than bullet.

As they approached each other, Ted evaluated the position of the opponent's knife, the narrow width of the alley, and the limited number of attacks that could be made unless conditions changed. He decided it would be safer to walk down the right side of the passageway and keep his attaché case in his left hand.

The messenger cursed his bad luck at having to approach his mark face to face and with a reverse grip on his knife. To make matters worse, the foreigner had stepped to the right side of the alley, making it difficult for him to try to furtively puncture his kidney as he passed by. He would have to make an obvious cut or wait until the American had passed him, then try to quickly turn about and catch him in the neck from behind. Difficult to do quickly, he estimated.

He watched the American walk steadily toward him looking occasionally at his face and totally unaware that he was about to die. The messenger marveled at man's amazing lack of perception, that people did not even know someone was about to do away with them. When they were five feet from each other, the mark looked at the Thai again and smiled gently as he stepped closer to the wall so his attaché case would clear the Thai's leg when they passed. Deciding his chance had come, the assassin pounced.

When the Thai's right shoulder snapped forward and around toward Ted, he knew the attack had come. He felt unhurried and saw the knife emerge and turn away from the assassin's right forearm as his weapon gained momentum for the downward slash against Ted's neck. Ted dropped his attaché case. The sudden lightness of his left hand propelled it upwards to intercept the Thai's muscular upper arm, interdicting his cut. Ted grabbed the man's biceps and sank his thumbnail deep into the muscle to find a nerve he knew throbbed beneath. The knife dropped from the messenger's hand and Ted pivoted to the left, launching a powerful elbow blow plowing a furrow of pain from the man's solar plexus to his chin. The Thai doubled over, expelling a breath.

Ted locked his right arm around the exposed neck of the killer and snapped his waist to the left, driving the man's head into the brick wall . Instantly, he reversed the direction of his pivot, shifting right, leveraging the man's head backward until he heard a distinct cracking sound and the body of the Thai went completely limp.

Ted looked both ways down the passage to be sure no one had seen the confrontation, propped the body in a sitting position against the wall, picked up his attaché case and walked with quick, stealthy steps further into the alley. He dared not pick up the knife for fear of leaving his fingerprints on it; at any rate, the Thai was dead or paralyzed and would attack him no more.

He had a choice on returning to the intersections that led to the larger alley with the massage parlors. He could go left toward the *klong*, right, as he had before, or straight. Turning left would probably lead him straight to the schoolboy.

He turned left and walked toward the opening that led to the sidewalk on the bank of the canal. As he approached the intersection he slowed until he reached the edge of the building that formed the corridor passage in which he was standing. He slowly looked to the right down the sidewalk. Forty feet away there were only two old women carrying their burden of vegetables and fruits down the walkway away from Ted. He cautiously moved his head around the wall to peer to the left. The schoolboy was only fifteen feet away and saw him, immediately breaking into a sprint towards Ted.

Ted put his case down just inside the corridor where he was standing and retreated two steps.

The Thai came charging around the corner into the alley. Too late, he saw the attaché case and tried to kick it out of the way. Instead he unbalanced himself and continued his lunge forward, his knife, now drawn and held at heart level, extended out before him.

Again, Ted felt the movements of the attacker were immensely slow. He even deliberated on the recklessness of the killer's technique as the Thai plunged forward toward him. He sensed his own legs stepping to the left and knew his right arm was rising to seize the wrist of the hand that held the knife. He did not worry when the point of the blade rushed by his breast because his feet and body had shifted properly, as if his mind were a spectator only.

He was now standing to the outside of his opponent, had grabbed his right arm by the wrist, and locked it with his right hand, his chest pushing against the frantic man's elbow. The Thai predictably jerked his extended arm back to retract it and try to break the American's grip. Ted obliged his momentum, but turned inward the wrist that gripped the knife. The Thai had no time to realize his mistake. His heart was already punctured and a crimson spray intermittently coated the already red bricks.

When the knife entered the chest of his opponent, Ted was behind him. As he released his grip and let the body drop, he noticed that he had only two or three small drops of blood on his hand and one on his shirt. He knew the Thai still clutched the handle of his own knife. Now the wisdom of the Butcher's teachings which had emerged so spontaneously the moment before became clear. It was a clean kill. He could walk away without detection.

The interpreter could not believe his eyes. He had walked quickly to the second alley he had seen Bergman furtively enter after the messenger. He expected to see the two hirelings picking Bergman's wallet and wristwatch from his blood-drenched body. Instead he saw what looked like the messenger taking a nap. But the man was dead, his neck cleanly broken. Suvannathep hastily retreated and looped around to retrace the steps he had seen the schoolboy take toward the *klong*.

Walking along the canal he reached the first side alley and cautiously peered in. If he had been incredulous at the sight of the first body, he was both awed and frightened by the sight of the second. A man dressed in schoolboy's clothes lay slumped in a rapidly enlarging pool of his own blood. There was a painful look of dismayed surprise frozen on the corpse's face. Suvannathep looked down the end of the alley and saw someone step quickly out into another corridor and disappear. Though he saw only a silhouette, he knew it must be Bergman heading back to the main road.

Ted turned into the alleyway from where he had originally

espied the two stalkers. He passed the fruit vendor with his fragrant durians and the two massage parlors. The overwhelming need to be away from all the strangeness in which he had immersed himself for so long engulfed him. The differences here, the sight ahead of him of a crowded, fume-choked street leading over a pungent lifeless canal and the dark, tanned, shirtless fruit seller who spat on the stones beneath his feet, the sexual amusements and the spicy food, all had grown tiresome. Not the least were the two corpses that lay behind him. He longed desperately for some familiar sign of his youth, a blue-suited police officer, Walter Cronkite, a McDonald's store. Even something Japanese would be an emotional anchor at this time when he most needed a firm grip. He had to get out. Perhaps he should go straight to the airport and catch the next plane to anywhere, he thought as he reached the curb by the street and waved his hand emphatically at an empty cab about to pass. The taxi stopped and Ted climbed in, commanding the driver to hurry to the airport without asking about the price.

A realization made his heart sink. His passport was securely locked in the hotel safe-deposit box where he had returned it the day before after going to the bank. Checking in at the ticket counter, much less getting through Immigration, without it would be impossible. He told the driver to take him to the hotel first, then sat back and plotted the course of the next two hours.

Suvannathep had emerged from the alleyway just as Ted closed the door of his taxi and it pulled into the sluggish traffic. He signaled the next empty cab and told the driver to follow the other vehicle, which was now many cars ahead in the queue that stretched over the bridge, waiting for a red light. The driver objected, saying that he wanted a destination and a price. Suvannathep tossed a hundred baht note in the front seat and told him he would get the same every ten minutes. The driver asked no further questions and pulled into the traffic, hoping he could keep up with the driver ahead through the next green light.

Nishida's interpreter quickly surmised that the American was returning to his hotel. He could not understand why a person who had handled himself so expertly a moment ago would be stupid enough to go back to his known place of residence. He was thankful for the opportunity it gave him, though. He could now count on a little more time before the American disappeared into another country or his embassy.

When they both arrived at the hotel, the interpreter watched the foreigner retrieve his key and rush nervously to the elevator. Positioning himself where he could watch the elevators while making a phone call, he inserted his change in the coin box and dialed.

The secretary who answered was instructed to connect him with Nishida.

"This is Nishida."

"Nishida? Suvannathep here."

"How is our friend?"

"At his hotel."

"Your workers are taking their time."

"They're dead."

"What!" Nishida said with more exasperation than he could afford. Nero was sitting in his office and his bushy eyebrows rose when he heard the cry.

"You should have told me Bergman's a pro. But don't panic."

"What do you mean, 'don't panic'?"

"I have a plan."

"Anything. Just take care of the situation."

"Yes. He will be taken care of." He dared not tangle with

Bergman unless it was with the extreme of a gun or in some much more subtle way. He decided the subtle way would be safest for himself and at least as effective.

Nishida hung up and turned to Nero, who had a concerned look on his face.

"Some plans not quite turning out, eh?" he asked.

"No problem. Just a delay."

"By the way, I got word from Singapore about Bergman," Nero added.

"Eh?"

"Yes. My contact there looked into Petrotools International. Must be legitimate. Bergman registered the nontrading rep office himself several years ago. There are distributors for his equipment in the phone book. Apparently before the boom went bust he was one of many employees in a larger operation."

"You don't think it could be a front?" Nishida asked, his spirits low.

"My contact even called the MD of his distributor, like he was an immigration official trying to get information on Bergman. He checks out. Unless he's CIA."

"What!"

"If he was planted into the U.S. business, you know the type. But he wouldn't have met with Brody if he was CIA. I still say he is just a salesman."

Nishida urgently desired to disprove Nero's case by telling him about the dead assassins, but he was still in jeopardy. His triumphant announcement, and the chance to push out the Count, would have to wait until Bergman was silenced.

Ted emerged nervously from the elevator onto his floor and looked left and right down the hallway before proceeding to his door, key in hand. He slid the key in quickly, turning the knob, pushing the door open, and rushing into the room in one movement. He was alone. He had dreaded that this would not be the case. He threw his scuffed leather bag on the bed and opened his valise. Taking his dirty clothes from the bottom of the closet in one armful, he deposited the pile in the open case. As he gathered his toiletries from the bathroom, he looked in the mirror. His mouth was pulled into a taut frown and his eyebrows were drawn down, wrinkled and stern. He closed his eyes and swallowed. Opening them, he looked at his hands and the several small drops of blood on his cuff. His hands were trembling; the physical aftereffect of his seconds of combat. He returned to the bedroom, realizing that he would soon begin to feel morose if he remained inactive.

When his bag was full, he called Thai International Airways. They did not have a flight that afternoon. He learned that Singapore Airlines did and called their reservation desk. Their flight left in two and a half hours and a seat was available but he would have to leave soon in order to have time to get his ticket endorsed and check his bags. Confirming his intention to take the flight, he got the reservation clerk's name and hung up.

He stripped off his shirt and threw it into the bag. Slipping into another, he felt slightly relieved. The other had worried him. His fear magnified the size of the spots and their weight burdened his thoughts. Now he had shed them. Washing his face and hands helped also. He was surprised that a symbolic gesture could be so effective. He hurriedly closed his suitcase, made his way downstairs, and got his passport from the safe-deposit box while clearing his bill with the cashier. He paid with his credit card and went to the transportation desk.

Suvannathep watched from across the lobby as Ted checked out. He had made another call after speaking to Nishida and a delivery had been made to him while he waited. No questions had been asked by the delivery man and the drop had been handled quickly and smoothly. He knew he owed his friend now, but it was worth the elimination of a treacherous type like Bergman. If the American was on his way out of the country by air, this would do. If he remained in Bangkok, as only a fool would, coarser means would be engaged.

Now the weapon of Bergman's destruction was in an airline bag next to the interpreter's feet. He was not sure of the best way to get it on Bergman, but he was sure as events unfolded he would determine a way.

He stood up and walked to the transportation desk as he overheard Bergman's request to go to the airport.

"Is he going to the airport?" the interpreter asked the clerk in Thai.

"Yes."

"Excuse me, sir. I have to go now to the airport also. Can we share a ride?" he asked, turning to Ted with a shy Thai smile.

Ted looked more carefully than he normally would at the man. He was not handsome, but was well-built and his lightweight business suit was tailored to fit him. He was almost Ted's height, which was unusual, he noted, but seemed legitimate, airline carry-on bag in hand.

"OK, but I have to leave right now." He turned to the clerk, "Do you have a car ready?"

"Yes, sir. Which airline are you going to?"

"Singapore."

"To Penang?" the interpreter inquired pleasantly.

"No, Singapore."

Suvannathep noticed that the lock had not been closed yet as the bellboy took Bergman's bag. He watched as Bergman got in the back door of the limousine, then turned to the bellboy and said in Thai, "Excuse me, I need to check something for my friend."

He went to the trunk of the car and quietly pulled open the spring catches that held Bergman's suitcase closed. He opened it up and judiciously examined the contents as the bellman looked on. When the bellman turned away to get a tip from Bergman, the interpreter smoothly transferred his small package from the airline bag to Ted's, opened it, and closed the suitcase.

"It's all OK," he said to the bellboy as he slid into the car by the American.

Ted was not in the mood to talk to anyone in his present state of anxiety and he regretted agreeing to let the Thai ride with him. He sat close to his door and stared out the window, hoping the other passenger would sense his disinterest and not try strike up a conversation.

"You do business in Singapore?" the intruder asked amiably.

"I live there." Ted's answers were merely reactions to frequent queries, lifeless and uninviting to further conversation.

"Singapore nice place. Clean."

"Hmm."

"Safe, too"

"Umhmmm."

"You came to Thailand business too?"

"Yeah."

"Thai girls nice, huh. Did you enjoy Thai girl?"

Ted turned to the man, and the desperation to be away from

all the strangeness he had brought upon himself for so many years returned and a look of disgust contorted his face. "I'd really rather not talk about it," he spat, turning to face the window again.

The view outside offered no respite to his tired mind. The squalor and promiscuity of the Asian urban scene slowly gave way to the squalor and destitution of the semi-rural vista along the highway. He realized that the situation was no different than it had ever been and he was not now somehow more enlightened, seeing it with new eyes. He was merely tired of it and needed the security of ordered surroundings to give him rest and perspective. He grimly understood that he would eventually love it all again.

At the airport, Ted took his suitcase from the trunk and went to the Thai Airways desk to have his ticket endorsed. The clerk obliged him quickly and he proceeded to the check-in area. Airport security used an explosives sniffing device next to the key holes on his bag and pumped the side wall several times, then allowed him to continue to his flight's service counter.

He was greeted warmly by the receptionist who smiled as she asked for his ticket. Staring at her closely as she examined his ticket and prepared his boarding card, he wondered why it was that his immediate feeling toward her was one of desiring possession, and he wondered, too, why he had never possessed anyone, nor been possessed. His brushes with romance had been commercial. As she handed his travel documents back to him and smiled again, he realized that her glow, too, was paid for by the airline and was nothing personal. The thought of not being able to communicate his loneliness and desperation to her, or anyone, depressed him as he went through Immigration.

Immediately after the passport check, an X-ray machine swallowed carry-on baggage and expelled the digested contents on the far side where several customs clerks searched suspicious bags for illegal exports of gold and guns. Ted idly put his attaché case on the strip and walked through the security archway electronically searching him for metal. Ted's whole body jumped as a clerk grabbed him by the shoulder and demanded he open his carry-on bag.

Lifting the lid he realized they must have seen the knife. He fawned and explained and presented them the receipt, and after being assured the *tanto* would travel first-class, was given a baggage-claim check to retrieve it in Singapore.

Thoughts of his loneliness followed him onto the plane. The stewardesses smiled in the same personally familiar way and he longed to reach out and take one by the hand and ask her to sit for a while and talk. What would I tell her, he asked himself. That I am a murderer, a horny salesman with a nice apartment they could visit? A young, international businessman, bachelor, a murderer? It was self-defense, he justified.

He closed his eyes and remembered the taut, sickly feeling in his stomach when he had realized what the Japanese at Ital-Siam were saying. The sense of impending doom as he waited for the elevator. His memory played out in slow motion the attacks and deaths of the two assassins. The sound of vertebra separating from one another and the first hiss of blood and air from the punctured chest roared in his ears. He was only just able to get the sickness bag to his lips before his stomach rebelled.

Bill Brody had been busy all afternoon. He had not welcomed the call from Ted, coming as it had in the middle of his preparation of a long report he had to send coded via satellite to Washington. His stomach protested about the missed lunch. He was not certain it was not a prank. He called Chuck Hatch first to ask his impression.

"Do I think he's a wise ass? What do you mean?" Hatch asked disbelievingly over the phone.

Brody told him about the call.

"No shit! Look, I don't think you should treat it as a prank. The guy's young, but he's a businessman anyway."

"What kind of business was it again?"

"Petroleum refining and exploration. He wanted information on a company. I'm afraid I couldn't help him a whole lot though."

"OK, thanks, Chuck."

"Any time."

If Bergman was mixed up in drug trafficking, he most certainly wouldn't have called me, Brody reasoned as he sat back at his desk. So he must have accidentally seen or learned something. So who did he pick this up from? The distributor? A customer? He called a friend on the Thai homicide squad.

"Khun Prinsep? This is Bill Brody."

"Hello Bill. It's been a long time."

"Yes, it has."

"I heard about your wife. I'm sorry to hear about it."

"Yes, thanks."

"What can I do for you?"

"I just had a call a few minutes ago from a young American businessman. He was a bit panicked. Said 'they' were trying to kill him, they being people who suspected he knew of their drug operations."

"Do you know this fellow?"

"Not well."

"Did he ask you to meet him anywhere?"

"No."

"So it's not a trap for you or anything."

"No. Not possible. Look, could you alert your men to be on the lookout for an American about six foot tall, well-built, blond hair, dressed in business clothes — especially any dead ones."

"Is that a joke?"

"No. It would be hard for you to screen all the live ones."

"Mmmm. Shall I put an alert out at the airport and train station?"

"No. If he is able to get safely out of the country, he said he would call. I don't think he's broken the law, but I would like to find out what it's all about. If your people find him, put him under protective custody and give me a ring."

"I think I can arrange it. Again, I was sorry to learn about your wife. If there is anything I can do to help, just call."

"Thanks, Khun Prinsep. Goodbye."

Brody hung up and sat back in his chair. There was nothing more he could do until he got some word on Bergman.

He tried to turn his attention back to the despatch he had been preparing. Rumors had been picked up that Khun Sa, the drug lord of lords, was stricken with a kidney ailment and would be seeking overseas medical assistance. Whether he tried to bring a specialist in or had to leave his lair himself, the situation could be exploited by the agency. His wording of the many options, some of them bound to be controversial, had to be as polite as he could manage. He found it difficult to concentrate as his mind inserted images of Bergman being stalked on the street or of him being shot dead, another innocent bystander mauled by the trade in mind-altering chemicals.

He had few outside interruptions as he labored on the despatch, but each time the phone rang he grabbed for it anxiously, hoping that it might be Bergman or Prinsep. In frustration he swore that if this was Bergman's prank, the young man would regret it. Finally, after two hours Prinsep called again.

"Bill, Prinsep here."

"You find him?"

"No. Something came in but I'm not sure it has anything to do with your American. By the way, he is not one of your agents, is he?"

"No. Why?"

"We found two bodies. Thais. Both were armed with knives. One had his neck broken, the other had fatally stabbed himself. We're trying to confirm their identities now. There were about a half block from each other."

"Fatally stabbed himself?" Brody asked incredulously.

"Well, it wasn't a suicide. Someone helped him bury that blade into his chest up to the handle. But no fingerprints other than the corpse's."

"What makes you think this has to do with the American?"

"On a hunch I asked people near the scene if they had seen a tall, blond, young foreigner. One fruit vendor recalls seeing some-one with that description carrying an attaché case minutes before the lady who found the first body started screaming."

"Did the lady see anyone besides the bodies?"

"She didn't, but the fruit vendor did. Someone came out of the alley about a half minute after the American, in a hurry, too."

"Thai?"

"Yes. Also dressed in business clothes."

"Thanks, Khun Prinsep. I owe you again."

"I'll consider it settled if you'll let me question your friend when you catch up with him."

"You're not going to put out an alert for his arrest?"

"Look, you didn't give a name and you said he's clean. If he put these guys away, it was self-defense. There were no witnesses and no prints. It stays simple as long as it's low life killing off low life. Gang war."

"Your flexibility is appreciated, I guess. I'll let you know when I find him. Let me know if anything further comes in."

"Will do. Bye."

"*Sawadee krap.*" Brody hung up the phone and tried to mentally assemble the jumble of data he had received so far. Bergman was probably alive. Indeed, if he had killed his two assailants, that raised another question. How? Brody dismissed the thought that Bergman might be a CIA agent. He would never have called on Brody for assistance. He assumed that his own agency would not send out an undercover operative without notifying him. Unless, he realized, as his feelings became very cold, the agency suspected him of complicity with the drug trade or perhaps incompetence. Either way he was angry and determined to track Bergman down. He also prepared a special cable to Washington and requested all information from DEA and FBI files on the young American.

After his stomach had settled and a drink had cleared the sour taste of vomit from his mouth, Ted tried to relax. He declined the offer of dinner from the stewardess and watched queasily as the man seated next to him chewed loudly on the tough steak that had been served. He tried to lose himself in the routine of preparation for landing.

When I get in Singapore, let's see, go home first and lock myself in. Get a good night's sleep and call Brody in the morning.

220

It's his problem, not mine. He should be able to take action quickly if I tell him who and where. Where the bodies are. What am I saying? The Thai government may charge me with murder. Don't worry about that. You're free and clear. It was self-defense.

Disembarkation into Singapore Changi Airport was always smooth. The airport was beautiful and functional. He paced himself as usual, exiting the plane as fast as possible and racing to the immigration counter ahead of the first-class passengers. He felt a twinge of anxiety as he recalled the possibility that he was already a wanted man for the two murders.

"You're free and clear," he repeated to himself.

The lightness returned to his step after the immigration officer handed back his passport and told him to proceed to Customs.

I am free and clear, he emphasized, bolstering his spirits. He wondered how he should celebrate his brush with danger. He considered taking a vacation or perhaps just picking up a girl, having a nice dinner, and getting laid. He chided himself for such base considerations after a narrow brush with death. Then his conscience replied, "To hell with philosophy. You're alive. Enjoy it." He smiled at the conclusion as he entered the vast baggage-claim area.

As he only had two items to retrieve, the *tanto* and his suitcase, he did not get one of the carts offered to passengers. After three minutes, the long, U-shaped black plastic conveyor began to circulate with a loud jerking noise. The silk-lined wooden box taken from him at the gate was the third item to emerge.

Picking it up, he inspected the box and then placed it into his attaché case.

He anxiously awaited his large suitcase. Most of the other passengers from his flight were now pressed around the conveyor

221

craning their necks for a view of the luggage emerging from behind a rubber curtain. Everyone was startled to see the large head of a German Shepherd dog poke through the curtain after a bag, then duck back behind.

The dog was a symbol, Ted considered, of Singapore's hard line on illicit drugs. One could not avoid seeing the warnings printed in bold letters on the back of the immigration cards: mandatory death penalty for possession of even minute quantities of illegal drugs. After his encounter in Thailand, he was glad to be in a safe haven. He had no such worries here.

He continued to wait as the crowd began to thin and move on toward the customs clearance tables. He hoped his bag had not been lost, but admonished himself for worrying so easily.

Suddenly, the large, black and tawny dog appeared again, jumping after a suitcase which had just emerged. The dog scrambled to get to the bag, its claws clattering on the black plastic conveyor. Ted's heart sank and the nausea returned.

It was his bag.

SIX

The tall, black, car-rental attendant stared indomitably back at the cowed college student. "We don't rent cars to drivers under twenty-one without two credit cards," she pronounced for the second time with finality.

"I'll be twenty-one next week. I only have one credit card. Give me a break," Ted implored, pushing the credit card his father had obtained for him back across the counter toward her.

"Hey, child, ain't no breaks in this world 'less you make 'em," she said not unpleasantly, suddenly the worldly philosopher.

Ted ignored the fact that she was only several years his senior and thought for a moment. Surely the company had considered this type of situation when they invited him down to Dallas. "I do have a reservation, right?"

She flapped a contract folder in the air with his name on it.

"I was invited down here by a company, Petrotools International, for an interview. They said they have an account with your company and would handle all this," he improvised. "Could you check to see if it says anything about that in the folder, ma'am?"

She opened the jacket and laid the contract on the counter, then slapped some figures into a computer keyboard and waited for a result on the screen. "You just got a break. Let's see we've got a …"

Driving down the highway in a Buick Regal, he settled back into the upholstery and tried not to be intimidated by the bewildering highway that lay ahead. He was reminded of something the Butcher had said that he had failed to write down at the time. When you start training, you're nervous and your attention must be glued to your body, what the muscles are doing, the angle of your edge and direction of your point, he had stated to an exasperated pupil who was angry at not being able to catch up with the old man. It is like driving a car, he had continued. The first year or so, your attention must not divert from the road ahead and behind, your speed, and so on. But after a while you can relax and begin to enjoy the scenery, the old man had said.

Ted's fighting art had developed to the point where he could enjoy the scenery. But his driving had not, especially on convoluted urban highways. He had to turn off the airport access road onto a larger highway east, then south onto another expressway and east again onto yet another. Despite the fact it was Sunday afternoon, the highways were fairly congested, but at least at a slow speed he probably would not overshoot his exits.

The hotel where he had a reservation turned out to be the standard roadside traveler's chain with no features to distinguish it from the competition. His room had the standard beige shag carpet to hide the dirt and one of the standard steel-framed double beds that were known to viciously attack unwary ankles and toes. Cable television, a white plastic ice bucket, and glasses. Formica and vinyl everything. He had heard about life on the road from his father. As a child on vacation with his parents he had, of course, found such places veritable amusement parks. Candy machines in the hall, swimming pools, and a guaranteed choice of fast food for dinner. But he entered this domain now with trepidation.

He was not really sure he wanted a job with Petrotools. He was not guaranteed one anyway, so what the hell, take the interview at least, he reasoned. The alternative he had in mind both excited and depressed him. He had thought he would go back to Japan to apply for graduate school, perhaps take an MBA there. But he knew in his heart that what excited him, the dream of finding a Mieko, would depress him, living so intimately within the environment of their tragedy. Anyway, his parents were excited about this flyback to Dallas.

Almost two years before, he had begun what had brought him to this hotel room in Dallas this night. It was in Washington, D.C., but his father had been with him then. Japan had been there. The Butcher had been there. He had seen an opportunity.

"I thought I told you to dress well, Teddy," Thomas remarked as his son appeared in the lobby of his dormitory wearing a flannel shirt, tight jeans, and loafers.

"Hello to you, too, Dad. Don't we have half an hour?"

"Yeah?"

"I thought I'd let you take a look at what I've got to wear. I'm not sure how formal this is supposed to be." Ted figured his father would be happy with that answer. It was not often people his age gave their parents carte blanche to dress them up like clowns.

"Oh. OK," Thomas said, defused.

They walked up the cement steps to the second floor then down the long, dimly lit hallway. His father sniffed the air with exaggerated volume.

"Is that what marijuana smells like?"

"Yes, Dad."

225

"You're not into that stuff, are you, Ted?" he asked hopefully.

"I told you about the run-in I had with my first roommates, didn't I?"

"The ones selling dope? You threatened to put them out of business, right?"

"That was their room back there. I've had new roommates for the past year and a half. In short, I'm still straight and they're still in business."

Thomas touched his son's arm and stopped him walking down the hall. He looked him in the eyes and said seriously, "Thank you, son."

Ted was touched by the sentiment and nodded, but then realized it was nothing to be thanked for. It was his body and mind that would be dulled and that was his choice to make. Congratulations were in order perhaps, but not thanks. He opened the door of his room with his key and stepped over his roommate who was sitting on the floor talking on the phone.

Seeing a parent enter the room, Isaac Goldblum hung up on his girlfriend after an abbreviated, if suggestive, farewell and stood up smartly, "Good evening, Mr. Bergman."

"Good evening … uh …"

"Isaac, umm … sir." The young man fumbled.

"Isaac, of course. How are things going?"

"Fine, sir."

"Studies?"

"OK. Not as good as Ted's though."

"Isaac is too modest," Ted enjoined. "I saw a paper the teacher had graded on his desk. It had 'brilliant' and 'good points' written all over it," he said, supporting the ego of his shy but sharp friend.

"Keep it up," Thomas said, as if he were reviewing troops. "Let

226

me see what you've got to wear. We've got to get going. You have showered already, haven't you?"

"Yes, Dad, yes. What do you want me to wear, already?"

"Let me see …" Thomas fumbled uneasily through the small closet.

Ted filled the gap left by his father's hesitancy. "How about a sport jacket, shirt with tie, a pair of chinos, and these shoes?" Ted said, pointing to his loafers.

Glad a suitable decision had been made for him, Thomas quickly assented. He sat down at his son's desk and looked at the stray pin-ups that littered the corkboard on the wall. Samples of Chinese calligraphy, the silhouette of a fist, a call-in pizza delivery menu, his own name card. His eyes stopped on a picture of Mieko standing in a pink and white ski suit about to catch a lift, bright white teeth in the sunlight set against pink lips and the snow-tanned face, wisps of black silky hair windblown. He sighed and turned to look at his son who had stripped down to his undershorts and was pulling on his slacks. As Ted bent over to pull them up the muscles of his back stretched taut and his lats flared from his ribs. When Ted stood up, his father could see the lattice definition of his stomach muscles.

"You're looking fit. Still practicing karate?"

Ted ignored the fact that he had never trained karate per se and replied, "Yes. Sometimes four times a week."

"Say, do you ever see that girl you introduced me to last time? The European?"

"Anna. No." Ted left it at that.

"She seemed nice," his father encouraged.

"Yes, she did."

"And good-looking."

"That she was."

Thomas found talking to his son like communicating with the Sphinx. His answers so often only reflected the question being asked. He decided not to pry. Ted had been quite sensitive ever since they left Japan. It was understandable, but time was supposed to heal all wounds. "Any girlfriends right now?" he asked, unable to resist the urge.

"Nope. I'm ready to go. I look OK?"

"A big improvement," Thomas conceded. "Let's go."

They were going to an engagement related to the business that had brought Thomas to Washington, D.C. He was working with federal government trade negotiators on the question of exports of beef to Japan. This evening they were to dine with a Japanese restauranteur who owned a chain of teppanyaki houses across the United States. He had started buying beef from Iowa sources after Thomas had canvassed him on his return from Tokyo.

"You may just be able to help me tonight, Ted," his father said brightly, as if he had just thought of the possibility as they sat down in the taxi now stuck in traffic on Connecticut Avenue.

"How's that?"

"Sonny Toyama is ..."

"East Mountain," Ted interjected unconsciously.

"What's that?" the interrupted man asked, fumbling for a start to his sentence again.

"East Mountain. His name. It means 'east mountain.'"

"Oh, yeah? Well, he's built like it, too. About five foot six, 200 pounds. Used to be a pro wrestler in Japan. Then he came here for a tour, liked the people, and decided to cash in the chips. Anyway, we're gonna eat with him at his place. I get along pretty well with him, you know, understanding the customs and all, but I think he'll be real impressed with you," Thomas said with a smile and a nod. "Watch his handshake, though. Phew! It's a killer."

The taxi eventually threaded its way through the evening dinner traffic and pulled up to a large remodeled restaurant with white stucco walls and swooping, blue-tiled eaves mimicking Japanese castle architecture. A large, hand-carved and -inked wooden signboard hung above the double doors proclaiming "KANTO TEPPANYAKI — The Fastest Knives in The East." Ted smiled at the prospect. He had rarely been able to afford good Japanese food while studying in the nation's capital.

They entered and immediately crossed a small wooden bridge over a Japanese goldfish pond of diminutive size. Thomas had a word with the Korean maitre d' who raised his eyebrows and nodded his head crisply. They were led past a full house of Western diners seated in groups of eight around teppanyaki grills while Asians of various ethnic backgrounds pretended to be Japanese grill masters.

In the rear corner of the restaurant was a raised room with *shoji* and *tatami*. Father and son slipped off their shoes and entered. Sitting down cross-legged on the floor, they heard the maitre d' leave them, saying, "Mr. Toyoma will be here shortly."

A kimono-clad Japanese-American woman gave them some hot towels and retreated from the room, sliding the *shoji* closed. Almost immediately, it slid open again and a short, husky Japanese man dressed in white slacks and polo shirt, with a black V-neck sweater and socks, all Arnold Palmer brand, entered smiling broadly, a thin mustache turned up to his nose by his grin. "Bugman-San!" he shouted jovially as if to say "banzai!" and rushed over to greet the American who struggled to regain his stance from the floor.

Toyama grabbed his hand and hauled him up, then shook the

hand like a water-pump lever, jarring Thomas. Toyama's attention turned to Ted who rose smoothly from the floor straight from the cross-legged position without using his hands. It did not escape the former wrestler's notice. "This is your son!" he exclaimed positively.

"Toyama-sama," Ted said, bowing from the waist and then extending his hand. The wrestler seized it and began to squeeze, friendly, but firm. Ted had made sure to get a good grip deep into the man's hand to prevent his fingers from taking the pressure, and matched the Japanese ounce for ounce. As they pumped, the mutual contraction became unpleasant, but they continued to smile. Ted added some selective pressure from the inside of his thumb joint to the outside of the host's hand. He felt a slight let-up on Toyama's grip from his inflicted twinge of pain and immediately released his grip, shaking his hand and proclaiming, "You're right, Dad, he's got a super handshake."

"Ha ha," Toyama beamed, happy that the young man had let him have face. "You do your father proud."

They all sat down again, and hot saké and a large, woven, prawn-shaped basket of fresh, sizzling tempura was brought in with a platter of raw fish slices and sushi rolls. Ted stared at the feast, his mouth watering.

"A few appetizers," Toyama said deprecatingly, "We'll have our master chef prepare teppanyaki for us later … . What's wrong, boy, what? Don't you feed him, Thomas?" he asked, amused to see the hunger in Ted's eyes, but not expecting an answer. "*Kampai!*" he said, enthusiastically downing his first tiny cup of the hot rice wine. The Bergmans followed his gesture.

After four toasts and a meal's worth of appetizers, they moved to a teppanyaki grill. A middle-aged man, the only other Japanese Ted had seen in the place, was waiting behind the hot metal counter dressed in white with a red apron and headband that had the kanji for "*kan to*" written inside a rising sun emblem. Ted recognized the headband as the type worn by Japanese fencing students under their helmets. The Japanese introduced himself in rough English. "I am Kishi, your chef tonight; sank you for coming," he bowed. The chef quickly set about his work and efficiently started preparing various meats, seafoods, and vegetables for cooking. The knife he wore in a scabbard by his right side flashed in and out of the sheath as he would cut, spin, and return it. His fingers deftly maneuvered as the knife shucked and deveined a dozen prawns.

Ted was amused by the performance and a thought entered his mind. By now he was on good terms with Toyama, who enjoyed the young man's brisk and mature conversation in his native language. He turned to the restaurant owner and said admiringly, "Kishi *sensei*," using an honorary title of master teacher for the chef, "is truly skilled. I have noticed some of the others here are not Japanese."

"All the rest," Kishi smirked. "I have had to teach all of them."

"And I regret to say I have seen some grease slinging and tidbits flying from misplaced strokes," Ted appraised.

Far from bristling at the comment, Toyama shook his head and said sadly, "Regrettably, we cannot afford to have all-Japanese staff. It is a sacrifice to economy. Kishi-san trains them as best he can, but true skill and flair take years to cultivate."

"How long to train them in the basics?" Ted asked, getting closer to the question he was setting up for.

"We apprentice them in the kitchen for four months. Then they get a trial two months, after which they go on full salary."

"And may I ask if Friday and Saturday are your busiest nights, when perhaps your patrons must wait at a grill for a chef, reducing your turnover?"

Toyama looked at the bright college student, wondering where this was leading. "You are correct. Do you have a solution to my problem?"

"A modest one, perhaps. Following in my father's footsteps, I became intrigued in your country by knife handling and was apprenticed to Chief Master Butcher Obara at Tokaido Meats for a year and a half. Although my skill lacks flair and is a mere shadow of Kishi *sensei*'s, I believe you might find it amusing."

Toyama laughed. "You, a blue-eyed American, are asking for a job at a teppanyaki restaurant?" It was not a put-down; he just could not believe the lad's audacity.

"I only seek to help solve a problem you mentioned you had. It is unfortunate that it is not economical to train a chef to work only part-time, Friday and Saturday night. But in my case, I can begin immediately to serve and entertain your customers those two nights a week. Imagine the joy of your Japanese patrons when I converse with them, perhaps increasing their bar tab by telling some saucy drinking stories."

Toyama pursed his lips and looked at Kishi who had stopped cutting and started listening.

Thomas, who had followed none of the conversation in Japanese, asked Ted, "What's going on?"

Ted politely waved his father silent and waited quietly.

"Please, show us your skill," Toyama requested. Ceremoniously Ted placed his hands on the counter together and bowed his head into the triangle formed by his fingers, once to Toyama and once to Kishi, then stood up and took off his jacket, leaving it behind the chair. He extended his hand to Kishi, who drew his knife and reversed his grip, presenting it to Ted by the handle. Ted took the knife and felt its balance. He tapped the tip on the grill experimentally to test the springiness of the metal. With a flourish, he spun the knife around its center with his finger, returning it to the point-out position. He tapped it smartly on the grill as he had seen Kishi do, using the spring back to time a bounce out of his hand into a somersault and back with handle in his hand. He smiled at them. "A new piece of steak please," he requested.

Not wanting to waste a good cut, Kishi selected one of the fattest pieces and slapped it on a cool portion of the grill. The gauntlet, in the form of a raw piece of meat, had been thrown.

"How lean do you like it, sir?" Ted asked in English to Toyama.

"Completely fat free. My doctor says I should cut down."

"As you wish." With a move Kishi had not even considered before, Ted deftly reversed the knife in his hand, blade along his forearm so he could not see the edge. The knife disappeared as he moved his hands over the plank of beef. Withdrawing them, the three onlookers could see that all the fat had been stripped from the perimeter with minimal wastage.

"Could you cut out that piece of gristle?" Toyama requested in English. "It shouldn't be there in the first place," he added. The mock accusation was directed at Thomas, who turned away sheepishly and shrugged playfully.

Ted righted the blade and considered the angle, thickness, and convolution of the hard gelatin, then set point and edge to work freeing tender meat from tough.

"What do you think, Kishi-san?" the owner asked.

Kishi was impressed, but it would not do to express it, especially if the boy was going to work for him. "You're the boss," he said unenthusiastically.

"You may not like the wages," Toyama warned the young

233

American.

Ted expected the minimum, but said nothing.

"You have to stay late both nights, no dates."

He was silent.

"OK. Start next weekend, one week in the kitchen to learn how to cook and then hit the grill. I can only pay you $9 an hour plus tips and a meal. OK?"

"Thank you, Toyama-sama," he said with deep bow, the pay double what he expected, the Japanese food a bonus.

"Ted, would you mind telling me what is happening," the nervous parent said, anxious that the son he thought would please was not screwing up one of his better restaurant accounts.

"I now work for Kishi *sensei*," he beamed as he sat down and toasted the two Japanese and his father.

His brief apprenticeship had gone very smoothly, aided by an expensive gift of Japanese tea he had bought for Kishi-san. Within the month he was at the grill and found the work to his liking. He had never been put in the role of the performer before, the extrovert, and he enjoyed it. He was especially appreciated, as expected, by the Japanese customers. They viewed him as somewhat of an oddity. He liked them because he could practice his Japanese and they tipped him liberally.

Eventually, he was automatically assigned to Japanese customers unless they had requested Kishi, who normally entertained large groups of Westerners who wanted a genuine samurai chef. With his earnings from the first six months, he was able to pay for extra tuition to summer school which his parents had not set aside. Not completely sure of what he would do with a degree in Japan studies, he took courses on accounting and management theory, marketing, and audited a class on Southeast Asian history.

His senior year had come upon him faster than expected and he was required to do a thesis on Japan. He had a choice of almost any topic and any age. He considered doing a paper either on Japanese teenage suicide or the *burakumin* subculture, but decided both would be too difficult, emotionally and technically. Instead, he prepared a thesis on Japanese businesses' use of an obscure text on strategy written by a Chinese 2,000 years ago. His professor approved, as it combined classic and modern with relevant conclusions to be drawn.

One cold February night when the wind funneled down the Potomac and branched its cold fingers through the city, he entered the restaurant after classes, his heavy coat pulled up tight. After changing and washing, he set to the preparatory work, precutting and weighing meats, scoring mushrooms for visual effect, washing bean sprouts. At 6 o'clock, some early diners, usually smaller groups and lighter tippers, were brought in, and as usual the other chefs were assigned. At 7, Ted was "on deck," as he referred to it.

He came out to his assigned Hibachi grill dramatically and bowed deeply from the waist. There were only two customers, a Japanese and an American, both in their early fifties. "*Konbanwa.* Good evening to you gentleman on this cold night. I hope the mama-san has brought you some spirits to keep you warm while I light the fire. I am Ted Bergman, at your service."

The two men stared politely at him while he finished his spiel, both thinking it was rather eccentric to have a tall, blue-eyed young man in a space expected to be occupied by an older Japanese. They resumed their conversation.

Ted could see the Japanese man was indeed from Japan and he took the opportunity of a break in the conversation to say politely, in the man's native tongue, "May I ask if this is your first visit to

235

America?"

The surprised man looked up and answered, "You speak Japanese?"

"Poorly."

"Amazing. No, this is my third visit," he smiled.

"We welcome you for many visits in the future. If I can be of any special help to you tonight, just let me know."

The American interjected with a heavy Texas accent, "Do you speak that language?"

"Yes, sir."

"Does he speak Japanese?" he asked his friend incredulously.

"Very well."

"I'll be damned. How come?"

"I studied there, and here. I'll be graduating in several months. Let me know if I can help you in any way tonight."

Following lessons from the Butcher, he had learned to observe people minutely and discreetly. The Texan was very handsome and well-tanned, with greying blond hair and a craggy masculine face. His hands had seen hard labor, but the jewelry he wore indicated he was wealthy and its flamboyance suggested he might be the owner of his business. The Japanese man was dressed in a conservatively tailored dark blue suit. The cut and material suggested that he was well-to-do and Ted wondered if the corporate pin on his lapel was of his own company.

Trying to follow their conversation over the sounds of the ventilator hood and sizzling foods was not easy. He picked up some discussion about some fun nights in Tokyo they had shared. Later in the meal the talk had turned slowly to business. Southeast Asia. Construction and exploration, petroleum. During breaks in the conversation, Ted entertained them with asides and small bits of humor that translated well in either direction.

The Texan CEO could see his customer's favorable impression of the American chef through his tone of conversation and facial expressions. A thought occurred to him. "Did you say you were graduatin' soon?" he drawled to Ted.

"Yes, sir. In three months."

"And what all d'ya study?"

"I majored in Japan studies, but I also took up extra courses in economics, accounting, and marketing," Ted promoted, seeing a chance. "You know, I couldn't help but hear you mention you're in the petroleum construction supply business. I spent two summers on a pipe-laying crew in Texas working for my uncle."

"What's his name?"

"Bob Bergman."

The American executive, who had built his business up from scratch over a twenty-year period partly through his memory of customers and keeping them, fitted the name through his mind's eye of faces, jumping from industry to era to locale until a face fit. "Sure I know him. He's a good ol' boy. We've tossed down a few beers. How's he doing?"

"Fine. I haven't seen him in two years. I spent the summer with him right out of high school," Ted said, recalling the bitterness with which he had attacked the hot, heavy outdoor work. The labor had channeled his sorrow over Mieko's death and burned it, refined it, until constant pain and reminder was transformed to numbness with only an occasional flare-up of inconsolable grief.

"Tell you what," the Texan said, smiling generously. "Right now we're lookin' for a fellah to take a sales position in Singapore in a couple of months. Exciting job, and I think you've got what it takes. Would you like to come in for an interview?"

Ted was shocked. He had sent a dozen résumés out with no reply and had only promoted himself this night as an amusement, practice. "I'm speechless. I'm overwhelmed by your generosity."

"It ain't a job yet. But let's get you down to Texas for some talk. Get you a big Texas steak," he said with a chuckle. "Looks like you know how to cut it pretty good."

"Thank you."

Ted hesitated. What about the air ticket? "How shall I arrange my air transportation, sir?" he asked noncommittally.

"Give me your address, I'll have Personnel drop you a line and get one of the prepaid tickets. OK?"

"Yes, sir. Thank you."

The Texan liked the "sir."

The headquarters of Petrotools International was smaller than Ted had expected. It occupied one floor of a commercial office park building in east Dallas not far from his hotel. Approaching the tinted glass door straight ahead of the elevator, he examined himself one more time. Shoes shined, sort of. His tie was on straight and did not hang out of his collar. The night before he had reviewed the material about the Southeast Asian natural resource boom. He had called his Uncle Bob and found out a little more about Petrotools and Jezek, the owner/president he had met in D.C.

The receptionist took Ted's name and phoned back to Personnel. Soon, a tall, balding man with a paunch that hung over his large silver belt buckle came out and greeted him. "Come right in," he said after shaking Ted's hand and pulling him in the direction of a corridor of partitions. "Well, you're Ted Bergman. We heard a lot about you from Mr. Jezek. By the way, I'm Bill Towers, V.P. Personnel. But you can call me Butch."

"Thank you, Mr. Towers,"

"Whoa, Butch! My father was Mr. Towers. I'm just Butch."

"Butch, thank you," Ted corrected, and continued. "I had a very good impression of Mr. Jezek. He seemed to be both friendly and authoritative."

Friendly and authoritative, a good, if risky, choice of words, Towers thought. "That he is. Self-made man. We all look up to him here. Here's my office," he said pointing the way in for Ted. "Liz, can we have some coffee in here?" he said to his secretary outside, then stepped in and pointed to a chair next to his desk for Ted to take. "She's the last of a dying breed. A secretary who's willing to do more than just type, file, and phone," he said wistfully. "Anyway, Mr. Jezek said he thought you looked to be the kinda fellah we're lookin' for." Towers paused to see if Ted would fill the gap.

"If he means the kind of fellah who's college-educated, willing to live in the Far East, who speaks some of the languages of your customers, and who's got some background you can use, then I'd say yes, I'm the kind of fellah you're looking for," Ted responded brightly.

Towers smiled slightly, but suppressed a nod. "Say, I got your résumé here and I've got a couple of questions."

"Good. I was hoping I would have a chance to expand on some things," Ted replied confidently.

"Well, then tell me. How does a farm boy from Iowa find himself in Japan? And what does he find when he gets there? I mean, what kept up your interest in Japan these years?"

Washington, D.C., was unlike any city Ted had been in before. It served no other purpose than the management of a nation and its defense. It was unlike Tokyo, which served as a multipurpose city for government and business, or Osaka, which served industry and finance, or Kyoto, which served cultural imperatives. It was almost what he imagined a European city such as Paris to be. Malls, museums, memorials. It was also an international city. Embassies everywhere and people from all over the world concentrated in the twenty-by-twenty-mile square. The local universities catered to the political and international flavor of the city, and it was for this reason Ted had enrolled at George Washington University. That and the fact that he felt he would not fit in with what he perceived the West Coast set to be.

He had come from his summer of hard labor in Texas tanned and muscular, but still morose over Mieko's suicide. He longed to dive into his studies of Japan, unconsciously hoping to find some clue in the language or culture that would tell him why she had left him. There had to be a reason. Something he did not understand about the Japanese, or possibly, he feared, something he had done.

He tested into advanced Japanese language classes and found even those rudimentary. The social studies were slowly beginning to delve more deeply into aspects of history and culture than the high-school courses in Japan had. The rest of the time he had to take mandatory overview courses to "broaden his perspective."

In the second semester he signed up for a Korean tae kwon do class for credit. He thought that giving himself a chance to train in a more disciplined environment and fulfill a physical-education requirement at the same time was a good idea. He was disappointed on the first day to see a relaxed crowd of wide-eyed teenagers in oversized uniforms hacking through some prearranged movements. By the various shades of their belts he knew they had been there from one to several semesters. The highest-ranked student had a black belt and may have been there two years. The "master," a Korean, called the class to order with a sharp clap of his hands.

"Line up," his senior student barked. "Bow."

Wow. Ted's thoughts finished the voiced command sarcastically.

Everyone was asked to sit cross-legged on the floor while roll was called and uniforms were issued. When they got to Ted, he explained that he had one.

"Is it a tae kwon do uniform?" the black belt asked aggressively.

Ted suppressed saying do you mean does it have that shit printed on the chest, and answered instead, "It's just a white training uniform."

"You need one of these," he said dropping one down in Ted's lap and moving on.

The first lesson after bowing was blocking. Arms snapping up over the head as if to attack the opponent with B.O. or smell it oneself. Single practice was followed by practice against an opponent. The newcomers like Ted were lined up facing the old-timers. He was paired with a melancholy looking red-headed coed whose belt color matched her frizz.

Expecting her to be able to block by now, he snapped a punch out to the target indicated by the "master," a point just below the nose. When the predetermined block did not rise in time, he triggered braking in his muscles and regulated the shifting roll of his hips and shoulders. A punch that would have decked her, he judged, was moderated to something less damaging.

"Shit!" she cried out holding her hand to her mouth. "Fuck," she said through her fingers. "You're not supposed to punch that way." Ted was dumbfounded. She was not supposed to not block

241

that way. He had done nothing to surprise her. It had just been a good, clean, committed strike.

The black belt came over and looked accusingly at Ted who shrugged helplessly as they tended to his wounded, who it turned out had suffered from a slightly swollen upper lip, no broken teeth.

It was now Ted's turn to receive her punch. He expected that she would be seeking revenge and would try to hit him back. He was right.

Looking at her rear foot, he could see the rising wave of muscle and bone that propelled her fist to a target far behind his lip. He bobbed and the punch blew past his ear.

The black belt had seen Ted's evasion from the end of the row and called out, "Block the punch, two!"

Ted complied, his brain trying to catch up with the commands and attacks. Instinctively his hand rose in approximately the form the "master" proscribed, but he caught the coed with his thumb knuckle in the funny bone before following through and up. It had been a hard point to hit and he sensed he could not have done it volitionally. He was responding from muscle memory.

The red head winced and then whimpered loudly, holding her elbow and rubbing it.

The black belt and the "master" came over. "You think you're tough, huh, tough guy?" the "master" jeered in a Korean-American accent.

"No … sir," Ted replied, wondering how long it would take to finish the semester.

The "master" clapped his hands and directed them to sit down again. He asked his four senior pupils in the class to get up and demonstrate some of the skills the new people would learn. When they had finished with these prearranged function forms, the "master" looked over the class and asked a belated question. "Have any of you trained martial arts before?" He resumed his scan of the pupils.

Ted remained silent. He knew it was semantics, but he felt he had not trained in "martial arts" because purists in Japan used the term to describe only arts for use on the traditional battlefield.

"Nobody? What about you, tough guy. What did you train?" Nervous snickering rippled through the class.

"Nothing you would have heard of," Ted answered, realizing too late that his answer sounded more insulting than he meant his response to be.

"Try me."

"I mean, what I trained has no name. It's not a school."

"Why don't you come up and show us some. … I insist."

Ted hesitated and then got up and walked in his jeans up to the front. "There's nothing to show. No forms."

"Demonstrate on Kelly." The "master" cued his black belt to attack.

Having observed the truculent lieutenant for forty minutes, Ted suspected he knew his mettle and favored techniques. He waited as the attack commenced. He hoped he could avoid hurting Kelly, if only to extricate himself smoothly from the mess he was in, and parried or avoided the first several highly telegraphed blows.

"You're just dancing. Show us something," the Korean taunted.

Ted waited for the next attack, a roundhouse kick to his head. It was met solidly by Ted's advancing body and elbow jamming into the flesh inside the knee while an uppercut to the jaw lifted the surprised black belt off his single supporting leg and sent him crashing to the mat, reeling.

Ted stormed over to his seat, picked up the uniform and

dropped it on top of Kelly, then started for the door as he heard the Korean scream the class dismissed.

The "master" ran over. "Hey, you!"

"Hay's for horses."

"You smart guy, too, huh?"

"No. Just fed up."

"You must not have trained with a real Asian master. They wouldn't let you behave this way."

Ted stifled a dry reply and remained silent, then said "Look. This is not going to work. I don't think you want me in your class and I don't want to be here. Do you have a suggestion?"

"I can fail you."

"I have a better idea. Why don't you just mark me down as having attended every night, give me an A minus for the semester and I won't come back and bother you or your black belt. It wouldn't do for a complaint to be lodged about the competence of the tae kwon do instructor. After all, there are more tae kwon do masters than there are students; the competition for good work must be fierce."

The cold, coal-black eyes stared back at him, evaluating. "What your name?"

"Bergman, Ted. Freshman."

The Korean exhaled. "OK."

"Yes, I believe I have a flair for negotiation," Ted responded in answer to another of Towers' questions. "Of course, you have to gauge the style of the man facing you. Sometimes hard, sometimes soft, but there's always some buttons to press."

"But besides buying trinkets at a Japan market, have you had

244

any negotiations you can recall?"

"You mean besides asking my girlfriend's mother for a first date with her?" he asked as a joke.

Towers nodded with a smile.

"Perhaps I shouldn't admit this," Ted said in a confidential tone, sliding closer, "But I once got an A minus for not attending a P.E. class all semester."

"How d'ya do that?" Towers smiled, egging on an admission.

"I persuaded the instructor that, though I knew what he wanted to teach, I might 'distract' his students and prevent them from learning what he was there to teach."

"What class was that?"

"Korean tae kwon do."

"Oh, you know that, too?"

"Only the principles."

"But you've got 'Asian fighting arts' down here as a key hobby."

"Yes, but not that."

"Something you trained in Japan?"

"Yes, sir."

Towers listened and looked and thought for a moment. The next question wasn't supposed to be part of an interview. He had seen drafts of the various laws coming out about interviewees' privacy. Can't ask sexist questions, can't ask about marital status, can't ask if they're fags, he lamented. But, by God, some questions had to be asked. I mean, he debated internally, Singapore's not cheap, especially for a married man, especially for a married man with children. The cost effectiveness of a marginal single salesman, which they expected any new man sent to Singapore to be, would be obliterated by the cost of a spouse. Damn the laws, he decided again. "Any sweethearts?" he asked, as brightly as Ted's grandfather

245

might have.

Ted tried to control an impulse that pulled his business smile down as the first face that came to his mind was Mieko's. To counteract the melancholy, he tried to change the direction of his thoughts. There had been a sweetheart, sort of.

Ted was thoroughly looking forward to his afternoon workout. He was in a foul mood, brought on by criticism he had received from his Japanese teacher on an essay he had written. He had tried to include some more sophisticated phrases, even attempting a double entendre, but Minamoto *sensei* was unimpressed. She was a crusty old bird, he swore to himself, and she can't get her mind out of the textbook set. Japanese is a living language, he believed, growing all the time with new phrases and patterns.

He changed rapidly into his training uniform, went to a corner of the gym where a heavy punching bag was hanging, and began to hit, each strike a relief of some tension built up since his last workout. As he moved in and out on the bag, striking lightly at imagined points he targeted, his mind wondered what sort of tension it was he was trying to get rid of. There was the drive to succeed, which to him meant at least living up to his capacity if not trying to exceed it. He did not think he was smarter than the average students around him. It's just that he saw a lot of burned-out, bewildered, or just plain lazy, fun-loving peers who treated college like summer camp without counselors. So his challenge was with himself, not them. Internal tension. He did not consider the source of his drive, but went on as he punched to think of other stresses. There was the undeniable pressure which built up from time to time from his sex. Actually, he seemed to almost always be on edge. His life lacked the softness of emotional attachment, except to a ghost.

He stopped and got out a rubber practice knife, and began moving and feinting, cutting, and piercing, the empty hand baiting, feinting, and grabbing while the knife hand did its work. After several minutes, the precision and concentration required exceeded the limits his mood would allow and he turned to put the knife back down.

"Don't stop on my account," he heard a lightly accented feminine voice say behind him. He turned to see an attractive blond woman, about his age, in dancing tights and a sweatshirt. He was immediately struck by the dichotomy of the attire: tight, revealing, formal, shiny, and baggy, obscuring, casual, dull. He looked up from her feet into her eyes and they stared at each other for a moment longer than he was comfortable with.

"I was going to stop anyway," he said, at loss for words.

"It's fascinating what you're doing. You're quite gute," she said in a tone of knowledgeable appraisal.

Ted laughed self-consciously and shook his head. He was intrigued by her accent. It sounded Scandinavian. He had never met anyone from his family's ancestral homeland. "Have you studied some method?"

"Yes! I have studied quite a bit yu yitsu, but I don't think I could stop your knife attacks," she added.

"Ju jitsu is not designed to fight a defensive knife man, only someone coming in with a committed attack," he said factually, unable to let his voice warm to her.

"You know yu yitsu, too?" she asked, walking over closer, her step light, like an acrobat's.

"Only what I have seen. Never trained it."

247

"Could you show me some more?" she asked, now standing facing him.

He looked at her mane of blond hair pulled back into a thick ponytail, her clear skin, blue eyes, and pert nose. His eyes followed down her cheek to a strong muscular neck.

She pouted her lips. "Well? How about it?"

"Umm, yeah. OK. What do you want to do?"

"I'm game for anything. What's your best technique? Perhaps if I put a lock on you and you break it."

He had done some seizing technique in Shorinji *Kempo*, but Butcher Obara had disparaged trying to defeat the opponent by solely relying on grabbing and joint locking. It was too complex and time-consuming, he had said, affording the opponent too many chances to retaliate. "You lock me up and then I break it? I wouldn't let you lock me up," he said, not meaning to be insulting but stating a fact of tactical principles.

She did not take the comment badly and said, "OK, then how about this. You grab me, I'll try to lock you up, and you either prevent it or break it."

"I don't want to hurt you."

"Of course, not. I won't try to hurt you either," she said smiling. He began to feel at ease with her. It seemed she had been through this before and was coaching him.

"How should I hold?" he asked shyly, his arms opened up to prepare for some aggressive embrace.

She laughed and shook her head as if to say "silly goose!" "Like your teacher attacked you, yes?"

If that's the way you want it, Ted decided, and lunged without warning, sweeping her right arm across her body and stepping behind her, trying to set a choke hold on her neck, his face and left hand buried in the cascade of perfumed blonde hair.

Her response was fast but not frantic. She slid her left hand up between her wind pipe and the crook of his elbow as she buried her chin down, cutting off the choke. With her right foot she stepped back between his legs as she slammed her elbow into his floating ribs, loosening the neck lock he maintained. She peeled the choking hand off her neck and twisted out of his rear embrace, now facing him.

Ted could feel his hand, wrist, and elbow being rapidly manipulated. A twist was applied and he could feel the beginnings of pain quickly growing in intensity. She had the lock, now she was going to drive it home. To relieve pressure he bent over and realized this brought him closer to a target. He gambled with breaking his distended joint by simultaneously striking a nerve in her knee and sweeping the leg out.

She released her grip and fell backward, breaking the downward momentum into the mat with a slap. Ted, because he had lost his balance, followed her down, his arms extended toward her to break his descent.

She did not relent and renewed the attack, parrying his groping arms and reaching for his throat with thumb and fingers. Caught by surprise at her persistence, he brushed the claw away and rolled her over on the mat, again putting a rear choke on her, this time entwining her flailing legs with his and controlling her free arm. Sensing that she would not give up, he steadily increased the pressure on her neck until she slapped the mat to signify submission. She was dead and she knew it. He relaxed and released her and they rolled apart, now both lying flat on their backs looking at each other, both thinking the same thing: Jesus, that was intense!

"Anna! Are you OK?" a worried coed's voice called from

249

nearby, breaking their interlude.

"What?" the blonde said, rolling to her feet smoothly and extending a helping hand to Ted. "Oh, sorry to worry you. He was showing me some yu yitsu." She turned to Ted. "You are gute."

"So are you. Whew!" he replied sincerely.

"See you around," she said with a wave as she trotted off the mat.

"Hey, umm. What's your name?"

"Anna Perrson"

"I'm Ted Bergman. Can I see you again?"

"I'm here three nights a week after dance. Bye," she chimed, as she took her friend's arm and walked off.

Lunch was taken at a classy grill room restaurant not far from the office park where Petrotools made their headquarters. Jezek, the president, invited the international marketing manager and Butch Towers to the lunch with Ted.

Ted was aware that the meal was as much a part of the interview as the office questions. Despite the fact that he was not inclined to eat heavily at lunch, he ordered the same eighteen-ounce "cowboy" cut steak they had, rather than the fourteen-ounce "countrygirl" cut. He followed their lead on an appetizer and ordered raw oysters which he thought would be sufficiently Gulf States macho to suit their perception. He turned down a cocktail.

"Do you drink, Ted?" Ed Reese, the international marketing manager asked, sipping on a Bloody Mary.

"Sure. I'm not a fiend about it, but I can hold my liquor pretty well, as well as the next guy."

"Those Asians are tough drinkers."

"Yes?"

"Oh, yeah. And they like some pretty fancy stuff out in Singapore, too. Cognac, VSOP."

"Cognac is fairly strong, but sweet, isn't it," Ted asked, letting the man talk on about a topic that interested him.

"Yeah. What is it?" he asked no one in particular. "The distilled dregs of champagne grapes? Something like that. What about Asian booze?" he queried Ted.

"I've had some in Taiwan and Korea. Tough stuff."

Jezek broke in and changed the subject, "Living in D.C., did you ever see the president?"

"Well, there was one night he was at a reception at a building across the street from our dorm. I remember it was snowing that night and some of us were waiting for him to come out. When we were getting too cold and just about to give up, he came out of the building with his wife and the Secret Service agents, ran down the steps waving to us, and ducked in the car. It wasn't much to see."

"But it was exciting, I'll bet."

"It was exciting," Ted added, following the executive's lead.

"What kind of politics are you?" Towers added.

Ted thought for a moment, "Conservative, but I suppose I'm still thinking about it."

"If you really love me, you'll be willing to give up these silly things and help me," Anna pouted as she traced her finger around the hair on his nipple.

Ted lay back with his eyes closed and drank in the moment while he could. His fingers also played with her erect nipple and he could feel her hot, wet pubic center cupped against his thigh. He

251

could imagine the sweetness of the taste of it, and although he had enjoyed many such moments of afterglow with her, he felt their time together was coming to a close.

Anna Perrson was a piece of ass. That's what it came down to, he realized with resignation. She had everything to be desired. She was intelligent. She had been educated around the world, spoke four languages fluently, and came from a good family. Her father was the Swedish ambassador to the United Nations and had provided very well for her. She had a private apartment in Foggy Bottom, of which they now lay in the bedroom. She wore fine clothes, some of which he had taken off her again tonight. She wore her hair and had her nails and facials done with professional attention.

The fashions fit because she had an overbuilt dancer's body. "Mama, who had been in the Royal Ballet, said I had the grace to be a great dancer, but my teats are too big," Anna had commented. Dancing's loss, my gain, Ted had thought at the time, which had come quickly and early on.

He had seen her the week after their first meeting and invited her to a movie in Georgetown. After a decent Italian dinner, the film, and some ice cream, he had walked her the one hour home. During their walk they had learned more about each other, their majors and interests, and discovered they overlapped most strongly in their flight from the domestic mundane to the international bizarre.

Feeling they had arrived too soon at her apartment door, he had been uneasy. What should come next? Should he ask her out again then? Or maybe try to kiss her goodnight? They paused awkwardly at the entrance as she opened the lock and turned to face him.

252

He had clenched his teeth lightly and leaned over to kiss her. To his dismay she put her fingertips on his lips, stopping him, crushing him, until she said, "Would you like to come in for café?"

Coffee had led to the first of many nights spent at Anna's. In retrospect, he was glad they had discovered their physical compatibility at the start. If they had waited until they had known more about each other, they probably would not have made it to bed.

"Are you thinking about it?" she asked breaking into his thoughts about their past.

"What's that?"

"Ted, you have no consciousness. Is there anything happening inside that brain besides your dreams about Japan, martial arts, and getting laid?" she scoffed. Now she was propped over him, her pendulous breasts hanging straight in his line of sight.

"Yes, Anna. I have a consciousness. I think it's just … maybe … I'm on a different track from you."

"That is where you are wrong. We are all on the same historical track at this moment. Those who deny it, like you, do so because you are in a dream world of materialist bourgeois values. That is not reality. That is what Madison Avenue wants you to think is reality." She waited for his reply.

Ted looked out the door of the bedroom past the black leather-upholstered sofa to the rainbow light refracted in the crystal hung up at the wet bar in the living room. If she had followed his eyes and seen his vision, an answer would not have been necessary. As it was he hesitated to voice his feelings.

"You see I am right. Exploitation exists everywhere. There is no freedom here. It's at all levels. Look at the condition of the poor calves used for veal. You should appreciate that at least. Pumped up with chemicals, never to see a sunny patch of green field, or to test their wobbly legs. And do you think it is any different for the workers? Management will do anything to get them to work faster, harder, longer."

The three words tripped off Ted's thoughts about the sexual engagement they had just finished. She had implored breathlessly for the same effort on his part and he had complied joyfully. Was he exploited?

"And do you believe Japan is any different? Just remember the discrimination toward your girlfriend's family. Japan is a feudal society, still is. Don't think there is freedom or democracy there. Everything is controlled by capitalist *shoguns* behind the scenes. They call them *kurumaku*, you should know."

"Anna," Ted said, interrupting her, "how do you know? When we first met you didn't know anything about Japan. Now you are always talking about the details of class and feminist struggle there, all kinds off stuff."

"I know because I care. I care because I want you to understand, to open your mind. Because I love you. I cannot love a man who turns his back on the oppressed. How can he love me if he doesn't find any realization in loving them? I want you to love me, but it has to be pure. Come with me this summer to Europe. Open your eyes. See what I am talking about."

Ted did not relish the idea. Europe sounded all right if he could afford it. But six weeks of working with radical minority groups in Ireland, England, France, Italy, and Greece did not sound like his idea of fun.

"You're thinking it won't be fun," she judged, reading his face. "There is more to life than fun."

He lifted his head up and tugged gently on her aureole with his teeth, his tongue lapping short strokes. He wished she would get off

254

the subject, but he knew she would not abate. She was dedicated, God only knew why, to her revolution. On any given day she would eventually turn the conversation around into a harangue on historical struggle and dialectic. He could not understand the source of her discontent or, indeed, if she was truly unhappy.

He stroked the blond fuzz beneath her navel gently with his palm. He had two theories, both unvoiced, about her dedication. He had first surmised that she was trying to get back at her father and mother for something they had or had not done to or with her. She was high society to the bone and had never suffered or been exploited. What was her beef? That had led him to the realization of the second possibility, she felt guilty about her own position in life and sought the masses' forgiveness. But if either supposition were true, why did she lead the kind of life she did? Even when she had taken him to campus "political orientation" meetings she had not dressed down. Why were there no homeless, exploited workers out on strike staying at her apartment, or boxes of foodstuff being shipped off to Biafra? If he had asked the question of a normal person, it would be ludicrous. But the plateau on which she carried herself and her campaign above him demanded answers to the contradictions.

"Ted! Stop!" she demanded sharply.

He withdrew his mouth and hands abruptly and surrendered.

"You are just a sexist exploiter of women, aren't you?" She preached the question in a tone he found absurd under the sheets.

He quickly re-examined his convictions again. In his heart he knew he was willing to accept women as equals. Different, but equal. To deny difference was as unjust and absurd as to deny equality. Value had to be identified, balanced, weighed. A piece of steak and beans with rice were different, though he had read somewhere, probably in one of Anna's texts about the capitalist food chain, that their nutritional value was equal. "I don't think so," he replied simply.

"Perhaps not, but what are you going to do to help correct the injustice?"

He wanted to ask why it was his fight. He wasn't a woman. It seemed that if indeed they were equal to the task and "held up half the sky," that they did not require a man's help to achieve recognition. When women relied on themselves alone to achieve the goal of their liberation, they would succeed. They might find freedom lonely though. "I cannot help you, Anna."

Her eyes turned down and her face grew stormy. "I do not want your help. I do not need your help. I have already achieved a breakthrough in my consciousness. You are the one who is blind to suffering."

Ted sat up and pulled on his underwear. "Anna, Anna," he said with resignation, "I have thought about the things you've said. I do sympathize with all the unhappy people. But I don't agree with you enough about why they are unhappy. And I especially don't feel guilty or responsible for their plight. If you want to right the world, you can do more with your time than try to jack me around. Give up all this, donate it to somebody who needs it, work with poor, pregnant single women. They need your help now. I don't." He stood up and pulled on his pants, then struggled into a tight pullover sweater. "You're wasting your time, and so am I."

Kyu: Conclusion

SEVEN

Ted stood at the head of the luggage ramp, stunned, his eyes wide in horror as the drug-sniffing dog was called from his bag by two security officers who appeared from nowhere. Not being sure he could maintain his composure, he feared his knees would buckle beneath him. The dull, choking pain rivaled that of a punch to the solar plexus. Violence he could cope with. He had proven it to himself that day. But treachery. He fought to believe people would not be so cruel as to trap him this way.

Shifting his focus from the bag to the ceiling and around the arrival hall Ted tried desperately to regain some foothold on the situation, his vision reaching out for the sight of something reassuring, a toehold, a way out. The memory that his name was not on the outside of the bag flashed through his mind. Planning for prevention of another crime had compelled him to use a pseudonym. He took a deep breath low in his stomach and tried to relax his arms and shoulders until they hung loose by his sides. He forced a small smile, turned slowly to face the customs clearance queues, looked at his watch nonchalantly, and proceeded to the customs tables.

He handed the officer his passport and placed his attaché case and the bound wooden box containing the *tanto* on the stainless steel counter.

"Where you come from?" the officer asked, looking at the document.

"Bangkok."

"Anything to declare?"

"No."

"No liquor, cigarettes?"

"Nope."

"OK," the man said waving him through without asking to see the inside of his bag.

"Thank you," Ted said as he picked up his case and walked briskly out the sliding doors and into the crowds of bystanders awaiting returning relatives. He looked at the crowd as they milled about him. Less unruly and better dressed than the hoards waiting for *balikbayans* at Manila airport, but colorful nonetheless. Turbaned Sikh youths walked with their girlfriends while sari-clad Indian matrons tried to control the flocks of children they had brought with them. An arriving Indonesian businessman walked with an attractive woman half his age clinging to his arm. Thais, Malays, Indians, Chinese, and white round eyes all mixed without ever really homogenizing in this most cosmopolitan of cities.

He longed to be a part of the staid sanity for which the city-state was famous, but he knew circumstances had now put him on the other side of the fence. He was a criminal in Thailand, probably wanted for murder, and in Singapore soon to be wanted for drug smuggling, a death-penalty offense. He had to get out of the country.

He walked to the escalator and went up the long ramp, past a waterfall chandelier and onward to the departure lobby. He stared at the huge signboard looking for a suitable destination. Somewhere far away, safe, but perhaps a place where he had contacts. Definitely not Thailand. Best to leave ASEAN entirely. Only one destination stood out as being most appropriate: Tokyo.

He wondered briefly as he proceeded to the Japan Airlines ticket counter whether there was something beyond chance compelling him to go back to Japan. Destiny. He had never really believed in it. He felt men created their own futures, good or bad. But the events of the day had shaken that conviction. He had meant no harm, nothing, to Ital-Siam Exploration, but they were bent on destroying him.

He waited as a balding American tourist and his wife bickered first with the ticket girl and then between themselves about some discrepancy. When they had satisfied their need to quarrel, they left the counter and Ted stepped forward.

"I'd like a ticket to Tokyo on this evening's flight."

"Any reservation?"

"No."

"First class, business, or economy?" she asked as she tapped the computer keyboard, summoning up the flight details.

"Econ."

"We have seats. Name?"

Ted was about to speak out and then paused. He didn't want to use his name. Perhaps he should use his first initial B, last Theodore. Then a thought came to him. His initial reaction was that the idea was too bold, but it might help to signal his innocence. "Brody. Initial B."

She tapped the name in. "Cash or charge?"

Again Ted paused to think about which would be best. He was not used to traveling surreptitiously. If he used his credit card it would be traceable, he realized, and, of course, the names would not match the ticket."Cash. Uh, how much is it?"

"One thousand four hundred and ninety-five dollars."

"U.S.?" he blurted painfully

"Sing dollars."

He breathed a sigh of relief as he checked his passport case and then got the remaining money from his wallet. He had enough with $50 to spare.

"Please proceed to the check-in counter," she said with a smile as she handed his ticket to him.

At the check-in counter there were no passengers waiting because it was still an hour and a half before the flight was scheduled to leave. The attendant took his ticket and again began snapping data into the keyboard.

"Mr. Brody, do you want smoking or nonsmoking."

"Nonsmoking, aisle, toward the front," he said out of habit.

"Do you have a visa for Japan?"

He anxiously remembered that he would have to show her the document, and worse, that Immigration would have to see his boarding pass. "Umm. Yes." He fumbled with his passport, opening it to the page with his visa stamped into it. He extended the document over the counter holding it open to let the girl look.

She took it from him, flipped through the pages and opened to the page with the photograph. She glanced at the picture, at Ted's face, and scanned the data quickly, snapping shut the blue book and handing it back to him.

He took a deep, relaxing breath, trying to ease the tension accumulating in his stomach, and restrained himself from snatching the document.

"Any bag?"

"No," he said as he remembered the boxed *tanto* in his attaché case and started to worry about that.

"Here you are, Mr. Brody. Have a nice trip."

"Yes. I'll try."

Ted went to the men's room and locked himself in a stall. Sitting down, he stared at the black formica door, into its depth, and his nervous bowels erupted suddenly in a round of diarrhea. He knew it was nothing he had eaten. It was only stress. Sitting there in the shadows, in the stench, he began to feel sorry for himself. So far from home, he lamented. Totally alone. I am wanted by criminals, by the law. I have no money and can't use my credit cards. No one can help me, he thought as he lost control, no one loves me, he sobbed silently. His sobbing grew louder as the weight of the day's events pressed in on him, his face in his hands pushed between his knees. "Mieko!" he choked, seeing her face as he had a thousand times since her death, wishing she was with him. The vision departed, leaving him more alone.

Hearing the door to the men's room being pushed open, he realized where he was and the need to contain himself at this critical moment. What would his pursuers do now? Search the airport? They would probably open his suitcase first. He tried to concentrate on the contents of the bag. Was there anything inside with his name on it? He remembered some correspondence from his head office that was sandwiched between catalogs. Hotel laundrys had printed "Bergman" on his collars. So, they would have his name. He had to get through Immigration before they were informed to be on the lookout for him.

He stood up and hitched up his pants. Looking down at the attaché case, he remembered the *tanto*. He didn't want to go back and check it and especially didn't want to have to register it at Narita Airport in Tokyo when he arrived there; that would draw direct police attention to him. He sat down again and put the attaché case on his lap. He opened the lid and looked inside. If he sent the bag through the X-ray machine, the knife would show up. If he carried the blade, the metal detector he would pass through would trip and a body search would reveal the weapon. He examined the lining of the bag. Along the inside back of the case, which was the base when the bag was closed and standing up, was thick cloth material riveted to the top and bottom halves of the base in several places. When the bag closed, this material then became looser, loose enough to accommodate the blade alone.

Ted unpacked the *tanto*. Upon seeing it he felt an unexpected resolve return to his heart. He realized that planning for his escape was calming him. The *tanto* merely reminded him of his training and his ability to remain cool. The first owner of this blade, he thought, could not have been a coward. He had been a samurai when samurai had been men of the sword.

He drew the knife and used its keen edge to cut the cloth liner closely and carefully around one of the rivets on the edge. Using a pen, he pushed out the bamboo pin which held fast the blade to the handle and dismantled the assembly, placing the pin, handle, and plain scabbard in a file folder. The blade alone could now be slid under the cloth in such a place that it would be between several metal pieces of the case's frame. He prayed it would show up on the X-ray as just another part of the luggage. He opened and closed the lid several times, checking to see that the weapon was secure.

Satisfied, he left the stall and discarded the box in which the *tanto* had been packed. Passport and boarding pass in hand, he went through the archway leading to the immigration checkpoint. Not many passengers were being processed and he was able to go straight to a counter. Handing his passport to the clerk, he retained his airline pass, but kept it visible to the inspector who methodically looked at his photo, flipped through the pages of the passport and slipped the arrival/departure form out of the book with a stapler remover. "Boarding pass, please," he instructed, his hand reaching up while his eyes still examined the documents.

Ted put the card into his hand and waited for the worst, sensing it had been unnecessary, and perhaps a bad idea to use a false name on the boarding pass.

"These names aren't the same," the clerk said looking up and pointing out the name on the card.

"What?!" Ted said incredulously. "Let me see." He looked for a moment at the card, thinking fast. "Oh, Jeez! That's my boss' pass, and he's already gone through. The girl at the check-in counter must have mixed them up when she gave 'em back to us."

The clerk looked back and forth several times between the three documents and Ted's face, then pounded the departure chop three times, snapped the book shut and handed it back to Ted, waving him on.

Ted swallowed and closed his eyes for a moment as he turned his back to the immigration officer and headed into the departure mall, hoping the weakness he felt in his knees was not visible.

Bits and pieces of information had been coming in all evening and by dawn Bill Brody felt no closer to determining whose side Bergman was on than he had been at the start.

I meet a guy who emphatically denies any ties to the drug trade and the next afternoon he calls me up and says he's being chased. Two Thais turn up dead and an Occidental answering Bergman's description was at the scene of the crime. Bergman departs for Singapore, and lo and behold Customs discovers two

265

ounces of heroin in his locked bag which suspiciously had someone else's name on the outside.

The thought that he might have ridden in the back of a car with a person who may have played an instrumental role in organizing the distribution of the white powder infuriated Brody. But why would Bergman carry a passport with his real identity if he was a criminal who could afford a false one? And why would he call on me, of all people, for help?

After hearing from Khun Prinsep about the double murder the night before, Brody requested files on Bergman from several government agencies cooperating with the DEA. After getting Bergman's passport number from Thai Immigration he sent the information on to the Justice and State departments. By midnight some facsimile documents began to arrive over the wire. Bergman's record was totally clean. He had never been arrested, suspected, ticketed, or fined. There was no mention of drug- or alcohol-related violations.

Bergman had once interviewed with the Foreign Service but had not shown up for the government service examination. A copy of the résumé he had given the interviewing officer was included in the file. Brody scanned the academic record. Double major at George Washington University, Japanese and business administration. Above-average grades. Worked at a Japanese restaurant, did some oil fieldwork. Even the Petrotools employment checked out. There was no sign that the American was anything but what he had said he was.

But two men were dead and a suitcase had heroin in it.

The phone rang, shaking Brody out of his reverie. He lifted the receiver. "Hello, Brody here."

"Brody, this is Prinsep."

"Oh, g'morning. Got anything for me?"

"Yeah. We dug around and found that old vendor again. Showed him the passport photo of Bergman. He felt it was definitely the one he had seen coming out of the alley."

"So, Bergman did the killing."

"I figure at least one of the guys was killed by him."

"What are you going to do with this?" Brody queried.

"As I said before, these two who died were low life anyway. If you think Bergman moved out of self-defense, I'll try to keep the lid on it while you track him down, find out what the hell happened."

"Remember, I didn't ask you to do it, but I owe you again."

"Forget it. Just try to get a deposition from Bergman and make some sense out of it."

That was just what Brody was trying to do and it did not make sense. When he had been informed over the wire about the seizure at the Singapore airport, he had telexed immediately for details. When he learned that Bergman's files were in the bag with someone else's name, he requested copies of departing-flight-passengers manifests. Bergman had passed through Immigration forty minutes after having entered Singapore. Brody had scanned the seven lists when one name stood out. His own. The flight was the same one Bergman had listed on his departure card, and as his name did not appear on the list, Bergman may have been trying to tell Brody something, or taunt him. Why Japan? Why a one-way ticket?

He remembered something he had seen on the material Chuck Hatch had sent over. He checked the one page again to make sure. Yes, Ital-Siam was part-owned by a Japanese firm. During the night he had run a cursory background check on the firm, finding nothing unusual except the makeup of ownership. Part Italian, part Japanese, part Thai. What a mix! he mused briefly, but then his serious side caught him again. What, if anything, was the connection?

Bergman serves as a liaison for Japan? Then what? He decides he wants a greater percentage and they try to do him in? Or he works for the Italians investigating the cheating going on by the Japanese? Unlikely. Why would he visit Hatch to get a meager bit of information on a company he worked for?

The more he looked at the situation, the more confusing it became. On reflection, he was glad he had made a special request to the Japanese authorities earlier in the evening. If Bergman was clean, he would probably settle down in Japan and make an effort to contact him. If he was the son of a bitch the evidence pointed to, then the tail Brody had asked the Japanese to put on him might be led to something big. Now all he had to do was wait and, despite his fatigue, pay a call on Ital-Siam Exploration.

He hated lines. Especially when the lines had disintegrated into masses of pushing, unruly people. Especially when the pushing, unruly people were dark, sweaty Thais. Soon, at least, he would be back in Japan.

The last eighteen hours had been hell. Of course, it had begun days before when they had first heard of the American "salesman," but yesterday had been a total loss. Thinking he could rely on his bodyguard for the completion of something so simple as the disposal of an American, he had been sorely disappointed. I panicked, he chastised himself in retrospect. I should not have given him a vague order the second time. I should have told him what to do about Bergman. Or done it myself. Instead he did the stupidest thing I can imagine. Character assassination! If they had caught Bergman in Thailand or Singapore, he would have told all about us. And if he was DEA, he would have come down on us like a truckload of shit.

The guard is a total fool to have thought his plan would destroy Bergman.

Was a fool. I'm glad he's dead. When he came back to the office yesterday he must have expected a rebuke. No words could curse his stupidity enough though. Poor man must have been so dense he couldn't keep his shoelaces tied. That is why he fell from the top of those steps, Nishida chuckled to himself, seeing that he was now at the front of the line to check his bags at the airport.

The night before he had called Yamashita from a hotel phone to inform him of the events that had transpired, the European's lack of concern, and Nishida's attempts to eliminate Bergman. He had planned what he would say, but Yamashita, his voice cold and distant cut him off short.

"Do not lie to me, nephew. Nero has already informed the *oyabun* about his concern over the salesman and the action he has taken. It seems you and Suzuki disagreed with Nero over a proper course of action. Did you act independently?" Yamashita said forcefully, his statement an accusation rather than a question.

"Yes," he replied, choking on the word. "We tried to … to eliminate the foreigner."

"Tried?" Yamashita bellowed.

"Yes."

"You failed in an action you should not have taken?"

"Yes."

"What happened?"

"Two men are dead." Three, he reflected, including the body-guard.

"And what happened to the foreigner."

"He has gone to Singapore, but we tried to set him up."

"Tried?"

269

"He did not take his suitcase which had drugs planted in them."

"You failed in another action you should not have taken."

"Yes."

"You will return to Japan immediately."

"Yes," he said, hearing the line go dead.

Recalling the grim tone of Yamashita's voice, Nishida felt a surge of hateful energy push up from his stomach to his brain as he waited in Immigration. He hated Bergman for coming along, for being American, and for escaping his traps. He hated Nero for being right and for being his boss. He hated them both for making him fail his *oyabun*. He was never to be trusted again by his organization, he felt for sure, and might even have to perform some drastic act of penitence even to be considered worthy of living. He knew he would perform as he was told and face whatever punishment was proscribed. If they do not punish me, then I must take the initiative, he vowed stepping through the immigration booth out of Thailand, and on to Japan.

Ted had slept fitfully between meals during the overnight flight from Singapore to Tokyo. It had been a dreamless sleep, which left him feeling more fatigued than when he had first closed his eyes. He prayed he could find some respite from the terror that had pursued him the past twenty-four hours.

He had worried about getting through Immigration, but had not been detained. Against his better judgement, which told him not to look suspicious, he had glanced back at the immigration clerk as he left. The man had called over an officer who went to the booth. I hope that's not about me, he began to fret again.

Without a suitcase to wait for, he had gone directly to Customs. Everyone in the line save himself and a Japanese businessman who stepped in behind him had large bags to be examined.

After waiting for an attractive Chinese girl to have her personal belongings rummaged through, he stepped up to the stainless counter and handed the inspector his passport.

"Where are you coming from?"

"Singapore."

"Anything to declare?"

"No."

"Any liquor, drugs, weapons?"

Normally Ted felt at ease answering the absurd question, but this time his stomach churned. "No," he returned impassively.

"Open the bag."

Ted complied, clicking open the chromed locks and raising the lid, imagining for a moment that the shiny blade would lay exposed. It did not.

"OK," the inspector replied handing back his passport. Ted was too anxious to leave to notice that the businessman behind him was not examined and that, indeed as a Japanese he was in the wrong line.

After exchanging his remaining dollars for yen, he entered the main arrival lobby at Narita and realized he had to decide how to get to Tokyo and where he would go. He had a choice of a taxi, bus, or train, in descending order of expense, so he chose the train. That would get him to Skylines Station in the Ueno section of town, from where he could make some calls.

He threaded his way to the ticket counter through the crowds awaiting arriving passengers. "Ticket for the next train," he ordered in Japanese.

"You get your bus outside to the line station. There you can get your train ticket," the girl answered in English.

He queued up outside behind three old Japanese women returning from a trip abroad, their large, wheeled bags stuffed to capacity with gifts, hardly manageable by them. He let the driver help them with the bags, then stepped on board behind them.

As he sat down in front, he noticed a nondescript Japanese man board after him and sit across the aisle from his place. The man wore a navy blue single-breasted suit, black leather shoes, white shirt, and red and blue tie — a corporate uniform. What caught Ted's attention was that though he was probably only 35, he wore an earphone in his right ear. The wire lead ran close to his neck and disappeared into the collar of his jacket. If it was in both ears, Ted would have assumed it was a compact stereo headset but it did not look like a hearing aid either.

He stared at the man, his face expressionless. The Japanese slowly turned his gaze to Ted, looked him in the Adam's apple, then quickly darted his eyes away. Ted was not sure if he noted a trace of recognition, or fear of recognition, in the man's face, but decided to keep a watchful eye out on him.

The ride to Tokyo on the train was uneventful. Anyone on the bus was necessarily destined for the train, so when the Japanese man in blue followed him down to buy a ticket and board the train, he took no special heed. "If only to keep in practice after yesterday, though," Ted thought, "I'll keep him in view."

Getting off the train in the Ueno section of Tokyo, he walked briskly toward the Japan National Rail station, about five minutes away. Stopping at a phone booth he looked back to see the man in blue enter the corridor and walk toward a ticket machine. Feigning confusion, Ted checked his pockets for change, looked about distractedly, and headed back the way he had come. Halfway back to the Skyliner station, he trotted up some stairs to the sidewalk above and walked to a vantage point behind where the stairs emerged. Several seconds passed and the man in blue ran up looking nervously from left to right.

Ted turned, not letting the Japanese see that he had been spotted, and walked toward a subway station entrance. It was the Ginza line, which he knew would take him close to Mieko's house. As he visualized the residence, he also saw the face he hoped would greet him and a burst of anxiety momentarily flared in his heart. She's dead and you need her father's help, his mind said to his heart, stifling the emotion, but not killing it.

He walked quickly down to the subway ticket machine and looked to see what the fare would be to Shibuya, deposited the coins, took his ticket, and walked through the gate, letting the man there punch his coupon. Then he proceeded to the track going away from Shibuya. A train must have just come because the platform was not as crowded as it should have been at this time of morning. The Japanese with the earphone shortly followed behind and stood in place to board two doors down on the same car as Ted. They stood at each end of where a car would stop.

Ted felt the movement of air before he heard the increasing din of the approaching chain of cars. He was in first in line to board at his door, and when it opened he waited momentarily for the press of people to exit, then pushed his way against the tide of stragglers and turned right, walking through the passageway to the next car.

The man in blue would not be able to see him here unless he pushed his way to the length of the car. Ted waited by the door, looking back through the passageway he had just traversed. He heard the warning buzzer that the doors were about to close as he saw the man look at him through the portal between the cars. He was only ten feet from Ted, but nowhere hear a door. As Ted heard the hiss of the pneumatic drives on the door, he leaped through and it closed fast behind him. He looked over his shoulder into the departing subway to see the frantic man hastily drawing a microphone to his lips to report that he had lost his mark.

Ted realized he had seen this stunt pulled in more than one movie, and the prey would normally smile wryly at the predator and wave as the car pulled away. For him, there was no humor in the situation. He was definitely being followed by someone, someone who was calling to others perhaps not too far away. And he did not know whose side they were on, but it did not really matter now, he lamented.

Business as usual or panic? That's the question that had tormented Nero throughout the evening until he had phoned the brother of the *don*.

"Paolo, Paolo. How are you, eh? Good to hear from you."

"I'm afraid it will not be good to hear from me."

"Eh? Problems? Is it that 'investigation' you mentioned briefly in a fax?"

"Yes. I need your advice, perhaps your permission, too."

"Tell me, simply, what has happened," the elder said cautiously, hinting for Nero to choose his words carefully.

"Our Japanese partner went beyond his authority in his counterinvestigation of a competitor disguised as an American salesman. As a result … as a result several contracts did not pan out and the competitor got back to his source," Nero began, not used to the imperative of burying his meaning.

"Please, explain again," came the bewildered reply.

"Ummm ... my counterpart took the matter into his own hands, and rather than come to a definite conclusion, allowed the problem to get out of hand, literally and figuratively."

"Was this really a problem?"

"I was never sure. But Nishida was determined and now we really have a problem. I wanted to play the scenario out, he wanted to force the hand."

"Where is the problem now?"

"The Japanese thought they could arrest the problem in Singapore. But that apparently did not happen. Now the problem is spreading, we can't really be sure where."

"The Japanese wanted government help in solving this problem?" the man on the other end of the line, 7,000 miles away, asked incredulously.

"They thought the Singapore authorities would execute quickly."

"Bad news travels fast, Nero. Perhaps you should make a trip to Tokyo to cut our losses with the JV partner or see about getting that pig-headed junior reassigned back to street accounting. When the dust settles in Bangkok, you can come back to pick up the pieces or close shop."

"I was hoping you'd say something like that."

"And Paolo, make sure you put our exploration charts and seismic findings in a safe place. We don't want other firms stealing our work."

"I understand. Thank you, Signor Giovanni."

"Give my regards to the Japanese."

"Yes. And my regards to you and your family."

"Thank you. Ciao."

"Ciao."

So the verdict last night had been "panic." But it had to be controlled panic. Not a rout. Not a disorganized sloppy retreat, but a quick evasive move to a relatively safe vantage point.

He called the *oyabun* first, before Nishida. He wanted to make sure the leader of Great Star Construction was aware he had not been remiss in guarding their interests and to confirm he was welcome to make a personal visit. His call was cautiously passed through two intermediaries who did not want to disturb their *oyabun* at night, and finally the older man came on the line.

"Paoro Nero?"

"Yes, sir. Is that you, sir?"

"Yes. How can I help you?"

"I believe Nishida will be calling Japan shortly about some problems we are having. I have tried to be fair and act in your interests, but it seems Nishida and Suzuki have conspired against my express orders and taken on a contract I did not authorize."

"Will 'des business vencha be a success?"

"No. Indeed their contract failed to be completed and the whole enterprise has been put at risk. I cannot report the details to you over the phone. You understand."

"Yes. Yes."

There was a silence while Nero hoped the *yakuza don* would suggest he come to Japan.

"What do you suggest, Mr. Nero?" he finally asked.

"We have several matters to discuss. I think I should fly up to Tokyo tomorrow to cover them with you."

"Yes. I see. It is serious then?"

"Definitely. ... Then I will telex you with my arrival time and flight tomorrow morning?"

"Yes, we will put you up in one of our own hotels."

"Thank you, sir. I look forward to seeing you again. Goodnight."

"Goodnight, Mr. Nero."

It was now tomorrow. Nishida was at the airport, having gone out first thing in the morning. The urgency of his departure worried Nero. He surmised that the bungling thug wanted to get back to his organization first to poison the well prior to Nero's presentation. The treacherous hood would no doubt make up some scenario in which his decisions would have represented the logical choice of actions. But Nero knew this would backfire on Nishida. He had sent several messages to the *oyabun* about the Bergman affair as it had unfolded and his case was further strengthened by the failure of Nishida in his insubordination. Beyond crude, rudimentary treachery, true deviousness required intelligence that Nishida could not claim, Nero considered soberly.

He had booked his seats on the Cathay Pacific noon flight to Hongkong where he would change planes for the Japan Airlines flight to Narita. The tickets would be delivered shortly. His office was yet in disarray as he packed boxes with certain files that he would put in a safe house unknown to others in the organization. He was busy with this task when his secretary interrupted him from the reception area.

"Mr. Nero, there is a visitor here to see you," she said meekly, knowing Nero did not want to be disturbed.

"Can you tell him I can't see him?"

"He is a journalist for a petroleum magazine," she said, handing him the visitor's name card.

Nero thought for a moment. He really did not want to waste his time, but his job was to provide legitimacy for Ital-Siam and if they survived the current crisis, a little press would add to that; not enough to draw a lot of attention, just a blurb to show to snooping bureaucrats and nosy salesmen.

"OK. Show him in," Nero ordered with a wave of his hand.

Nero sat behind his desk and waited for the writer to be ushered in. He was preparing to stand as the man entered the office but his legs failed him as he looked into the unmistakable face of "Wild Bill" Brody.

Stifling his panic, he looked down to some loose papers on his desk to avoid allowing the Thai section chief of the U.S. Drug Enforcement Agency to see his startled look. He picked up the disorganized stack of papers and cleared his choked throat as he tapped the loose sheets together into a neater pile, which he placed methodically face down in the center of his desk pad. These short, mundane, reassuring movements bought him several seconds as his mind raced through awkward conclusions.

The game's up, he asked himself. What the hell is he doing here. I should ask! Of course, it's about that snitch Bergman. I'll kill Nishida if I see him again. And he's not even here to take the heat, that shitty little yellow bastard. But why would Brody present a phony name card if he had a case, Nero realized. Even without an airtight case raids can be made in Thailand. So he has no case! Brody is on a fishing expedition and I am the first one he's going to hang a worm out to. OK. This game I can play. He looked up from his desk and rose to greet the American who had stood patiently there for several moments examining the room, its decor, contents, momentos, and business appliances.

"Mr. ... Blaylocke?" he said, looking down quickly at the card again as he held out his right hand, gripping the agent's hand firmly, pulling him confidently closer to himself, nearer a chair. "Won't you sit down?"

"Yes. Thank you." Brody said as he found the seat next to Nero's desk and put his attaché case on the floor beside him, its tape recorder operating inside. So far he had seen nothing particularly suspicious. The reception was decorated with colorful and dramatic photographs of offshore and onshore oil rigs in various parts of the world. Each photo had a name tag beneath it indicating its Japanese or Italian owner. There were drafting tables in some offices, many large grey filing cabinets used to house blueprint-sized documents and one room with a large refrigerator, several microscopes, and a personal computer.

When Brody had been led into the office, he had seen nothing unexpected at first. Nero looked like an Italian version of a lot of the oil and construction types he had met through the years in Asia. He was tall, well-tanned, and fairly muscular, with large, tawny eyebrows that matched the color of the mat of sun-bleached hair on his chest showing through his open collar. There was a similarity to others in his profession, but the style was definitely Italian. Rather than a large gold I.D. bracelet and heavy diver's chronometer, he wore a thin gold chain around his neck and a more elegant gold Rolex, which Brody guessed was from the Cellini collection. The clothes were well-tailored and well-matched, color, texture, and fit all having been taken into account. The shoes were low-heeled, black leather with narrow toes, cut low around the ankles.

The executive had made him stand for a moment as he imperiously arranged the papers on his desk to establish the rank in the meeting. He can sit and trifle with papers while I stand and wait. "Whose time is more important?" was the implication. Brody understood. Then Nero rose and aggressively shook his hand, propelling him in the direction of the plain, fairly uncomfortable chair beside his desk, not toward the deep cushioned ones in the corner.

279

The only odd thing he saw were several cardboard boxes, full and semi-full, of documents, randomly placed around the room. Packing up something. For disposal? Last year's files? He looked back at Nero as the man sat down again and spoke up.

"Well. What can I do for you, Mr. Blaylocke?" he asked with the half cheerfulness of a man who welcomes but does not want to spend a lot of time at it.

"Mr. Nero, I am sure you've heard of our magazine, *Energy Facts Monthly*," Brody declared, placing a copy of the latest issue on the Italian's desk.

"Yes, of course, but we do not subscribe, I am sorry to say."

"Perhaps later, but I'm not here to sell you a subscription."

"I hope not, good man," Nero chuckled, glancing at his watch, pressing Brody.

"Our winter edition will feature a regional review of exploration, drilling, and supply firms. We have very little data about your company and we think it's in the interests of the industry and your company that we provide some details. Nothing confidential. Business statistics, ownership, exploration capabilities, and territory. That sort of thing."

"I see. Well. I am quite busy this week. I'll tell you off the record that we have had some signs of a substantial gas deposit, but we are conducting more tests. I've got all my people in the field now. That's why it's so quiet here," he said, waving his hands widely, palms up. "If you could leave a list of questions with my secretary, I will see to them as my time permits."

"One question. You do have a lot of lab equipment here; what are the microscopes for?"

"You should know that they're for examination of core micropaleontological samples," Nero chided, playing with the imposter.

"I just wasn't aware of any firms in Thailand doing that sort of work locally," Brody quickly rebutted confidently, hoping to turn the tables on the Italian rather than further reveal his ignorance.

"Actually we have only limited capabilities here. Most work is done by our labs in Italy or Japan."

As Nero completed his explanation, his secretary came to the door, an envelope in her hand.

"Yes, Devine?" he asked, always amused by her chosen name — less so today — but he instantly regretted giving her permission to speak.

"Your air tickets to Tokyo are here. The delivery boy would like you to sign the charge form."

"Oh, yes, all right," he said gruffly, his mood undisguised. "Can't they put this on our account?" He looked back at the man he knew was an agent and added, "I have to attend the board of directors meeting in Tokyo in ten days or so."

Tokyo? Again? Brody thought. Too coincidental. He glanced around the room once more. It was normal for an executive's office, except for the boxes. Nero seemed fastidious, not the type to leave cartons around or embark on a job that would disturb his office setting during normal working hours. He would have planned for the disruption and taken care of filing at night or early in the morning. So this was an unplanned disruption, like his moving out anything incriminating before he heads to Tokyo to either meet or bump off Bergman, for instance.

As for the date of departure, the secretary was probably following her standard procedure to get him to sign the form. The comment about crediting their account could be a ruse. Which meant Nero was actually angered by the fact she had brought the tickets in

281

at an inopportune time. His departure date was imminent, if Brody's line of reasoned suspicion was correct, which meant there was no big gas field about to be plumbed. Someone had to stay and mind the ship after all, he concluded. So it was probable Nero was abandoning ship. But what was the ship's cargo?

"If I can be of further assistance, Mr. Blaylocke, please make an appointment with my secretary," the Italian said, concluding the interview, as he stood up and pointed a friendly hand to the door.

"Yes, of course. I'll ask her now to write down the questions for you to answer. Thank you, sir."

"My pleasure, I'm sure. You can find your way out?"

"Yes. Goodbye," Brody said as he backed out the door. He stopped briefly at the secretary's desk and recited a list of basic questions. He then hurried down to his car which was parked around the corner and in an alley. He anxiously called upon another unit over the radio to establish a lookout post prepared to follow the European and his boxes of files should they move.

He had not been so positive about a hunch in too long a time, certainly since before his wife had been killed. It smelled so fishy he could taste it. Whether or not Bergman was an international drug dealer and murderer, he had to thank him for putting him on the trail again. It was a trail he wanted to track personally, not refer to someone else. He began to consider the difficulties and knew he had some calls to make. It would be a very busy day, the kind of day that would let him forget the ghost of his wife. He thanked God.

Certain he had lost all tails, Ted circled once more through some small scattered lanes in Shibuya. It was a painful journey full of doubt. What right do I have to involve the Yoshidas in this? They haven't seen me in practically ten years. I haven't written them. They may despise me, loathe me. I don't know what they think of me. Maybe they blame me for Mieko's death. They never said so, but they never said anything. The funeral had been so quiet and austere. But perhaps the vicious supposition his own mother had implied was true. It had always strained him in the back of his mind. "I hope you didn't ... do ... anything to that Yoshida girl," she had said after they had learned of the girl's tragic death. "I mean I tried to warn you, but you had to have it your way. Because of this, there's a good chance we'll have to go back to Iowa now." Had he "done anything" to Mieko? Not in the crude way his mother suspected. There was no way she could have been pregnant short of an act of God. Their love had been pure. Although the attraction was also physical, there had been no consummation on that plane. Had their love been too strong or too forbidden that Mieko had not been able to cope with it? He knew she had been worried about the future and whether their parents would condemn the possibility of a marriage. But suicide was so unlike the spirit of Mieko she had shared only with him. God, he loved her, even now.

He had hated his mother ever since she had stained him with Mieko's blood. But perhaps he was stained. There was no way for him to know except by walking up the path that lay ahead of him off the driveway of the Yoshida residence. It was a journey he should have made a decade ago to put Mieko's memory to rest or accept the responsibility and deal with his guilt. But to have carried suspicion, doubt, and veneration for those years had been a toilsome burden.

He steeled himself, looked about once more to make sure there was no one suspicious about, and walked up the driveway. Each step brought more painful memories. The smell of the pine trees and the uneven texture of a stepping stone he had tread on before all flashed through his memory, bouncing off other experiences, the tumult of the past snowballing. He rang the doorbell and waited, the surge of the past playing itself out.

The door opened and a vision stood there, a rapidly growing smile spreading over her face.

"Mie ... Yuko?" Ted exclaimed, confused. The young woman before him was everything he had imagined Mieko would have become, but he had to believe it was the younger sister.

"Takabashi-san!" she cried out, as surprised, and seemingly as happy to see him. "Come in, please," she said in flawless English, taking his hand gently and leading him in, where he reflexively removed his shoes.

Ted was at once ecstatic and taken aback by her touch. Mieko would never have led him into the Yoshida house that way. He looked at all the familiar objects and alcoves that had once been part of a romantic fantasyland for him as he followed Yuko back to her father's *tatamied* study.

"Takabashi-san, what brings you back to Japan after so long?" Yuko asked as they kneeled down together on two sides of a low wooden table.

"An emergency of sorts, I am afraid."

"You came from the United States for an emergency."

"Well ... jeez, it's a long story and ... are your father and mother here?"

"My mother is dead, Takabashi-san. She passed away several years ago. My father is here. I'll call him. He will be surprised to see you," she said, the welcome tone of her voice having changed to imply the surprise was not one her father would enjoy.

She rose to find her father, then paused at the *shoji*. "I have

284

missed you." She was gone.

Ted pondered her words and her grasp of English in his solitude. He had never thought about Yuko except as Mieko's sister and as a part of the Yoshida family. He couldn't say he had missed her. Still her words carried a sincerity he found hard to place. He was also impressed with her unexpected use of English. Her pronunciation, cadence, and structure were all well-measured, better than Mieko's had ever been. Of course, she was eight years older than Mieko had been then, but her speaking was way above average for a Japanese.

He heard Yuko and her father padding down to the hall and stood up on seeing Yoshida enter the room, a look of incredulity on his face, doubting the news Yuko had brought him.

"It is you," he said solemnly. Yoshida looked tired. He had gained weight and the kilos did not sit well on him. They hung in rolls of flesh from his neck, jowls, and waist. His hair was thinning and grey, and wrinkles deeply furrowed his brow. Age spots dappled his forehead and hands.

They sat on the *tatami* while Yuko prepared tea.

"How is your father?"

Ted did not expect this as a first question and found it odd. "Fine, I suppose. I haven't seen him in about a year. He's getting ready to retire soon."

"Your mother?"

"She had some cancer treatment several years back and seems to have come through well enough."

"Mmm." There was a pause. "What have you been doing all these years?"

"I continued studying Japan and took a degree in business. Then I was hired by an American firm and sent to Singapore. I've been there several years, traveling around the Asian region."

"What kind of business?"

"Petroleum tools of various kinds."

"How did you keep up your Japanese?" he asked, a touch of interest in his voice.

"Alas, my Japanese has dwindled, Yoshida-sama," Ted said, humbly expressing the wretchedness in his second tongue.

"You have indeed improved," Yoshida appraised. "But I am not surprised, Takabashi-san. You were always special," he said wistfully, looking through the *shoji* which led to a small deck and his garden. There was silence as Ted watched Yoshida who closed his eyes and lowered his head. The old man shook his head slowly back and forth, regrets welling up and forcing the action. He took a deep breath to control a sob.

"Forgive me if I make you feel unwelcome, Takabashi-san, but you bring back many of the most painful and regretful memories of my life. I find things hard enough to cope with just looking in the mirror or at a familiar object from the past. But to unexpectedly face you after all these years and remember my fatherly hopes then … then everything gone. You will forgive me if I am overwhelmed."

"Yoshida-sama, I am glad we are men now and can share this. There is nothing to forgive. For a decade I have been carrying a chain around my heart tied to the love of an angel. My memories are painful even in their beauty and happiness because I have felt that there will never be that beauty again. We both lost someone dear."

Yoshida now had his eyes closed and his head tilted toward the ceiling, Ted's words entering his mind and exploding as bursts of recollections — fast, bright, and crisp.

"Forgive me that I have come back to you and made you

remember this shared past. I realize now I had a choice yesterday in an emergency to go back to America to see my father for help or to come to Japan to see you. I came here. Please, take that to mean what you will."

Knowing of your sorrow has made mine even deeper, Yoshida thought. "What is your emergency?"

"It is a long and involved story. I will let you know first, in fairness to you, that I am probably being hunted by the police. My problem is so terrible: murder, drugs, *yakuza*."

Yoshida looked toward the young man at the sound of the word for "gangster" and the constant fear that had raked at his heart for so many years sunk its claws deeper. They had taken his dignity. They had taken his daughter, and still they had managed to acquire controlling interest in Tokaido Trucking. Like *Noh* puppet masters dressed in black, the color of darkness, they hid behind him and controlled his arms and legs and mouth. His father despised him. His wife had died rather than live with him. He was a man totally alone. His daughter stayed with him and served him, but she could not love him. Perhaps she even hated him. And now here was this young man he had enjoyed so much and the *yakuza* had been mentioned. He could only listen to Ted's story and hope that more misery was not in store for him.

"Tell me how you are involved," Yoshida ordered quietly.

Ted told them everything he could remember in as much detail as he could. How he had learned of Ital-Siam. How he had investigated them and finally gone to see them, and the two Japanese he saw there. He stopped from time to time to gather his thoughts. Yoshida asked him the name of the Japanese he had met.

"The senior fellow was maybe five years older than me. He was missing the end of his little finger. His name was Nishida Yoshikazu."

287

For a brief flash Ted thought he saw recognition of the name in Yoshida's eyes. Yuko looked at her father, her lips pursed.

"Continue with your story."

He told them what the Japanese had said, about his being stalked and about killing two assassins. Finally, he told them about his surprise at the Singapore airport and his flight to Japan, along with the tail he had eluded on the way from Narita airport.

"You have not reported this to the police?"

"No. Well, I called Brody up when I was being followed in Bangkok, but I couldn't give him any details and I couldn't call him back. I want to get in touch with him to try to prove my innocence."

"Of course you do," Yoshida said, and sat thinking. If Yamashita ever found out that he knew Ted, there would be hell to pay. Of course, he might be able to use the information. Get something back from Yamashita. In return for what? Well, Ted didn't have to get hurt. He could keep the *yakuza* just behind the American. Cooperate but not quite fast enough. That, not to mention the fact that he could use his knowledge of the whole affair to extort concessions from the dogs who had tormented him so long. Perhaps this was just and balanced anyway. After all, it was Ted's father's inability to arrange financing that had caused this whole chain of unfortunate events that had befallen his family. Yes, he would have to call on Yamashita.

"I think you should stay here tonight," Yoshida said. "Let's not call the authorities just yet. I think you should have some time to get some rest and collect yourself."

Ted breathed a sign of relief. "Thank you, Yoshida-san. I knew you would understand. Besides, I have no money to put up in a hotel with."

"Yuko, can you take care of Takabashi-san for a while? I have some business calls to make. Then we can spend more time together." Yoshida got up.

"Yes, father," she said emotionlessly.

When her father had left she turned to Ted and slid closer to him on the *tatami*.

"Takabashi-san, let me change and get my sweater and purse. I think we should take a walk," she said quietly.

"I don't think it's a good idea to go out on the street."

"Do not argue with me, Ted. Just wait here a moment," she ordered firmly as she rose. It was a firmness he did not expect and she had called him Ted. He had never been called Ted by them. He was left to sit alone and bewildered with his thoughts.

Shortly, Yuko reappeared. She carried a voluminous shoulder bag of natural soft tanned leather, and wore a baggy sweater with wide shoulders that rounded her form. The top three buttons were not clasped and he became aware that she was wearing a low-cut tank top under the sweater and no bra. Her pleated silk pants broadened her hips and accentuated her very feminine curves.

"Let's go quietly. Don't forget your briefcase," she said, pointing to the bag he had left by the *shoji*.

He picked it up and followed her quietly into the hall, slipped his shoes on, and went out the front door without a sound, confused, and upset.

"You know what I've been through the past six months!" Brody shouted down the long-distance phone connection to Washington.

"Bill, cool your jets. It's precisely because I know what you've been through that I don't want you to go. I don't want you up there light years away from your post chasing down an improbable lead. You're just anxious about this, grasping at straws."

"I'm rational. The lead is solid and we're getting more information right now. But I want to be in this investigation. I need to be. Can you appreciate that?"

"I want you to demonstrate that you are in charge of yourself," his superior added forcefully.

His assistant walked into the room carrying a message which he handed to Brody. "Wait a minute, I've just got something."

Brody read the message. The contents would normally have enraged him, but he was ecstatic as he lifted the receiver back to his mouth. "OK, I'll ignore your last comment. Listen to this. The guy who tipped me off on all this, the guy I was having followed in Japan."

"Yeah."

"He lost his tail. Very slick, very professional. They don't know where he is."

"That's another thing that bothers me about this, Bill. You won't tell me this guy's name. That's not like you."

"I got to protect my source," he said lamely.

"Come on! A murderer. You know I can find out the guy's name from half a dozen places by now."

"OK, OK. But they lost him."

"And you can find him."

"Yes."

"How?"

"He called me and told where to meet him," he lied.

"What?" his boss whined. "You didn't tell me before."

"I wanted to see if you'd go to bat for me on this one. You really let me down, Joe," he said, trying to appeal to his senior's paternal management sense.

"OK, you listen, Brody. Head up to Tokyo and report in to our office as soon as you get there. No messy street tactics, right? If the case has developed further by that time, I'll let you go for it. Otherwise, it's vacation time. Hope you like touring Japanese shrines."

"This is a big one, Joe. I can feel it. Thanks."

"Yeah, yeah," the man in Washington said, winding down. "Where is this American fellow held up anyways?"

"Jeez! Joe, there's no time to catch the last flight out of here. I'll call you from Tokyo. Bye," he said hurriedly, hanging up. Brody took a deep breath. He was going off the deep end. He had to get in better control of the situation. He had to find Bergman. He called his assistant in.

"Where's the Italian now?"

"On the road. He loaded some boxes in the trunk of his car. You were right."

"Good. That makes me feel better. Keep a tail on him. If he drops the boxes anywhere, have an agent there. Then, keep following him."

"We know where he's going."

"What?" Brody asked, puzzled.

"I'm sorry. You were right. He's booked on the noon flight to Tokyo."

"Good, good. Make sure he gets on the flight and arrange with the Japanese authorities for observation. Not the kind of muffed-up job they did with Bergman."

"Right. Anything else?"

"I'm going to try to dig a little deeper into Bergman's background. See if I can't find out where he's likely to be in Tokyo. If I need you to take over for me before I hit the airport, I'll let you know."

"Ho-kay," his assistant said breezily. "I wish I had your instincts," he added admiringly.

"Shit. If I'm wrong, it's my ass and you know it."

"Yeah, but you're not," the younger man said confidently as he left the room.

Brody desperately wanted to share the young man's confidence. He was way out on a limb and it was not only his job status that would suffer if he was wrong. He feared for his sanity. The circumstances, like pieces of a broken plate, fit so well together. He thought he could begin to see the outline of the reality like the form of the plate. But pieces were missing: a hole here, a gaping shard left off the edge there. It was not yet a functional hypothesis; it was still a broken plate with missing pieces. Still he found himself trying to will the missing pieces into place.

This was not good investigation, it was wishful thinking. It was a wish fueled by the fire of revenge that had consumed him for months, eating away at his heart with each small failure, each dead-end. Finally, by accident, he had been led into this path. But perhaps it was a trap for him. He had not even considered that. That would explain why Bergman had come to the embassy. But his meeting with Bergman had been chance, an accidental acquaintance that occurred through Chuck Hatch. Or had it been accidental? His mind raced through the options suspiciously. Maybe Hatch is one of them, he considered, remaining momentarily incensed by the thought. His rationality caught this line of inquiry and froze it. If Hatch is part of this, I'll deal with it later. The first step, friend or foe, is Bergman.

He lifted the phone and, looking down at Bergman's eight-year-old résumé, dialed the Iowa phone number that was at the top of the page.

"Hello," a woman's voice answered the phone.

"Hello, Mrs. Bergman?"

"Yes. Who's speaking, please."

"This is William Blaylocke speaking. I'm calling about your son, Ted," he said, using the false name to avoid any repercussions.

"Teddy?"

"Yes, ma'am," he said officiously, hoping to increase her anxiety, counting on it to get the information he needed.

"Oh, dear, has something happened to him?"

"I'm afraid so, but you can help me if you can give me some information."

"What do you need? His blood type, what?" she asked, flustered.

"No, ma'am, he's not hurt, yet. But he's become a factor in a drug investigation ..."

"Oh my God," she gasped.

"And if he's innocent, I need to know how to find him."

"Well, he sent us an itinerary. He always does."

"No, ma'am. He has made a sudden unplanned trip to Japan. Can you think of any reason he would go there? Anyone he would contact?"

The mention of that country's name brought back more painful memories than Sarah cared to face at the moment. Her son's seduction by the culture, the devious and unfair ways they did business that had resulted in her husband's recall and disgrace, and the unhappy circumstance of the Yoshida girl's promiscuity and subsequent suicide that had shattered her boy's life.

"Mrs. Bergman ... are you there?" Brody called across the

293

silent connection.

"Yes. Umm ... there is a place he would probably go. The only place I can think of. My husband's previous business contact. A man called Yoshida something or other."

"You wouldn't happen to have the whole name and address, would you?" Brody pried, the surname alone being useless.

"Let me ask my husband," she said as she put her hand over the phone and silence ensued again. Brody waited.

Another voice took over the line, "Who is this?"

"Mr. Bergman?"

"Who is this?"

"William Blaylocke here."

"And who are you?"

"Interpol."

"Where?" he asked brusquely.

"Asian section chief," he said impatiently, "Mr. Bergman. Your son's suitcase was found with heroin at the Singapore airport. As you may know, that carries the death penalty there, and he rather deftly eluded the authorities and escaped to Japan. I have reason to believe he's innocent and I'm trying to help him, but ... I need your cooperation now."

"Why do you think he's innocent?" the father asked.

What kind of a man would rebut his son's presumed innocence, Brody wondered as he said, "He called me from Bangkok and said someone was after him. Later several men were found dead and your son was reported at the scene of the crime."

"How?"

"How what?"

"How were they killed?"

"One with a knife, one with bare hands."

"Hmmph," Thomas snorted.

"So where can I get in touch with your son? You are not obligated to tell me, but I am trying to help him."

"It sounds so preposterous. But it won't hurt, I guess. Let me get the address."

Thomas returned to the phone after a short interval. "Are you in Japan now?"

"No."

"I'll give you the phone number first."

"The whole address and phone if you have it."

Thomas gave the complete address to him.

"Does anyone at the Yoshida house speak English," Brody queried.

"Yes. Yoshida Tsuji does. I don't know if you'll find him at the office or at his house."

"You've been very helpful, Mr. Bergman. I 'll do my best to get to the bottom of this."

"Thank you, Mr. Blaylocke. If Ted phones us, I'll tell him you called."

"Please. Good day."

"Yamashita. This is Yoshida," he said, a touch of defiance in his voice as he dropped the formal verbiage he had resorted to for so many years and addressed the mobster as an equal.

Yamashita was taken aback by the unexpected phone call and even more so by the insolent tone in the *eta*'s greeting. "Yes, Yoshida. Why are you bothering me?" He had so many more important things on his mind than to talk to an unreliable debtor. His head was on the block over the Ital-Siam debacle and he was anticipating Nishida's arrival at the airport in several hours. He would roast his bungling subordinate's testicles on a skewer if no good explanation was forthcoming.

"I have something you want very badly."

"The remaining interest in Tokaido Trucking?"

"No. As a matter of fact, you will have to return your shares of Tokaido Trucking to me in order to get what I have."

"Speak quickly and politely, you defective, or you will join the carcasses hanging in your cold storage."

"Hmmph. I am not scared. Without my company, my family, and my dignity, my life has little meaning anyway. But what I do have will mean much to you if it is kept silent."

"Speak up about this silence before I hang up."

"Let me first say that everything I know about I have recorded and it will be distributed to the authorities and the papers both Japanese and Western, should anything unhappy befall me or any member of my family." He hoped the lie would hold. He continued, "You have business operations in Thailand."

Thailand again! "We have business all over the world."

"I am referring to a specific business, a very dirty one. You know the one."

"We don't get involved in dirty business. What makes you think there is anything illegitimate about any overseas operations we may have."

"The fact that an animal of a man is in charge. You know the one. Your nephew, Nishida Yoshikazu. The one who defiles children."

Yamashita was enraged and he could feel the blood rising to his head, his lower lip trembling. His rage was twofold: the insolence of the *eta* to address him and his nephew in such familiar, insulting language and by the chain reaction caused by Nishida's stupidity that was already reverberating back to Japan. But how could Yoshida know anything about it? "He has traveled to Southeast Asia as a tourist on occasion. That's a matter of record and no crime."

"Perhaps the name Ital-Siam will remind you. The name should recall something about smuggling, and about a twice-failed effort to murder an American just yesterday."

Yamashita's hopes that the *eta* knew nothing of substance faded. He could not deny the man knew everything, but how had he found out?

"The source of your information is as defective as you."

"I think not. I have the American you seek."

"Seek, have? We are searching for no one."

"Ask Nishida when you speak to him if he would like to see Bergman again."

"Suppose he has a need to meet with this Bergman. What will it cost?"

"Nothing you have earned. I want all shares of Tokaido Trucking back unconditionally, my debt to you totally erased, and a guarantee against reprisals. All documented in advance through legal channels."

"I don't suppose this American is with you now."

"He is away at a safe place," Yoshida lied. "There is no use searching for him, but I can lead you to him at any time."

"I will ask Nishida if he would like to arrange an appointment. By the way, did the American say whether he had discussed this supposed affair with the authorities."

"As a matter of fact, he has not."

"We may be more amenable to your offer if that remains the

case," Yamashita calculated. Perhaps the whole mess could yet be contained, Bergman quietly disposed of off a rocky beach in Shikoku, or perhaps bumped accidentally in front of an oncoming Shinkansen. The thought of dealing with the *eta* to accomplish this disturbed him thoroughly.

"I await your call. But don't delay. I might find more pleasure in going public with this and dying honorably than getting my company back. Do you understand?" Yoshida asked imperiously. He heard nothing but the sound of a telephone receiver being gruffly hung up.

Yoshida smiled faintly and drew a deep breath as he hung up the phone. It is done, he thought. Now all he had to do was contain Ted for a little while. If the *yakuza* would deal with him, then so be it. Once he got back his company, he could tip them off on Ted's prearranged whereabouts. Of course he would tell Takabashi-san at the same time that he heard the *yakuza* were after him and give him a sporting chance to get away. But the *yakuza* would discover where he had been too late. Yes, this will work. If they don't want to deal with me, then we go to the authorities. I have nothing to lose by that either.

He stood up and stretched his legs, rolling his shoulders once. Despite the kilos he had put on, he suddenly felt lighter. He padded down the hallway in his stockings to rejoin Ted and his daughter. He had many questions to ask, many answers to obtain to strengthen his negotiating position with the gangsters. He could spend the whole night loosening up the American, perhaps get him drunk — that would let him sleep long and well — anything to give Yamashita time to get very worried and call back.

Reaching the *shoji* leading into his study, he became aware of an alarming silence. No talk, no sipping tea sounds, no knees shifting place on *tatami*, no breathing. Sliding open the screen quickly and peering into the empty room, the silence was the worst thing he had ever heard.

The thunderous ring of a telephone shook him from his panic. He reached for the receiver, hoping that Ted and his daughter would come back through the front door at any moment, a neighborhood stroll concluded.

"Moshe moshe?"

"Person to person call for Mr. Yoshida Tsuji."

"Speaking."

"Your party is on the line; go ahead." the operator said to an unannounced caller.

"Mr. Yoshida Tsuji?" the American voice asked. It was not a voice he recognized.

"Yes."

"I tried to call you at your office but they said you were at home today."

Most days, Yoshida thought sadly. "Yes. Who is speaking?"

"This is William Blaylocke. I am looking for Ted Bergman and I was told you might know where he is?"

"Bergman!" Yoshida gasped, letting his astonishment slip out.

Brody heard the unwelcome surprise in the man's voice. "Yes, a young American. He said he was going to Tokyo and asked me to contact him through you."

"Regarding?"

"I am at the American Express office in Bangkok. He had some traveler's checks stolen along with his passport," Brody improvised. "He didn't have the check numbers or purchase receipts so it took some time to get his refund processed. There's still one or two questions though. Can you have him call me?"

"If I see Ted Bergman, I will tell him you called."

"Thank you. Can you think of anyone else he might contact. Where can I reach him?"

If I knew that, I wouldn't be in the mess I'm in, the Japanese man's mind railed. "I'm sorry. But I really don't know where he is now."

Hearing the man add "now" to the end of his sentence, Brody felt an opening. "But you have seen him today," he pried.

"Ummm. No. He has not been here," Yoshida said lamely.

"Thank you again, Mr. Yoshida."

"Yes. Goodbye."

Hanging up the phone, Brody turned toward his assistant. "Bingo. The guy's gotta be lying. You got my tickets ready for Tokyo."

"Yep. They'll be at the airport waiting."

"Good. Get your hands on those boxes of the Italian's. Any pertinent information should be faxed to me in Tokyo. But I need it by tomorrow morning. OK?"

"Will do."

"Good. Then I'm off," Brody said picking up his attaché case.

"Hey! Good luck! You're on the right track."

"Thanks. See you when it's all over."

"Yuko, what's this all about?" Ted questioned after a long, fast walk that had winded him, not her.

"You are not safe in our house. That is all I can say now."

"But I just got here. How can it be dangerous for me?"

"Takabashi-san, do not ask questions now which I will answer when we have reached a safe place," she commanded. "You said you are low on money?"

"Yes, I have less than 10,000 yen?"

"I have brought all my cash, enough for several days at least. But I'd feel better if we had more to work with. Let's go to the bank."

Ted thought for a moment, his mind made clearer by the show of strength of the woman with him. "I can use my credit card to get a cash advance."

"Would that be risky?"

"I used my real name coming into the country."

"And you were followed."

"Yes, but I lost them."

"If they were *yakuza*, we want to keep them lost. If they were police, also better to keep away from them. How long does it normally take to get your money?"

"Twenty minutes at the most. For a small amount, less than $500, it's even faster."

"That should be enough. You have a VISA card?"

"Yes."

"Good. That's accepted at my bank. Now listen to my plan."

As they walked into the bustling core of the Shibuya section of Tokyo, Yuko told him what they would do. As they neared the bank, she directed him. "You go in that door. Don't look at me once we go in."

"Right."

They separated. She went to the cash dispenser, inserted her card, keyed in her code number and withdrew 250,000 yen. The money came out in a steady brown stream of twenty-five crisp 10,000 yen notes. She put them in her wallet and went into the bank lobby. She found a seat on a lounge sofa and began to read a magazine. She saw Ted fill out an application form, sign it, and give it to the girl at the counter for approval along with his passport. She examined the travel document and handed it back to him, taking the card and form to her supervisor, giving him a red numbered disc in exchange. Ted looked at his watch. Five minutes elapsed and Ted began to get anxious.

Yuko could see no unusual activity taking place at the supervisor's desk. Ted's card number had been keyed into a computer pad and the man awaited confirmation. No calls had been made. Then his phone rang. Yuko craned her neck to see what his facial expression was as he received the call. The man stood up as if being addressed by a superior and his head bobbed up and down in sync with the chorus of yeses he gave the caller. She decided this was probably not about Ted. The man hung up the phone, looked down at the LED display on the credit card monitor, scribbled a code number on the form, and called the teller over to collect the documents.

Ted was relieved to see her returning. It had been nine minutes and with each passing minute he had expected the bank guard to be called over to detain him. He collected his card and money and thanked the teller as he stood up and walked out the front door to meet Yuko at the street corner.

"Good," she said as he approached her. "Now, let's get out of here." They walked quickly to subway station one block away and descended into the fluorescent world of the underground trains.

"Buy a ticket to Shinjuku," she said as she pulled out her monthly rail pass.

"Wouldn't it be easier to just take the JNR?" he asked, referring to the more direct surface train.

"No, we go indirectly. Buy the ticket."

302

They continued on to the platform. There were several dozen people waiting along its length. He saw her look at each one and his eyes followed hers. When the people waiting had been examined, she looked to the steps they had used. Each arriving commuter was scanned. The rush of wind preceding a train began to play with her fine, straight black hair. Ted looked at her as she brushed a wisp out of her face with her hand. She glanced at him and gave him a brief smile as she chuckled to herself, then resumed looking at the steps.

When the train stopped Ted moved to step in, but she touched his arm and gently restrained him.

"We wait."

The platform cleared completely and the train doors closed.

"OK, we can take the next train."

Ted then understood her motive. Anyone who could have followed them down had gotten on the train. There was no one remaining, no enemies. He smiled at her, admiring her foresight.

They got on the next train and went four stops to Akasakamitsuke where they changed for a line toward Shinjuku. Emerging into the skyscrapers and sunshine beside the Mitsukoshi department store, she asked him brightly, "What's for lunch?"

"Mmm," Ted thought for a moment. He had not had a chance to even consider the growing hunger he felt in his stomach. And it had been so long since he had been in Japan. There was so much food to enjoy: where to begin? He realized that some calm had returned to his stomach since the night before in Singapore. He willed himself not to begin worrying about his situation anew and said, "I'll leave it to you. I could eat a horse."

Yuko thought for a moment and said, "I think there's a restaurant down this street that has horse *sashimi*," as she began to walk in the indicated direction.

Raw horse? Ted had not indulged in that when he had lived in Japan before. "I was only joking! How about tempura?"

"Fine." She changed direction and they walked down a side street next to the department store. They passed an American ice cream store, and two hamburger restaurants on the way to a small tempura shop on the corner. Japan had certainly changed its eating habits in his ten-year absence. They went in and were led upstairs by an old woman in a dark blue kimono. They found their seats overlooking the street of boutiques and fast-food restaurants below.

"Don't you think it would be better to get off the streets and into a hotel or something?" he asked her.

"We'll go there next. It's too early to check in unless we pay extra. Anyway we have to eat," she smiled. "Why don't you order?"

He placed an order of a large mixed plate of tempura served with *sashimi*, pickled vegetables, rice, and soup. She ordered the same.

"So, Yuko, what have you done with yourself all these years?" he asked, looking across the wooden table at the young woman who so reminded him of his lost love.

"No, you first. I want to know everything you have done since I last saw you."

"Not much," he smiled, looking down at her.

"Please. I'm sure your life has been filled with adventure ... and romance."

He looked up at her again and tried to understand the intensity of the eyes that looked at him.

"Where do I start? I went back to the U.S., I entered college. Studied what I wanted. Got the kind of job I thought would suit me, sort of. I've done it well and I've been paid pretty well. But there's no upward mobility, I'm afraid."

"But you travel everywhere in Asia. Surely you must have a lot of stories to tell."

"Actually, the one I told you and your father is the most dreadfully exciting thing. I wish it was just a story."

"We'll work it out," she said.

"What about you! I just can't believe how you've grown ... and your English!"

She shook her head, dismissing the compliment. "I have no special achievements. I am waiting really. Waiting for the right opportunities."

"To do what? What have you been doing?"

"I helped my mother as best I could when Mieko died, but it was more than she could bear. She gave up living. She told me she wanted to join Mieko and leave my father ... . Takabashi-san, I'd really rather talk about this later," she finished, her face stony.

"Yes, let's talk of something more cheerful."

"Mmm. I guess you have kept up your training from the Butcher?"

How did she know, or remember that, he wondered. "Yes, I suppose so. Actually I became quite good during college. But when I went to work it sort of fell by the wayside. I kept hoping that I could find a way to restore my devotion to it, but something was missing. I grew tired, I guess."

"But it is all still there. All your skill." It was not a question.

The food arrived and they ate silently. Ted was famished and the crispy fried shrimp and vegetables were better than he had ever found outside Japan. The contrasting flavors, texture, and temperature of the raw fish, with its stinging green radish paste, was also a welcome delight. Finishing off his rice with the soup and pickles, he found himself sated.

305

"You look tired, Ted," Yuko said. "Let's go now."

He settled the bill and they walked out onto the busy street.

"Follow me. We're going to a fairly new hotel I've read about. It's interesting. Fully automatic."

He walked with her down the crowded sidewalk, drinking in the sights of the new satellite city within Tokyo. The shopping area gave way to a vista of elegant skyscrapers set graciously apart from each other. Some were hotels, some were office buildings. They walked up to the base of a tall, pure-white building with rounded ends and a flared waist.

Entering, they proceeded by elevator to lobby level. Yuko walked uncertainly for a moment, then saw the check-in computer panel and went directly toward it. He stood by her as she typed in a name. She had not used her real name but had chosen Matsuda Naoko. She typed in a request for a room with two single beds. The tariff flashed on the screen. She slid yen notes into a slot and was given a magnetic key card which also contained coded information regarding how much she had deposited, how much time was remaining, and her name. The room number, 3117, had been printed on the paper card, which was shaped like a short ruler.

"Let's go!" she said.

"That's it? No reception counter or anything?"

"That's it. We're paid up for four nights."

We? It was the first time it had occurred to him that she was going to stay with him. A flush of sexual energy suddenly made him somewhat weak and he chastened himself for thinking such things. I must have misunderstood what she meant, he thought.

"Do you mean … I mean, umm, are you staying here? Too?" he stammered, flustered as they got alone in the elevator and pushed the button for the thirty-first floor.

306

She turned to him without a blush and said earnestly, "Yes. I can't go back to see my father now. I will tell you why shortly."

"But if I'm wanted by the law, I don't want you to get into trouble."

"I won't. You'll just tell them you picked me up at a restaurant and we've been spending time together; just a stranger, you see."

It can't be what you're thinking, Ted's internal dialogue railed. If she's here just for a lay, then she hasn't been listening to the kind of trouble I'm in. I mean, getting laid wouldn't be bad, just the timing is poor. She must have another reason. Why all the secrecy?

She put the paper key in a slot and pulled it downward slowly until the click of the lock's solenoid indicated the door could be opened. They walked into a tiny nine-by-twelve-foot cubicle with two beds, a small desk equipped with a clock and radio, a small color television, a refrigerator, a built-in closet, and a tiny prefabricated plastic bathroom.

"All the comforts of home," Ted joked, "though I'm glad we're traveling light."

She looked at him with only his attaché case and snickered. "Yes, But a little too light. I want you to stay here. Shower up, get in the *yukata* and go take a nap. You must be exhausted. I'm going back to the shopping area to get you some things you'll need."

Ted looked at her as she left and closed the door behind her, shaking his head. What a remarkable woman, he thought, turning to the tasks she had assigned him.

Four men. They sent four men to meet me, Nishida thought. He squinted his eyes through the crowd of greeters to see who they were as he pressed on toward them. One was definitely Omori; his great bulk and hands the size of small bushes were unmistakable. Good. I know Omori. The second looks like Watanabe. Just muscle, no command. The third was ... his luck was with him. It was Suzuki's younger brother. The fourth he did not know. So, Yamashita must not have totally given up on him. He had sent friendly soldiers to pick him up. Good. Perhaps things were not so bad after all.

When Nishida reached them, they collectively bowed elaborately in their Great Star ritual and then again individually as he greeted each one, save the fourth younger man, by name.

"And who is this?" Nishida asked, arms akimbo, smiling at the new face.

"Tanaka-san, at your service, Nishida-sama," the man replied, bowing. Nishida gave Tanaka a short bow, a nod really, as he smiled approvingly at the man's obeisance.

"Nishida-san," Omori said. "We have a car waiting."

They walked out into the darkening sky around Narita and as they approached the curb, a black limousine pulled up, the symbol of Great Star Construction on its doors.

Nishida sat in back with Omori and Watanabe while Suzuki and Tanaka got up front with the driver. There was a partition separating front and back that gave them some privacy.

"Thank you for coming tonight," Nishida began.

"It is as it should be."

"It's nice to be back in Japan, if only for a few days," he said looking out the window. "Back to civilization."

"Soo, life in Bangkok is not paradise?" Omori asked, a lascivious grin on his face.

"Good and bad, up and down, but it's not Japan."

"But you like the up and down part," Omori laughed, thrusting his right index finger repeatedly through a circle made by his left

308

thumb and index finger.

"You sex-crazed *sumitori*," Nishida laughed, referring at once to Omori's size and fabled libido. "It is occasionally entertaining."

"*Soo des neh*. I had the good luck to be assigned to orientation for one of the women you had recruited. Lovely! Breasts like melons, a twat like a hot rabbit, and no end to her excitement. We played for hours!"

"What was her name?"

"I don't know her real name. We gave her the name 'Tropical Pond.' Inviting guests for a 'swim,' neh."

"I hope you enjoyed her."

"Yes, yes. Nishida, why are you back?"

"Because a fox of an Italian Mafiosi has been trying to subvert our activities."

"Is he the one that's coming in tonight?"

"Must be. Nero?"

"Yes."

"Coming to tell lies to the *oyabun* about us. It's really a disgrace that he should even be allowed to come and go ... unless it's in a burial shroud."

"Nishida, this man is your enemy?"

"He is our enemy."

There was silence in the car as it sped down the highway toward Tokyo. The men in back were all thinking about enemies, and friends, and the value and power of belonging to an organization such as theirs.

"Where am I to be put up?" Nishida asked breaking the silence.

"The Biwa Cruise Hotel," Omori replied, referring to a love hotel they owned shaped like a cruise ship.

"And the Italian? Not with me I hope?"

"No. He will be closer out to Narita side."

"Good. Where?"

"Castle of Romance."

Appropriate place for the Count to stay, he thought, and then asked, "Can you trust your men?"

"Completely."

"And can I trust you?" he added.

"Totally."

"I think it would be best to eliminate the Italian before the dawn."

"It can be done."

"It must be done very naturally. No one must suspect."

"Yes."

"We don't need a murder investigation, neh," he said hating to have to ask others to do his bidding again, still smarting from the mistakes he had made over the last several days, and yet unable to do the work himself.

"Yes."

"Can you do this for us?"

"Yes."

"Perhaps an opening will be coming up in Bangkok I could recommend you to, neh?" he said, smiling.

"I will try to live up to your confidence. He will not see the dawn, naturally."

Ted awoke with a start as he felt a soft touch on his cheek and heard the words, "Teddy, wake up." Blinking his eyes several times, he raised his groggy head, uncertain of where he was or what time it

310

was. It was dark outside and in the soft light he saw a young woman. Focusing his eyes, he started to remember everything.

"Yuko?"

"Yes."

"What time is it?"

"Seven o'clock."

"When did you get back?"

"Over an hour ago. I just sat watching you sleep as the sun went down."

"Exciting, huh."

"Yes," she answered, her eyes widening. "I've got you some things here," she said, putting several large shopping bags on the bed as she sat down next to him. "I hope they fit."

She pulled out a dark green, baggy pullover sweater, a fashionable blue jean jacket with many pockets, several pairs of brightly colored socks, one package of undershorts and -shirts, three flannel shirts, and a pair of baggy khaki pants with a drawstring top. In another bag was a pair of dark canvas shoes with rubber soles.

He tried on the shoes first. "Yep. Just right. How did you know?"

"I checked your shoes at our house."

He shook his head in wonderment. "I don't think the rest of the clothes will be a problem. They're all cut pretty full."

"Yes, it's the fashion here among young men. I suppose they wish to make the most of their slight physiques. And I think you should blend in."

She took out another bag. In it were black, heavy-framed plastic sunglasses, hair dye, and some styling gel. "We'll use this later. And then, no more Ted Bergman. When I am finished you may even pass for an *ainoko*," she laughed referring to children born of Japanese/Western parentage.

"Jeez, it's 7 o'clock! I wanted to call Brody. It's 5 there now."

"Teddy. Wait. It is time for us to talk and you may still want to call Brody tomorrow morning after you hear what I have to say. Then again you may not want to call him."

"OK," he said, leaning against the padded headboard as she lifted her legs up on the foot of the bed and put her large leather bag between them.

"I don't know how to begin."

"I have no idea what you are going to say, so you'd better start at the beginning."

"There's so much, and several different stories. I don't want to burden you with them all, but I feel I must."

He nodded for her to continue.

"Life has been very difficult since Mie-chan died. My mother was shattered. I told you this before. My life was shattered, too, but for a different reason." She paused. "You asked me about my English. I studied in America. I took my degree in languages with a minor in Oriental philosophy. I took one year of college in the U.S."

"Really. Where?"

"In Iowa."

"Is that so? Which school?"

"Cornell College."

"*Soo desu neh.* I'd heard they had an exchange program."

"Yes. ... Ted, are you married?"

"Me? No. Never got close."

"There is no one in your life?"

"Not now. Not for many years. Since Mieko, my love life has been a wasteland. There was one girl in college. We pretended at

312

love. But she was so committed to some personal fantasies that she couldn't really love me. I suppose I was, too. Our love lacked passion. Mostly it was a physical thing; a college-level course in sexual relations with lots of lab work," he laughed, and realized that he had not had such an intimate conversation in years, and that he felt very much at ease talking to Yuko.

He looked at her and continued, "No love life for me. I have been degenerating really, going from one willow-world playground to another. I've never been satisfied and I've frequently regretted going, but I never found anyone to love outside, in real life."

"I'm sorry to hear you have been so lonesome. You sound like me. I have been chased by many men. But I have never found one who I did not think would reject me if they found out I was *eta* or whom I felt I could love. There was a boy I loved. I still do. But he went away."

"That's too bad. Like Mieko leaving me."

"Yes."

"Maybe he'll come back."

"Maybe." She smiled softly at him. "After you left … after Mie-chan's death, our lives were shattered. My mother became very depressed. So much so that she died several years ago, just slowly burned away her spirit. I, too, was broken. I blamed myself in part for Mieko's death, because part of my girlhood jealousies with my sister had surfaced and I had frequently thought of eliminating her. Not seriously, but, you know, as children do."

"I suppose I can understand. Why were you jealous of her?"

"I saw a psychiatrist for several years but he did not really help," she said, ignoring the question. "When I began to study philosophy, my teacher recommended me to a master outside of school with whom to study. The teachings were very private, very intense, and very enlightening."

"Zen?"

"No. You know what appeals to most people about Zen is its relation to esoteric Taoist teachings. My master was a Taoist. So I think the study was closer to the heart of the matter."

"So you learned a lot?"

"Yes, I did. Perhaps more than you can imagine. I found myself again — or for the first time. And I learned the value of love and the value of waiting, patience. Traditional Japanese and modern Western concepts of romance are both flawed, I think. The restrictive, arranged traditions here are not suited to love, only child-rearing. And the promiscuous detachment of the Western joy seeker is also a corruption. There is a mean somewhere, where one knows what one needs and seeks it without compromise. The love of life, of love, of sex or movement, breathing, is made all the more intense by the realization of the proper path and adherence to it. Not a dream world but ..."

"Yuko," Ted said, interrupting her.

"Yes."

"I'm not sure I understand what this has to do with my current situation."

"I'm sorry. I guess I'm lecturing you, but, as I said, there so much to say, and several different stories, paths, coming together."

"OK. Proceed." he said leaning back up against the headboard and closing his eyes, to concentrate on her words.

"Perhaps I should just get to the point and hope you do not become too preoccupied to want to learn the rest."

"Suit yourself, but you are confusing me."

"Then I will make it clear, now. Why did Mieko take her life?"

Ted bit down and pursed his lips. The abruptness of the

sentence and the fact that it was a question bothered him. He wanted answers and his suppositions were most painful. "Don't you know?" he asked in a low, half-swallowed voice.

"Yes, but why do you think, what have you thought all these years?"

"I don't know. But I have thought about it so much, so much until it made me sick sometimes. How could she do that? How could she leave me if she loved me?" he choked. "I mean, I always believed, naively I guess, that love could solve problems and bridge gaps. What could have been so bad that we could not have overcome it? I felt our love was that strong, especially in retrospect. But she killed herself, mutilated herself. Someone hinted maybe it was because I had made her pregnant, but that wasn't possible. Or maybe because your folks wouldn't let us get married, but I can't believe that was the reason. And she never let on she was depressed, never told me. She would have told me! God, I loved her," he sobbed, "and she didn't even say goodbye."

"She did say goodbye, Ted," Yuko said soberly, pulling a book from her leather bag.

"What!" he gasped, recognizing the diary he had given Mieko.

"Not in here, but in a letter I have kept here. I must tell of certain family matters first."

Ted slumped back, his eyes wide as he listened.

"After Mieko died, I took her diary from her room and kept it. After you gave it to her she was always very quiet about it, so I suppose my parents had forgotten it existed. In my guilt, I read it so many times, to see if it said anything to relieve the pain I felt. It did not. It spoke of her life and her growing love for you. There was nothing, no hint, that she was so depressed about something that she would kill herself. This made me feel worse, that maybe somehow, my childish dreams had come true."

"Just before my mother's death, she called me to be with her. She told me many things. She said that many years ago my father had a mistress who had threatened to kill herself if he did not pay her off. To do this my father was forced to borrow money from a loan company controlled by gangsters." She stopped and watched for Ted's reaction, seeing that his eyebrows had raised at the mention of organized crime.

"He was never able to pay off the debt. It just got worse. Mieko's death is tied to this. When my mother died she left me several things. She left me a small fortune she had privately accumulated over the decades by saving family spending money, and she left me a letter she had received from Mieko after her suicide. I have often thought that perhaps my mother felt responsible for Mieko's death because the money she willed me would have covered at least part of the debt. But she hated my father for his conduct and never thought her family would be hurt. She certainly did not want to pay for his affair herself."

"Anyway, in order to force my father to pay up, the *yakuza* kidnapped Mieko and treated her … terribly."

She unfolded the letter. "This was written when she had escaped from the love hotel where she had been held. Are you sure you want to hear it? It's very painful."

Ted nodded his head weakly. He was finding it impossible to concentrate, to think, as his emotions, memories, dreams, and nightmares collided in the churning cauldron of his heart. He felt any pain worth bearing as long as he learned the truth.

"Haha-chama," Yuko began reading the opening to the letter addressed respectfully to her mother. "I do not understand why the men have done this to me. They said Daddy sold me to them until

316

his money is paid back and I was to do anything for them. I do not know what to believe. But my body hurts and I am not clean. The men have done things to me again and again and I am lost.

"Their leader, Nishida Yoshikazu, said I would have to make him happy every night for six months to pay him back. Mommy, why does it hurt so much? Even though I have escaped them and am running, my heart is held captive by them.

"I dare not see Daddy again, I am too ashamed to see you, and I am too unclean to see Takabashi-san. I love you all. Pray at the temple for me.

"Your daughter, Mieko."

Hearing her words for the first time calling across a decade, with their condemnation of Nishida, Ted could no longer control the tumult of emotions he felt, and the feelings manifested themselves as he choked on his sobs and streams of tears dampened the sleeve of his *yukata*. The only sense he was aware of outside his wretched self was the sense of touch — the warm and comforting embrace of Yuko.

The vestiges of a very tense day were being deftly removed from Nero's shoulders, back and arms by the Japanese girl in her mid-twenties. If he had ever needed a relaxing massage it was on this day. The calls to Italy and Tokyo, the crazy meeting with Brody in his office, the long and tensely boring flight from Bangkok to Tokyo had all taken their toll. But, now I am fed, sated, saké'd, bathed, soaked ... and eaten, he thought as he felt the girl begin to expertly consume his sex.

The involuntary flexing of his muscle punctuated his thoughts about the coming day. "I'll crucify that ... uh ... cock-sucker Nishida.

He and Suzuki both. They'll learn not to … aah … fuck with me."

The sense of power of the aggression he felt aroused him more, and as the woman lapped away faster and faster, his heart sped up. The thought of her accepting his climax raised his pulse higher until he was clawing the sheet. At the high tide, suddenly, his heart raked at his chest from within, as if it had imploded, and his eyes grew wide in horror as he gripped his breast. With each beat the pain grew more excruciatingly intense. He knew he would be dead in a matter of moments, and as he thrashed on the bed, the horrified masseuse covering her body with a doffed uniform, screaming, he saw the cup of strange-tasting Japanese tea that the room boy had brought. Nishida, his mind cried out. *Bastardo!*

EIGHT

Since you've gone I've been lost without a trace
I dream at night I can only see your face
I look around but it's you I can't replace
I feel so cold and I long for your embrace
I keep crying, "Baby, baby, please ..."

The forlorn song broadcast into his room over the Armed Forces Far East Network turned Ted's thoughts to Mieko for the thousandth time since he had talked with Yuko the night before.

His head buried in the pillow, he saw her face floating in the deep purple void of his mind's eye. He saw her greet him at Shinjuku station on his return from the United States. He saw her kimono-clad figure kneeling serenely with hands folded neatly in her lap, a shy smile her only makeup. He imagined he saw her at the hands of *yakuza* and he could not stop his mind from repeating the scene of her defilement.

His dark mood was not lifted by the sound of the powered lock on his door clicking open and the sight of Yuko entering with a small plastic bag of groceries.

"Ted?" she asked, seeing him scowling as he looked out the window.

"Yeah. Morning Yuko."

"What's the matter?"

"You should know. The same as always."

"Mieko?"

He nodded his head as he continued to look out the window, avoiding her eyes.

"I have brought you some breakfast," she said as she sat down on the bed between him and the window, putting the plastic bag next to her. "Care for an orange?"

His view interrupted, he looked at her silhouette with the morning sunshine at her back, a piece of golden fruit extended to him. With the face darkened, he could imagine seeing Mieko there before him, in modern attire and fully grown. But the woman seated in front of him was not Mieko, no matter how much he wished he could make her so. It was another woman in another time; a woman that he did not find lacking when compared to his lost love. She might even be more than Mieko could have been. Her life had been harder and this had given her more practicality than he had seen in her older sister, he reasoned. She was intense, but not tense. Wary, but relaxed. Her face was at once serious and gentle, softly beautiful and impervious to assault. It expressed no doubt.

"Yes, Yuko. Thank you," he said taking the fruit, his mood softened. As he peeled the skin away he thought about the day ahead. "I think I'll try to call Thailand soon."

"You have decided to contact the American?"

"I think I've decided. I don't know what's best, but that seems to be the only first step no matter what."

"Why?" she asked, as she peeled her orange carefully, wanting to make sure he had thought through his plan of action.

"Because I want to explain what happened in Thailand and let

320

him track Nishida and Nero down. That way I can clear myself of this matter quickly and cleanly, before it destroys me."

"Do you think the American can do anything about Nishida?"

"More than I can."

"You think so," she said, her tone between a question and a statement.

"Yes. I mean, I hope so."

"Then let's get ready to call Thailand," she said decisively. "What will you do afterwards?"

"Call on Butcher Obara."

"*So na no*. Good idea. I am sure he will want to see you after so many years. ... Let's do your hair now," she said, rising from the bed and skirting around it into the small plastic bathroom. Ted followed her in and realized there was hardly room for the two of them.

"Sit on the toilet and lean your head back over the sink."

It was not difficult to do as they were placed right next to each other. She put a towel under his neck to cushion it and turned on the bathtub faucet.

"Can't you use the sink faucet?"

"The hand-held shower will reach here," she said, lifting it from the wall and testing the water temperature, pointing it into his hair and turning on the spray.

He felt the bite of hot water dig into his scalp and the amorphous touch of steam rising against his cheek. The scent of Yuko wafted into his nostrils and he became acutely aware of her presence next to him. Her fingers clawed gently, moving the skin with them and raising a lather. He looked up at her and she smiled back, wiping a drop of suds from the tip of her nose. Rinsing her hands off she pushed up her loose baggy sleeves. As she turned to adjust the

321

water temperature, his eyes followed up the arm that remained on his head. The baggy tunnel of cloth led up ivory arms and he could see the definition of her ribs and muscles. As she shifted forward, so did the cloth, and a firm breast, unsupported yet defiant and crowned with a rosy pink confection of a nipple, hung in view. Ted swallowed hard and turned his eyes away. He hated himself for being attracted to what he saw. This was not some rented lover, he screamed within. This woman has tried to help you, to explain things to you, to protect you. How can you see her this way? She does not want you that way. She has a love she lost and waits for. She said so. Don't ruin this friendship, his mind admonished. She is a friend.

She turned back to him to rinse his head and saw his closed eyes and stony expression. "I'm sorry, did I get some soap in your eyes?"

"No. No, Yuko, I'm just a little depressed."

"Ted," she said, turning his face towards her with her water-hot fingertips. "Things will work out."

"Yeah," he said, smiling half-heartedly.

She applied the hair dye and let it set then rinsed the excess and blew-dry his hair. Not letting him turn to see the mirror, she applied some styling gel and curled his hair into a slicked up pompadour. "Wait a moment," she insisted, as she ran into the bedroom to retrieve something. She came back with the black heavy-framed sunglasses she had bought. "Just a moment yet," she pleaded for him to restrain himself from looking in the mirror while she added a hint of eyeliner to the corner of each eye, suggesting to the casual observer an Asian influence. Then she put on the sunglasses.

"OK, turn around," she said, smiling broadly.

He looked cautiously over his right shoulder to see someone

he did not recognize. Not only was the hair color different, the personality was different. He had always been very conservative in his hair styling; even more so since he went to work. The person in the mirror was a Tokyo Sunday rocker, a greased-back throwback to the 1950s, one of the *shinjinrui* generation who believed in personal gratification before corporate satisfaction, a person who found conformity in nonconformity.

"Try the clothes on," she said tugging him away from the mirror.

She did not avert her glance as he shyly doffed his *yukata* and slipped quickly into the clean undershirt she had bought him the day before. He buttoned up the plaid shirt and pulled on the drawstring pants.

"Button the shirt up all the way," she said, pointing at his neck. "Lots of young men wear shirts that way here without a tie."

He buttoned up the neck and pulled on the bright, baggy V-neck sweater and blue jean jacket, finally donning the sunglasses once more as he looked in the mirror and groomed his hair back.

"Pretty slick," he said, grinning, assuming the posture of a bad-ass rocker, snapping his fingers.

Yuko smiled approvingly. "Now, you still want to call Bangkok, right?"

"Yes, better do that now, eh?"

"Yes. I bought you a phone card with 10,000 yen credit on it. Let's walk over to another hotel and use their LD phone to dial that man."

"Ten thousand yen?"

"Yes. It should be enough to call him for 15 minutes or so."

"Yuko," he said, stopping her as she turned for the door.

"Yes?" she asked turning to face him, her eyes meeting his, the corners of her mouth upturned.

Ted paused a moment, smiled back at her, and said falteringly, "Nothing … just thank you … OK?"

A sleepless flight had not diminished Brody's anxious excitement. He was sure he was tracking something larger than appearance would suggest and was waiting for a few more bits and pieces to fall into place. His Tokyo counterpart with the DEA had met him at the airport and brought him directly to their office within the American Embassy compound, offering him the use of his facilities. Brody had briefed the man, George Peterson, about what he suspected so far.

"Bill, when are you going to call the U.S. about this?" Peterson asked apprehensively.

"Well, the boss is at home now settling down after dinner," he said looking at his watch. "No reason to rile him. I'll call him late tonight when he gets to the office."

"He told me to 'remind' you that you were to call on arrival."

"George, I need a few hours. Answers will be coming in."

Peterson didn't like the look of the Thai section chief. His clothes were slept in and his delaying was a thinly disguised excuse for having nothing to go on. He also had a hungry, desperate look in his eyes.

"Bill, we haven't worked together very much, face to face. You know, Japan isn't Thailand and I've gotta lot of rules I have to follow … you understand."

"Sure, we can cooperate with the local authorities, if that's what you mean."

"No, it goes beyond cooperation. It's not the Wild West here.

324

I don't do anything without the local authorities, and that usually means I don't do anything at all, enforcement-wise. This is their country, they have their ways."

"Yeah?"

"Yeah. Washington doesn't understand that too good, I guess. If I had known you had requested to be sent here, well, I gotta tell you, I wouldn't have allowed it."

"I'm sorry to hear you don't think going after the core of a smuggling empire is worthwhile."

"Don't change about what I said — you know what I mean. I want to kick ass as much as you do. But, I don't need you here personally trying to stir up a lot of trouble. All I need is your intelligence reports and maybe your recommendations. Capiche?"

"Hey. What am I gonna do? Run amok?"

"Just no 'Wild Bill' stuff, huh? All right?"

Brody's stomach tightened at the mention of his unwelcome nickname. "And what does that mean?"

"You know. Do I have to spell it out?"

"Yeah, what did you hear?"

"Something about a raid you participated in, some said directed, in Chiang Mai. What was it? No one in the building came out alive? Fifteen to twenty dead? Justice, huh?"

"Yeah. I went with the Thai police to bust up a place. It was a place some junkie whores had mentioned. You know what happened when we busted in? There were bullets flying all over the place. I only killed one guy who came around a doorway with an armalite. Some of the girls who came there for fixes got hit by the bad guys, some were shot when they got hysterical and clawed at our boys takin' aim at somebody about to shoot them. Yeah. It was a mess. But only six were brought out in bags. A couple were

325

wounded, including policemen. And anyway, that raid was lauded in the Thai papers, so where do you get off giving me shit about it?"

"I don't have to get off your case, Brody. I didn't ask you here in the first place and I don't want anything going down without my consent. Why do you suppose those guys started playing hardball right after the raid, with your wife and all, anyway?"

Brody looked at the man coldly, his lips taut as he tried to contain the rage he felt. Of course he had realized the consequences of his actions too late, he screamed within. Of course they had taken his wife in retaliation. Taken her. Blown her apart. Destroyed the one woman who loved him despite his obsession, only making him more obsessed. He would not let a functionary stand between himself and revenge, he began to consider when his sanity stepped into his consciousness. You're going out on that limb again. It's going to break and they will have won: point, game, and match. If you're going to play this out, you've got to play through Peterson.

Peterson saw the anger build in the DEA section chief and said, "Look, Brody. That was out of line. I'm sorry. We were all sorry to hear about your wife. But do you read me loud and clear? You act with my consent or you go home."

There was silence as Brody listened to the distant traffic outside the embassy compound. "Yeah, George," he said resignedly, "I hear you. Anyway, I don't think there's much I could do here on my own. No language, no culture, no contacts. I'm tethered to you."

"Just so you understand."

"Yeah. Can you do this for me, just so we don't end up looking stupid. Don't clue the locals on the possible link between Bergman, the Italian, and Great Star until I say so."

Peterson looked at the Thai section chief skeptically but answered, "OK."

326

"Good. Now I've got to get down to work."

"What can I have my secretary do for you?"

"I'd like a report on Bergman's disappearance, the current whereabouts of Nero, the Italian, and ask her to bring any faxes I get as soon as they get here."

"Will do."

"I'm gonna call Bangkok now."

"I'll have her get you a line," Peterson said as he turned to leave Brody with his thoughts.

He would follow Peterson's game plan as best he could. Keep him informed. He knew he was at a disadvantage trying to pursue this case here and began regretting not just turning it over to Tokyo. But an underlying need fueled by the power of his instincts told him that the criminals he pursued would not be brought to justice unless he acted. And that might mean disobeying Peterson.

The phone on the desk in front of him rang. He lifted the receiver, punching the third button which was lit. "Your call is through to Bangkok, Mr. Brody. Through the scrambler."

"Thank you. ... Hello? Jackson?"

"Yo, Jackson here. You got to Tokyo in one piece?"

"Sure did. Got anything for me?"

"A reminder from D.C. to call as soon as you get to Tokyo."

All right already, Brody thought.

"And some big news on our exploration firm. Boy, you got a nose, boss."

"What d'ya get?"

"Everything. Enough at least. Seems Nero was keeping a vacuum cleaner dustbag full of dirt on his partners. Plus, we got some detailed maps of their exploration concession. Looks legit, except some places marked on the map which are definitely drug country."

"Doesn't sound like too much to me," Brody said nervously.

"No, listen, one of the maps is marked just where the army raid took place a week or two ago. You know, the one where the chopper took off from."

"OK," Brody said, his tone asking for further news.

"Ital-Siam's got a chopper. Same type that was seen there."

"Bell's pretty common out there, Jackson."

"We're trying to get a hold of the pilot but he's up-country now."

"Anything else?"

"Well, we've gotten some more info on the investors in Ital-Siam. The Japanese side is a division of a subsidiary of a holding company with directors who also sit on the board of Great Star Construction. Peterson can probably tell you more about them.

"The Italian side is likewise a long way down the chain from a big Italian company, legit, but on the board are some definite bent-nose types. Either side could actually benefit from real petroleum exploration, but there's also a lot of shadow here that needs some light."

"Good. Keep digging."

"Will do. What's the Italian up to?"

"They're checking on it for me now."

"Bergman?"

"No word, no sight. Please get on the horn as soon as anything breaks."

"Sure. Hey! Wait. Don't hang up. There's a long-distance call coming in for you."

"If it's D.C. I'm not here."

There was a moment of silence and then Jackson excitedly

shouted through to Brody, "It's Bergman. What shall I tell him."

"Can you connect me through to him?"

"It won't be easy, shall I just ask him to call you in Tokyo?"

"Talk to him, see what you can find out. Keep trying to think of a way to patch me through." Brody leaned over his desk until he could see Peterson's secretary. "Hey ... hello. Excuse me. Can you tape this conversation?"

"Yes, sir."

"Please start."

In Bangkok, Jackson pushed the lit button on his second phone and lifted the receiver. "Hello. This is the Drug Enforcement Agency. Can I help you?"

"I would like to speak to Mr. Brody, please."

"Who is calling, please?"

"Ted Bergman."

"Yes, Mr. Bergman, Mr. Brody has been expecting your call. Can you hold for a moment please?"

Thousands of miles away in the lobby of the Tokyo Hilton an anxious Ted Bergman stared at the sweep second hand on his Rolex. He wasn't sure how long it would take to trace his call, or even if it could be traced easily. His mind had wrestled with the memory of tracing times he had heard of in movies and crime dramas. Was it three minutes or thirty seconds? It had already been one and a half minutes since he had been connected with the embassy, and he had been put on hold twice.

He was about to hang up and change booths when a familiar voice called out, "Bergman, is that you?"

"Yes. Mr. Brody?"

"Yes. Are you all right? We've been concerned ever since you called."

329

"I'm OK. But I'm in a mess."

"I know. How did you get in it."

"I don't want to talk on the phone. Is there someone I can meet in Tokyo?"

"Tell you the truth, I've been so worried I flew up here myself to look for you."

"You knew I was in Tokyo?"

"You left a pretty clear trail."

"Was that your man yesterday at Narita."

"The one you lost?"

"Yeah."

"Yes. Not exactly my man. Japanese authorities. Where are you holed up now?"

"No. I want to meet you somewhere else. We've got to talk first. Some place neutral. How about Ueno Park?"

"I don't know Tokyo."

"Where are you?"

"The embassy."

"Have some one put you on the Yamanote line at Tokyo station on the most forward car, and plan to arrive at Ueno station at … 5:45 sharp; no earlier. When you get off the train head for the park exit. Turn left and cross the street, go into the park and follow the path around to the museum. Come alone and follow these directions. You will be watched."

"Isn't this a bit much?"

"Look, Brody, I've been attacked, framed, and chased. When I know you and we have a mutual understanding, then we go to the embassy together."

"Look, I'm just looking out for you. I'd rather have backups there in case some bad boys come after you again."

"I plan to handle that," Ted said without hesitation.

"Like in Bangkok?"

"What does that mean?"

"You know. The two dead guys."

"What two dead guys?"

"Don't bullshit me, Bergman. You were positively identified at the scene of the crime. You need me, Bergman, more that I need you."

"Cool your jets, Brody. We'll talk at 5:45. Since I suppose you're recording this, I won't repeat the directions. And even if you succeeded in tracing to this phone, it won't help. I'm miles from where I'm staying. Don't waste the effort. Goodbye."

Brody heard the phone signal indicating one line had been hung up. "Jackson? You there?"

"Yo! We got it on tape. Do you need it back?"

"No. I got it here, too."

"You gonna meet him?"

"Of course! It's not a trap ... I don't think."

"Let me know what happens."

"Yeah. And you, too. As soon as anything breaks."

"Yep. Goodbye and good luck."

Brody hung up the phone and rubbed his eyes, concentrating for the moment on his planned meeting with Bergman. *It's probably not a trap. Bergman wouldn't bother calling me if it was a trap. Unless he is using the obvious to obscure the intention. Nah. Anyway, Peterson's probably got some Japanese boys who can blend in pretty well and keep an eye on me. Except Bergman's done a number on anyone who has followed him so far. He's too fucking sharp to be what he says he is, just a salesman. So, you bring Peterson's backup boys anyway and let them know about Bergman.*

He leaned through the doorway and called to the secretary. "You got that call on tape, right?"

"Yes, Mr. Brody."

"Where's Mr. Peterson?"

"Here!" the Tokyo section chief called from down the hall. "What can I do you for?"

"The reports on Bergman, the Italian, etc."

"Got 'em right here." He said, smiling as he came into the office. "Where do you want to start?"

"Bergman."

"Nil. He hasn't been located yet. Either he is staying with friends or using false name at a hotel. We've got local police boxes screening foreigners with his basic description for their papers."

"You can do that here?"

"Sure, drives the local expats batty."

"Can you have Immigration run a check on his past trips to Japan?"

"I'll take a run at it."

"What about Nero?"

"Very interesting." He paused to let Brody's suspense build. "The man arrives last night. He is picked up by a car owned by the Great Star group. They take him to a hotel, a love hotel by the way, and five hours later an ambulance picks up one dead Italian."

"What!?"

"Yep. Cardiac arrest."

"Psshit," Brody swore letting out a breathe. "Autopsy?"

"We're onto it. I'll let you know what the results are."

"What is the Great Star group? They're related to Great Star Construction?"

"Good guess. One of several large 'alleged' *yakuza* organiza-

332

tions. Benign on the surface, malignant at the core. Not easy to go after."

"*Yakuza* are the organized-crime groups."

"Yeah. Japanese Mafia. Like the warlords you deal with except city based and very flashy in a tacky sort of way. Elaborate codes of conduct harking back, supposedly, to the samurai code of honor. Most of them are real low-class toughs with no future in any other job. Maybe they're nonconformist or ultra right, but they get sucked into the gang slowly and find some regimentation and group security there. Both seem to be important to all Japanese. They all want to belong. It's just a matter of whether their orbit finds them with a big legitimate company, a student radical group, or *yakuza*."

"What do they deal in?"

"You name it, they deal in it, though some things are definitely more risky than others. Mostly loan sharking, gambling, prostitution, stockholder meeting disruption, protection rackets, some drugs."

"Only some."

"I mean, they're not as heavy into the drug scene as the Cuban and Colombian Mafia in the U.S. The government here really frowns on that. It's not that they keep their hands off; it's just they are very discreet."

"Have you had any run in with them?"

"Nothing violent, nothing dramatic. The Japanese agents have taken me around to observe them. Shown me how to pick them out in a crowd, what some of their rituals are. I saw some films they made of *yakuza* meetings. But I have never been in on a bust."

"They just don't deal in drugs that much?"

"Well, I should add, the biggest worry I have with *yakuza* is reporting on intelligence we get here about their activities in the

U.S., especially Hawaii."

"So, even if they were not working to export drugs from Thailand to here, they might still be working to sell them in the U.S.A."

"Sure. Possibly."

"I hate to say that's a relief to know. I mean, otherwise my idea about the Italian, the Japanese, Bergman, would be much less plausible."

"Sounds as though you're beginning to have some solid tie-ins. Even the death of — was it Nero? — adds to your case, and I understand you got a call from Bergman this morning."

"Yeah. Have you heard it?"

"No." Peterson called his secretary in and had her play the recorded phone conversation.

"You want me to arrange a backup?" Peterson asked after listening to the tape.

"I was hoping you'd offer. Do you have any really good Japanese boys?"

"I got two who are pretty good."

"They're going to have to be. Bergman's slick as snot. Well, you read the Japanese tail's report."

"Umhmm. But this time we know approximately where he is going to meet you. I know that station. We can put one guy on the train with you and one out by the park side exit. Even if Bergman's waiting on the platform for you, he won't suspect anything because he won't see anyone else wait for the train but not get on it when you get off."

"You know the place, I don't."

"What do you want my men to do with Bergman? If you want him taken into custody, then I have to bring the Japanese authorities in on the surveillance."

Sure is different from Bangkok, Brody thought. This pussy's got his hands tied by the locals so tight they have to hold his dick for him so he can take a leak. Jesus. "No, just watch him and be ready to follow him after he leaves me. Of course, if it looks like the situation is getting a little rough, I suppose it would be too much to ask them to prevent Bergman from killing me, huh?"

"Actually, they could call the police for you, or intervene in a civilian capacity."

"I feel so much safer already," Brody said snidely. "No chance I could get a gun, is there?"

"You're right. There's no chance. Not now, at least. Has to go through channels, but my men will be packing."

"Just thought I'd ask."

The meeting was one he had dreaded having for several days. But, now, standing before his uncle Yamashita the dread had left him. His explanations were prepared, Nero was dead and could not tell any lies, and Suzuki was there to back him up. He knew the worst that could happen would be death, by his hand or another's, and that thought had never bothered him. For his mistakes, perhaps it was even justified.

"Yamashita-sama," he said formally, taking a half step forward and bending his knee while bowing from the waist, his hands extended downward, palms up in the Great Star salutation.

Yamashita's stony expression was unchanged by the obeisance.

"I have returned by your command to report on the treachery of the Italian fox who will shortly give his story to you. I urge you to listen carefully to his words ..."

"His words," Yamashida bellowed. "The words of a dead man!"

Nishida feigned concerned surprise and looked to Suzuki for an explanation.

"Don't act as if you did not know Nero-san was dead. I know you too well for you to disguise your plots. His death reeks of your trace."

Nishida hung his head low. There was nothing he could say. He could not deny it. Yamashita already knew. To admit his guilt would only have belittled Yamashita's intelligence. He stood there, numb. He should have expected this outburst from his uncle, he thought.

"I am ashamed you are my nephew. It makes me think ill of my sister for having had such a useless son. What a waste of manhood you are. Sons should be sources of prosperity and happiness. You have brought upon yourself and your family nothing but ridicule and moral indebtedness."

Nishida was unprepared for the abuse Yamashita heaped on him. He could not even raise his head to glare at the old man, though.

"Tell me about the American," Yamashita ordered in disgust.

All of the explanations he had prepared seemed empty or riddled with inconsistencies he thought, as they raced through his mind once more. He began as factually as he could. "We discovered an American was investigating our front operation. We advised caution; Nero wanted to wait to see what kind of person the American was. Some photos were taken of the American in the company of the DEA section chief in front of the American Embassy. We felt the investigator should disappear. We failed twice."

"Your use of 'we' is interesting, Nishida. I think you must have learned the tricks of the fox from Nero himself. 'We discovered'? Nero had the first hint. Who took the photos? Nero. 'We failed twice.' No. You failed twice. Where is the American now?"

"We are not certain."

"How totally ignorant can you be, Nishida, and still claim to be above the plant kingdom? Even I know Bergman — yes, I even know his name — is here, in Tokyo, right now."

Nishida looked up, startled. Something he hated to express, fear, showed in his eyes.

Yamashita saw the weakness and continued, "Yes. Bergman. The man you cannot kill. Perhaps he is here to kill you. Is that why you are so scared that I can practically see the filth draining from your pants leg?"

Nishida stiffened up. "I am not afraid of Bergman. He is just an American."

"Perhaps you should be afraid. Perhaps he knows something about us, or you, that could be very damaging to our organization. The organization which has treated you so well. So well, even when you were a boy. Even when you grew up into a useless man who makes bigger and bigger errors. The organization has lived for you. And yet you are not afraid of a person who can hurt us with a few words. I am afraid," he said, touching his fingers to his breast. "I suppose it is just the way a useless dog treats the tree that gives it shade and drops fruit down to it. He just pisses on the trunk ..."

"Yamashita-sama, what would you have me do? I give you my life. Please take it."

"I do not need or want your life, you useless piece of goldfish shit. You deserve to live in shame."

"Is there nothing I can do?"

"There is only one thing that can set right all of the wrong you

337

have brought upon us and if you die succeeding, all the better."

"Anything."

"Get Bergman, discreetly, and without fail."

The neighborhood around Sumida had changed, Ted remarked to Yuko as they mounted the three flights of steps to Butcher Obara's apartment, but his building was still the same. The streets and alleyways leading from the train station now were crowded with convenience stores and fast-food shops, which were slowly squeezing out the mom and pop specialty grocers and sundries shops. Now the plastic and fluorescent took over for the wood and lantern. The modern street scene gave way to post-World War II utilitarian apartment design as they entered the side entrance and walked up the narrow unlit steps. It was small, but it was home for Obara, and he had always taken pride in having Ted visit his home. "I own this place, you know?" he had said without modesty more times than Ted could count. Looking back ten years to the challenging time he had spent with the Butcher, Ted now felt a surge of nostalgia flood his heart. He swallowed hard and knocked on the outer metal gate. There was no answer. He listened to hear if there was anyone at home but could discern no movement. He knocked harder. "Maybe he is taking a nap after lunch."

"Or maybe he is not home," Yuko rejoined.

Ted knocked harder one more time.

"Yes, yes, yes. Who is it?" a disgruntled voice bellowed from within.

Ted wanted to surprise his *sensei* so he nodded to Yuko to reply.

She giggled, shrugging her shoulders, and said, "Obara-san," in

338

her cutest, schoolgirl voice.

"Who is it?" the voice bellowed again.

"Obara-san … flower delivery for you," she said, thinking quickly and restraining a laugh.

"Flowers? Go away."

"Obara-san, there is someone here to see you!" she chimed.

The Butcher opened the inner door a crack and peeped through to see two people he did not know, a degenerate college student wearing sunglasses on the dark steps and his cheap-looking girl-friend. He slammed the door again, "Go away."

"*Sensei*, don't you recognize me?" Ted spoke up, suddenly remembering he was in disguise. "I'm Takabashi."

The door opened again wider as Ted removed the sunglasses.

Obara looked at him long and full with the eyes that had once pronounced Ted unfit to become a pupil. Again they drilled into Ted as Obara squinted in the shadows. Slowly Obara began to shake his head back and forth in disbelief and a smile turned up the corners of his mouth shattering his face into a thousand wrinkles. "Takabashi-san. I just can't believe it," he said stunned, the gruff edge gone from his voice.

"Will you not let us in?," Ted urged with a grin.

"Oh, umm, yes," Obara said, confused, as he reached for the lock on the outer door.

They removed their shoes while Obara found some well-worn slippers for them to put on. They then padded single file through the narrow passage to his *tatamied* sitting room.

The place was a mess, the same as Ted remembered it. Full ashtrays overflowed onto month-old newspapers used to wipe up spilled beer from a recent but forgotten night of excess. Obara looked at the filth, looked shyly at Ted and Yuko, then bit his lip as he scratched his head, sucking in his breath in embarrassment. "One moment, please," he said as he trotted back to the tiny cooking area.

Ted heard what sounded like Obara dumping cans, bottles, and trash onto the kitchen floor. The old man then returned with an empty plastic pail. "One moment, please," he grinned as he pushed past Ted and cleared everything off the low table into the bucket with a sweep of his arm. He emptied the ashtray, discarded the newspapers, beer cans, used plastic noodle bowls, then stacked the sex magazines neatly on top of the television.

"So, my apologies. I did not expect any guests. No one visits the old anymore," he rued. "Now, who is this you have brought with you? Mrs. Takabashi?" he grinned, his teeth even more tobacco-stained than Ted remembered.

Unembarrassed, Yuko replied, "You don't remember me, Uncle Obara?"

He looked at her more carefully as thoughts, memories, and feeling exposed themselves. He briefly smiled, then looked saddened. Finally, a small wistful smile appeared. "Yuko-chan?"

"Yes."

"I don't even remember the last time I saw you. Perhaps at … at," he looked at Ted, "At Mieko's funeral."

They were all silent for a moment. "Yes, Uncle Obara," she said.

Ted looked again at the two of them. "You're not really her uncle, are you?" he asked, wondering if something else had been kept from him so long.

"No, Teddy," Yuko replied in English, with a laugh.

"I have beer and tea; which would you like?" Obara asked.

"Tea, please."

"I'll go make it," Yuko volunteered.

When she had gotten up and left the room, followed by four eyes, the two men turned to face each other.

"She reminds me, painfully, of Mieko," the old man said, looking for the reaction in the younger.

"Yes. Me too. But she is different. Even stronger, even smarter, even more … attractive," Ted said, glad he could finally say to someone what he had been thinking. "I understand you are retired now?" he asked changing the subject lest it lead to factors he was not prepared to let surface yet.

"Yes. What a bore. No meat to cut, no camaraderie with the packing crew, no student like you."

"I've missed you, too, old man."

"Is that so? How come so few letters? What? Five postcards in ten years. I still have everyone of them too. You want to see?" he added, defiantly.

"I am sorry," Ted said, meaning it. "I have no good excuses."

There was silence for a moment as they both thought about the other.

"How about you? You're not a degenerate, are you? What's with the clothes. And the hair? Disgusting."

Ted laughed until he remembered the purpose of the hair and clothes. "No. I am a fairly successful businessman. Still with the same company I mentioned in my last postcard. But things are not going well all of a sudden, and that is why I am here and why I am dressed this way."

"Sales bad?"

"No, I am in real trouble and I may need help from you. I should tell you that what you taught me has saved my life twice in the past week."

"That kind of trouble," Obara said settling down, his smile replaced by a concerned look.

Yuko returned with a plastic tray and three cups of green tea. She kneeled down and placed them on the table, then shifted over to kneel by Obara.

"I was just about to tell him about the trouble I am in."

"Yes, carry on," she said as she distributed the cups.

Ted launched into his story while the old man sat and listened. He pursed his lips at the sound of the word *yakuza* but remained silent. When Ted told him about the two men he had killed, Obara stood up and asked him to demonstrate what technique he had used.

Ted told Obara to lunge at him as the first man had. Ted expected the move, folding Obara's elbow and hand back into his sternum. The older looked at him and shook his head. "Again." This time when Ted began to fold his elbow, Obara shifted it inward and dropped his hand down, unbalancing Ted in the process. Ted felt a slap to his left inner thigh and then searing pain as the man's fingers dug in and grabbed a roll of flesh. Ted sucked in a breath of air and contained a wince.

"If I had a knife, that grab would have been a deep cut to your artery. You'd be dead now."

Ted could not contain a rebuttal. "Teacher, the man is dead. His heart was pierced. The technique worked."

"Just be careful. And don't forget your manners. What about the other attack?"

Ted showed him how he had broken the assailant's neck.

"Good. Clean and safe. I didn't teach you that, did I?" he asked, puzzled.

"It's the essence of your strategy, but the adaptation of a move

342

I saw in a magazine."

The old man nodded approvingly. "OK. So why are you here now?"

Ted continued with his story, omitting the part about his visit and stealthy departure from the Yoshida residence.

"I suppose if Yuko's here, you've been to see Yoshida-san already?"

Ted paused before answering and looked to Yuko for advice.

"Out with it. What's the story?"

"Yes, there is a story. Do you know how Mieko died?"

Obara was confounded by the change of subject, especially when it was obvious his pupil was in danger. "Suicide."

"I mean why, how?"

"There was no explanation and I never asked. Baseless rumors from uninformed gabs I never believed said it was school or boy problems. It has frequently troubled me, all the more so because I had a fondness for her through you," he finished, looking at Ted and briefly at Yuko.

"Yuko, please tell Obara-san what you told me yesterday," Ted said turning away, afraid of facing the raw, unrefined truth again.

Yuko told of Mieko's demise quickly and factually, referring to what she thought Obara would remember to bolster his impression. As she spoke, he sat in stony silence, only his long breath audible in his flared nostrils. When she neared the end of the story he sat with his eyes closed, his head shaking back and forth wishing to deny the truth his ears reported. Eventually he spoke up in a quiet but firm tone. "I was taught that there is a wheel of life. We are born, live, and die, and then repeat the cycle, perhaps in an altered way, better or worse, in the next life. But I think not anymore. We all died a little when Mieko did. Your sister was taken away. Your heart's companion was taken away, and that led to me losing you, the only student I had ever had and someone I loved as a son. Yes. A son I never had.

"And yet, we are all brought back together in this life and another cycle is here. It's not one cycle, it's two. Or more. Wheels within wheels. It's not karma of past life. It's karma of our lives within this life. I just don't understand."

"*Sensei*, I need your help today."

"No. Don't interrupt me. I know you need my help. And that's part of the cycle, I guess." He paused. "When you were young, Yuko, did you ever hear a legend about a *shinheimin* who took care of his own? Who defended us against the excesses of prejudice and exploitation?"

"The Butcher?"

"Yes. That's the one. And Takabashi-san, did you ever wonder why I had all these terrible skills to teach you in the first place? I am not a professional instructor of a lofty Japanese philosophical martial way. I am a poor street man."

"You're the Butcher?" Yuko and Ted asked together.

"Most every one of the techniques I showed you has seen its use. Of course, not recently."

"Why? How did you become him?" Yuko asked.

"I didn't become him, I am him. It's not a cinematically monstrous transformation, you know. ... Why? Because a human being can only take so much. Then he either has a choice of ceasing to be human or fighting back. The government had repealed our class designation when I was a sprout, but still there was discrimination. It was a time of growing patriotism and emperor worship. I grew up between the contradiction of a country I loved above all else and a country that loved me less than anything. I was able to

344

stand it until it was time to serve my country. I wanted to be a soldier and honor my country with my blood in battle. Instead, somehow, they knew I was *shinheimin* and I worked at the usual job: butchering. After the war I came back … I suppose I was lucky to have been on kitchen duty. There has to be more food and less bullets there … anyway, I came back bitter. My country was defeated, I was defeated, the enemy occupied my homeland — no offense," he said to Ted, "But a strange thing happened that pushed me over the edge. The Americans wanted to re-emphasize the elimination of class. I was hopeful, but with so many jobless men returning, the competition for jobs was stiff. Needless to say we did not get washed clean of our taint and were pushed into ever more undesirable work. It was a very hard time. In many ways even harder for us than the war.

"I saw many of my friends who had survived the war, some having served like myself for the imperial cause, destitute." Obara uttered a short, curt laugh. "Yuko. You cannot know how lucky you are to be in the Yoshida family, your grandfather was a very far-sighted man. Most of us look like me, or worse, even now.

"But then …" he paused, as if wondering whether to continue. "Then I saw a man I knew beaten to death. Why? He was one of us. A friendly, easygoing boy really, who had no enemies. Why? Because he presumed to enter a cheap whorehouse for sport one night where one of the pimp guards at the entrance recognized him as one of us and said to the other guard in their dialect, '*kabu*,' a derogatory expression for *shinheimin*, and gestured at my friend with the four fingers hand sign. The second guard did not like the idea of a *burakumin* despoiling their women, so he set upon my friend. The first guard joined in, and as a rape rumor circulated through the inebriated evening street crowd, more joined in, kicking and spitting.

"I could do nothing to help him and, as a crowd was involved in his death, no one could really say who started the rumor, besides myself who had no credibility. No one was brought to trial or arrested.

"But the two guards were brought to account. Remembering back, it always amazed me how easy those kills were. Perhaps a butcher's expertise with his instrument transcends the medium being cleaved. I waited one late night until they were getting off work and tired. I followed until they split to go home separately. I took out one from behind within a minute in an alley approaching his home and ran to catch up with the other. I passed him on the other side of the street, crossed over, and approached him casually from the front. As I passed on the narrow sidewalk, I buried my knife up to the handle in his chest. He made much less noise than a cat at night and no one noticed. The police, seeing an otherwise unmotivated crime, probably suspected gang warfare."

"The Butcher wasn't just a folktale hero?" Yuko said incredulously.

"No."

"You only killed 'bad guys,' but how did you determine that?" Ted asked.

"I don't want any moralizing questions from you on how I chose my marks," Obara said sternly. "Every one of them deserved what he got. Would you argue any differently for Nishida?"

"No," Ted said in a low, chastened tone, "I understand."

"*Soo*, you see the cycle. We all come together again in a different way, but the same. I am the Butcher again, you are my pupil, and Yuko … well my old brain can't see where she fits in again exactly, except Mieko was your sister and you are the daughter of Yoshida, my former boss, around whom this whole mess revolves."

They all sat quietly with their thoughts until Ted said, "The first thing I need your help on is this afternoon. I am scheduled to meet the American drug agent. I have warned him to come alone, but most certainly he will bring others. Can you help take care of them without killing them? I'm in enough trouble already."

"Don't be impudent. You know damn well I've put you out more than once, but you're still around," Obara said with a feigned huff.

"Good. We can work out a plan."

"It's not the American I am concerned with. It's Nishida."

"How so?"

"He has hurt enough people. You won't let him live, will you?"

The thought had crossed Ted's mind with increasing frequency, first in Bangkok and then the revelation about Mieko. But he had thought he would report what he knew to Brody and let the authorities mete out the punishment. "Can't the police take care of it?"

"You disappoint me ... deeply. You sound like an American. First of all, this has gone beyond the police... above the police. The authorities know the *yakuza* exist, so why aren't they shut down? Even if you can pin something on Nishida, it won't be the rape of Mieko-chan or your attempted murder in Bangkok. He might go to jail but his sentence will be short and he will return unreformed. The sentence you face in Singapore is much worse.

"Second, this has become an affair between you and him. If he finds you, he will no doubt try to kill you. The police cannot prevent that. And if you let him live, psychically, he will always be there attacking you, in your memory, the man who defiled the

347

sweet flower Mieko and ruined your life in Singapore. I certainly could not live with that. I hope you are not so weak-bellied that you can," Obara concluded, his arms folded across his chest.

Yoshida had hoped Yamashita would conveniently forget the prior day's phone call or not have any interest in what Yoshida had to offer. He regretted having been so coarse with the man who had ruined his life, but knew apologies would not be accepted. He would not further seek the attention of the *yakuza* and if they called, he could only play the scenario out.

It was with much dread, then, that he received a call at his office after lunch.

"Yoshida. Do you still have the American?"

"Where you will never find him." Nor I, he thought.

"We want to meet him."

"Fine. I'll arrange it, as soon as I get all the legally executed documents from you. Our deal, remember?"

"Don't try my patience."

"Don't threaten me. I will properly advise our young American friend to go to the authorities. My remaining wealth can at least hire a good lawyer."

"You won't need a lawyer in hell."

"Now you try my patience."

"OK. We will prepare the document."

"Good. Shall we say tomorrow night. Perhaps 7 o'clock?"

"You will have the American with you?"

"Of course not. I shall tell you where to find him. A place where he will be waiting for my phone call. He knows to leave there if my call does not come in."

348

"I am sure you know better than to try and fool us. We will be there at 7 p.m."

Yoshida hung up the phone slowly, his mind occupied with other thoughts. There were countless affairs that had to be put in order, legal matters to review, the disposition of Tokaido Meats, not to mention an impossible search for Ted. A man with no family is hard put to plan his own funeral, he lamented.

Bergman had chosen the wrong time to arrange a rendezvous, Brody decided. Tokyo station was packed, seas of people flowing in neap tides through the corridors, surging, dividing, rejoining. He supposed Ueno would be the same and it would be impossible for Bergman to pick his tail out among so many thousands of nondescript office workers.

Brody turned to the young Japanese liaison agent who was to follow him from the train and expressed this view.

"Yes, we all look alike to Westerners, anyways," the Japanese man joked, without seeing the humor in the comment he had heard before. He looked around the crowded train platform nervously despite himself. He did not want to be made a fool of as his counterpart was on the trip from the airport. "I think we should separate after we get on the train," he cautioned.

"OK, Tanaka-san. No more talking," Brody agreed as he stepped back away and others crowded in around his tail on the queuing area.

In the distance a train appeared. Tanaka looked back over his shoulders and flicked his eyebrows up to signal Brody that this was the train they were to board. The din increased as the first car of the train rushed past them and subsided as it came to a stop. The door opening reminded him of the starting gates at Aqueduct Raceway. The people spilled out, propelled by those behind and their own frenzy to catch a connecting train on another platform. Brody was pushed to one side and waited until almost all the arrivals had disembarked, then was propelled on board himself by the mass to his rear as the high-pitched electronic whistle reported the imminent departure of the vehicle.

Once on board, Brody was unable to move. He stood "facing" a Japanese businessman, one head shorter than him, who was trying to read his newspaper and hold the strap at the same time. The newspaper was practically resting on Brody's chest. Occasionally the old man would look up at Brody with tired eyes, then go back to scanning the sumo news.

At the next stop some people got off in front of him and an unequal number boarded. He used the interval to move further into the car. He regretted changing places. After taking a strap and preparing himself for the start of movement, he began to smell something. He looked over his left and then his right shoulder when he saw the source of the odor.

An old panhandler, Brody thought at first. I didn't know Japan had bums. The man reeked of sweat, old beer, and nicotine. When Brody looked back at him again he realized he was either retarded or drunk. He swayed expansively with the train and sang a song in a low tone with his eyes half closed. He noticed Brody looking at him and his eyes opened wider as if trying to focus and a cigarette-stained smile broke across his wrinkled face. He started to sing more audibly as if to serenade a new American friend. Brody tried to ignore him and soon the volume of the singing went back to a mumble obscured by the sound of the train.

He glanced past Tanaka who was standing five shoulders to

his left. Tanaka had pulled a folded newspaper from his coat pocket and was reading it.

After the next stop Brody began to maneuver back toward the door, for he knew by counting the number of stops Tanaka had mentioned that Ueno was next. Tanaka would get out the rear door and he the center. He pushed his way up close to the door as the train began to brake. In front of him was a young couple, together but not cuddling. Japanese conservatism, he assumed, but felt the pair were a little unusual. They were both dressed very colorfully; he was tall for a Japanese and well-built, she petite and well-proportioned with an innocent-looking face that nonetheless had a come-hither look. He caught himself thinking she would be good in bed.

The doors opened and Tanaka was spilled out onto the platform. He looked left and right, saw Brody emerge from the center door and get pulled along with the crowd toward the steps. It was difficult to see anything more than Brody's head and he certainly had no time to look for Bergman. Ahead a drunken bum was reeling through the crowd, bumping and bowing. As he approached, Tanaka tried to step around him. The drunk suddenly veered into Tanaka who held out his arm to catch the man. As the man's weight settled into his forearms, a wracking pain suddenly imploded from his ribs into his lungs. His knees buckled underneath him and he fell gasping to the cement. As he choked on the ground he saw the drunk turn away from him and his whole body sober up as he yelled, "This man's having a seizure; call the medic, he's sick. I'll call a medic, you stay here," he said, grabbing a businessman. "Give him some room, he's sick," were the last words Tanaka remembered hearing before blacking out.

At the steps, Ted and Yuko looked back to see a commotion on the platform. They knew Brody was right behind them and

351

having confirmed their diversion had worked, Ted grabbed him by the elbow. "Brody-san, no tricks and follow me."

Brody was stunned. It was the Japanese couple who had stood in front of him. He felt a firm, commanding grip behind his elbow which steadily became more firm until the pain was quite intense. "Let up, OK," he squirmed.

"Just no tricks."

At the top of steps they turned right and Brody began to get worried. Bergman had said the park exit so they should have turned left. He knew his second tail was supposed to wait at the exit and they were heading the other way. He tried to look back, but during the brief glimpse his escort allowed him he did not see Tanaka.

They turned abruptly and went down a long flight of steps to street level, exited through a ticket gate and crossed the street. Brody looked more carefully at his abductors. The woman was definitely Japanese. But the man on closer examination looked like ... "Bergman!" Brody exclaimed.

"Shut up, Brody, and keep walking; we'll be there soon."

They led him through, down and around several intersecting alleys which did not seem to meet at right angles. He completely lost his sense of direction. Unexpectedly, the firm grip on his elbow jerked and redirected his entire momentum to the left, propelling him into a small restaurant, giving him no time to look left or right or even memorize the restaurant's facade. They immediately went upstairs and found a table in the corner.

Ted directed Brody to sit with his back to the wall and the stairs to his left, while Ted sat in front of him, the stairs to his right. Yuko sat between them and called the old kimono-clad waitress over.

"This is a *Yakiniku* restaurant. Broiled meat on skewers. Hope you like it," Ted said amiably, his tone a complete reverse of what Brody had heard on the street.

"Quit jacking me around, Bergman, I'm not here for the cuisine."

"Mr. Brody. It's dinnertime, we have a lot to discuss, and since we'll be undisturbed here for quite some time, I think we should relax as best we can and eat a little. Beer?"

"Jesus. Yeah. Beer. OK. What have you done to my tails?"

"At least you admit you disregarded my instructions. The tail. We got one of them for sure. Right now he is probably in an ambulance and the medics are trying to decide what's wrong with him. By tomorrow they will determine that he merely suffered a very abrupt blow which caused a very small bruise. In other words, he's out of commission for the night, but no harm has come to him. As for the others, if there were others, they are probably waiting at the park entrance, possibly in the train station, but I don't think we were followed.

Two large bottles of beer were brought to the table and a glass was poured for Brody by the Japanese woman.

"Who's your friend?" Brody asked.

"Just a friend."

"You've involved her in quite a mess by bringing her along, you know."

"Mr. Brody, I am involved in 'this mess' more than you suspect."

Brody looked at the young woman, her eyes looking straight into his until he averted his glance. They were defiant eyes, not the contemptuous eyes of a laborer who hates the man exploiting her, he considered, but a confident defiance.

Brody decided to soften up. He felt he would get nowhere with the two if he remained aloof, and they had done nothing to harm him.

"OK, Ted and Miss Japanese-san." They both laughed at the improvised name. "Can we mend some fences here, and see where we can help each other?"

"Yes. What don't you know yet?"

"Are you innocent?"

"Am I involved with organized crime? No! Did I kill those two hoods? Yes. In self-defense, as you know. Did I smuggle drugs to Singapore? No. It was a plant."

"I'm going to believe you … for now."

"Thank you. I need that at least, right now."

"So if you're so virgin, how come you're involved in this at all?" Brody asked and sipped on his beer.

"Because I'm thorough. I work hard to prepare for a sales call before I ever see the customer. In this case, I think the customer mistook me for you, or someone like you."

"Ital-Siam?"

"Yes. You checked with Hatch?"

"Yep."

"What have you found out?"

"I'm asking the questions now," Brody rebutted. I have some surprises for you later, though, he thought.

"OK. So I was getting ready to see Ital-Siam. They must have picked up on it. Anyway …"

"Who did you go to see to check up on them?"

"Besides Hatch, I went to the Petroleum Ministry, the Concessions Department to see Khun Phansaeng"

"What did he tell you?"

"He said he hadn't heard of Ital-Siam. In retrospect, he acted

354

kind of queer about my visit but I didn't make a connection about it then."

"How so?"

"Just a feeling, nothing I could pin down, then or now."

The wizened woman in her dark blue kimono brought over a lacquered tray bearing several wooden serving dishes with queues of aromatic skewers covered with barbecued meats and vegetables. She placed them one by one quietly on the table and backed away with a short bow.

"You went to see Phansaeng before you came to the Embassy, right?"

"How did you know?"

Brody flicked his eyebrows and said smugly, "We found the pictures they took of you and me together."

"At the embassy?!"

"Yeah. Do you remember when we pulled out in the car and I jerked around? There was someone shootin' our picture."

"Shit."

"Yep. At least they weren't shootin' bullets. So then what."

"I went to see Ital-Siam. I had made a morning appointment and showed up on time. It was going smoothly, if not successfully when I overheard some Japanese talking about me."

"In Japanese?"

"Of course!"

"Hatch said you speak the language."

"Yeah, good thing, too, otherwise I wouldn't be here. These two Japanese were talking kind of low and secret but when I definitely heard that they were going to kill me, I about dumped in my pants," he laughed nervously, relieved to be telling the story to Brody. "I got out of the meeting as smoothly as possible and when

I was sure there was really someone following me, I called you."

"How did you manage to kill the two Thais?"

"You've probably seen the autopsy, I haven't."

"I mean how did you manage? What are you, ex-serviceman?"

"No. Just luck."

"You're jacking me around again," Brody said changing his tone of voice. "Both toughs died, probably without a sound, certainly quickly. I couldn't have done it better myself," he said, grinning trying to open up Bergman again.

"It's just a skill I picked up along the way. Karate, high school, college."

"That wasn't karate, Ted. What are you, CIA?"

Ted pursed his lips. "It's the same thing that took out your man tonight."

"Ninja?"

"Don't make me barf."

"Kung fu?"

"In the sense that it is an acquired skill, yes, but Japanese, not Chinese. Look, don't play a guessing game. It's really nothing you've heard of before and nothing I have ever used before. All right?"

"For now. So then what did you do?"

"I went back to the hotel and packed and checked out."

"You didn't pack any drugs in your bag? Didn't notice any?"

"No," Ted took a deep breath and signed. "When I rode to the airport, though I shared the limo with a Thai. He looked business-like enough. Could have been him, though, that made the plant."

"What did he look like?"

"He was well-cut and well-dressed, tall for a Thai, about my height, and lean. He could speak English."

"Do you normally ride with strangers?"

"Well, you save a buck here and there. It adds up."

"Why didn't you call me before you left? Or come straight to the embassy?"

"Hindsight is twenty-twenty, right? But I was scared and rushed and I thought I could call you from the relative safety and sanity of Singapore."

"Why did you come to Japan?"

"It was the furthest destination in the right direction I could get to with cash. And I have friends here," he said looking at Yuko and smiling.

Brody looked at the two of them and bit a piece of chicken from a skewer. "Anything else you two want to tell me?"

"I've got some questions I need answered before we talk more."

"I'll see what can I do. Shoot."

"Have you arrested the people at Ital-Siam?"

"Hell no. That's why I'm talking to you. So we can build a case."

"Are they under surveillance?"

"You know Nero? He's dead. Last night in Tokyo. Probably poison."

"What about the Japanese?"

"They're in Tokyo, too. We're not sure where right now."

"Am I in real trouble, Brody? It is something I can get out of, something you can get me out of. Can't you?"

"Yes, you are in trouble. Real trouble, if everyone looks to find you, but not close enough to see your case. Everything you've told me could be a fabrication. You might be the Italian's trump card against their Japanese partners, or vice versa, or just someone who deals with them. What better way to cover your ass than to contact me when you realize you're being cut loose."

"You don't believe that, do you, Brody?" Ted asked incredulously.

"No. But someone else might."

"So who do I have to convince?"

"I think we should handle it through Thailand. You haven't broken any laws in Japan yet. And we can prepare a report for Singapore to clean you up there. The Thai authorities are only interested in getting the record straight, not prosecuting, and besides, you acted in self-defense. It may be messy for a while, but it can be worked out."

"What about Ital-Siam, the *yakuza*. Will they be stopped?"

Brody chuckled. "No, I doubt it."

"Why the laugh?" Ted asked in a low snarl.

"Because, I can't do anything here, my hands are tied, my counterpart's a pussy, and the locals are afraid to move, I guess."

"You're just going to let them get away, business as usual," Yuko spoke up in an accusing tone backed by Ted's glare.

"We finally hear from you, Miss Japanese-san."

"Yes, and it sounds like you are the pussy, Mr. Brody," she said sharply.

The agent focused his eyes narrowly on hers, not averting his stare this time for her words stung him like cold sea spray. "Let me tell you something," he began in spite of himself. "I want to catch these buggers as much as anyone. You don't know," he shook his head. "Less than a year ago this kind of scum killed my wife. My wife! Since then I've had no good leads, until Bergman came along. If I didn't care, if I didn't want their peckers nailed to the wall, do you think I would have come here. You think I would have come myself? I'm not supposed to work Japan. But I want something to happen. But my hands are tied. Anyway, what's it to you?"

"Indeed, Mr. Brody. What is it to me? Let me tell you."

"No, let me start, Yuko." Ted interjected.

"You probably know I lived in Japan before, as a teenager," he said to Brody.

"Yeah."

"Well, at the time I fell in love with the daughter of my father's business associate."

"Yoshida?"

Ted and Yuko's eyes widened. "You work quickly, Mr. Brody. Yes."

Yuko continued, "My father owed a lot of money to the *yakuza*. When he didn't pay, they kidnapped Mieko, my sister, and … used her … sexually. She could not bear the shame and took her life."

"Yuko's got a letter," Ted added. "Mieko wrote it before she jumped in front of a subway train. The man who did this to her … is the same … the same one who tried to kill me," Ted said choking on the words, his teeth clenched.

Brody's stare softened but remained fixed on the two young people. "Jesus," he said under his breath. "You're sure?"

"She uses his name in the letter."

"Jesus God."

"He must pay, Brody. I know you agree. And you said there is no chance of prosecution here."

"That's what I've heard."

"So what do we do?"

"Can you give me a day? Let me find out what more they found in Thailand and the autopsy report on the Italian. You keep low and I'll try to keep you out of any more reports. Will you do that?"

"I'll lay low," Ted agreed, but even as he spoke, he was calculating how revenge could come to him.

"Ted," Yuko said, emerging from the bathroom of their cramped hotel room, brushing her long hair. "Do you think we can trust Brody?" she sat down on the bed opposite him.

"It's a little late to reconsider now. But yes, if you're talking about him being square with us. If you mean 'Can we trust him to bring in Nishida,' no. I don't think it will happen."

"So we will still go after Nishida?"

"I suppose, only I don't know how to get to him."

"That's not too difficult. We can get him to come to you probably."

"How?"

"Through my father. He'll know how to contact Nishida. We can make him do it once he knows you understand the whole past."

"The least he can do. I'm so disappointed in him. You know I used to think he and I had a rapport. That he liked me. And I respected him, even more than I respected my father sometimes. All these years of being torn up about Mieko and thinking maybe I had something to do with it and feeling bad because I might have taken his daughter away from him and all the time he was the one. God, it's a lonely piss ant world and I hate to say it about your father, but he's a fucking coward."

"Don't apologize. You have been pained living without the knowledge of his real face. I have been pained living with it. But soon enough we will put all this behind us," she said, putting her hand on his, making his pulse jump. "We can stop Nishida from hurting us, or anyone, again. And get on with our lives."

Ted looked into her eyes and drank in the resolve he saw there. "Yuko, you are an extraordinary person."

Yuko was aware of his conscious choice of a nonsexist term and his reason for it and said, "Woman, Ted. Extraordinary? Not unless you have spent your time with lesser 'persons,'" she smiled. "You at least deserve a me."

Ted swallowed hard as his mind raced through a dozen years of emotion, devotion, denial, and rejection. This goddess sitting before him could not possibly want him, he thought. What had he done to deserve her love?

"Yuko, I …"

But she touched her fingertips to his lips. "Ted, I told you the other day I was waiting for someone. I have been waiting for you, or at least someone as good as you. I have never found anyone."

Ted shook his head involuntarily, "I can't believe you could love me too."

"You remember I said I felt guilty reading Mieko's diary," Yuko said as she stared down at their joined hands. "It was because I thought my crush on you had caused her fate. It was just a matter between sisters, my infatuation with her boyfriend, but it developed into more than that. When I read her diary and why she loved you and how she loved you, I loved you too, more and more, and even now. Why do you suppose I tried to perfect my English. I even went to study in the U.S.A. and look for you, but you were abroad already and your parents would not give me your address.

"When I opened the door to you yesterday, my heart almost stopped. I had resigned myself to a life alone. That is why I studied philosophy, to try and make some sense out of my fate. Do you believe me now?" she implored, looking into his eyes. They were shut tight and pent-up tears broke through the seal to roll down his

361

nose.

His answer was physical as he pulled her to him and embraced her as a drowning man grasps at a float. Their arms wrapped tightly around each other as they rocked gently. Finally, Ted said quietly "I, too, have waited long years for a love. Thank you for waiting."

She gently pushed him down to lie on the pillow, her head above his, a long wisp of silky black hair tumbling across his cheek and neck. "This may be our last night alive," she said seriously.

He thought about the strange statement a moment and realized it was possibly true. "So?"

"So, don't let me die a virgin," she quipped with a shy grin.

NINE

Morning light illuminated the pure white sheets and Yuko's golden body next to Ted's. Looking at her through half-opened eyes, the warm glow of the memory of the night before swept through him. After making love, they had fallen asleep in each other's arms, the small size of the single bed a welcome confinement, flesh warming flesh. His sleep had been sound and now, with the dawn, his mind contemplated what his heart had realized.

All these years I have been searching. Searching for the perfect lay, for something sexually special. What a waste of time. He smelled Yuko's natural musk and scented hair and his heart jumped. Technique is not important. It is secondary. There is no perfect lay devoid of emotional bond. Love is the aphrodisiac, he realized. He laughed to himself. Why did it take me so long to know what any good poet could tell me?

Yuko woke up to see Ted's gently smiling face next to hers. It was a beautiful face, she thought, as she smiled back at him, no less so in the morning light. She had not been prepared for the passion he had unleashed in her the night before. She had thought she had an idea of what physical love would bring her. In the past she had many dreams that awakened her at night, excited, and she had touched herself until the flush of high tide consumed her spirit. But nothing had compared with his soft touch, here and there, and his breath and lips and tongue. She had feared an impatient lover, but he had waited and touched and rubbed until she could stand to wait no more. Then he had taken her and she was helpless to control the surges of pleasure that shuddered through her body. He had felt her release and then she had felt his insistence, and as his excitement had built up, so again had hers. She had cried out uncontrollably as their ecstasy peaked together and they slumped into the pillows, one perspiring body.

The two lovers' warm reflections were extinguished by a crisp knock on the door. Ted's heart pounded furiously and he whispered urgently in Yuko's ear, "You get it." He drew the *tanto* he had reassembled, its matte-silver, patinaed edge a hardened razor, and stood out of sight in the bathroom.

Yuko quickly pulled on her *yukata* and tied the sash loosely, then looked through the viewhole and opened the door quickly. "Obara-san!" she exclaimed grabbing his arm and pulling him in before anyone appeared in the hall to see him. Obara obliged her tug and came quickly into the room, his movements smooth for a man his age. He looked about, assessing the room. Only one bed had been slept in. He smiled inwardly, then grinned broadly as Ted emerged from the bathroom, one hand holding up a small towel wrapped tightly around his waist, one hand holding a fine knife.

"Just as I would expect," he began with mock sternness. "Armed, naked, and sated. Let me see that blade," he concluded with a grin.

Ted obliged his request, handing the knife to him butt first after deftly reversing the blade's position in his hand with a smooth, gravity-guided motion.

The precision and naturalness of the movement was not lost on Obara, who admired the amount of skill his disciple had retained, but he pushed that thought aside as he stared minutely at the gleaming steel. "You are paid well enough to afford such a treasure?"

"I haven't had it checked to see if it is real valuable or not," Ted replied modestly.

"Very nice, neh? And this nick here on the edge, a good sign for a fighting knife."

"Why?" Yuko asked, also mesmerized by the beauty of the dagger.

"Barring neglect, and a samurai would not have neglected such a knife, it means this has seen and survived real combat. It has tasted blood, maybe killed a wounded samurai."

"Not a sword?" she asked again.

"No, maybe two samurai on the field of combat who have lost the measure they need to fight with long weapons." He sheathed the blade. "They are at close quarters, grappling. One of them, the owner of this weapon, draws the *tanto* quickly as he seizes his opponent's right arm, jamming it before he can draw his." He stepped into Ted, shoving the taller American's right elbow into his body and slamming him against the wall. "He struggles and raises his arm to escape and draw at the same time, but ..." Obara scooped Ted's foot up with a kick to his heel upsetting him, then the wiry old man jammed the wooden sheath into Ted's armpit as he fell. "The sweep opens up the unarmored underarm. Did I ever show you that one?" he asked as he pulled Ted up off the floor.

"No, you old fox. What else are you holding back on?"

"Enough to still beat you, you little prick," he replied jovially, pulling off Ted's towel. "Well, maybe not so little," he appraised. "Put that tool away now," he said as Ted blushed and Yuko suppressed a laugh. "We have got to get you back in shape so you can be worthy of the weapon you carry. Also, we have to do some scouting." He turned to Yuko. "I am afraid we will need your help, Yoshida-san, but at the same time I hope you will not accompany us. We must work fast and without … distractions."

"Obara-san, say what you want done, and it will be done. Anything," she said with a resolve he appreciated.

"First, we must call your father. He is the only one we know who may know where we can find Nishida."

"Is it wise to engage Nishida so openly?" Ted asked.

"We have no other way of taking care of this business quickly. Do you agree?"

"Yes."

"And we must act fast. Your American friend will get anxious, neh?"

"Yes. What should I do about Brody?"

"Let's finish this first call, and then I will tell you. Yuko, please, call your father. Don't tell him I am here or that Takabashi has seen me. Tell him you have told Takabashi the whole story and he knows the Nishida who killed our Mieko and the one who tried to set him up are one and the same. Yoshida must help to arrange a meeting."

"What's the meeting for?"

"Anything, let them suspect, they'll come, especially if what my belly tells me is right about Nishida."

"Where and when do we meet?" Yuko asked.

"Ted and I have to find a place. Tell him you will call back at 7 o'clock this evening to confirm a time and place. Don't tell him where you are."

"Yes," she confirmed as she picked up the phone receiver and dialed the number of her family's house.

366

The phone rang only twice and was snatched up by Yoshida.

"Moshe moshe …"

"Father."

"Yuko!" the voice exclaimed its relief on the phone. Yoshida had given up hope of finding Bergman in time.

"Yes."

"Where are you?"

"Never mind. We must talk."

"Where can we meet?"

"We must talk now, on the phone. I have told Ted everything about Mieko. I have shown him the last letter she wrote."

"You … have it?"

"Yes. He knows all about your *yakuza* debts. He is sure the Nishida who killed … who abducted Mieko is the same one who tried to have him killed."

"And?" Yoshida asked, wondering where she was leading.

"He wants to meet Nishida, alone."

"That's it, he wants to meet him?"

"Yes."

Yoshida's mind raced through the implications. He was off the hook, for the time being. He could deliver Bergman, but what was the American up to? Surely he did not think he could take out a *yakuza* clan alone. Blackmail? Equally dangerous.

"When?"

Yuko was disturbed by her father's immediate acquiescence to the scheme. So I was right, she thought, he was going to turn Ted over to Nishida. "We will call again at 7 o'clock to confirm a time and place."

"How about here at 7 this evening?"

"No, Ted will fix the time and place. This will not be any

367

problem for you to set up?" she asked.

Realizing he had been too enthusiastic about the aim of her call, he awkwardly changed his tone, "I don't know. Perhaps it won't be easy. I have been out of contact with those dogs for ... so long."

She found his about-face laughable, but held her tone steady. "Be waiting for the call at 7. Goodbye, father."

"Goodbye, Yuko."

She replaced the receiver and looked to the two men who waited for her word. Obara-san was like a grandfather. Not the stuffy, all-business grandfather she had once had, but like the jovial, retiried, golf-playing, karaoke-singing grandfathers she saw on T.V. Obara, however, was too poor to play golf or enjoy karaoke, she lamented. Ted was her love of loves. The man she had waited for, the person she had dreamed would return to her life. Both of them waited on her word like orders to do battle. She knew death would be born from her words; either the death of her friends or the death of her foes. But she knew, too, that none of the three of them could consider a life of nonaction.

"Well?" Ted blurted out shaking her from her meditations.

She laughed bitterly, "I am glad I got you out of my father's house the other day. For surely he would have turned you over to the *yakuza*."

Obara shook his head sullenly, ruefully acknowledging the descent of his old friend from humanity. "So he will arrange a meeting."

"I think he already had!"

It was Ted's turn to shake his head in wonder.

"Cheer up," Obara said, "It's good news. If the *yakuza* wanted him to help them find you, then they won't suspect any trap when we do meet them."

"OK, so what's your plan for Brody."

"If you were he, what would make you suspect the least?"

"An admission of something, coming clear."

"Yes, and what is his jurisdiction? Thailand, neh?"

"Yes."

"Call him now and leave a message for him. Tell him you will call back at 6 o'clock."

"Between now and then book return flights for you and him to Bangkok tomorrow morning. When you call him, tell him you trust him and feel safe enough to return with him to Bangkok the next day. Tell him you will lay low and meet him at the airport. I think he'll go for it. After our work tonight you'll be safe to leave with his escort. As far as they know, you have broken no laws here."

"Old man, what if I'm cut up bad, or dead?"

"If you're dead we'll cancel your seat," he chuckled. "But you're not going to die," he said. "Wounds can be bandaged. You must not concern yourself with your death or injury or they will surely come. Concern yourself …"

"Only with cutting down the opponent." Ted finished the line he had heard many times before. Looking at Yuko, he suddenly found it hard to wish conviction into his words.

Brody sat in stony silence, looking at the Japanese calendar girl's photograph superimposed on a picture of Mount Fuji. This is the umpteenth time Peterson has just left me sitting in this cubicle cooling my heels, he fumed. I can't do anything on my own, he's so fucking slow he makes a turtle look hyper, and that ditzy secretary won't get me anything without asking him first. He forced a tense grin as he heard Peterson re-enter the room.

"Sorry, another call," the Tokyo section chief apologized with a shrug. "Where were we? Your meeting with Bergman?"

"No, let's not continue on that. I want the info on the Italian."

"Aren't we rushed?" His question was a snide statement.

"Aren't we an asshole?" Brody retorted in the same tone. "Look Peterson, you haven't given me diddly shit since I got here. I think I've demonstrated that with Bergman's help we are pursuing some decent leads, and what kind of help are your people?"

"What kind of help can they be? One guy was laid up yesterday while with you. You wanna explain it?"

"I didn't even see what happened. He wasn't looking where he was going, he was lookin' after me. He ran into a column or someone's umbrella or something. Why? What do you think happened?"

"I don't know, you were there. He just reported passing out when he bumped into someone."

"Your guy is good, right? Observant?"

"Yeah. The best I have. He's OK."

"So no one would have noticed him. How could they have picked him out? It was probably an accident; if it had been criminal, he'd be dead, don't you suppose?"

"So why didn't you stop to help?"

"I was already going up the steps and didn't want to draw attention to him by looking back."

"All right. Let's not beat a dead horse 'til the maggots fly. Did you learn anything from Bergman?"

"Nothing that will help out hereabouts, but he was able to give me everything he knew about the Thai side."

"Where is he?"

"Somewhere safe. I told him to lay low and give me a call today."

"Why do I have the feeling you're not squaring with me, Brody."

"Because you're an asshole, like I said." He laughed to break the tension and let Peterson know he was joking. "I made a promise to you yesterday. And, by the way, there's nothing I can do here on my own because No. 1, I am not on my own turf; No. 2, I doesn't speak the lingo; and No. 3, I can't start without information from your people, which I ain't getting."

"You make me nervous, Brody."

"Let's hope the bad boys feel that way, too, eh?"

"OK," Peterson said, putting the shock of Brody's rudeness behind him. "Here is the autopsy for Nero." He handed a manila folder to Brody marked:

> Nero, Paulo, autopsy, see also Great Star Construction
> Nishida, Yoshikazu
> Willian Brody, investigator.

Brody scanned the translation the police department had faxed to the DEA branch. "Poison?"

"Looks like it. Well-done too. Herbal and made to react potently with his alcohol and excitement."

"Not just rat poison, huh?" Brody quipped.

"No. If murder had not been suspected by us, a normal autopsy would only have revealed a heart attack and some hemorrhaging in the brain. I just got off the horn with my Japanese counterpart. The girl who was jacking off the Italian hadn't served him the tea, and said it had been delivered while she was in the bathroom. She didn't see the guy who brought it."

"The plot thickens," Brody smirked

Peterson scowled, "Yeah, yeah. Don't bust my chops. What d'ya suggest?"

"See if we can tail Nishida and his No. 2 for a while. Unless we can get him on some charge here, tie him to Nero's death, we'll have to try to get him extradited to Thailand. Do Thailand and Japan have an extradition treaty?"

"I don't know. Let's check. Do you suppose it would be easier to convict in Thailand? Here they'll have the support of established *yakuza* networks from top to bottom."

"If we can get him back to Thailand, then we might be able to convict. But the judicial system there has been known to occasionally bend rules."

Peterson's secretary peeped around the door, "Mr. Brody," she said shyly, trying to gently interrupt the brusque man she sensed her boss did not like. "You had a call a moment ago from a Mr. Ted Bergman."

"Great! Put him on the line."

"Had a call, sir. He said he just wanted to check in with your office and said everything was all right and that he will call back at 6 o'clock."

Brody concealed his concern about the odd nature of the call and said confidently to Peterson, "You see. Everything's straight. Bergman's laying low and keeping safe until we can make a move."

"Mr. Brody," the secretary interjected again. "You also just received these fax messages from Bangkok over the scrambler."

He took the sheaf of papers from her and scanned the points his assistant Jackson had delineated.

Peterson saw Brody's eyes widen and his head shake when reading a certain conclusion. Finally, when Brody clucked his tongue lightly and said "Bingo" under his breath, Peterson could no longer stand to wait. "You wanna share these revelations with me or what?" he said impatiently.

"I'll think about it. Yeah. OK. This is good stuff, what we've been waiting for. I think you heard that we had seized some documents Nero left behind, presumably in a safe place."

The Tokyo section chief, sitting back in his chair, his two hands together with his fingertips supporting his chin, nodded affirmatively.

"We've had a chance to file through them. A vague, but significantly clearer, picture is coming together."

"Which is?"

"You know what Bergman was doing snooping around this company, right?"

"Fill me in."

"He was trying to sell them some gear for petroleum exploration. On first glance the owners of the company look legit. Their office looks legit, they have all the right authorizations. Even I was almost fooled when I went to their office. Nero is, was, a petrochemical engineer."

"But?"

"But they're not legit. If Bergman hadn't stubbed his toe on them, we probably wouldn't have noticed."

"Noticed what? What were they up to?"

"This is great. It's still just a strong theory, but we think we figured out how they were going to export a semi-refined opiate mud to Europe, Japan, and the U.S. in twenty-foot freight-container quantities."

"Impossible."

"Listen. Apparently a vital part of oil exploration is the examination of fossilized micro-organisms from prehistoric sediment. They bore hundreds of deep holes and bring up the core intact. It has to be specially packed and marked according to the depth and the place and refrigerated to prevent spoiling. Later, micropaleontologists — there's a $10 word for you — examine the cores under microscopes to see what lived at what depth, at what age. They can use this to try to determine where and how deep to drill."

"Bill, this is interesting, but ..."

"Hey, I'm getting to the good part. This group was really trying to find oil and gas, but on the side they planned to have opiate mud cores packed and marked the same as the real ones and shipped out with the real ones to their 'research labs.' Do you think these big, obvious, expensive, refrigerated vans being imported by legitimate concerns would have come under much scrutiny? No way."

"You said 'they planned.' It hadn't been put into effect yet?"

"Looks like we caught them just before it was expected to start up. They were delayed by a Thai government attack on one of their suppliers' refineries.

"There's more, too. A guy answering the description Bergman gave me of the Thai who he thinks put the drugs in his bag was found dead, apparently from a fall down the steps ... of the building where Ital-Siam is located.

"And," he said animatedly, holding up his index finger, "there's more. Thai authorities have taken in for questioning the helicopter pilot employed by Ital-Siam. That's still ongoing, but could lead to some conclusive details."

"So Bergman is just what he said he is," Peterson said, his tone between a disappointed statement and doubting question.

"If you're asking me, I'd say yes. His business connection

checks out, he has no record, I met him accidentally before the whole thing started and he impressed me as being rather conservative. And, within the limits he feels he can take due to the danger he thinks he's in, he has cooperated with us."

"OK. Let's get the tail set for Nishida. They may have already put him under surveillance because of our inquiries and Nero's death, but let's double check."

Yamashita sat quietly in his office after a late lunch, trying to meditate and let his hastily eaten meal of Japanese fast-food noodles settle in his upset stomach. The pressures of executive life had unavoidable drawbacks. His mind was constantly evaluating deals. Big deals, new deals, old deals, legal deals, shady deals, the people who played as factors in these deals, customers, markets, competition; an endless stream of mental interruptions as one thought created another. He liked to try to meditate for at least ten minutes every day after lunch. It helped put his morning's activities into perspective and keep lunch in place.

However, today the misty shroud of peacefulness did not descend over his meditation, isolating it, and stopping his internal dialogue. His thoughts were varied, deep, and led him to conclusions he was not sure he liked.

I don't know how much longer I can stand Japan. It's just not the same country as before. The younger generation is just farting around, not driving themselves. Is there anywhere in Tokyo I can go and find what used to be Japan? Even at home my son talks badly to me and listens to obnoxious music. My married daughter ignores me and my wife rarely seeks to please me alone. It's good I am getting old. I won't see the final degradation of Japan when these

375

youngsters who have forgotten how to be Japanese find out they aren't good Westerners either. The West will eat us alive. Our markets will be decimated, our technological edge eroded, just like what happened to America. Maybe even the Chinese and Koreans will assume leadership. The thought of those fatherless hoards getting an edge up on us makes me want to vomit. His thoughts realized their form and his stomach gurgled nervously. The food is lousy, too. When I was a boy, a bowl of noodles was a poor man's rich meal. Thinking back, he could taste the cold, salty brine and the raw, satisfying taste of buckwheat noodles his grandmother had hand-made for him. But these instant noodles today, though anyone can have them any time, are worthless. They have no taste beyond basic salt and starch. I'm sure they have no food value, and they only fill an empty pocket in one's stomach. Even so the empty pocket cries out for something more. I bet a bowl of real *soba* like grandma used to make would cost an hour of a working man's wage. Ridiculous. Criminal!

At the thought of robbery, his attention turned to Nishida who he then realized was the object at a subconscious level that had brought on his indigestion. Nishida. To have such a nephew. Such an anachronism. As a foot soldier in old Japan, he would have excelled. He would have trained hard, fought brutally, and died early, thinking he had done well serving his master. But this world presents few opportunities for such as he. He chose his profession well, but even this profession needs him less and less, at least at the level of management to which he would like to think he belongs.

In a flash of inspiration which made Yamashita blink with shock he realized that his meditation had been fruitful. He had seen something in a new, clearer way. Even crime in Japan is getting soft. Cash rich, pot-bellied: soft crime. Salary-man crime. Even crimeless crime. He laughed inwardly at the thought. We invest our funds in legitimate businesses. Are they criminal because of the source of their investment? Crimeless crimes.

So where does that leave Nishida? Alone. A nasty brute, a hardened criminal in a world of gentle, middle-class salary men. A man whose principal tool for social intercourse is violence. He hardly has a place in our organization anymore, much less in society. We cannot return him to the street; he would kill himself rather than lose so much face. We can't promote him; he has proven totally unable to handle any but the coarsest actions requiring the least finesse and subtlety. It is time to cut our losses with poor Nishida.

He sensed the mixture of cold calculation and sentiment in his thought and examined it. This is a business. As an employee, he is a failure; as an investment, he has turned into a liability. Still, he is flesh and blood. Even I cannot order the trigger pulled on him. After this Bergman affair is concluded, perhaps Nishida will see fit to seek his own penance. Perhaps it would even be correct to hope he does not survive his encounter. Better to die than to err again.

His secretary's quiet knock at his desk told him his time of meditation was through. He slowly opened his eyes and looked at her.

She smiled back and bowed at the waist slightly, her hands folded in a triangle, her round, firm belly covered by her palms and the large manila envelope she held to her lap. She extended it to him. "The legal documents you asked to have prepared, Yamashita-san."

Yamashita sighed. If this was all it was going to cost to stop the hemorrhaging of the Thai business they had so carefully developed, then it was a reasonable price. At any rate, he was glad to be rid of the Tokaido Trucking shares. They had never obtained majority ownership anyway. Yoshida's treachery had seen to that. And then the unfortunate accident surrounding Yoshida's daughter had left a bad taste in his mouth about the whole affair. His own daughters had been the same age and … listen to yourself. Soft crime. You can't even stomach the consequences of your own actions. Where's the brutally ruthless edge you once had? Gone with the need for it, he reflected. Gone like the need for Nishida is gone. He picked up his chop and corporate seal, inspected the documents carefully, and imprinted his and his company's name; another deal done.

Ted had been hard put to keep up with Obara as his mind raced over the details they had to cover. They had sent Yuko out to buy some dark-colored track suits and sat discussing preparations in his hotel room. First Obara had considered the weapons.

"We have to do it quietly and we have to do it quickly," the old man said.

"Knives?"

"Of course. That's our specialty, eh, 'Little Butcher'?"

Ted recoiled at the name.

"What? You don't like the name? Get used to it. Remember it, assume it as yours; it is yours. If you are going to remain soft on these animals, they will devour you, and very possibly Yuko as well."

Ted's eyes narrowed as he balanced yet again in his mind the terror of killing once more and the need for it. "OK. Knives, 'Big Butcher.'"

"That's the spirit. But knives aren't enough. This time Nishida may come prepared. I shouldn't even speculate. He will come prepared. How?" It was not a question he expected Ted to answer. "He will probably bring a minimum of two, maximum of four, toughs with him, I'd say."

"How do you know?"

"He doesn't want to parade around with an entourage, especially if he's up to no good. And besides he doesn't deserve the coverage. He's not so high up in the gang, and he is, by your accounts, a bungler."

"A bungler?"

"Yes. He's a loser." Obara could see Ted still did not understand. "He let Mieko escape from her bondage. She was less than no good to him dead. Not only did he lose the collateral he had obtained from Yoshida, but he lost a good lay." Obara's eyebrow lifted as he looked at the American for a reaction. Like swiftly moving storm clouds, he could see Ted's mood grow turbulent and dark.

"And you're alive, aren't you? If Nishida was good, you'd be dead. No, I think he is an overrated street hood who won't get more than four hands to help him."

"So he'll be easy to knock off?"

"No. He's a loser, but no one wants to die or be humiliated. Never underestimate your opponent. Not in preparation, his or yours, or in execution. Assume he will do anything to kill you."

Ted recalled the wracking pain in his chest as he looked up at Obara on their first meeting so many years ago. He had said the same thing then. "That's lesson No. 1."

"Very good, Bugman-san; it only took you how many years to learn? Just don't forget it today. I would expect one of the four we face to have a handgun, but he will be very hesitant to use it. I expect they will have knives, like ourselves. Perhaps one will have a sword or a short sword maybe. That's the one we have to be careful of. He has range, silence — powerful blows."

"What can we do against a *katana*?" Ted asked, a worried tone filling his voice as he considered that he had never trained against a live sword.

"We have no time to teach you a new repertoire of techniques so your old ingrained ones must suffice. However, we can give you some armor they won't expect."

Ted envisaged himself laced from head to foot in a suit of bamboo, leather, silk, and lacquer samurai armor, striking a fierce pose with sword in hand. "Won't armor be bulky and obvious?"

"Not what I have in mind. I have some ready I made for myself. I just hope it fits you. You'll see it later. Now, about our weapons; have you registered that knife of yours?"

"No. No time and no inclination. I didn't want to draw attention to myself at the airport when I brought it in by registering it."

"You would have brought more attention to yourself if you were caught smuggling it."

"Yes, I suppose."

"Can you afford to lose that knife?"

"If it saves my life and I have to ditch it, it will have been money well-spent."

"Good. Are you comfortable with it as fighting blade?"

"Yes. I wish the handle was a little better for gripping or it had a wrist thong or something."

"No problem. We'll bring it with us. I can fix that over at my place."

"OK."

"Let me carry it, though. They may have police boxes on the lookout for you. If you get stopped, it's best you don't have it."

"Aren't you going to be with me?"

"With you, yes, but if they stop you, I don't know you. You were a foreigner asking directions of me, or better yet, just let me walk away like we don't know each other."

"Why?"

"And another thing. If we get separated, I still want you to call Yoshida at 6 to tell him where to have the thugs to meet us."

"But we haven't decided!"

"It will be the last field we will have looked at. Keep them in mind as we check out a few places."

"But if the police have me?"

"They'll at least let you make a call. Anyway, I will go to face Nishida alone if you are indisposed. I'm sure I can at least take him out before the others get me."

Ted looked at the old man, the implications of his words slowly sinking in.

Seeing that Ted was about to comment with some unwanted sentiment, Obara waved him silent with a flourish of his hand. At that moment they both turned their heads at the sound of the solenoid lock clicking open in the door.

Yuko stepped through quickly and closed the door behind her. She was carrying a large shopping bag and a plastic bag from a grocery shop.

Obara took the shopping bag from her and emptied out two black track suits with maroon-striped sleeves. "Good. Perfect. The right choice of color. They have pockets, too," he said, examining their construction. "I hope I don't get cut up too badly tonight. I'd kind of like to have a chance to wear one."

Yuko, quite moved by the innocent declaration of sincere appreciation and poverty, said quickly, "Don't worry, Obara-san. If it gets cut up or can't be washed, I'll buy you a new one."

"You will?" Obara asked, genuinely touched.

"Anything you want, Grandpa Obara."

The old man smiled. "Did you get the other things?"

She emptied the plastic bag onto the bed.

"Bandages, antiseptic, adhesive. It was tough to get just what you wanted in this season. I had to go to a big department store. Here they are." She pulled a large-sized pair of black, unlined leather gloves from a bag.

"These will do. Try them on, Takabashi."

Ted slid his hands into the soft compartments and flexed his fists, the leather becoming shiny and taut over his knuckles. "Feels good. How did you know my hand size, Yuko."

With an unabashed smile, Yuko cupped her breast in her palm as if weighing and measuring.

Ted's eyes looked toward the ceiling as he shook his head and laughed.

"Very practical, isn't she?" Obara commented with mock dryness. "Now we have to get going. Yuko, are you going to stay checked in here?"

"It's too early to go home. My father will pump me for answers. I think I'll stay checked in here one more night."

"OK. You bring these things to my place a little before 6. We'll call Yoshida-san from my house and then you can return here and wait for our return. Ted, you can spend the night here or in Narita. If you stay here you've got to get up real early to get out to the airport. Which will it be?"

Ted's response was prepared before Obara phrased the question. "If it's all the same with you, I'll stay here tonight."

The old man returned a broad, cigarette-stained grin. "Let's go."

Their first stop had been reached by two short walks before and after a train ride.

"This is Shinagawa. I think," Obara huffed, his breathing heavy with the quick pace he maintained, "ther's a small shrine up here that might be a good meeting place. It is closed at 9, but after 7 it's pretty deserted."

"Not Sengakuji shrine?" Ted asked.

"You know it?"

"I know of it."

"What?"

"Isn't it dedicated to some samurai."

"Not exactly. It is where the forty-seven *ronin* are interred, where they committed their final acts of piety to their deceased lord."

"I read the novel. It's really there?"

"Of course."

"I don't really understand the term 'ronin,' though. 'Wave man,' 'man on the waves.' They felt that because their lord had died in disgrace they had to degrade themselves, that they were no longer samurai, that they were set loose as a man floating in the ocean?"

"Until they could avenge his death, yes, they felt they were no longer samurai, though they were not stripped of their class. They behaved degraded to make those on whom they sought revenge lower their guard. This took years. Finally, they killed their lord's foes all on one night and came to the shrine up this hill," Obara said as they turned off the main road and walked up an incline. "Here they all killed themselves."

"But did they really feel like men afloat loose in an ocean?"

"You ask me? I wasn't one of them. But think of yourself. I

think you are a *ronin*, too."

"What?"

"You were a lad well on the way to becoming master of yourself. Then what happened? The lord of your heart was brutally taken from you without reason. I feel you have lived the past decade aimlessly. Of course, you have had your mundane material goals, but there has been no higher purpose to your life, no dedication. You were off track, afloat."

"Old man, how do you know all this?" Ted asked incredulously.

"You reek of it, and I know you. My heart bled for you when you had to leave. I, too, have been a *ronin* of sorts since you left. And we have only one chance to become men again."

Ted touched Obara's arm, "Old man, I want to hug you."

"But you won't because you're smart, you don't want to be too familiar with me here. Thank you for your thought though; it has been a long time since anyone has hugged me."

They entered the shrine. There was a souvenir stand off to the right and the main shrine straight ahead, its old, weathered, wooden construction a welcome anachronism within the steel and concrete background. To the right of the shrine was the erection housing the large drum with the family crest of the lord of the forty-seven *ronin* painted on the head.

"What do you think?" Obara asked, obviously testing his disciple's judgement.

"There may be some good shadows at night, but I am worried about two things," Ted said, rapidly analyzing the pros and cons of the venue. "If it was one-on-one, this would be good, confined enough to be easy to find him, open enough to be able to arrange an ambush. But you speculate there will be four, plus us two; that

384

makes six in this small area. Too crowded."

Obara nodded and waved his hand for Ted to continue.

"The second problem is that there is no easy alternate way out. Only the front gate. It might be difficult or impossible to get out any other way and that might mean having to go through them or the police to get out."

"You are correct on both points, however, we will not leave 'through' them. Either they will retreat or die or we will die. You are correct about the police though. So, maybe next time," he smiled. "Let's go on to the next place."

They walked back to the main road, Daiichi Keihin, and Ted asked, "Where to now?"

"Shiba Park."

"Isn't that just up the road, not too far?"

"Yes."

"Shall we hail a cab?"

"No. I don't think we should take taxis tonight. People who see us together for extended periods may remember us, and where they took us. Let's get on the subway. Though it's close, I think we have to change lines once; but it's better this way."

Two brief one-stop subway rides brought them to Shiba Park. They emerged to see the golden, late afternoon sunlight reflecting through the shiny walls of medium-rise buildings and the Eiffel-like Tokyo Tower beyond the elevated Capitol Expressway. They walked under the expressway and soon came to the park.

"Let's try up here," Obara suggested, turning left and walking up a sidewalk that led into a small, densely forested area. They walked along a path, noting entrances, side paths, naturally lit areas, and areas where lone street lamps would shine at night. It was evident by the smell, the occasional pieces of debris, and by the several solitary figures they saw sleeping on park benches and against trees that this was a park frequented by some of Tokyo's homeless.

They walked up and around a slightly steeper hill. Into it had been leveled an area for picnicking, prayer, and relaxation. It was unpaved natural ground. There was a small prayer shrine where people had frequently burned incense. Ted and Obara paused, each quiet in his thoughts and observation. Turning toward each other, they realized that even a nod of agreement was not necessary. This was to be the place.

As Nishida stared at the black walls of the love hotel suite he occupied, he had an odd feeling of having lived through this sense of total frustration once before. Twice before? Of course, there had been the time he was forced to quit the judo team for teaching his judo opponent a lesson. He felt he had been right to demonstrate that he was the best judo player in school. For that, he had been punished without recourse. Though he had not done well in school, he had intended to graduate, something his mother had encouraged and his parents had not had the opportunity to do. When graduation on time became impossible, he had justified quitting, staying out to deny himself further failure. In his dark, contemplative mood today, though, he realized that decision had generated a greater failure.

The other instance he had felt such a caged-in, burning frustration, was during the affair with the Yoshida girl. Despite the circumstances under which they had met, he had felt a strong attraction to her. Though an *eta*, she was the kind of girl he had sought to befriend. Of course she was young, ten years younger than he, but that had only added to the sweetness of his captivity of her.

For years he had kept his memory of her hidden from his *yakuza* brothers until he had managed to turn love into hate and know that she and those like her had seduced him, turned his mind, distracted his attention like magic vixens. He had never admitted to others that she may have escaped because he had been too relaxed in security, his affection for her clouding his judgement.

But he had had to pay nonetheless for her escape. She had killed herself and Yoshida had threatened to go to the police. His uncle, Yamashita, had felt there was room to negotiate and was able to get some concessions out of Yoshida, but certainly not enough to cover his debt. This left Nishida to submit to Yamashita for penance.

The pain, deserved though it was, of severing his left little finger at the third joint and presenting the partial digit to Yamashita was only the beginning of his dismemberment. He had been reduced in rank and exiled to work for a country *yakuza* cousin, sweeping out *pachinko* parlors and watching for cheaters on the floor. Having endured this for three years, he had then been brought to Osaka and finally to Tokyo.

Yamashita had met with him on his return, the first time they had seen each other in five years.

"Nephew. You look well."

"Yes, uncle. I have been busy."

"I know. I requested those who led you to report to me regularly on your every infraction of their word and code," he paused as Nishida's eyes widened, wondering what he had done wrong. "Fortunately, they had little to report. ... You know, Nishida, you are like a troublesomely buoyant piece of shit that refuses to be flushed. You keep floating back to the surface, still smelling, but there, a reminder of one's waste. Do you agree?"

"Yes."

"Perhaps such a piece of shit should be spread around the fields as fertilizer rather than jettisoned to the drains. What do you think?"

That conversation had led to his slow redemption and initiation into a further scope of Great Star activities, including a six-month trip to Hawaii for which he had studied English. On his return from Hawaii he had been told by his uncle that he was needed to develop a project in Thailand. It was the opportunity to make up what he owed to Great Star and he had thanked Yamashita for his dispensation.

Yet here he was one year later, in the toilet again, waiting for the flush cord to be pulled. He had failed the *oyabun*, he had failed Yamashita, he had failed himself. But this time he was not going to be sucked down alone. He would take the American with him. That was the least he could do.

"Omori," he called out.

The corpulent tough shortly came to the doorway and looked in at Nishida. "Yes."

"Are those police snoops still outside waiting for some action?"

"Yes. They have been there for two hours."

"Bad for business."

"It's the slow hour anyway," Omori chuckled. "We better get rid of them before nightfall though."

"They will leave very soon."

"Yes?"

"Yes. When I go, they will go."

"Mmm. It does seen they may be here for you, yes. We heard back from a contact in the police department that an autopsy was called on the Italian. That's not usual. They said it was because he was a foreign tourist, but I don't believe it."

"He was done in well."

"Very well. Very expensive. We know of no one who could confirm that any of our people were near him. The girl he was with saw nothing."

"Good. I like dead ends. We have to be at Yoshida's at 7. How long will it take us to get there?"

"Normal traffic; an hour. But we have to get rid of your chaperones first. That may take an extra forty-five minutes."

"Let's see if we can do it clean and fast."

"You have an idea?"

"Get two cars ready." Nishida peeked through the drawn curtain to examine his options. The love hotel was an L-shaped building and the undercover police waited in their car parked on the inside of the long leg of the L.

"Pull the two cars up to the front door parallel to each other and the building," he said, pointing to the inside foot of the L. "We will go three in one car, two in the other. Let me get in the outside door of the car nearest these cops. I'll slide over and through the car with two more getting in behind me. I'll go out the inside door and into the next car. You get in behind me and I'll keep low. We'll pull up at the gate with the other car right behind, but let's turn opposite directions and see who these fatherless public servants follow."

"Where do we meet up?"

"Do these cars have phones?"

"Yes."

"I will tell them where to meet us after we have seen Yoshida. Are your men packing?"

"Yes. I have a pistol …"

"With a silencer?"

"Yes."

"And?"

"One other, Suzuki's brother will have a gun. The rest have short swords or knives. What do you want?"

"A good, sharp knife."

"Would you carry mine?" Omori asked respectfully.

"It would be an honor. May I see it?"

Omori's left shoulder jolted downward and the wooden handle of a short fighting knife appeared out of his sleeve caught in his left palm. He removed the weapon gently and held it high in both hands as a gesture of obeisant presentation.

Nishida similarly received the blade with two hands, bringing it close to his forehead with a short bow as sign of respect. He examined the knife. It was a new blade of a high-tech alloy, this he could see, but the lines of a traditional *tanto* had been retained. It was obviously well-honed and came to a sharp, armor-piercing point. He took it in one hand and felt the heft and balance. It was centered but heavy; not a flashing slash knife, he thought, but one that would move with deliberateness and cut through anything in its path. He touched it to his forehead once more. "Thank you, Omori-san."

"My pleasure," Omori said as he removed the wooden scabbard strapped to his left outer forearm and handed it to Nishida.

"Is everyone ready?"

"Yes."

"Bring them here."

Omori returned in several minutes with the same greeting party that had met Nishida at the airport two days ago.

"Watanabe. I have heard much of your prowess. The amount

390

of beer you have consumed is only equaled by the amount of others' blood you have spilled."

"You are too kind."

"Do not fail to live up to your deserved reputation tonight."

"Yes," he replied crisply with a brief bow.

"Suzuki. Your brother is a loyal and capable member of our gang with a good future. Live up to his standard tonight."

"Yes. He is coming in tonight from Bangkok."

"Eh?"

"Yes, I heard he felt the police were close to making some arrests so he is returning, at Yamashita's request."

"I see," Nishida said as he began to consider the consequences. It meant that the whole Bangkok operation may have been compromised, his work ruined. It meant that no matter what happened tonight, he was a nonentity at Great Star. The best he could do would be to die honorably, die taking Bergman with him.

He looked deep into the eyes of the newest soldier they were to bring. "Tanaka."

"Yes," he barked.

"You can do no better for yourself or this organization than to do well tonight."

"You will not be disappointed."

"See that I am not," Nishida commanded solemnly.

"We are going on an excursion to dispose of some American trash that has washed up on our shores. He is being introduced to us by a Japanese man he does not suspect. Therefore, he will not suspect that we will come for him. How do you feel about that, Tanaka?" he asked darting his eyes to the newest man.

"Confident that we will succeed, Nishida-san."

"No. We must not be confident. This American is a snake

who has bitten and killed two of my Thai men in Bangkok with his bare hands. How do you feel now, Watanabe?"

"He has not met me. Two Thais are not up to one Watanabe," he said with a cruel smile. "Still, forewarned is forearmed. The more we know about him the better."

"He is tall, that means he has reach, probably strong, though he does not look or carry himself like a fighter."

"What will he be packing?"

"I have no idea, though possibly a knife."

"And what do you want done with him?" Suzuki asked.

"We would prefer to dispose of him discreetly. An American who just vanishes while at the seashore perhaps. That would be best. But if he puts up too much of a fight, then we may have to kill him first and discard him later, a climbing accident in the Japan alps," Nishida chuckled. In his heart he hoped Bergman would resist. Resist enough so Nishida could kill him then and there. "When the time comes to take his life, I insist you wait for me to do it. He has troubled me too much. You all understand?"

They nodded their solemn assent.

"Omori and I will take one car, you all in the other. We have worked out a diversion to escape our police friends. I will call you around 6:30 with word on where to meet me. When you get there, do nothing until I arrive." He paused and looked into their faces. "Let's go."

Obara was obviously proud of his creation which he extended to Ted as if holding a crystal chalice, kneeling on the old, dirty *tatami* in the living area of Obara's flat.

Ted took the heavy copper forearm guard from him and looked

carefully at its construction. A three-inch diameter section of one-eighth-inch thick copper had been halved along its axis, making two half-moon shaped troughs. These had been shaped and cut to fit Obara's arm, and two wide straps were attached. Some thin foam had been glued to the inside diameter.

The outside showed signs of use. There were two areas where copper had been peeled up by the force of blows and then pounded back into place. "What happened here?"

The wiry old man grinned, "That guy was tough. Nearly killed me."

"You were cut up?"

"No. In a real fight you can't afford to get cut up too much and still win. But there comes a point in the confrontation where it's you or him. He almost won."

"What did you do?" the American asked, his attention fixed.

"Let him take his best shot on my arm, damn near cut through the copper and even so almost broke my arm. But his blade, a heavy one, got caught in the copper, and when I recovered upward it opened him up, and I opened him up. From here to here," he said tracing a line across Ted's abdomen from left to right. "Cut him about three inches deep. You know what he did? Maybe it was the stomach force of him trying to hold his guts in, but he looked at me and spit in my face. Then he fell dead."

"Jesus," Ted exclaimed, involuntarily reverting to English.

"What?"

"Nothing." He tried the guard on his outer forearm. Despite being a much shorter and wiry Asian, Obara's forearms were massive for his size, the result of years of handling meat. Therefore, Ted was not surprised when they fit, although they didn't cover as much of his arm back to the elbow as on Obara. "They're great! How do

I use them?"

"You can hit him with them, block almost anything. Best to let him be surprised about them though." Obara looked at the cheap black plastic, Taiwan-made digital watch on his wrist. "It's about time to call the American at the embassy, isn't it?"

"Yes." His ears detected the sound of steps on the cement stairs leading to Obara's door. "Yuko?"

"Probably. I'll check." Obara got up and opened the door as cautiously as he had the first day, admitting Yuko who carried his shopping bags.

"Any problems, anyone follow you?" Obara asked.

"No, not that I know of."

"Good. Takabashi-san, call your friend."

Ted went to the phone and dialed the embassy. The switchboard answered.

"May I speak with William Brody, the visiting DEA chief from Bangkok?"

"Who is speaking?"

"Ted Bergman." He waited while the call was connected, looking at Yuko. She was turned away from him and talking to Obara, who handed her an envelope. He made a mental note to ask her about it later.

"Ted? Brody here."

"Bill? Hi. Look I'm calling to say I want to cooperate with you completely. I think you can take care of this if I do."

"OK. I thought we had that understanding?"

"Yes. But I want to go back to Bangkok with you. I feel like a fugitive here. I'm running out of money and Bangkok's where it all started. From there we can go step by step over everything. And maybe you can help me clear the air with Singapore."

"Umhmm. There's been some progress on the case there and we feel we can prosecute better from that end, too."

"Good."

"When can you be ready to go?"

"As a matter of fact, I took the liberty of booking you and me on tomorrow morning's Thai Airways flight at 10 o'clock. I hope economy's OK. It's coming out of my pocket so I couldn't afford business class."

"Economy's OK. Tomorrow morning, huh?"

"Yeah. You'll need to leave your hotel around 7 a.m."

"Where can I meet you?"

"I'll be the nervous looking fellow waiting for you at the Thai Airways ticket counter at 8:30."

"OK. Eight-thirty, Thai Airways ticketing counter."

"Yes. And Bill? I'm counting on you."

"Everything will be fine, Ted. You settle down and lay low, and I'll see you in the morning."

"Thank you. Tomorrow." Ted said as he hung up.

Yuko and Obara were staring at him. "He will go, yes?"

"Yes. We meet tomorrow. He is probably just now beginning to think about what he agreed to. I hope he doesn't think too much and back out."

"That is not a worry now," Obara said, forcing Ted's thoughts off the unconstructive sidetrack they had taken. "Change into your track suit. Yuko, take his clothes back to the hotel. I'll carry the knives to the park."

As the two men changed, Yuko helped them on with their forearm guards and put away Ted's things. "We make a strange pair dressed like this. We should not travel there together. I'll leave first and scout it out. You come fifteen minutes later. Call Yoshida from the park and explain where to meet us."

"Yes."

"And you take this old coat. Wear it when we go into the park. You will want to look like a bum." Obara saw and heard Ted's nostrils flare as he whiffed the odor of the never-washed garment. "And smell like a bum," he grinned.

"Old man," Ted interjected, as he drew nearer to Obara who pulled away reflexively.

"What?"

Ted closed the gap that separated them and wrapped his arms tight around the man who stood motionless. "You can't leave without that hug. I love you."

Obara rested his head on Ted's shoulder and patted the American's back. "This is not a good time for sentiment. But thank you, son. Now I'm getting out of here," he added, shaking himself free. You follow soon," he ordered as he disappeared down the stairwell.

Ted looked into the blackness of the unlit, descending passage and turned, shaken, to Yuko. "How he can leave like he is going to the corner for a bottle of beer, I just don't know."

"He is just like he is going to buy beer. That is why he has a chance of surviving. His mind is clear," Yuko replied sternly.

Ted was further taken off guard by her tone. "But he might not come back. I may not ever see you again," he said getting closer to a deeper concern. He began trembling and closed his eyes. "How can I lose my love now!" he cried out. "How can my mind be clear now? What do you know about it, anyway?" he cursed as his spirit cascaded downward.

Suddenly Yuko lashed out at him, slapping him squarely on the cheek. "I know something about your fighting arts. I know something about your clarity of mind. If you want to act clearly,

396

love clearly, fight or kill, you must empty your mind of all the dreams and nightmares. You didn't block my slap just now because you were preoccupied. Preoccupied with your self-pity. You might as well be dead, because you have ceased living, stopped experiencing what is happening to you now," she growled as she struck out viciously at him again with her palm, this time hitting him even harder, one of her fingernails digging into his cheek, drawing blood. "Destroy Nishida because he is evil. Like Butcher Obara said, if you do not he will destroy you, physically or psychically. But pursue him with resolution and a clear mind; otherwise you will fail."

She attacked again with her left hand, but this time the motion of her arm was stopped at the wrist with a jolting, hard-hitting pain up her arm, making her blink and bite her lip.

She inhaled slowly to suck in the hurt. "Yes."

As the large American automobile carrying Omori and Nishida pulled up to Yoshida's house, Nishida found himself dreading the meeting. The evasion of the police had been successful, traffic had been normal and they had arrived in the area a little early. Everything was going smoothly. But he felt uneasy at the pit of his *hara*, his spiritual and physical center. This house which he had visited before and the man inside were at the root of his own failure. The memories of his glaring ineptitude came back to him. This time it had to be different. It had to be.

Omori and he walked through the unlocked gate and up the short driveway to the path that led to the front door.

Yoshida was waiting for them at the door, having heard their approach. "Good evening."

"No pleasantries, Yoshida."

397

"All right. Do you have the documents?"

"Yes. Do you have Bergman?"

"Perhaps Yamashita did not make it clear to you, or maybe the rot in your brain has overflowed into your ears, but I said you deliver the documents first. Then I tell you where he is."

"Yes, you maggot. We have them."

"Please," Yoshida requested with his hand out.

Nishida glared at him, then signaled for Omori to deliver the documents and removed a thick envelope, handing it to Yoshida who opened them and began examining each one.

"Shall we take a walk?" Yoshida asked pleasantly.

The two *yakuza* looked at each other. "Where?"

"To the place where I can tell you about Bergman," he replied.

"Go."

As they walked, Yoshida looked over each document. Sometimes he stopped and squinted in the fading light to make out a passage. Finally, when they had walked about three blocks toward the main road he put them in a larger, stamped envelope and suddenly thrust them into a postbox they were passing.

The two *yakuza* were caught by surprise and each restrained a move to attack the debtor in public. Nishida snapped his finger angrily and waved his hand to the curb and the large white car that had been following them pulled immediately up to where they stood. "Get in, dead man," he ordered.

When they had gotten in the car, Nishida grabbed Yoshida by the throat, "Where is Bergman?" he growled.

"I'll tell you. Let … go," he gurgled.

Nishida let up on his throat.

"I always meant to tell you where he is. Go to Shiba Park. The southeast corner. Enter and head west until you reach the center.

There is a raised area and a small shrine. He is waiting there until 8."

"Alone?"

"Yes," he replied after a pause.

"Alone?" Nishida demanded to know, almost screaming, tightening his grip on Yoshida's throat.

"My daughter may be with him." After a moment he said, "Don't hurt her."

They had pulled back up to Yoshida's house. "Omori-san will keep you company until we have Bergman. He understands that if I don't call him by 8:30, you die, a victim of suicide. Do you understand."

Yoshida looked into the squinting eyes of the man smiling in anticipation of seeing him dead and replied evenly, "Yes. Bergman is where I say. I understand the threat."

Darkness and relative quiet had settled over Shiba Park like a heavy cloth cover over a bird cage. Despite the solitude, Ted could not feel peaceful. Despite how smoothly everything had gone, he could not feel confident.

He had left Yuko with a kiss, a hug, a pledge to return, and the stinging reminder of her lesson still wet with blood on his cheek. Strapped to his left arm beneath his sweatshirt was the custom forearm guard Obara had put to use in a former life. He had been conscious of the lack of one on his right arm and hoped the unbalance did not show in his walk. Over his left arm he had draped the musty, unwashed trench coat Obara had given him to wear in the park. He was conscious of the smell and hoped his gait was not made even more awkward-appearing in avoiding the rank odor.

The subway ride had been uneventful, almost humorous. He had watched the other passengers through his dark sunglasses as they had tried to determine for sure if he was a foreigner whom they could malign with impunity among themselves. Other passengers had muttered comments about bathing. Some had just sniffed and turned away. One older businessman who had drunken several *biru* after work belched and farted almost simultaneously, sniffed the result cautiously and chimed with inebriated pride, "My farts smell better than this kid."

Ted had been relieved to arrive at the proper station before further militancy could evolve. Ascending into the golden street light and cool night air, he had quickly found a public phone and called Yoshida. Ted had played with him, asking questions to upset him. "Why do you sound surprised, didn't you think I'd call?" And "How can I thank you enough for arranging this meeting?" Yoshida had even asked him if he had seen Obara. "No," replied the American guilelessly, "I thought I heard he was dead. Didn't you say that the other day?" When his old friend had asked if Yuko would be at the meeting he had not been able to contain his disgust and had jibed, "No, one pure thing sacrificed to your lust is enough." The old man had not answered. After telling him where the meeting place was to be, Ted had hung up the phone without signing off. There was no one he recognized on the other end.

Obara had roused several bums who usually bivouacked there and had given them each a thousand yen note with the instructions to find another spot in the park for the night. When Ted had arrived at the appointed place, there was no one but the Butcher waiting.

"Here's your knife," Obara said. "It's clean. I took all the fingerprints off so just handle it with your gloves on."

The disciple took it in his gloved right hand. The handle was much more textured than it had been that morning. Had it only been a half day ago? Ted marveled at the compression of so much life experience.

"I didn't have time to wrap or put a strap on the handle so I carved grooves in it and coated it with a thin veneer of rubber cement. It should give you a good enough grip. Just don't get it too bloody. How does it feel?" The old man asked, not revealing that he had imprinted his fingerprints into the tacky coating.

"Good. Thank you," Ted said with a short bow. "Where do you want me to wait?"

"I'll be here," Obara said, pointing to a stone bench as he pulled down his sweat pants and proceeded to urinate liberally around the perimeter of his "hiding" place.

"And you just sit down and lean up against that tree over there. Don't wear the coat, just pull it up over you to conceal the knife and be ready to spring."

"When?"

"Right after me, unless they go for you first." Obara was deliberately vague. He knew the more specific he was the more limited his pupil's range of immediate response would be. "Relax ... and take off those stupid sunglasses!" he demanded quietly.

Ted had forgotten he had them on and was relieved to find his eyes super-adjusted to the shade of the night forest.

It was a half-hour ago now that he had taken his seat leaning against the tree. Obara lay on the stone bench snoring expansively. Ted was not sure if he was really asleep or pretending. He hoped it was pretense and began to worry that he, too, might fall asleep. His mind animated the dark forest and he found images of Dorothy, the Scarecrow, the Tinman, and the Cowardly Lion waiting there.

"Lions and tigers and bears, oh my!" Ted shook his head and became aware that his pulse had quickened. He recalled a night when he was four years old and his parents had left him to go shopping while he watched "The Wizard Of Oz" on television. They had come home to find him closed in the kitchen closet, wailing. "It's just a story," they had said, but he had not felt that then, he did not feel that now. As a child he had not been afraid of the images he had seen on the television screen, but of the evil symbolized. He was still afraid of evil, and of being led down yellow brick roads, of being used by other people.

He fingered the narrow scab on his cheek and Yuko came to mind. The image turned negative, as if she had started out smiling pleasantly and slowly evolved into a bitch queen. He could feel a pain in his stomach and his breathing became short. She's choking me, he thought, breathless. What the hell am I doing here? I didn't come to Japan by choice, I just want to put this behind me. I don't want to kill anyone. She's using me to get back at these people. Wake up Obara, get out, his mind's emotional center screamed claustrophobically as the walls of his misperception closed in.

Ted closed his eyes and tried to take a deep breath, and another. Slowly the panic began to subside. He asked himself if the Butcher and Yuko were right. Would he never be at peace with himself if he did not destroy Nishida? The thought of Nishida, became fixed in his mind, stronger and clearer than any image he had ever had of Mieko or Yuko. He was looking up at Nishida's cruelly smiling face, a smirk of dominance glaring downward. Ted followed down from his head as the image of his tattooed *yakuza* body materialized into view. His arms were pinning Ted to the tree, his male tumescence ready to plunge. Ted's thoughts pulled him away and he could see Mieko in his place, her violated body limp

402

and submissive under the Japanese.

Ted took another deep breath and realized his teacher and his lover could not be wrong. He could exist without destroying Nishida, as he had for ten years, but he would not live. It was a distinction he suddenly found very important.

He slowly opened his eyes and trained his ears onto the sound of the forest in the city. All was mechanical. There were no natural sounds reaching him behind Obara's rough breathing.

Suddenly, to his distant right he heard the rustle of leaves and the crack of a twig. Two men, he estimated. Then from far away and directly ahead of him he heard muffled conversation and more steps on the path. Another two men at least. He suddenly found the Butcher's snoring very irritating, both because he could not single out the sounds of the men on the path and he was becoming more convinced the old man Obara had really dozed off. He wanted to make some noise to rouse Obara, but he stayed still and quiet, turning his attention back to the interlopers.

They were now only fifty-five feet away down the hill and Ted could see their outlines clearly. Four large men dressed in suits, unbuttoned. One was very husky, another big for a Japanese, and the other two average in size and build. He figured Nishida to be the bigger, well-built man. Ted was glad he had on gloves; he would not need to wipe the sweat beginning to drench his palm. He fixed his half-open eyes and waited.

"This must be it," Nishida said in a hushed voice. "Watanabe, you go up first and see if the American is here. Clear out anyone else."

The burly leg breaker grunted, drew his knife in a reverse grip along his right forearm, keeping it out of sight for the moment, and stalked slowly up the hill.

"There's a couple of bums sleeping it off," he rasped down the hill to his senior.

"Hustle them out."

Watanabe first approached an old man lying on a stone bench. He had spent his share of time in sweaty, rank judo uniforms and dirty urinals, but the smell coming from this unwashed street person rivaled anything he had encountered. He was not repelled by it; it was just a mental note he made. Bums stink.

Coming closer to the man he turned his right side away slightly, keeping his weapon close to his body. With his left four-fingered hand he tapped the old man on the shoulder.

The sleeper was caught in mid-snore, grunted, and fell quiet.

Watanabe shook his shoulder and said brusquely, "Wake up. Move out."

The old man blinked his saké-laden eyes and tried to focus on Watanabe's face. He smiled faintly and lay his head back down.

Watanabe asked himself why he had been so soft on the loiterer and grabbed the small, frail man by his left arm, lifting him from the bench. His right arm came around to support the Jello-legged drunk.

In a blur that only afforded Watanabe time to think about his mistake, not correct it, he felt a cold piece of steel slash a hot trail across the veins in his wrist deep down through the tendons. He saw his knife drop slowly from his hand, its path downward the opposite of the one that arced up smoothly from his wrist to his neck cleaving a deep red furrow across his right jugular and through his wind pipe. Slumping to his knees silently he realized the master stroke that even now drained him of life also prevented him from shouting a warning.

After a minute without word from Watanabe, the toughest

man Nishida had brought, he began to get worried. "Let's go up. Suzuki, you take the lead with the gun. Tanaka, you cover his left flank. I'll be between you," he ordered with authority in his voice.

Suzuki nervously drew the silenced revolver. It felt heavy in his hands. He hoped he would not have to use it. He had never killed before, only maimed. Tanaka pulled the *wakizashi* from under his coat and drew it anxiously. He admired the confidence he saw in Nishida and Suzuki as they strode forward and hoped he could emulate them. But he had never used a short sword, only bamboo and dull, long metal swords in practice. He figured he could get a power cut but he wished he had practiced more before.

Nishida shook his left arm and freed the blade Omori had given him. Transferring it to his right hand he felt confidence return. He would kill the American if he was here, and if he wasn't he would kill Yoshida. Both of them had been equally destructive to him. The night was guaranteed to be satisfying. He pushed the thought of his satisfaction from his mind and cleared it, only hearing each sound, seeing each movement.

As they reached the leveled recreational area, they could see Watanabe's body slumped over a bench and a bum about fifteen feet away, sleeping up against a tree.

Nishida stopped and looked carefully, then signaled Suzuki to go to check Watanabe while Tanaka roused the sleeper with the point of his sword.

The Butcher waited, hardly breathing and without movement, buried behind the bleeding mass of Watanabe. He was ready at any moment to let the body slide off, and the release of energy would propel him up into his next victim. But he was getting tired. He was getting old. He was old, he thought, too old for this. He found it hard to quiet his breathing as he inhaled heavily to keep his strength up. Then he realized it did not matter. They did not know their friend was dead. Raspy deep breaths might bring them in faster, close, and more recklessly. He breathed loud and deep, adding a small cough for effect.

At once he could hear quickened footsteps getting nearer, very near. He tensed. He felt the body being touched. Letting it slide away, he came face to face with the extended barrel of a silenced gun. His cramped leg failed to push out and he stumbled forward on his knee, his blade a brief crescent moon in the forest. His cut to the exposed wrist of the young frightened man holding the gun was on target but not deep enough. The hand tensed, squeezing the sprung trigger involuntarily. An explosion erupted in Obara's face, heard as a loud spit by the others, and he felt a large piece of his neck burst in a shower of flesh and blood. The intense pain he focused on the tip of his knife and drove it home, as he fell forward, deep up under the man's sternum.

The sound of the loud expectoration and the sight of three corpses heaped where there was one before, momentarily caught the attention of Nishida, Tanaka, and Ted. Tanaka was between Ted and the man he had come to destroy. Not thinking, but acting suddenly, instinctively, Ted sprang at the man he judged with almost omniscient objectiveness, to be ten years his junior. As their two bodies came closer, Ted realized it was as if his mind was just along for the ride, as an observer, recorder, but not as an actor. He could clearly see the opponent raise his sword from a low position. Ted the observer noted this was a mistake; he should have cut on the rise, but what did the man-boy know, anyway? He was obviously getting ready to cut from high to low, diagonally. Ted's fortified forearm rose to meet the descending arc of hardened steel. Ted the observer pitied the queer look of confused desperation that clouded the man-boy's face as he realized that he had not cut off his opponent's arm and, worse, his blade was caught. A quick, precisely angled punching thrust up under the man's chin pushed Ted's knife clean in to the opponent's brain, fast in and fast out.

It was Ted's turn for a brief flash of panic as the dead youth collapsed, still grasping the short sword buried in Ted's armor. His left arm was dragged down and the tip of the blade dug shallowly into his pectoral until the *wakizashi* freed itself.

He looked up to see the expressionless Nishida stride nearer.

The *yakuza* stopped just out of springing range, his left hand forward, his right hand and knife a shadow somewhere behind. "You are Bergman?" he jeered the question.

"Yes. You are Nishida? Rapist of small girls?"

The criminal's eyes narrowed with faint recognition of a forgotten event. Bergman was the boyfriend he had seen with the Yoshida girl, he realized fitting his opponent's face over the memory of a photograph he had seen years ago of a teenage foreigner and his Japanese girlfriend. That explains how he knew the debtor. He smiled. "Yes, and she loved it," he taunted.

Ted the observer flared with anger, but the actor intervened, calm resumed. "Yes, so much so she has sent me to kill you so you can join her forever." Ted prayed Mieko would forgive the taunt; the thought repulsed him, but he hoped it would have the desired effect.

Nishida stepped forward, not liking what he saw, an undisturbed, fearless opponent. Closer, he saw a wet tear in the American's clothing. "If the kid Tanaka could cut you, then I don't expect much of a fight, you are no match for me!" he growled, grunting as he lunged at Ted, trying to extend his knife long enough to find flesh or to cut arms or legs on the way out.

But Ted was not there. He had disappeared into a crouch and Nishida's attention dropped to a piercing pain on the inside of his left knee. A five-inch-long opening appeared on his pants leg and a purple oval patch widened. Ted recovered with a step back, out of range again.

"You missed," Nishida sneered. "You couldn't have hit the artery if you tried. That's because you're weak. That's what she said, too. His knife is so thin and short and dull, no fun for a Japanese girl," he said in a mocking girlish tone.

"You sound afraid," Ted consoled. "But of course, you're afraid. Everyone knows Japanese are cowards. Losing the war, then bowing and scraping, kissing American boots. Don't be afraid. It will all be over for you …" Ted's taunt was interrupted by another assault. The *yakuza* extended his left foot and hand forward as bait then slashed from left to right laterally, hoping to catch Bergman's counter. Again he was surprised. The American had not gone for the bait and had outflanked him to his right, stopping his lateral cut with a jolting elbow block and cutting his forehead slightly as Nishida recovered away quickly.

"Weak, a weak cut. You are no match, American," the wary street fighter said as a trickle of blood oozed through his right eyebrow. Nishida knew the time had come. It was him or Bergman; maybe both. That would be acceptable. He took a deep breath, clutched his knife in both hands, a reinforcing double grip, and took an experimental step forward, changing the whole relationship between the fighters. He was prepared for a desperate *kamae*, the "posture of throwing your body away."

Ted noted all the changes and remained still, his knife hidden in his right hand behind his left arm.

Viciously, Nishida plunged into Ted, a freight train with a

knife for cowcatcher in front.

Ted gasped as his feet pulled him to the left and his back arched his stomach inward, narrowly avoiding the deep thrust of the unstoppable assault. He knew Nishida could cut out of his lunge and he observed in minute detail the unfolding encounter.

As Nishida turned his right elbow out to move his point closer to Ted's side, Ted was racing to get his edge to the leading elbow. As the *yakuza* dug laterally, his elbow met Ted's knife edge, and cut itself, severing the tendons behind the elbow and scraping deep into nerve and bone.

Ted observed the surprised look on Nishida's face as his hand opened up releasing his weapon. As the blade floated to the ground, Ted's *tanto* streaked up to the *yakuza*'s cheek slicing a Heidelberg-esque crag from jaw to brow, then followed its natural circular motion up, around and down, finally hooking up and plunging into the scrotum cavity. The knife remained there, buried to the handle, a stream of hot blood and urine flowing off it.

Ted stumbled away, leaving his knife, a ghastly penile pros-thesis, dangling red in Nishida's crotch. He watched for what seemed like minutes as Nishida tried to stay on his feet, the pain of moving and falling more excruciating than locking his stance. Finally, he toppled forward, dead.

Ted trudged slowly over to the heap of bodies by the bench and found Obara's wrist. There was no pulse. He forced himself to look at his teacher's face. Despite the gaping crimson cavity that had been his neck, his face was not pained, the eyes closed, the lips gently pursed, a small line of blood tracing across his cheek.

Ted knew what the Butcher would want him to do. He quickly attended to his own wound with a large wad of gauze and tape which Obara had insisted Yuko zip into their pockets. He then looked one more time at his teacher, picked up the trench coat he had been given, and left the park and all its trauma behind him, his past, present, and future clear, his step light.

EPILOGUE

"Ted, you're off the hook," Brody said after they had sat down for drinks in the lobby of the Bangkok Dusit Thani Hotel, a large manmade waterfall roaring outside the window.

"Everything?" Ted asked, the incredulity pretended in his voice, added so as not to upset the American who had had no conscious choice but to help him.

"Yep, Bangkok side was easy. Singapore took some explaining, but they accepted an affidavit from me. Don't make me regret it," the agent smiled, pointing a finger of warning at Ted.

"Japan?"

"Well, some minor infractions were cleared up ... unofficially. Shouldn't be a problem."

"Will you shut down Great Star?" With my help, Ted added in his thoughts, knowing his intent would be received.

"Thanks to you, I suppose, we've already shut them down here. They collapsed on their own anyway when so many principals died."

"Who besides the Italian?"

"Oh? You didn't see the article in yesterday's *Trib*. Sorry. Jeez. The day we left there was a big *yakuza* bloodbath. Vengeance killing. Really interesting, I'll see if I can find it for you to read."

"What happened?" Ted asked, taking a sip of Perrier.

"It was the cap to a chain of gangland assassinations stretching out over decades. Some old fart had taken it on himself to knock off hoods every so often since the early 1950s. He bit off more than he could chew this time though. Tried to knock off four toughs at once — with a knife no less!"

"What does this have to do with Nishida?" Ted asked, conscious of his slip, testing the man he faced.

Brody looked at him slightly askance, "I didn't say it had anything to do with Nishida."

Ted unhurriedly scratched the itching stitches a Tokyo emergency room had sewn for him. "Then he will be arrested after your investigation, won't he?" Ted asked with concern, instantly bolstering Brody's impression of his innocence.

"Actually he was one of the four hoods. They all died. The old man must've known he was gonna buy the farm. A postmortem confession of his dual life was received by a Japanese tabloid the next day."

"Sounds very Japanese," Ted the actor said thoughtfully, leading his current opponent further from the truth.

"Yeah, I suppose so."

"Can I be of any further help to you, Bill?" he asked sincerely.

"Not for now. Keep your eyes out. If you're ever in trouble again, let me know."

"I will. You know, Bill," he said personally. "It seems you've changed a bit in the past week."

"Yeah? I feel better. Better than I have in months, since ... you know ... my wife died. I've been too busy to have nightmares."

"You're back on track."

"Something like that. What are you going to do now? Back to

the grind?"

"Yes … no … maybe," Ted said with a shrug and a smile. But he knew exactly what he would do and where he would go. Yuko needed help with her father's estate. There was the rest of his life, their life, to live; carefully, with love and disciplined attention to each other and their future. He smiled at the man across the table from him as a parent smiles at a child and let the conversation, but not his mind, drift.

GLOSSARY

All words in Japanese unless otherwise indicated.

bakana — equivalent to "bullshit"

balikbayans — (Tagalog) Filipinos returning from overseas

biru — beer

budo — martial way, philosophical schools of physical training derived from traditional martial arts

daruma doll — a wooden doll with a round bottom that rebounds when pushed over. Named for the Buddhist patriarch Daruma

dhoti — (Hindi) long white cloth wrap worn with a shirt. Worn by Indian men

dojo — a place for training in the "way," usually a martial way.

don — (Italian) head of an Italian Mafia family

farang — (Thai) tourist/foreigner

futon – mattress

gi — training uniform for judo, karate, ju jitsu

hajimemashite — polite expression used when meeting a person for the first time.

iie, wa karimasen – no, I don't know

kabu — "defective"; dialect slang for *burakumin*

katana – sword

khap khun krap — (Thai) thank you (male version)

kinilaw — raw fish marinated in vinegar to chemically cook the fish

klong — (Thai) canal

konbanwa — good evening

kurumaku — black curtain from Noh drama; refers to political kingpins who work behind the scenes

mai ben rai — (Thai) no matter; no problem

o-jama sasete itadakimasu — may I trouble you for a moment

obi – sash

oyabun — head of the *yakuza*

pachinko — Japanese version of pinball, a mild form of gambling controlled by the *yakuza*

Porca Madonna — (Italian) Pig Mother (Mary)

randori — free wrestling in judo, as opposed to prearranged practice

samisen — stringed instrument resembling a banjo

sashimi — fish and other flesh to be consumed raw

sawadee krap — (Thai) greeting used for both hello and goodbye

sensei — teacher

shinjinrui — "new generation"; derogatory

shira-saya — the plain, white, wooden mounts used for sword storage

shoji — sliding screens made of wood and paper separating living areas

soi — (Thai) lane, side street

soo desu neh — "is that the way it is"; an exclamation equivalent to a strong "hmmm"

sumitori — sumo wrestler

tatami — mat

tsuba — ornately carved steel hand guard on a sword

wakizashi — short sword carried by a samurai

weii ... Ten Hong Wu Jin — (Mandarin) "Hello ... Ten Hong Hardware"

yakiniku — skewered grilled meats

yakuza — gangsters. Japanese equivalent of the Italian Mafia

yukata — light cotton house/bath robes

zori – slippers

ABOUT THE AUTHOR

For the past twenty years, Christopher Bates has designed his life around his interests in Asia, martial arts, business, and his family.

He holds a third-level black belt in Bando (Burmese fighting arts) and has had 18 years of training in Chinese martial arts, including Northern Shaolin, Hsing-I and Tai Chi. He has been scrupulous in seeking instruction only from masters of repute. He has received awards and honors at various tournaments for demonstrations of his skill. He is also familiar with traditional Japanese martial arts and is an expert in Kukri combat techniques used by the Gurkhas.

Since graduating with degrees in Asian studies and international management, Christopher Bates has spent 13 years in Asia, residing in Singapore and Taiwan and traveling continuously throughout the region. He lives in Singapore with his Taiwanese wife of 15 years and their three children.

Christopher Bates' previous writing experience includes the series "Philosophy of the Bando Discipline" for *Crossed Swords* magazine and "The Burmese *Dha*" for *Hoplos* magazine. Fluent in Mandarin, he has translated part of *Tales of Chivalrous and Altruistic Heroes* from Mandarin into English. He is presently at work on a book on martial art, a novella, and a philosophical children's book. *The Wave Man* is his first novel.